PATRICIA H. RUSHFORD
HARRISON JAMES

DEAD
FALL

INTEGRITY®
PUBLISHERS

Nashville

Library of Congress Cataloging-in-Publication Data

Rushford, Patricia H.
Deadfall / by Patricia H. Rushford and Harrison James.
  p. cm.

ISBN 1-59145-150-7

1. Police—Oregon—Fiction. 2. Oregon—Fiction. I. James, Harrison. II. Title.
PS3568.U7274D385   2004
813'.54—dc22   2004005458

Printed in the United States of America
04 05 06 07 08 PHX 9 8 7 6 5 4 3 2 1

To the families of violent crime victims nationwide,
who find the strength to carry on.

To the finest Southern belles Texas ever produced,
my grandmothers Mary Lou and Clora May.

—HARRISON JAMES

*In the early 1900s Samuel Lancaster, an engineer, said of the
Columbia River gorge: "I was profoundly impressed by its
majestic beauty, and marveled at the creative power of God,
who made it all. There is beauty in the bare angles of the rocks
that look down from the heights, where His fingers broke them.
Here He rent and tore them asunder, to make room for one of
earth's great rivers."*

Acknowledgments

Thanks to our agent, Chip MacGregor.

To our editors, especially Jennifer Stair and Kris Bearss.

To Integrity Publishers for believing in us.

And a special thanks to our Lord God,
in whom we place our trust.

1

*S*OMETIMES DEATH *is the only option.*

Brad Gaynes stood on the precipice overlooking Wah-kella Falls, in the Columbia River Gorge. He jammed his clenched hands deep into his pockets, willing himself to calm down. Anger wasn't going to solve anything. How many times had his dad said that?

Brad thought about his girlfriend's comment again—about death being the only option. Why would Jessica say something like that? She could be weird at times. What had she meant? Had she been talking about herself and how life was no longer worth living if they couldn't be together? Was she thinking about a suicide pact?

"Nah." Brad watched his warm breath turn white as it hit the cold November air. Jessica didn't seem like the suicidal type. More likely, she made the comment to manipulate him. She did that often and well. He probably should have stayed with her and talked things out, but he couldn't stand it anymore. He needed to get away before he did or said something they'd both regret.

He breathed in the fresh, earthy smell of rotting leaves, rain, and rich, woodsy soil. He'd stopped at the top of the falls to catch his breath after practically running up the mile-long trail. As he stood tall, face into the wind, he let his gaze roam across the

Columbia River and up the cliffs and hills on the Washington State side. Even now, with fog and rain, the spot offered one of the most spectacular views in Oregon, made even more beautiful by the gold and red maple leaves and the setting sun. The clouds had just opened to the west as if offering a gift of vibrant colors to make up for the persistent rain. The climb and the view calmed his anger and helped him to think through his dilemma. He knew now what he needed to do to make things right. Still, something about Jessica just didn't sit well with him.

Brad emerged from his deep thoughts and heard an odd guttural sound along with the rustling of brush in the woods behind him. Had Jessica followed him? Or maybe that trucker had come back to make good on his threat. Brad had been in a fighting mood when the trucker tried to intervene in his and Jessica's argument. She'd assured the trucker she was okay and he'd gone back to his truck, but not without promising to get even.

The thrashing grew louder.

"Who's there?" Brad's heart accelerated again, and this time it wasn't from exertion. He called out again, "Jess? Is that you?"

No one answered.

It had to be Jessica. "Come on. What are you doing? Quit playing games."

Something told him to get out of there—to hit the trail running and not look back. But Brad's curiosity overcame his intuition. He drew back from the edge of the falls and headed into the woods to investigate.

2

VICTORIA GAYNES YAWNED AND STRETCHED. Nine o'clock and she was exhausted. No surprise there, as she'd been up since five. "I think I'll go to bed early and read." She leaned down to kiss her husband's balding head.

The phone rang before he could respond.

Vicki frowned, suddenly hit with an odd premonition.

"Want me to get it?" Todd started to get up.

"No; stay put." She hurried to the kitchen and picked up the portable phone. "Hello."

"Mrs. Gaynes, it's Jessica. Brad is missing and—"

"What did you say?" Vicki's throat closed, nearly trapping the words inside. "What do you mean 'missing'?"

Todd got out of his chair. "What's wrong?"

Covering the mouthpiece, she whispered, "It's Jessica. She's crying, and I'm having a hard time understanding her."

"I don't know where he is," Jessica sobbed.

"What do you mean?" Vicki all but yelled at her. "Jessica, for heaven's sake, calm down and tell me what happened."

"Brad's missing."

Vicki forced back the bile rising to her throat. "All right." She deliberately slowed her breathing. Jessica wasn't making any sense. "Why do you think he's missing?"

"He went hiking alone, and he didn't come back. I waited and waited, but he never came and I didn't know what to do. I tried to call from the cell, but the battery is dead."

"Where are you?"

"At the cabin." The cabin was situated near Mount Hood.

"You said he went hiking. Where?"

Jessica explained that she and Brad had been parked at the base of Wah-kella Falls that afternoon. "We got into an argument, and he got really mad. He said he was going for a walk—only he didn't come back. Brad had been drinking, and he said he needed some air. He got out of the car, slammed the door, and started walking up the trail."

"When did he leave?" Vicki glanced at her watch.

"I don't know, around four-thirty or so. It was almost dark."

"And you're just now calling us?"

"I'm sorry—I . . ."

"Let me get this straight. You left my son in the woods in the dark with no way to get home?"

"I didn't know what else to do."

"You could have stopped somewhere to use a pay phone."

"Everything up there was closed. I couldn't think straight. I just . . ." Jessica's voice broke.

"All right." Vicki rubbed her forehead, wondering what had really happened. "Have you called the police?"

"Yes, I just did. I'm supposed to meet them at the falls in the parking lot."

"Then get up there." Vicki sounded as annoyed as she felt, and she didn't care. "We'll meet you there as well."

She hung up the phone and found Todd in the bedroom. Vicki's heart was beating so hard she could hardly hear herself talk. "We have to go."

"I gathered that." Todd, being his efficient self, had already put on his shoes and began gathering stuff for the drive.

"Brad's missing. Jessica said he went off for a hike at Wah-kella Falls and didn't come back." Vicki pulled off her lounging pants and got into her jeans, nearly falling as she tried to stuff two feet down the same pant leg.

"What's he doing walking up there at night?" Todd raked the car keys off the dresser.

"He knows that place like the back of his hand." Vicki frantically pulled her blonde hair into a ponytail. "Besides, it was still light when he left."

"Honey." Todd stilled Vicki's hands and wrapped his arms around her. "Take it easy. At the rate you're going, we'll never get out of here. Besides, it's too soon to panic."

Vicki sucked in a frustrated breath. He was right; she needed to keep her wits about her. "I'm trying, but our son is out there and . . ." Tears faded his image.

"I know, and I'm just as concerned as you are." Todd caught her tears with his knuckles and kissed her forehead. "Now take a deep breath and get your shoes on. I'll grab some water, snacks, blankets, our jackets, and some rain gear."

Minutes later the couple braved the rainslicked streets as they made the forty-mile trek east on I-84, the wiper blades taking up the lament of Vicki's heart. *Let Brad be all right. Let Brad be all right.*

OREGON STATE POLICE TROOPER Dana Bennett was about to head home when the call came in over her radio: "Eleven-twenty-three."

"Go ahead," she responded.

The dispatch operator gave her the details. A missing person in the Columbia River gorge—a twenty-five-year-old white male, last seen around dusk at the Wah-kella Falls trailhead.

Dana knew the area well. The Eagle Creek trail system was one of her favorite places to hike, and she didn't mind working patrol out there either. The gorge offered such awesome views, glimpses of nature at its finest; she couldn't help but feel good out there. But the area could be as treacherous as it was beautiful.

"I'm on my way. I'll be working overtime, if you could advise the on-call sergeant." She'd be working with no pay if overtime wasn't approved, but Dana didn't mind. She was trying to get as much experience under her belt as possible in preparation for the day she made detective. She thought for a moment about calling Mac, a detective with the Oregon State Police and a good friend, but Mac was probably either hanging out with his fiancée or working on a case. Mac had been mentoring Dana of late, giving her advice on making detective.

Still, he might be interested. She knew for a fact that Mac enjoyed hiking and that he often volunteered to help find missing persons. She put in a call and got his answering machine. Dana left him a message with the details, sketchy as they were, and asked him to call. Disappointment at his not being there drifted through her.

She tossed her feelings aside. *You have no business getting involved with Mac, even in your imagination. He's engaged, for heaven's sake.* Dana sighed. Some things were not meant to be, and a relationship with Mac was one of them.

If she were honest with herself, she'd admit that she had a thing for the handsome Detective Antonio "Mac" McAllister. He liked her too—she could tell. In fact, they had even dated briefly several years ago, before she became an OSP trooper. But they were both dating other people now, and Dana had made up her mind that she would not get involved with a cop. No way. In the meantime, they met on a regular basis for coffee or lunch and talked shop.

Dana forced her mind back on the task at hand and called dispatch to find out who, besides herself, had responded.

MAC WALKED INTO HIS APARTMENT at ten, ignoring his dog and the blinking red light on his answering machine. He headed straight for the kitchen and yanked open the refrigerator. Lucy, his golden retriever, followed, whimpering and sticking her head into the fridge. She backed out and sat next to him. "You want out?" Mac asked. He'd fed her and taken her out just before leaving for his fiancée's place around seven-thirty.

Lucy licked his hand. Mac backed out of his pitifully empty fridge and scanned his cupboard. He cleaned and filled Lucy's water bowl and leaned against the counter, his arms folded while he watched her drink. "Why can't all women be like you?" He sighed. "You're easy to please. Don't take a lot of maintenance. You're happy to see me when I come home, and you don't whine about my hours."

Anger and resentment along with frustration tore at his insides as he thought about the fiasco of a counseling session he'd just endured with his fiancée and her pastor.

"Not the smartest thing I've ever done," he told his dog. "If I were a drinking man, I'd have downed a pint of booze by now." But Mac didn't drink and had no intention of starting. He credited his father for that. Watching that stumbling drunk had cured Mac of ever wanting alcohol. Still, he needed something. His gaze fell on the coffeepot. He took down his stash of Starbucks ground coffee, put a couple of heaping scoops into the filter, filled the reservoir with water, and turned it on to brew.

"What happened, Lucy? I thought I loved her." He eyed the dog, who seemed more interested in something out on the patio than in anything Mac had to say. "Everything was going great until Linda insisted on counseling."

"We need to go to marriage counseling, Mac," he said in a falsetto tone.

Several days after he'd asked her to marry him, Linda had told

Mac yes, but only if he would see a marriage counselor with her. She'd quoted a Bible verse about being "unequally yoked." Mac said he had been brought up Catholic, but apparently that wasn't good enough. He'd made excuses and managed to avoid counseling for a while. Then, in a weak moment, he'd succumbed and Linda made an appointment with Pastor Jim. He'd gotten tied up at work and called the church, certain they'd have to cancel. But Pastor Jim said that the Sunday evening service was over, and his schedule was flexible. He agreed to meet them whenever Mac could get there, which was around eight-thirty.

Mac had liked the pastor at first, especially when he started talking about sports and staying fit and working out several days a week. They talked about marriage and family. Mac let Linda go on about her family: parents who were still married after forty years; siblings who, like herself, had gone through college and earned their degrees. She'd come from a normal, loving family—one without all the dysfunction he'd had in his.

When his turn came, Mac said, "My father was a cop, my mother died when I was young, and my grandmothers raised me." He didn't elaborate—didn't tell them his father had been an alcoholic. He didn't even mention his mother's family or why he never used his given name, Antonio. His brief explanation seemed to satisfy them. Apparently they had an agenda and were eager to get started with their project: changing Mac.

Linda kept her gaze on Pastor Jim as she explained how she felt left out and how days would go by without her hearing from Mac. "We're engaged, but I'm lucky if we see each other more than once a week."

"I'm a detective," Mac said in his defense. "When I'm on a case, I don't have a lot of extra time on my hands."

"I understand." Pastor Jim smiled in Mac's direction. "My schedule is overwhelming at times too, and I have to work long hours. I tend to be a workaholic, but we do need to compromise if we expect to nurture our relationships. I try to reserve Tuesday and Thursday evenings and all day Saturday as time with my family. We guard our time together closely." He chuckled. "If I slip up, my wife keeps me in line."

Mac wasn't amused. He shifted his gaze from Linda to Jim. "There's no way I can set aside specific days. I never know when I'll be called in." He struggled to keep his tone pleasant.

"You can't carve out a day or two each week?" Pastor Jim asked.

At the moment, Mac didn't want to spend an hour with Linda, and particularly not this hour. He should never have agreed to come. How could such a beautiful, sensitive, sensual woman have turned into such a pathetic snob?

Pastor Jim was patronizing and clearly on Linda's side. Mac fumed inwardly, not willing to give an inch.

"It's not even the time so much." Linda turned her watery, doe-brown eyes on him.

Oh, great. She was going to cry.

Linda reached for a tissue from the box conveniently placed on Pastor Jim's desk and dabbed at her eyes. "When he's working on a case, which is all the time, I go for days without hearing from him. I leave messages that he never answers. I worry so much about him—I mean, he's out there tracking down killers. It's a dangerous job, and sometimes I can't even sleep at night worrying about him. Would it be so hard for him to call me?"

"Mac?" Pastor Jim folded his hands and waited for Mac to respond.

"I suppose I could call more, but . . ." Mac hesitated. How could he tell her that when he was on a case, calling her was the farthest thing from his mind? Maybe it shouldn't be, but it was.

"You have your cell phone with you all the time." Linda had torn apart the tissue and then wadded it up. "Would it be so hard to take a minute when you're getting coffee or stopping for lunch or dinner to call me so I know you're okay?"

"Ah," Pastor Jim said. "Now we're getting somewhere." Again, they both turned their gazes to Mac.

No, it's not possible. I don't want to have to check in. Mac didn't express his thoughts aloud. After all, Linda's request was reasonable—annoying, but reasonable. Linda slid her hand over his, and he released his grip on the arm of the chair. "I might be able to do that. Not all the time, but when I can remember."

She smiled, her eyes still misty. "That's all I ask. You have such a dangerous job, and I really want to know you're okay. Besides, it's good to connect more often."

He caught a glimpse of the woman he'd fallen in love with in that smile. She really was a wonderful person. He'd met her in the hospital where she worked as a nursing supervisor. Linda had been so compassionate and efficient. Of late, instead of listening to her requests and acknowledging her concerns, he'd written them off, feeling smothered and put upon.

"That went well, don't you think?" Linda had asked on the way home.

"I suppose." Mac's annoyance returned, and he wasn't sure why. "Am I such a bad guy that you feel you need to change me?"

"Oh, Mac." She leaned over and kissed his cheek. The warmth of her breath and the heat of her hand on his leg almost made him forget his question. "Change is necessary in any relationship."

"For me, but not for you?" Mac didn't want to be upset with her.

"You want me to change?" She removed her hand and leaned back, shifting slightly in her seat to look at him. "In what way?"

He shrugged. "Stop acting like I have the worst job in the world. Some people think what I do is honorable."

"I do, Mac." She licked her lips. "It just frightens me."

"Well, if it's any consolation, you're listed as one of the people to contact if anything happens to me."

Linda folded her arms and leaned back against the seat, her dark, shoulder-length hair falling forward. "That's not exactly comforting."

After walking Linda to her door, Mac drew her into his arms and kissed her.

"Want to come in for some coffee?" She smiled up at him, her eyes shining with promise.

Mac wanted more than coffee—more than she would offer. He chided himself for thinking about sex when their relationship was on such tentative ground. Holding her close, his arms securely around her, he said, "You really need to decide whether or not you want to be married to a cop. Some women aren't cut out for it."

She leaned back. "Mac, I love you."

"That may be, but take a look at the divorce rate among law enforcement officers. I don't want you to get into a marriage you'll regret."

She frowned. "I can handle it. We'll just need to make some adjustments."

Mac dropped his arms to his side. "Don't expect me to change too much, Linda. I'm not sure I can."

He'd driven away, more upset with himself than with her. He was the one who had serious reservations about marrying Linda. Now he'd dumped his concerns in her lap. Why couldn't he just tell her how he felt—manipulated, coerced, unsure of himself and of their relationship?

The coffeepot sputtered out the last few drops. Mac filled his Mariners mug then took it into the living room. He listened to the answering machine. Dana's voice and her message about the missing hiker lifted his spirits. He took the wireless phone to his favorite chair in front of the fireplace and punched in Dana's number. When he got her voice mail, Mac left a message indicating that he had the day off tomorrow and if the hiker was still missing, he'd be happy to join the search.

Lucy padded in and gazed at him with love in her deep brown eyes. She put her head on his leg, waiting for his undivided attention. Mac petted her and took her outside for a brief walk in the rain.

Then the two of them settled in for the evening—Mac in the recliner and Lucy at his feet. Lulled by the fire and the sound of the rain on the windows, Mac drifted off, waking around midnight to stumble into bed. The image drifting through his head was not that of the brunette he was engaged to, but the blonde trooper, his good friend, Dana Bennett.

3

THE POUNDING RAIN HAD LIGHTENED to a steady drizzle when Todd and Vicki Gaynes arrived at the park just before ten o'clock that night. They scanned the lighted parking lot, hoping Brad would be there waiting, angry that Jessica had taken off without him. He wasn't there, and neither were Jessica or the police. Five big rig trucks had parked at the west end of the lot in the long-term parking area, their drivers taking a break or getting a few hours of sleep.

Todd grabbed a flashlight out of the trunk, and together he and Vicki walked the length of the parking lot on the creekside, looking for Brad. They were about to start up the trail when two deputies from the Hood River County Sheriff's Department pulled into the parking lot. On their tail was an Oregon State Police car. The three cops talked among themselves while they put on rain jackets. Then the trooper, a woman, left the men and approached the Gayneses. She reached out a hand and identified herself to Vicki and Todd as Trooper Dana Bennett, Oregon State Police. She hadn't needed to add the last part, as the silver lettering on her dark rain jacket made it clear.

Dana had a sympathetic smile and dimpled cheeks. Her long

blonde hair was neatly tucked into a braid and secured at the back of her head.

"How does this work?" Todd asked. "We were about to head up the trail to start looking."

"Are you the ones who called in the report?"

"No," Vicki said. "That would have been Brad's girlfriend, Jessica."

Dana nodded. "We've been told the reporting party would meet us here." She glanced at Todd. "To answer your question, sir . . . in Oregon, the search-and-rescue responsibilities fall to the sheriff of the respective county of venue. In this case that would be the Hood River County Sheriff's Department, which, by the way, is one of the best. These guys have had years of experience rescuing lost hikers on the Eagle Creek trail system and stranded or injured hikers on the north face of Mount Hood."

Todd glanced over at the two deputies, who were still talking. "There are just three of you?"

"The sheriff's office has a call in for volunteers. The deputies will lead the search effort, but we rely on volunteers to provide most of the muscle. Most of the searchers are seasoned outdoor types, men and women who enjoy Oregon's back country and look for opportunities to hone their skills with a difficult climb or challenging rescues."

Vicki didn't care about any of that. She just wanted to find her son.

"Will you be helping with the search?" Todd asked.

"As much as I can." Dana assured him.

Jessica drove into the parking lot in Brad's Subaru. "That's Brad's girlfriend," Vicki said, trying to keep the venom out of her tone.

Dana's gaze flickered toward Jessica. "You don't like her."

Vicki swallowed. "No, I don't." There was no point in lying.

"Anything we should know about?" Dana asked. "Do you suspect foul play?"

"N-no. At least not at this point. She told me Brad had gone hiking and didn't come back. There's no reason to suspect anything different."

"He probably just lost his way in the dark," Todd said. "It doesn't take much to get turned around in these woods."

Dana nodded. "Especially at night. I'd like to hear what Jessica has to say."

Vicki and Todd walked with Dana to the Subaru and stopped a few feet away. The two deputies joined them and Dana introduced Vicki and Todd.

"Deputy Hanks." The younger man extended his hand to Vicki and then to Todd, finally to Jessica.

"This is Deputy Miller." Hanks seemed to take charge at this point. Deputy Miller had a medium build with an ample spare tire while Hanks looked well built, with a broad chest and shoulders. Both men looked to be around Todd's height—over six feet.

Vicki listened as Jessica recounted her story to the deputies and the trooper. She talked about their argument and about how she'd decided to break off their relationship. "I told him I was moving out. Brad got really mad. He got out of the car and said he needed some air."

"What was he wearing?" Deputy Hanks asked.

"Jeans, tennis shoes, and a sweatshirt. He left his wallet in the glove box and the keys in the ignition."

Todd walked around to the passenger side of the Subaru and grabbed the wallet out of the glove box. He unfolded it and checked the currency compartment.

"What are you doing?" The younger deputy seemed annoyed.

"There's no money in here." Todd glanced over at Jessica.

She clenched her jaw. "So? You think I took his money?" Jessica turned away in disgust. "I didn't. I wouldn't do something like that."

To the officers, Todd said, "Brad is a ski instructor who makes good tips. He always has a wallet full of small bills. I've never seen Brad without cash. My son doesn't have a checking account, so he keeps his rent, grocery money, and whatever else in his wallet."

Hanks made some notes in a small notebook. "What else can you tell us about him? Do you have a photo?"

"There's one in his wallet," Jessica said in a small voice. "We're both in it."

Todd flipped through the plastic-encased photos, pulled out the photograph of Brad and Jessica, and handed it to the deputy. "He's about six-two and what, Vicki, about a hundred and eighty pounds?"

"Maybe a little heavier," Vicki added. "He's lean but very muscular. Brad keeps in shape."

"He weighed one-eighty-five this morning," Jessica offered. "He said he was getting fat. It was one of the things we argued about. I told him it was from all the beer he drank."

Thanks to you. Vicki kept the comment to herself. "When are we going to start looking for him?" she asked. "We're wasting valuable time standing around here."

"We'll get a ground search going tonight, folks." Hanks held his spike mic up to his lips and asked his dispatch to get a chopper from the Portland Airbase with FLIR.

Dana came up alongside Vicki. "Is there anything I can do for you?"

Vicki shook her head and pinched her eyes closed as tears invaded again. "I'll be okay. Just find Brad."

"If he's out there, we will."

"What's FLIR?" Todd asked Dana.

"Forward-looking infrared. It looks for body heat."

Hanks held up his hand, asking for silence. Then he held his radio mic up to his ear, trying to hear over the roar of the falls, the freeway traffic, and the pummeling rain.

"Looks like we're on our own tonight, folks," he said. "The weather's not going to permit an air search right now. You folks are welcome to come along, or wait here and we'll be in touch."

"I'll come," Todd and Vicki said together.

"Are you going with us?" Vicki asked Jessica point-blank.

Jessica licked her lips and in a whining tone said, "I'm not feeling very well. I'll stay here in case he comes back." She climbed back into the Subaru and closed the door.

Vicki didn't attempt to hide her fury. She hurried to catch up to her husband. "Can you believe that woman?"

"Leave it, honey," he told her. "Don't waste your energy on her. Save it for finding Brad. Besides, she has a point. Someone should stay here."

"Right." Vicki pushed her anger aside—as far as it would go.

Trooper Bennett and the two sheriff's deputies, along with Brad's parents, headed for the trail with their black mag lights illuminating the way. For the next three hours they searched the trails and creekbed that led to the Columbia River but found no sign of Brad.

Their initial search ended well after midnight, with Deputy Hanks recommending a full-scale search-and-rescue operation in the morning.

"How can you stop now?" Vicki could hear the desperation growing in her voice. "Shouldn't we go farther into the woods?"

"Mrs. Gaynes." Dana placed a hand on Vicki's arm. "I know how you must feel. But we need to wait until morning before we can conduct a thorough search. Maybe by then the rain will have let up. The search will be much more effective in daylight." As if to prove her point, a spray of water cascaded from her hat.

Vicki shrugged deeper into her warm jacket.

"I'll be leaving now," Dana said. "But I'll check with my supervisor and make sure it's okay for me to come out tomorrow."

You can't quit. My son is out there! Don't you care? Vicki bit into her bottom lip to stop the bitter retort.

"I know this is hard for you." Dana handed Vicki a card and said, "Call me if anything turns up or if you need to talk."

Vicki thanked her and leaned against their Ford Explorer. Todd opened the back and took off his rain jacket, tossed it into the trunk, and pulled on a sweater. "Might as well give me yours too."

Vicki nodded and exchanged her Gore-tex for a warm fleece jacket. Todd handed her a blanket, some trail mix, a couple of apples, a box of crackers, and some mozzarella cheese sticks. When he opened the passenger side door for her, she ducked inside.

Jessica opted to go home when the trooper left, mumbling some excuse about needing a shower and wanting to get some sleep. Vicki's anger surfaced again. When Todd climbed in behind the wheel, she pointed at the disappearing taillights of Brad's Subaru wagon. "Look at that! The least she could do is wait with us."

"Try not to be so hard on her, honey. She seems pretty upset. Must have been rough waiting out here for Brad all by herself."

"Are you taking her side?" Vicki ripped open one of the cheese sticks and peeled off a strip.

"No, of course not. But she said she wasn't feeling well, and I think at this point we need to give her the benefit of the doubt." Todd crunched into an apple.

Vicki didn't agree, but she didn't argue either. "I just don't see how Jessica can say she loves Brad and then leave like that."

"Maybe she doesn't love him. After all, didn't she say she was breaking up with him?"

"She told the deputies that, but I don't believe it." Vicki really didn't know what to believe.

After eating their snacks, they opted to spend the rest of the night in the car, waiting and watching in case Brad returned. Vicki noticed that Deputy Hanks had returned to his vehicle but was still in the parking lot. The green glow from the patrol car's mobile data terminal screen provided just enough light to see the deputy's dark silhouette through the drizzling rain.

Hanks was on the phone, maybe calling his wife or maybe arranging for more people to search for her son. His presence brought a sliver of reassurance.

At Todd's insistence, Vicki stretched out in the backseat under the blanket he'd brought. With the small car pillow tucked under her head, she closed her eyes. Todd dropped his seat slightly and folded his arms. "Let's try to get some sleep. Morning will be here before we know it."

"We should call Rachael." She sat up. Rachael was their daughter, and Todd had called her before they left the house. Vicki had promised to keep her informed.

"Relax, honey. We've been through that. Rachael will be here in the morning. No sense calling her when we have no news."

"I'm surprised she didn't come."

"She wanted to. I told her to wait—no sense in all of us going. I told her I'd call if anything developed. We can give her a call in the morning, but my guess is that she'll be here at the crack of dawn."

Vicki catnapped throughout the next few hours, impatiently waiting for morning to come. How could a mother sleep when her precious son was missing? Her mind kept conjuring up horrible images of finding Brad dead.

4

IT WAS JUST GETTING LIGHT when Vicki heard the beeping sound of a car door opening and the rumbling of a big rig. She rose up and saw that it was a large motor home with the Sheriff's Office Mobile Command Post insignia on the side. Todd stepped out of the car and waited for the man driving the rig to stop.

A sheriff's deputy jumped out and stretched out his hand toward Todd. "Morning. I'm Deputy Sam Wyatt." He glanced at the waterfall. "You must be Todd Gaynes. Deputy Hanks said I'd find you here."

Vicki climbed out of the car and waited for Todd to introduce her. Shaking hands with the deputy, she said, "Thanks for being so prompt."

"Got to take advantage of every minute of daylight. Too little of it this time of year."

Within minutes, dozens of officers from various agencies arrived to assist in the search. Vicki didn't know who was an officer and who was a volunteer. She recognized the sheriff's office personnel because they wore the same uniform as Deputy Wyatt, and the state troopers because of their traditional straw campaign hats, but beyond that she had no clue. She was simply grateful this many people would turn out on a Monday morning at daybreak.

Rachael arrived soon after sunrise. Vicki hugged her, choking up as she tried to talk.

"Have you heard anything?" Rachael asked. "Is he still . . ."

"Nothing yet," Todd said. "We're just getting started."

Vicki brushed back Rachael's bangs. "Where's my grandbaby?"

"At home with Daddy." Rachael smiled. "Kip took the day off to stay home with him. He would be here if he could, but I didn't want to bring the baby out in this mess."

"Wise choice." Vicki glanced around at what appeared to be growing mayhem and hoped they knew what they were doing. Deputy Wyatt seemed competent.

"I'm going to see what's going on," Todd told them. He turned and made his way toward the command post.

Vicki watched him go and caught sight of a familiar face as Dana Bennett and a young man stepped out of an Oregon State Police car. Maybe her boyfriend, she thought. With his handsome face and muscular frame, he reminded her of Brad. Only this man had dark hair. Brad's was blond. They made a nice-looking couple. Jessica and Brad made a nice-looking couple too. She chided herself for making comparisons.

Dana and the young man were dressed in layers, as you'd expect hikers to be in this part of the world. She was wearing a turtleneck under a black-and-red plaid shirt and fleece vest, jeans, and sturdy hiking boots. He was dressed in jeans as well, with a cable-knit sweater over a turtleneck. They both took official-looking rain gear from the backseat with Oregon State Police written on the backs in silver. After suiting up, they donned back-packs.

Dana saw Vicki and waved, then she indicated to her friend to follow her. As she approached, her dimples deepened and her eyes brightened despite only a few hours of sleep. "How are you doing this morning, Mrs. Gaynes?"

"Okay. This is my daughter, Rachael. Rachael, this is Dana Bennett with the Oregon State Police. She was here last night and helped search."

"Nice to meet you." Rachael extended a hand.

"This is Detective Mac McAllister, also OSP." Dana said freeing her thick, blonde braid from inside her vest.

"Detective?" Rachael frowned. "Are you investigating—did something happen? I thought Brad was lost . . ."

Mac held up a restraining hand. "I'm not here on official business, just as a volunteer. Dana told me about Brad, and since I have the day off, I thought I'd join the search."

"Thank you." Vicki looked from one to the other. "This is so nice of you—both of you."

"You're welcome." Mac nodded toward the mobile command unit. "We'd better go in and get our marching orders."

Vicki watched them go, warmed by their generosity. There were so many people here to help, like Dana and Mac, just because they wanted to.

"So what's going on, Mom?" Rachael asked. "What did Jessica say?"

As Vicki told Rachael about Jessica's version of events, the subject of their discussion pulled into the parking lot in Brad's Subaru. "Look who got out of bed before noon," Rachael sneered.

Vicki sighed. "Rachael, I know you two don't care for each other. I don't like her either, but we should at least try to be civil."

"She's a bad influence on him," Rachael muttered.

"I know, I know. But right now we need to focus on Brad and pray we find him."

Jessica came toward them, wearing Brad's wool mackinaw

jacket, which was way too big for her thin frame. She stuffed her hands in the deep pockets. "Any news?"

"No," Vicki answered. "Did you sleep well?" She hadn't meant to sound sarcastic but didn't bother to apologize for her snippy tone.

"No, I didn't." Jessica bit her lip. "I should go. You obviously don't want me here."

Vicki sighed in resignation. She'd told Rachael to be civil, and here she was, acting like a shrew. "You should stay in case the authorities need to talk to you. You'll want to be part of the search party, won't you?"

"I don't know. Maybe."

Vicki clenched her fists to keep from shaking the girl. Jessica didn't even have the decency to look worried.

MAC GLANCED BACK AT THE TWO WOMEN he'd just met and nodded toward the girl who had joined them. "Is that the girlfriend?" he asked Dana.

Dana nodded. "There's something weird going on with those people. I can feel the chill factor clear over here."

"Me too." He also felt something else. Excitement at being involved in the search and relief that he was out here and not at home. Here with Dana, who accepted him at face value, and not with Linda, who insisted he change his wicked ways.

Mac had been bone tired the night before, partially due to the distressing session with Linda and her pastor. They'd ganged up on him and he resented it. Linda had five more counseling sessions scheduled, but Mac didn't plan on going back. He had no idea how to tell Linda that or how she would react. Mac also had no intention of compromising on the amount of time he spent on his job—he had no intention of changing. If Linda didn't like him as he was, then tough. He'd compromised enough by agreeing to attend the premarital counseling session, and look where that had gotten him. Still, he had promised to call Linda every now and then to assure her he was still alive. And they were still engaged.

He wasn't especially happy about his decision or the way he wanted to cut and run. Nor was he pleased with his dishonesty in not telling Linda about his past. His behavior reminded him of his father and how he had broken Mac's mother's heart. That was the last thing Mac wanted.

Dana's voice had been pure heaven this morning, and the promise of a search had pushed aside his angst. "Of course I'll come," he'd told her.

"I'll pick you up at six." Normally Mac would have insisted on driving up himself, but he readily agreed to ride with Dana. Being a passenger would be a nice change, since Mac usually did the driving when he and his partner, Kevin Bledsoe, were working an investigation.

On the drive up the gorge, Mac had been as excited as a kid on his way to Disneyland. He'd done a stint with the Oregon State Police Fish and Wildlife Division and loved being outdoors, although most of his exposure in that field was limited to seasonal fish run assignments.

Now here they were, searching for the missing hiker. He couldn't say why, but like Dana, he had a bad feeling about this guy's disappearance. He just hoped they were wrong.

They got their orders from Deputy Wyatt. Most of the searchers would stick to the trail. "Don't pick up clues or evidence—clothing, food items, litter. Just mark it and report back to me." They received a small bundle of flags—footlong pieces of wire with plastic red or orange squares at the top—with which to mark items to be recovered by the police or search supervisor.

ON THEIR WAY OUT, Mac and Dana paused to talk briefly to Mrs. Gaynes and her daughter. Then they greeted the young woman who seemed to be catching the family's icy barbs. He felt sorry for Jessica in a way. Dana had told Mac about the girlfriend's report—how she and Brad had argued and how Brad had taken off in a huff.

"You must be Jessica." Mac tried to make eye contact with her, but she stared at the asphalt. She had a birdlike look about her. Small, delicate features. Cute and fragile.

"I must be," she commented in a stale, flat tone. She didn't seem overly concerned about her boyfriend. Jessica's oversized wool jacket and jeans with white canvas tennis shoes and no socks were not the kind of gear needed for hiking around these parts. Still, Mac felt he should extend the invitation. "You can come along with Trooper Bennett and me if you want. We're taking the upper trail."

"No thanks." She flashed him an almost frightened look. "I'll stay here. I'm not feeling well this morning. I shouldn't be out hiking."

"Up to you." Mac glanced at Dana. "Let's go."

When they were out of earshot of the others, Mac leaned toward Dana. "Does this case remind you of anything?"

"No. Should it?" Dana adjusted the shoulder straps on her pack.

"Ten years—maybe more. This gal called 911 to report that her boyfriend was missing. She waited eight hours before calling the police and then it was at the guy's mother's insistence. In that case, the boyfriend supposedly took off and never came back."

"He ran out on her?"

"Nope. The authorities suspected suicide for a while. But get this." Mac tossed her a conspiratorial look. "His body was found months later up north in Gray's Harbor, near Aberdeen, Washington.

Turns out she'd pushed him off the cliff—at least that's what the jury determined at the trial."

Dana grimaced. "I remember reading about that. Happened down at the Oregon coast, didn't it?"

He nodded. "Ecola State Park. Anyway, this gal is acting funny. I wouldn't be surprised if Jessica killed Brad."

"Let's hope not." Dana marched on ahead. "I prefer to think he just got lost. Easy to do out here."

Mac nodded as he glanced back at the parking lot and then up at the falls and at the helicopters churning the air above them. Good, the choppers were on the job. The search was starting in earnest now. If Brad Gaynes was out there, they'd find him.

TODD EMERGED FROM THE TRAILER and jogged over to where Vicki, Rachael, and Jessica were huddled against the wind and rain. "They've got at least one helicopter and more ground searchers," he told the women. "A guy with tracking dogs should be here in a few minutes. Deputy Wyatt says he's a local guy— from Cascade Locks—and that he's been pretty successful at finding lost hikers in the past."

Todd looked over his shoulder and pointed toward the mobile unit. "They've got coffee and hot chocolate in their command post if anyone is interested. You ought to take a look; that thing is set up better than our house. It has televisions, radios, computer ports, and fax machines. Looks like they are set up for the long haul if we need them."

"Let's hope it won't be too long." Vicki tucked her cold hand into her husband's large, warm one.

He squeezed it. "I know."

"I'll take some of that hot chocolate." Jessica turned away and ambled toward the motor home.

Rachael sneered at Jessica's back. "Let's go, Dad. I don't want to take time for hot chocolate or anything else. Where are we going?"

"Up to the top of the falls and on from there for as long as we can. Honey . . ." Todd gave Vicki an apologetic look. "They'll need someone who knows him to stay here. We could leave Jessica, but I'm not sure we can trust her to stay."

"I'll stay. I'm not sure I'm up for all that hiking anyway." Vicki bit her lip, tears stinging her eyes. "You two be careful."

Todd kissed Vicki's cheek and Rachael gave her a hug. Then they headed out.

Jessica climbed down the steps of the motor home with her hands wrapped around a steaming mug. Instead of joining Vicki, she opted to sit alone at a picnic table on the grass, just outside the parking lot.

Vicki eyed Jessica critically. *You don't want to talk to me, huh? Just as well. I don't want to talk to you either.* Vicki walked back to her SUV and settled into the passenger seat. Flipping down the visor, she winced at the image. She wore no makeup, and her hair looked as though it had been slept in. She undid the ponytail and finger-combed it back, securing it again and putting on the cap she'd worn the night before. Her heart lurched as she realized it was one of Brad's old ball caps.

Vicki leaned back in the seat, closing her eyes. "God, please let Brad be okay. Let them find him . . . alive," she added quickly. "Bring him back to me."

He may not be coming back.

"No. Don't even think such a thing," she said aloud. "Brad is alive and he's out there. He's just lost his way." Brad had never had a great sense of direction. "They'll find him. They have to."

Vicki tossed a couple of mints into her mouth, wishing she'd taken time to pack some toothpaste. Her thoughts were halted as she caught sight of a silver Dodge pickup pulling into the parking lot two spaces away between her car and the command center.

The pickup had an odd-looking canopy—a giant wood box with chrome trim. The box had four large, round holes on each side and reminded her of a giant birdhouse. On the hood of the truck was flat plastic platform, with fake green turf glued to its face. Four short pieces of chain, with clasps on the end, were mounted in the four corners of the platform.

The door opened, and a large man with a bulky frame exited the vehicle. The crudely made ad on the door read J. Clovis Logging, with a Cascade Locks, Oregon, address and phone number printed below. The three-quarter-ton truck rocked as the man stepped onto the asphalt. He walked to the rear of the vehicle and opened one of the small doors on the box. A brown-and-black hound leaped from the back of the truck and ran to the front of the vehicle then back.

"Kennel up," the large man said in a gentle tone to the hound, who obediently jumped onto the platform mounted on the truck. The man opened three more doors, releasing two more black-and-brown hounds and one blue tick—a muddled gray, white, and black-spot blend.

"Kennel up," he said to each of them, his volume rising as the dogs' excitement and barking increased. Almost in unison, the three dogs joined the first hound on the flat platform.

The big man reached for a box in the truck and returned to the hounds.

Curious, Vicki climbed out of the car. "What are those?" she asked as he took out four black boxes about the size of a man's wallet.

"Radio antennas." He glanced in her direction and then returned to his task, fastening the antennas to each of the dog's collars. He then checked the transmitters with the handheld device he grabbed from the dash of the pickup. "The dogs run free on the track, and I can monitor their location by their barking or by these radio-controlled collars."

Deputy Wyatt approached the man, and the two shook hands. Vicki stepped closer. "Can I give you a hand with anything?" she asked.

"I think we've got everything under control." The big man smiled.

"Mrs. Gaynes," Deputy Wyatt said, "this is Jack Clovis. Vicki is Brad's mother." Clovis removed his brown oilskin hat and shook her hand. She was surprised that such a giant of a man would have such a gentle handshake. "Pleased to meet you, ma'am." He winked and rubbed his thick black beard.

"Jack is a professional tracker," Deputy Wyatt told Vicki. "One of the—"

"I wouldn't say professional." Clovis interrupted, seemingly genuinely embarrassed. "Let's just say me and my hounds enjoy helping out." He pointed back to his truck, where his dogs gazed at him with impatient eyes that seemed to say, "Let's get going."

"He won't let me brag about him while he's around, so I'll tell you more later." Deputy Wyatt grinned.

"We'd better get moving if we're going to be any use to you today." Clovis put his hat back on. "My dogs have some of the best sniffers in the state, but they need something of your son's to start with."

"Maybe there's something in his car." She tried the door and it opened. In the back she found a blue sweatshirt with a Vail, Colorado, logo. "Brad wears this one a lot."

"Good." Jack took it from her. "As long as he hasn't washed it since the last time he had it on, it should be fine." He brought it to his nose. "This will do the job." He approached the hounds with the sweatshirt and allowed them to bury their faces in the soft material. Each hound smelled and licked the sweatshirt for only a couple of moments before Jack moved the garment to the next animal. "Now, fetch 'em up. Go fetch 'em up, babies."

The hounds exploded off the truck, each seeming to have a different idea of where to go. The group eventually raced downstream toward the Columbia River.

"Do they smell something already?" Vicki started jogging in the direction the dogs had taken.

"Hold on, there, Mrs. Gaynes," Deputy Wyatt said.

Vicki stopped and came back. "Why?"

"The hounds take off like that when they start out, but usually they're just running off some steam before they settle in on a track."

"How will Mr. Clovis know when the hounds are on Brad's scent? Does he use those antennas I saw him put on their collars?" Vicki watched the dogs for some sign that they knew what they were doing.

"Yes, ma'am. See that black thing Clovis has in his hand, that thing that looks like a cell phone?" The deputy pointed. "That's a GPS, or global positioning system indicator. He keeps track of his hounds with the antennas on the dog's collars. When they bark a certain way, he knows they are on to a track and checks his GPS to see where they are. You can hear those hounds bay for miles."

Clovis's dogs eventually headed up the trail. Vicki listened closely for their baying, but they remained ominously silent. With every minute that passed on that impossibly long morning came another layer of anxiety and disappointment—another reason to believe the premonition she'd had the night before.

5

HOVERING AT ABOUT SIX HUNDRED FEET, an Army Pavehawk helicopter thumped along the Oregon side of the Columbia River. The helicopter from the Portland Air Base had been dispatched to find a white male in his twenties, last seen yesterday afternoon at the base of Wah-kella Falls in the scenic Columbia River Gorge. All the pilot and observer had were a description of the man's clothing and his last known location. At that altitude, the name and other particulars were not important.

THE NAME AND PARTICULARS, however, were very important to Victoria Gaynes. The helicopter and countless others were not just looking for a faceless man without a name; they were looking for Bradley Gaynes, her only son.

Vicki scanned the endless November clouds for answers. There were none. The steep, fern-covered cliffs to the south and the meandering Columbia River to the north did not leave many places for a grown man to hide. But the thick, thousand-plus acres of forests with giant cedar and fir could hide a man for years.

"Oh God, please let him be okay," Vicki murmured under her

breath as she zipped her raincoat up to her neck. It had begun to rain again—or had it ever stopped?

Vicki covered her ears to lessen the almost painfully loud noise the helicopter made. The pilots were flying as close to the ground as possible, but to Vicki they didn't seem close enough.

Deputy Sam Wyatt stepped out from the mobile command post and approached Vicki with obvious concern in his eyes. He was a stern-looking man, lean and strong, a man who seemed to know his business and at the same time maintained an empathetic demeanor. His face had the leathered look of someone who spent a lot of time in the sun.

Vicki read the news in his eyes before he spoke. Not wanting to hear the negative report, she said, "I'll take that cup of coffee now, if it's still available."

"Sure thing, Mrs. Gaynes." His mouth curved into a tentative smile. Relief flickered in his eyes, but only for a moment.

SAM DUCKED BACK INSIDE, grabbed an empty cup, and filled it from the insulated carafe on the counter next to the small sink. He didn't want to give Mrs. Gaynes a report any more than she wanted to hear it. The morning's search had yielded nothing but a few articles of clothing and some trash; none of it belonged to the missing man. Brad's mother took her coffee black and strong. That request he could handle.

Sam grasped the mug and stepped back outside, feeling helpless and wishing he could give the woman a modicum of hope along with the hot drink. Sam wanted to be out there searching, but someone had to stay at the command post; and he'd been assigned that duty. Besides, he doubted his arthritic knee would let him hike for long. So for now, at least, it was up to him to keep the family informed and the troops in line.

Brad's mother stood there shivering, her lips almost blue. She barely reached his chest, maybe five feet at the most. Her blonde hair, partly caught up in a ponytail and covered with a baseball cap, hung straight and dripping onto her back and shoulders.

"Thank you." She took the steaming mug from him, wrapping her hands around it for heat. Mrs. Gaynes had been vigilant since the night before, waiting and watching, pain etched in her blue eyes and expressive face.

Sam knew what it was like to lose a son. His had been killed by a drunk driver three years ago. He hoped with all he had in him that Brad had just wandered off the trail and become lost in the woods. He offered up a prayer that Vicki Gaynes's son would be found alive and that the family could go home happy and relieved.

Removing his weathered baseball cap, Sam snapped it in midair to rid the bill of excess water. A useless gesture in this weather. He turned away from the distraught mother and tipped back his head to look up at the awesome sight Wah-kella Falls made with its thick wall of water cascading over the top of the sheer cliff. Rain relentlessly drizzled from the heavy, sunless sky. Clouds merged with water and mist, turning everything that hazy battleship gray so prevalent in the Northwest during November.

The Pavehawk dipped in again, churning up the waters. Although constructed for peacetime rescues, with winches and wire baskets within her hull, the helicopter was no less menacing looking than its military sister, the Army Blackhawk. How ironic that the plain helicopter was on a search-and-rescue mission in Oregon while in other parts of the world, its heavily armed relatives were on search-and-destroy missions.

Truth be told, Sam's hope for finding the missing man had faded as soon as he'd heard the location. The place had a reputation most people had never heard about. Sam and his law enforcement buddies referred to Wah-kella Falls as Suicide Point. Over the years it had earned its name.

An ancient Native American legend told of an Indian maiden who loved a young man even though her father had promised her to another. The young man attempted to prove his bravery to the maiden's father, but the father did not deem him worthy. So great was the young man's grief that he threw himself over the cliff, ending his life and his pain forever.

According to the legend, the maiden was so heartbroken, she sat on the side of the cliff and wept for days, her tears eventually becoming the massive waterfall that cascaded over the three-hundred-foot cliff and wound its way down to the Columbia River.

Deputy Wyatt was all too familiar with the legend, and even more familiar with the real-life tragedies that had occurred at Wah-kella Falls over the years.

The scenic waterfall was located close to the heavily traveled Interstate 84, only about forty-five miles east of Portland. The waterfall was easily accessed from the parking lot where they waited. Visitors could enjoy the haunting beauty of the waterfall from its base or, for the more adventurous, from the top. A mile-long trail switchbacked and meandered through the woods, eventually ending up at the fenced-off viewpoint. The trail went on from there, through the Mount Hood National Forest and up into the hills.

Most people knew only the beauty of the falls and came to capture its grandeur with their cameras and canvases. A few, however, came to the waterfall to end their lives. Four suicides had been documented at Wah-kella Falls in the past fifteen years—the last one, only eight months ago.

Sam and two Oregon State Police troopers had responded to the call, discovering that a despondent computer engineer accused of molesting a child at a swimming pool had leaped to his death rather than face arrest and humiliation. The officers found the life-less body facedown at the base of the waterfall. The suicide note in the man's car indicated his intent to end his life and proclaimed his innocence. He'd eventually been cleared of the offense, but the vindication came too late.

Sam, aware of movement beside him, snapped back to the present, breaking the spell the misty waterfall seemed to cast on him. He turned his attention back to the anxious mother.

"What are Brad's chances?" she asked. "When you came out of the trailer earlier, you looked like you were about to tell me something."

"Just wanted to bring you up to speed on our progress." Sam tried to sound enthusiastic. "We have two birds in the air, one flying with forward-looking infrared to look for body heat and the other with a spotter."

"Any sign of him yet?" Vicki asked without making eye contact. Her gaze scanned the rock-faced cliff to the top of the waterfall, as if knowing the answer yet needing to ask.

"No, nothing. But it's still early in the game." Sam zipped up his Gore-tex jacket. The mist from the waterfall and the low-hanging clouds could soak through the best of raincoats in no time at all.

A GAME? He thinks this is a game? The comment irritated Vicki. *My son has been missing for eighteen hours and he thinks "it's still early in the game"?* She bit into her lower lip to keep from voicing her anger aloud. It wasn't Deputy Wyatt's fault, or any of the people out there searching.

"In addition to the birds . . ." Sam paused while the Pavehawk flew overhead. "We now have almost sixty officers and explorer scouts working the trails and the riverbanks. We still have Clovis and his hounds working the area. If your son is out there, Mrs. Gaynes, we'll find him."

Vicki was not convinced. She shivered from the downdraft of the helicopter as it churned up the air and the water in and around the giant pool at the base of the waterfall that fed the creek. "Why does that helicopter keep hovering over the pool?" Vicki turned back to Sam.

The deputy cleared his throat. "The helicopter rotors try to stir up the water and . . ." Sam hesitated, taking off his cap again to adjust the brim. "Are you sure you want to know?"

She nodded. "I need to know everything."

He frowned, pulling his gaze from hers and fastening it on the chopper. "They're displacing the water. In the event there's a body floating under the surface, they should be able to spot it."

Vicki nodded, unable to speak. The familiar lump clogged her throat as unbidden tears filled her eyes.

"If he was in there, they probably would have found him by now," Sam said. "It's just routine; we want to make sure. Cover all the bases." Sam planted the damp hat back on his head. "We're still planning on finding him alive."

Vicki's watery gaze met his. "He didn't jump, if that's what they're thinking."

Sam stuffed his hands in his pockets. "Are you sure, ma'am? It wouldn't be the first time . . ."

"Of course I'm sure," Vicki snapped. "Brad would never take his own life, no matter what anyone may have told you." She turned to glare at the young woman huddled on top of the picnic table next to the motor home. If anyone could be blamed for Brad's disappearance, it was Jessica.

Voices from a radio inside the motor home sent Sam rushing back inside.

"No matter what *she* may have told you," Vicki muttered, more to herself than Sam.

Moments later, Sam leaned out of the motor home's door. "It's getting on noon, Mrs. Gaynes. I'm going to call the troops in for lunch. Can I get you anything?"

"No thanks. I'll probably grab something when my husband and daughter get back." Vicki walked over to the trailhead and peered up the trail. She couldn't see far, only about twenty feet, before it disappeared into the woods. She wondered what was taking Todd and Rachael so long. They had been searching the trails since sunup, if you wanted to call it that. She hadn't seen the sun all day. Waiting at base camp, Vicki decided, was far more difficult a task than searching.

Vicki turned her attention back to Brad's girlfriend. Jessica should have been helping with the search. Instead, she just sat there, staring into space. Sitting at the table she'd been sitting at all morning except for brief trips to the car or to the bathroom. Vicki wanted to shake her, to batter her with questions. *Why aren't you helping the others search? Where is Brad? What have you done to him?*

Instead, Vicki ducked into the trailer and refilled her cup; then she helped herself to a second cup, filling it with hot water and dumping in a package of cocoa mix. She drew in a deep breath and took the hot chocolate out to Jessica. Her upbringing superseded her desire to confront. She'd remain civil—at least for now. Besides, the mother in her had a shred of compassion for the girl.

Jessica acknowledged Vicki with wariness in her brown eyes. Undoubtedly Jessica could sense Vicki's animosity. She and Todd and Rachael had been rude, to say the least. Jessica had dark brown hair and smooth, clear skin. Even now, with no makeup and rain plastering her hair to her head, she was attractive. Vicki could see why Brad had fallen for her. But looks could be deceiving.

Handing Jessica the steaming mug, Vicki said, "Thought you might like something warm."

Their hands brushed as Jessica took the cup. "Thanks." Jessica didn't smile; she just turned her gaze to the marshmallows Vicki had tossed in the drink at the last minute.

Vicki climbed up on the table and sat next to the tall, shapely brunette, sipping her own drink, feeling the need to talk yet not knowing what to say. The questions damming up behind her inner control panel seemed too harsh, and Vicki didn't trust herself to ask them.

Jessica had grown up near Fresno, California, and moved to Oregon two years ago to work at the ski resorts on Mount Hood. That's where she and Brad met. He, a fun-loving snowboarder and accomplished downhill racer, had come up to Timberline Lodge to wet his whistle after a day of snowboarding with friends. Brad and Jessica had told her bits and pieces of how they'd gotten together, and Vicki let her imagination supply the rest. Her tall, handsome Brad had removed his ski cap in the entryway to the lodge and shook out the wet cap, running his hand through his long, matted blond hair.

Water from the hat sprayed several feet, landing on a waitress who stood near the giant stone fireplace taking drink orders. She turned and complained about the unwanted shower. "The minute I looked into Brad's eyes I knew we were meant to be together," Jessica had told her. That had been a year ago.

The two began dating soon after their chance meeting and, six months later, moved in together. They shared a small cabin in Brightwood, just a half-hour's drive from Mount Hood. The arrangement made Vicki uncomfortable. She was from the old school where people married first and then lived together. Still, she'd never encouraged Brad to marry Jess, which was what Brad called her.

She'd had reservations from the very beginning. It didn't take long for Vicki to discover that her reservations were well-founded.

Jessica was not the wholesome young woman she'd pretended to be when Brad first brought her home. She drank and smoked and used marijuana and probably other drugs. She tried to keep that side of her personality secret, but Vicki knew. Vicki also knew that Brad was involved in the drug and alcohol use, and she blamed Jessica for bringing him down to that level.

Oh, Brad, why didn't you break things off months ago?

"You blame me for Brad's disappearance, don't you?" Jessica's question startled her.

"I . . . I don't know what to think." Vicki cast a sidelong look toward Jessica then turned back to the waterfall. "Is there a reason I should blame you?"

"I feel bad. I guess I should have called the police sooner."

"Yes, you should have." Vicki stiffened. That was one of the disturbing things about all of this. Brad had been missing for more than four hours before Jessica finally called the police.

"Like I told the police, Brad went for a walk up the trail and I took a nap. We'd been arguing, and I was tired. When I woke up, it was dark and Brad was still gone. I took a flashlight and went up the trail to try to find him, but I got scared and came back to the truck. I locked the doors and waited and waited." She took a sip of hot chocolate, leaving a ring of foam on her upper lip. She licked it off.

"After a while, I began to think maybe something bad might have happened to him." Jessica's gaze met Vicki's and for a moment, Vicki felt they shared a common bond—love for Brad and fear for his safety. Jessica tore her gaze away. "Anyway, I tried to use the cell phone, but the battery was dead. Brad is terrible about charging it. I didn't know what to do, so I went home and called the police from there."

Vicki tried to drum up some empathy for Jessica but felt only numbness. "Had you and Brad been drinking?"

"He had a couple of beers. He wanted to quit. We talked about getting into some kind of recovery program." She paused again to sip her hot chocolate.

"I'd like to believe that, Jess. I really would. You told Deputy Wyatt that you broke up with Brad and that he got angry."

"That's true."

"But Brad told me he was thinking about breaking up with you. He wanted to get straight, and you were dragging him down, wanting to go to parties and do drugs."

Jessica set her cup beside her. "I don't expect you to believe me, Mrs. Gaynes, but I wasn't the one keeping Brad down. He did that to himself."

"You're right. I don't believe you. Brad wanted more than anything to get back to his Christian values and back to church, but you didn't want to go."

"You're right about that. I don't go to church, and I probably never will. But that isn't what we were fighting about." Jessica tipped her head down.

"What were you fighting about?"

Jessica pursed her lips and scooted off the table. "What's the point in my even talking to you? You have your mind made up that I'm a bad influence on your precious son. Nothing I say is going to change that." She left her cup on the table and headed for Brad's Subaru.

Vicki watched Jessica climb into the car and start the engine. Was she leaving? Apparently not, she decided after a few minutes. Maybe Jessica just needed to warm up. Humph. It would take a lot of heat to melt that cube of ice.

Vicki still couldn't understand why Jessica wasn't out with the rest of the searchers, even if she'd had a fight with Brad. Something was wrong with that girl. Vicki had heard Jessica's account of what had happened several times and was more convinced than ever that Jessica was not telling the truth.

6

VICKI HUGGED HERSELF, shivering from the damp cold as she listened intently for the hounds to start barking or howling. Four hours of wanting, hoping, and praying hadn't yielded the results she longed for. The hounds never howled. Besides freeway traffic, the waterfall, and the constant November rain, all she heard was the occasional crack of the police radio back at the command post.

The searchers drifted in and out now—getting food, warming up, and giving reports before heading out again.

After most of the searchers had gone back out, Wyatt invited Vicki and Jessica into the motor home for turkey sandwiches and coffee. Jessica declined, saying she wasn't hungry. Vicki thought it was probably because she didn't want to be in such close proximity to a police officer—or to her.

"Wish we had some good news, Mrs. Gaynes." Deputy Wyatt gestured toward a booth and placed a paper plate with a sandwich and some grapes in front of her. "But there's been no sign of Brad."

She glanced at her watch. Two o'clock. Todd and Rachael hadn't come back in yet. What was taking them so long?

"I haven't heard or seen the helicopter for a while," Vicki said.

"They're still up there. The Pavehawk is scanning the forested areas now, and the Coast Guard chopper is working the river."

Vicki nodded, taking a bite of the sandwich. "Thanks for lunch."

"No problem." Sam poured himself a cup of milk from the container in the fridge and offered her some. She shook her head. "I've had too much coffee," he said. "It's hard to hang around here and wait."

"That's for sure." The sandwich and coffee settled like a giant lump in Vicki's stomach and stayed there long after she'd finished eating. She and Sam talked for a while about the weather and the latest news happenings. He offered her a couple magazines from the rack in the motor home. She took an old copy of *Sunset* and scanned it, not really reading anything. Eventually, she tossed the magazine on the seat and went back outside, where she paced back and forth from the trailhead to the car, praying and going crazy with worry.

Finally, at four-thirty, she spotted Todd and Rachael coming down the trail.

She recognized Todd and Rachael's raincoats from a distance, even if her eyesight prohibited her from seeing their faces clearly. The steady rain made it impossible to wear glasses; she tired of cleaning them and left them in the Ford hours ago. Even without her glasses, she could read Todd's grim expression as he got closer. *Still no sign of Brad.*

Todd hugged her and draped an arm around her shoulders as he led her to the command post, where he opened a cooler and pulled out a bottle of water.

Rachael glared at the Subaru. "Jessica is responsible for this. I know it."

"Let's not jump to conclusions." Todd twisted open the lid to the water and handed it to his daughter; then he grabbed another for himself.

"What else am I supposed to think? We've had an army of people out there all day combing every inch of those woods. He isn't there." Rachael took a long sip of water.

"Maybe he just took off." Todd tipped back his head, his Adam's apple moving up and down as he drank nearly half of the sixteen ounces of water. "He could be back at the cabin right now, wondering where everybody is."

"Have you tried calling him?" Vicki asked hopefully.

Todd nodded. "Every hour. But he could have gotten a ride with one of the truckers. Maybe he decided to split for a while." He nodded toward Jessica. "Maybe he wanted to get away from her."

"He wouldn't do that without letting us know," Vicki insisted.

"We don't know that." Todd ran a hand through his wet hair, displacing his cap and knocking it to the ground. He stooped to snatch it up.

"Jessica said he'd been drinking." Vicki's voice trembled with barely disguised anger.

"Maybe we should check out places he likes to go," Rachael offered. "He could have gone up to Mount Hood or Bachelor to snowboard. With all this rain, there's bound to be new snow. You know how he likes to be out in that stuff."

"We should check with his friends," Todd said.

"I'll do that," Rachael offered. "I need to get home anyway. Kip and I can make some calls and go to all Brad's haunts—ask if anyone has seen him. Like you said, he could have come down and seen that Jessica was gone and then hitched a ride into town."

Vicki allowed herself to get caught up in their whirlwind of hope. She kissed her daughter good-bye and then grasped her husband's hand. Watching Rachael leave, she prayed they were right and that Brad was at home—or somewhere, safe and alive.

AT FOUR O'CLOCK, Mac's cell phone vibrated. He and Dana had been following the upper trail. Flipping open his cell, he answered, "Mac here."

"Fun's over, Mac." His partner, Kevin Bledsoe, sounded none too happy. "We got a twelve-forty-nine. Body was found by a real-estate assessor at the old Cazadero Mill on Faraday Road, east of Estacada. A guy was found in the old sawmill out here. Sawed in half."

"You're kidding." Mac glanced at Dana, who joined him on the trail.

"Wish I was."

"Have you ID'd him?" Mac wondered briefly if the murder victim might be their missing guy, then dismissed the idea. No reason to make that kind of connection.

"Not yet. The assessor said it was a male. I'm en route—M.E. should be there within the half-hour. Where are you?"

"Wah-kella Falls area—about two miles from the top of the falls."

"How soon can you get out here?"

Mac wished he'd taken his own car. He hated to pull Dana out of the search. "Hang on, Kevin." He told Dana about the murder. "You'll have to take me out there, or I'll try to catch a ride."

Glancing at her watch, Dana said, "I'm with you."

"We're on our way. Should be there within the hour."

"We?" Mac could picture Kevin's raised eyebrow. "Don't tell me; let me guess. You're with Trooper Bennett."

Mac grinned, not really minding the implication. "Yeah. You got a problem with that?"

"Not at all, partner. Just curious." Kevin chuckled. "This one sounds pretty grisly, Mac. Dana might want to think twice about coming in on it."

"I'll tell her."

As he and Dana jogged down the trail, Mac's concerns about

Bradley Gaynes returned, but he didn't voice them. He wanted to be wrong. He wanted Gaynes to walk out of the woods a few miles down the road. He wanted the girlfriend to be an innocent bystander. There was nothing thus far to indicate foul play, and he hoped it stayed that way.

"You think Brad might be the victim at the sawmill?" Dana asked after they had checked out with the command center and were pulling out of the parking lot. Her flushed cheeks, sparkling aquamarine eyes, and breathless voice made her more appealing than usual.

"Crossed my mind." Mac pulled his gaze from hers. *Down, boy. She's got a boyfriend and you—you're in limbo.* "Estacada isn't all that far away. They haven't ID'd him yet."

"Guess we'll find out soon enough," Dana said, merging into the freeway traffic.

"Are you familiar with the Cazadero Mill?" Mac asked.

"Yeah. The sawmill went out of business a little over a year ago. The owners left it as is, hoping to sell it, but nothing so far. There's still thousands of dollars in equipment in the building with a razor cyclone fence around it, but like any abandoned property, after a while it starts looking attractive to the bad guys. Some creeps were dealing drugs out of it for a while. We closed them down."

"Right. I heard about that." Mac glanced at her. "Maybe they started back up again."

She shrugged.

"Kevin said a real-estate assessor found the body. Makes me wonder how well the security guys are doing their job."

"I think it's one of those agencies that checks in once a shift. If the bad guys knew the routine, they could stay under the radar."

Mac shifted in his seat. "Kevin said you might want to stay out of the foray on this one. It's pretty gruesome."

Dana bit her lower lip. "Aren't they all?"

"Yeah, but this guy was sawed in half."

Dana sucked in a sharp breath and gave Mac a quick glance. "Sawed in half!"

"Don't know if it's postmortem or not. You sure you want to see it?" Mac raised an eyebrow, already knowing the answer.

"Not really, but yes. If you don't mind me tagging along."

Mac shrugged, "It's your time, Dana."

Dana cut through Gresham on Highway 26, then down to Highway 224 from the town of Sandy, turning off onto Faraday Road toward the condemned Cazadero Mill on the Clackamas River. They pulled off the road, parking between a Clackamas County Sheriff's SUV and an OSP Cruiser. Mac noted that the medical examiner's truck was there, as well as the Ford pickup belonging to the crime lab. The Camry probably belonged to the reporting party. It was hemmed in by two official vehicles, which in all likelihood belonged to the original responding officers.

Yellow crime-scene tape had been set in place over one hundred yards from the mill's entrance. Mac recognized Kevin's influence there. *"An outer perimeter to a crime scene can never be too big."* Mac could almost hear Kevin's deep voice. *"Start big, and you can always make it smaller. Start small, and if you need to go bigger, you're in trouble."*

Mac and Dana logged into the crime scene, waiting to make eye contact with Kevin before walking to the front entrance of the mill to avoid disturbing the evidence.

"Watch your step." Kevin peered at them over his clipboard. "Follow the yellow-brick road."

"Follow the what?" Dana asked Mac.

Mac chuckled as he pulled some rubber shoe covers from the trunk. "That yellow strip of crime-scene tape on the ground." Mac pointed to the four-inch-wide yellow plastic tape that ran from the parking lot to the mill entrance, where Kevin was standing with the chief medical examiner, Dr. Kristen Thorpe. With her usual getup and short, spiked burgundy hair, the M.E. was hard to miss. He smiled remembering the first time he'd seen her. He couldn't stop staring at her, and she'd fixed his curiosity good by accusing him of flirting.

"Humph. Looks like someone needs to tie their crime-scene tape a little better." Dana nodded toward the tape.

"Well, that's Kevin's yellow-brick road. He wants us to walk the same path to the mill entrance, which I assume he already searched for evidence. If we walk on the tape, it should be a safe path into the building so we don't disturb anything. Here, put these rubber booties over your boots so we don't leave any shoe prints in the sawdust. I think Kevin secretly likes seizing shoes for evidence from emergency personnel, especially firemen."

"Why does he take their shoes?" Dana asked, slipping the large rubber slip-ons over her small boots.

"If he finds shoe prints in the crime scene, he has to compare all the shoes that emergency personnel wore into the scene. It's a process of elimination. Sometimes they don't ever get their shoes back; they just sit in evidence for years if no suspect is arrested."

"Yikes. I just paid a hundred and sixty dollars for this pair. I'd rather keep them, so thanks for the rubber covers. They look like the boots my mother made me wear to the bus stop when I was a kid, except for the smooth soles."

"Perfect for not leaving prints. Here, wrap some duct tape around the top so they stay on your feet. We can just throw them away when we are done. I go through a lot of them." Mac tossed Dana a roll of tape.

When Dana finished securing the rubber covers to her boots, they walked the tape to the entrance.

"Sorry I'm so late, partner," Mac said. "We got here as fast as we could."

"No problem." Kevin looked pale, and Mac noticed a line of

perspiration on his upper lip. Mac had never seen Kevin get sick at a crime scene.

"You feeling okay, Kevin?" he asked.

"Yeah, nothing to worry about. I just need a little air." He glanced over at Dana. "How have you been?"

"Great. I just completed a crisis negotiation course last week. Should come in handy someday."

"Good for you." Kevin studied Dana a moment, then he said, "Listen, I don't mind you coming into the scene. Just don't get into hot water with your patrol sergeant if you should be taking other calls."

"Not to worry, Detective. This is all on my own time. He knows what my career goals are."

"All right, then. Come on in. This one is not for the faint of heart, so prepare yourselves." Kevin led the way into the lumber mill's main saw room. Once inside the enormous dark room, he gestured toward a large table where Kristen Thorpe was taking photographs. "Looks like we have a transient living in an office in one of the outbuildings. We found a cot, a few toiletries, and some clothing—nothing that helps us ID the guy. The guys from the identification bureau are hoping to lift some prints from the room where the guy was staying, but it's going to be tough with all this dust floating around."

"So we think the victim was the transient?" Dana asked.

We, Mac thought. *Didn't take her long to feel at home.*

"I think so. The victim is dressed in a camouflage shirt and jacket, with wool hunting pants. It's the same type of clothing we found in the room. He isn't wearing any shoes or socks, and we found a pair of boots under his bunk that look like his size. This old mill is up for auction, along with all the heavy equipment. An assessor from the auction house was the one who found the body. He came by this morning to itemize the mill's equipment when he made the discovery. I think the victim was living out here for whatever reason, killing wild game to stay alive. There are several deer hides and meat hooks in the back of this main room. I can't imagine one man eating that much meat, unless he's lived here for years, so I haven't quite figured that out yet. With his sleeping bag turned out and his lack of shoes, I think someone paid a visit to our victim last night—probably surprised him."

"Any clues from the body on cause of death?" Mac asked.

"There's no doubt about this one, Mac. Come take a look." The three stepped carefully over to Kristen, who was still taking photographs of the gruesome scene. The victim had been cut into two pieces, from the tip of his head through his pelvis, with a giant band saw that was designed for cutting heavy timber beams. The saw had dried blood on it, along with what were probably chunks of hair and bone dust. Blood spatter reached all the way to where they were standing.

"Hey, Mac. Welcome to the slaughterhouse." Kristen's broad smile showed under the large camera. "Looks like a case of split personality, if you ask me."

Dana grimaced. "Split personality?" she mouthed to Mac.

"You'll get used to her," Mac said. "Our Dr. Thorpe thinks she's a stand-up comedian."

"Oh, well in that case . . . breaking up is hard to do." Dana grinned. "I'm Dana Bennett. I was at the Tyson body dump scene working the crime scene tape."

Kristen chuckled. "I remember you, Dana. 'Breaking up'— that's a good one."

Feeling the need to add his own pun, Mac said, "I'm thinking maybe he was killed because he was two-faced."

Kristen and Dana both groaned.

"Enough with the gallows humor, guys. Maybe we all should just do our job." Kevin cast each of them a withering look. "Dying is rough enough without having you yahoos mocking his corpse."

Mac raised his eyebrows at Kristen, who shrugged her shoulders and continued to take photos. Nothing bothered her, but Mac was a little put off. Kevin and other senior detectives had made jokes like that dozens of times, and Kevin never seemed to mind. In fact, most of the detectives indulged in some sort of gallows humor. It made the horrendous tasks they had to face go down a little easier. Maybe Kevin wasn't feeling well. Or maybe something was going on at home. Mac decided to ignore Kevin's surly attitude. Instead, he focused on the crime scene, which was indeed horrific.

The band saw blade looped through a giant steel feeding table, around a floor guide, and then back into the saw engine that was mounted twenty feet above the table. The victim had been forced through the blade, nearly through the center of his head and torso, slicing through one wrist before completing the cut. The victim's wrists had been bound in the front by a heavy wrapping of silver duct tape. Mac made a mental note to secure the tape at autopsy in case the killer had left prints.

"I'm thinking the guy was alive when he went through the saw." Kristen lowered the camera. "It looks like he took a blow to the head prior to death; you can see the bleeding by the left temple. The tape on his hands leads me to believe he was knocked out and then bound, probably prior to the saw blade finishing the job."

"Whew." Dana shuddered. "What a way to go. I hope he wasn't conscious."

Kevin nodded and turned to Mac. "The latent guys lifted a partial boot print mold from the area around the saw prior to printing the room where the guy lived. They didn't have much luck around the saw blade or controls. The killer was probably wearing gloves."

"I've got plenty of pictures," Kristen said. "Let's load him into a body bag and schedule an autopsy. You guys go ahead and bag those hands now, so we can protect that tape and his fingernails."

"Why do you need to bag the hands?" Dana asked.

Since Kevin had elected to do the job, Mac answered. "We bag the hands with paper sacks so nothing is lost in transit. We'll examine his fingernails at the postmortem examination, in case there is forensic evidence under his nails or on the tape."

Dana stepped back as Mac donned gloves and helped Kevin and Kristen prepare the body for transport. They transferred the bagged body to the waiting stretcher and then wheeled it out to Dr. Thorpe's Dodge pickup.

"When can you get to the post on this guy, Doc?" Kevin asked.

"How does tomorrow look for you?" She glanced in Mac's direction. "Say, eight-thirty?"

"Fine with me." Mac ripped off his gloves and tossed them in the disposal box in Kristen's truck.

"Are you coming to the post, Dana?" Kristen removed her gloves as well.

"Um—you mean post as in autopsy?"

"Right."

"I'd like to, but I can't. Have to work. I'll take a rain check, though." She grinned up at Mac then let her gaze slide to Kristen. "I'm hoping to make detective, and Mac tells me I should get all the experience I can."

"Good," Kristen said in a clipped tone, her jocular manner gone. "Call me anytime. I'll arrange it."

Kristen climbed into her truck, put on her headphones, and started the engine. Strains of rock music lingered as she drove away.

"Interesting woman," Dana said. "I like her. She's eccentric and funny and very smart."

Mac watched the truck exit the gate and turn onto the road.

"Yeah. She's eccentric, all right."

"What do we do now?" Dana folded her arms, her gaze moving from Mac to Kevin.

"Go home," Kevin answered. "The crime lab guys will finish up and take care of the scene." He headed for his car. "See you tomorrow, Mac."

"Right. Did you want me to pick you up at the office?" Mac asked.

"Would you mind swinging by my house?" Kevin tossed Dana a smile. "Mac's been acting as my chauffeur, so I might as well take advantage of his generosity while I can."

Mac and Kevin worked as a team. Mac usually drove, but he'd never picked his partner up at his home. Though his gut told him something wasn't right, Mac didn't comment. "Sure," he teased. "I'll just put in for overtime and list chauffeuring Kevin on my time card."

"Smart-mouth." Kevin rolled his eyes at Dana. "See what I have to put up with?"

"Such a hardship. Hey, thanks for letting me observe."

"You're welcome. Anytime."

As Mac and Dana headed in a northwesterly direction across the Glen Jackson Bridge toward Vancouver, Dana chatted about Bradley Gaynes, saying she hoped the search party had found him by now.

"We could ask," Mac suggested.

"We could." Dana pulled up her radio and contacted Deputy Wyatt. The news wasn't good. They'd called in the searchers at dusk and would resume the search in the morning.

"That poor family." Dana sighed. "I wish I could go back out."

"I know."

"I also wish I could go to the autopsy. It would be nice to follow through with this case. See how you and Kevin operate."

"I'll try to keep you posted. Want to meet for coffee Wednesday morning before work?"

"I'd love that."

Dana's obvious enthusiasm made him laugh. She looked and sounded delighted. He wished Linda could be that excited about his job. Mac could relate to Dana. He'd been and still was eager to learn. Even now with some experience under his belt, Mac could hardly wait for tomorrow and for the autopsy. The evidence and the criminal process would eventually tell them who the unfortunate victim was, and hopefully the trail would lead them to the killer.

7

THE NEXT MORNING, Mac and Kevin let themselves in the old red brick medical examiner's building through the employee's entrance at the back. Kristen was already dictating the description of the body when the detectives walked into the small examination room. She clicked off her machine. "Welcome to the little shop of horrors, boys."

Mac let his gaze travel over the cap covering Kristen's spiked hair, the lace peeking above her rubber apron, and then stopped at her clear blue eyes. There was no laughter in them this morning.

"Can you tell if this guy's our missing hiker?" Mac had been thinking about Brad Gaynes all night. Brad hadn't been wearing combat fatigues when he'd disappeared, but he'd been gone long enough to go home and change. Kevin thought the victim might have been a transient who'd been staying at the mill. But what if the guy at the mill had been the killer? Kristen was quick to shoot down his theory.

"He's not, Mac. This guy has a scar running along his left cheek. He's older too."

Mac nodded, relieved that he wouldn't be having to face the

Gaynes family to tell them their son had been murdered. His relief was short-lived, though. The guy was someone's husband or son or father.

The two body halves were lying on the giant steel table. The victim's left eye was open, staring blankly, while the other eye was closed. Mac looked away for a moment, seeking objectivity. When he did look back, it was to view the torso. The victim's clothing had been removed to reveal heavily tattooed arms and torso. "Jailhouse tattoos," Mac noted. "Once we grab prints, this guy should be easy to identify. Looks like he's done some time in the joint, by the look of those cheap green tats."

"Just what I was thinking, partner." Kevin scrutinized the victim. "With any luck at all we'll get his prints into the Automated Fingerprint Identification System. We could use a break. The ID bureau only found a few prints at the scene—no telling who they belong to. Could be our guy here, or the killer, or could be employees who used to work at the mill. They found no real evidence in the guy's makeshift bedroom either. Looks like what we see is what we get until we put a name to this fella."

Mac and Kevin bagged the clothing for examination at the crime lab, in case it contained trace evidence that would help nab the killer. They found nothing evidentiary under the victim's nails or on the rest of his body.

Kristen peeled back the scalp, confirming her suspicion of blunt force trauma to the head prior to death.

"Looks like this guy took a pretty good whack to the head, guys. There's a large cranial bruise. I'd say it was enough to knock him goofy, but probably not enough force to kill him. I'm going to rule the saw as the mechanism of death. The cause can be your pick: laceration of the brain and virtually every internal organ."

"Okay to print him now, Kristen?" Kevin asked. He seemed in a hurry to get through the procedure.

Mac could certainly understand that, but they'd seen worse.

"Sure, I'll change the John Doe jacket once you call with a real identification. He's not matching any current missing-person reports in the region. I'll go out of state on the computer search if you don't come up with anything."

Kevin produced a small ink pad from his briefcase, inking the victim's fingers while Mac carefully cut the duct tape from the wrists and secured it in an evidence bag. After Kevin inked the fingers, Mac rolled each individual finger onto a print card. Rigor had set in, and the fingers were like concrete.

"Let's get this stuff down to the lab," Kevin said when Mac had finished. "See if they can get some prints off the tape and identify our dead guy."

"You got it. I'm ready." Mac glanced once more at the nightmarish scene on the heavy steel table before taking off his gloves.

"You guys taking off so soon? You don't want to stick around for some sewing lessons?" Henry, the medical assistant, walked in with a hook needle and heavy thread to sew the body back together for the morgue.

"Nope—sorry, we have to split." Kevin winked at Mac.

Mac groaned and shook his head.

"Not bad, Detective." Kristen saluted him. "Not great, but not bad."

"Humph. Better than the hash you guys were slinging last night." Kevin turned to Mac. "Let's get out of here. You two are rubbing off on me."

"I don't get it," Mac said once they were on their way. "Why would the killer use a saw?"

"Actually, the method of murder speaks volumes, Mac. I'm thinking the killer had a vendetta against him. From the looks of it, he was sending a message. Remember the horse's head in *The Godfather*?"

"Right. So you're thinking this might be a mob killing?" The thought struck Mac in the chest like an ice pick, bringing back memories of his grandfather. Mac didn't know many details surrounding Antonio DiAngelis's life—he chose not to know. What Mac did know was that his grandfather's money was as dirty as he was. Rich, powerful, and mean, Mac's grandfather might have ordered something like this done. Antonio DiAngelis was serving a life sentence for his connection to the murder of a federal agent who'd infiltrated the ranks of his organization. Mac wondered how a man so evil could have fathered such a decent woman as his mother or have married someone like Dottie. His grandmother, aside from her devotion to her corrupt husband, was a saint.

"It's something to consider," Kevin was saying when Mac tuned back in. "Maybe a drug dealer. I'm thinking our victim crossed someone big-time, and his killer used the saw to send a message loud and clear."

"Yeah, like, 'Cross me and you get the saw.'"

"Or something worse." Kevin sighed. "If we're right and this guy is a con, his list of enemies could be a mile long. I'm gonna let you take the lead on this one, Mac."

Kevin looked tired and distant. Not that being tired was a problem, but Kevin's weariness, accompanied by Mac's own instincts, set Mac on edge. "You feeling okay, Kev?"

"What?" Kevin fiddled with the crease in his slacks. "Oh, yeah. Fine."

The set in his jaw told Mac to butt out. *Fine.* If Kevin didn't want to talk, Mac wouldn't ask. Still, it hurt to think that the friendship they'd developed these past few months meant so little to him. Mac's thinking took an abrupt turn. What if Kevin had somehow found out about Mac's family history?

Mac glanced over at him. That might explain the surliness. Had Eric, Kevin's former partner and Mac's cousin, told Kevin about the McAllister family tree? Mac's father, Jamie McAllister, had been a dirty cop and a drunk. He'd left his wife and Mac when Mac was a kid. Worse though was Mac's namesake, Antonio: the mobster who thought he could rule Chicago. He did too, for a while. He had the mayor and most of the other politicians in his back pocket.

My past shouldn't matter, Kevin, he wanted to say. *I'm clean. I put myself through school. I never touched a dime of Antonio's money.*

That wasn't quite true. As a kid, Mac had been placed in a private Catholic school and given all he needed by his grand-mothers, Dottie DiAngelis and Kathryn McAllister. But getting into college was another matter. Antonio had expected him to become a lawyer and join the family business. Antonio had in-sisted on sending Mac to Harvard, but Mac chose a different path: law enforcement. Though he hadn't been the one to take down the old man, he applauded those who had.

MAC AND KEVIN ARRIVED at the twelfth floor of the Justice Center in downtown Portland in less than fifteen minutes. They walked into the reception area of the state police forensic lab.

"Anybody home in latents?" Kevin asked the receptionist.

"Well, hello yourself, Kevin, Mac. I'm doing fine, thanks for asking."

"Sorry, Sarah. We're looking to identify the murder victim from last night."

"Oh, yeah," she grimaced. "Heard about that. Let me check." She dialed a three-digit extension. "Hey, Pete. Mac and Kevin are here looking to talk with you. Okay, thanks." She turned back to the detectives. "Go on back. Pete's in the latent print office."

The Portland crime lab looked like a business office, filled with cubicles and work stations. The first tip-off that dozens of forensic scientists worked in the building were the wall hangings that depicted photographs of detectives from days gone by processing their crime scenes. The enlarged black-and-white photos showed stern-faced men wearing thin ties and fedoras, using what was then state-of-the-art equipment to catch criminals in the 1930s and '40s. "Things have changed a bit since then," Kevin said to Mac while they walked back to the latent examiner section.

"No kidding." Mac chuckled. "Do you still have your hat?"

"That picture was a little before my time, smarty, but a lot of the methods are still the best in my book." Kevin was sounding a little perturbed again, so Mac let it drop.

"Hey, guys." A slight man in a white lab coat looked up from his papers when Mac and Kevin walked in the ID office.

"Hi, Pete." Mac stepped inside the spacious room. "Sorry about coming in unannounced, but we lifted some prints from a murder victim at the post this morning and were hoping to get a name from you."

"Sure. Let's see what you've got."

Mac pulled the print card out of a manila envelope and handed it to Pete.

"We also bagged a length of duct tape that was wrapped around the victim's hands." Kevin set the paper bag on a steel worktable. "We were hoping you could find the bad guy's prints on the tape. A field team from your office didn't have much luck at the scene."

"This is the saw blade guy, huh?" Pete made a sour face while he examined the print card. "Not bad; you did a good job lifting these prints. Let's feed them into AFIS and see what comes back. As usual, you guys need to wait out here, though. The print computer is a clean room, so we minimize our foot traffic in there." Pete disappeared through a sliding door and returned moments later. "I'll let you know when we get a name. In the meantime, I'll get to work on this tape."

"Thanks. My pager number is on the card." Mac slid a business card across the table.

"I'll call you on the tape in a couple of hours, even if AFIS hasn't returned. It will take me a bit to separate the tape and search for latents, but I've had pretty good luck with duct tape in the past. Folks usually remove their gloves to work with the stuff."

"Let's hope that's the case," Kevin said.

"Want to grab some lunch, partner?" Mac checked his watch. Eleven-thirty.

"I'm not particularly hungry." Kevin pulled up his seatbelt and fastened it. "Tell you what, why don't you drive me back to my place? I have an appointment this afternoon. We can't do much until we figure out who this guy is. Maybe Dana can meet you for lunch."

"Sure." Mac turned the key in the ignition.

An uncomfortable silence rode with them as Mac maneuvered the crowded city streets. He missed his partner's bantering. He even missed Kevin's minisermons. What was the deal, anyway? Kevin seemed to be distancing himself more all the time. Was he planning to give Mac a bad review? Did he plan to ditch Mac and grab another partner? As much as he wanted to, Mac couldn't ask those questions.

He dropped off Kevin and went in search of a fast-food place, finally going through the drive-through at a Burger King. His aloneness and confusion turned to anger, which lasted until he got to the office. Mac took his lunch into his cubicle to eat it, then he decided to catch up on some paperwork and update Sergeant Evans. Once he disposed of his empty lunch containers, he headed out through the maze of cubicles. The junior officers, of which he was one, shared the big rooms with dividers, while the sergeants and senior detectives had private offices. It seemed everyone was always vying for primo space. Mac didn't really care at this stage. He was just glad to be there.

Mac knocked on the door to Sergeant Frank Evans's office, hoping to update him on the case and see if there were other assignments pending. He heard shuffling inside. Since the office door was slightly ajar, he pushed it in a bit farther. "Hey, Sarge, you got a sec?" Mac asked in a hushed tone, in case the sergeant was on the phone.

"Did I say you could come in?" A voice boomed back, but it wasn't Frank's. Mac pushed the door open all the way and found Detective Phil Johnson seated at Frank's desk, reading through a stack of paperwork.

"I wouldn't have asked if I'd known you were here. Where's Sarge?"

"Dunno." Philly huffed without looking up. "Just dropping off some reports. Thought I would tidy up his desk a little."

"Tidy up, or read his confidential memos?" Not sure what to make of the situation, Mac offered a tentative smile.

Philly slapped the paperwork back on the desk and tried his best to look offended, pushing back on the chair's wheels and sliding several feet back. "Sarge knows he works with a bunch of detectives. If he didn't want us reading his paperwork, he should lock it up in his desk."

"Would that keep you out?" Mac asked.

"Probably not. I have a key to his desk too." Philly went back to reading. "Where's Grandpa—getting his dress blues altered for his retirement gala?"

"Kevin? I don't know." Mac didn't think it appropriate to discuss his partner's business, whatever it might be. He sat on the edge of the desk and folded his arms. "I think I'll page Sergeant Evans and bring him up to speed on our case. You want to talk to him when he calls in, Phil?"

"You tell him I'm in here, Junior, and I'll string you up." Philly suppressed a grin as he stood up and poked Mac in the chest with his thick index finger. "I'd like to get out of here on time today without Frank loading up a bunch of admin junk on me."

Mac grabbed Philly's fingers and, with a half-hearted attempt, tried to twist him into an arm bar. He underestimated the strength in Philly's forearms and found himself in a choke hold instead.

"Don't try that ninja stuff on me, kid." Philly licked his finger and stuck it in Mac's ear before letting him go. "I'll let you off with a wet willy this time; next time I go for the wedgie."

"I give, I give." Mac raised his hands in surrender, mainly because the exertion had left Philly red-faced and panting. "Now go sit down before you pass out on me. I'm calling Sarge, but I won't mention that you were in here."

"Good. I owe you one." Philly slapped Mac on the back as he walked to his own office.

Mac went out to his cubicle, closing the door behind him. *Wonder what all that was about?* And that remark about Kevin retiring—was that just Philly's attempt at humor, or did he know something Mac didn't? Mac had said he wouldn't tell Frank about Philly's snooping, but he hadn't said he wouldn't tell Kevin—or Eric, for that matter. For a detective, Mac sure was having a hard time figuring out his coworkers.

PETE CALLED AT TWO-FIFTEEN. "Good news and bad news, Mac. I lifted latent prints from the duct tape, but AFIS didn't come back with a match for them. The prints came back on our victim, though. The guy is an escaped con from the Nevada State Pen. Name's Gerald Norton. He's got a rap sheet a mile long."

Pete promised to fax over the information. In the meantime, Mac got on the phone with the Nevada State Department of Corrections and got a lot more information than he'd expected. After hanging up, Mac retrieved the fax and scanned the report as he made his way back to his desk. He literally bumped into Kevin when he rounded the last corner.

"Hey, partner. I'm glad you're back." Mac waved the paper at him. "Got the results from Pete and have been on the horn to our buddies in Nevada."

"Good timing." Kevin motioned him toward his office. "Have you been in touch with Sarge?"

"Tried to a while ago, but he wasn't in his office."

"Okay, give me the info and we'll let Frank know what we have."

"We were right about the tattoos. The victim's name is Gerald Norton, an escaped con from the Nevada State Pen."

Kevin sat in his swivel chair and leaned back, placing his feet on the desk and crossing his legs at the ankle. "What was he in for?"

Mac lowered himself into the straight-backed chair across from Kevin. "According to the report, Norton has a lengthy Computerized Criminal History for drugs, guns, and person crimes. He's the real deal, Kev. Looks like a pretty violent dude. The feds tagged him as an armed career criminal back in 1996 after a number of robberies and assaults, all involving guns. His ACC status placed him on a higher sentencing grid, so he was looking at life even before he murdered a pit boss at one of the off-strip casinos. Got a life sentence for aggravated murder."

"So how did he get out?" Kevin picked up a pen and rolled it between his hands.

"He escaped during transport to maximum security from the state prisoner triage center. Nevada detectives think he had help on the inside, because he made it into the facilities contractor entrance and took off in a service truck without force or any broken doors. They think he paid someone on the inside to get him the keys."

"When did all this happen?"

"Mid-July. Norton's been missing since then."

"Humph. And he turns up in a sawmill, split down the middle." Kevin dropped his feet to the floor. "They have any idea who might want him killed?"

"Yeah. There's a laundry list of suspects in Nevada. Guy like that makes a lot of enemies. Most of them have mob ties. Their cops will take care of interviewing their local list of usual suspects. I told them I'd forward an electronic copy of our tape latents in case they have a local match."

"Sounds good, Mac." Kevin picked up the phone and dialed the sergeant's extension.

"Been slacking off this afternoon, boss?" Kevin said when the sergeant picked up. Mac could hear Frank's hearty laugh. "Hey, if you're up for it, Mac and I thought we'd bring you up to speed."

Sarge must have answered in the affirmative as Kevin got to his feet and signaled Mac to follow as he hoofed it to Frank's office.

"Hey, partner," Mac said. "Are you really thinking about retirement?"

Kevin stopped midstride. "Where did you hear that?"

"Philly said . . ." Mac stopped, unsure of how to continue.

"Mac, I know you've been concerned about me. I haven't been easy to work with and . . ."

The door to Frank's office opened. "Come on in, fellas." Frank settled his gaze on Kevin as if trying to read him. "You doing okay?"

Kevin cleared his throat. "Fine, Frank. Just peachy." Turning to Mac, he said, "Tell the sergeant what we have on the sawmill case, partner."

8

MAC MET DANA THE FOLLOWING MORNING at a coffee shop not far from the freeway on the Vancouver side of the river on 164th Street. Since they both lived in Vancouver, it was a handy place to meet. Mac had been glancing over the headline stories of the *Oregonian*, Portland's primary newspaper, when Dana came in. The sawmill murder had been relegated to the second page.

Setting her bag on the chair next to Mac, Dana greeted him with a touch to the shoulder and then stepped to the back of the line to order her coffee. The line was still short this early in the morning, and Mac opted to watch Dana instead of perusing the headlines. She was in her uniform, a blue shirt with the appropriate patches, navy blue slacks with a blue lateral stripe, and highly polished black leather boots. Her traditional gun belt and holster held her Glock .40 caliber, with two extra fifteen-round magazines. She wore her long blonde hair braided and wrapped in a tidy knot at the back of her head.

Mac had worn the same type of uniform day in and day out while he'd been on patrol. He didn't miss it a bit, though he had to admit it looked mighty fine on Dana's trim figure. Now that he'd made detective, Mac's uniform was slacks, a dressy shirt and tie, and a sports jacket to cover his shoulder holster and weapon, also a Glock .40 caliber.

Dana paid for and retrieved her coffee, then she took the cushioned chair across from Mac. "Anything new about the missing hiker?"

"No. I was hoping you might have some news."

She sighed. "Wish I did. Brad is still missing, and the search resumed at daylight this morning. I went up to the site yesterday afternoon since I was patrolling the area anyway." She took a sip from the covered cup. "Found out some interesting stuff about Brad, though."

"Oh, yeah?" Mac's eyebrow shot up. "Like what?"

"Deputy Wyatt did some checking in the criminal history files. It seems Brad ran into a little trouble a few years ago, with an arrest for possession of a controlled substance—marijuana. I asked his mother about it. She didn't want to talk about it at first, since she doubted it had anything to do with Brad's being missing now. I told her, maybe it did."

"So she talked?"

"Yep. It happened while he was on a ski trip to Bend. Mom says Brad had always been athletic, good looking, and popular. He grew up on the slopes and won an athletic scholarship to the University of Montana for downhill skiing. They never suspected he was into drugs until he was arrested. By that time, Brad was in his senior year and using marijuana pretty heavily. He admitted that he got rid of the prerace jitters by smoking a bowl before the competitions. He was arrested before a qualifying competition at Mount Hood when an anonymous informant called the local police and told them about the bag of marijuana in Brad's hotel room. He had little more than an ounce inside a sandwich bag."

"Not a lot, but enough to make it a felony in Oregon," Mac

commented. "Interesting. Kind of makes you wonder if he started using again and just skipped town."

"I wondered the same thing. His mom says absolutely not, but his history indicates that he might do something like that."

"He's run off before?" Mac leaned back, resting an ankle on his knee and adjusting the cuff on his gray slacks.

"Not exactly. After he was arrested, the racing circuit rumors had it that a competitor turned Brad in to avoid competing against him in the finals. The competitor was also a druggie. That's according to Vicki. Apparently he didn't make the team and dropped out. Brad was suspended from the professional down-hill circuit, forfeiting his goal to try out for the U.S. Olympic downhill skiing team."

Mac whistled. "What a shame. I thought his name sounded familiar. Such a waste. He loses his entire career over an ounce of pot."

"Well, that's been a few years ago. His mom says he went through some pretty hard times after that. Stayed away from the family and church. My guess is that he's one of those spoiled rich jocks who think the rules don't apply to him. He'd had it *his* way for so long it was a shock to him to get caught and actually be arrested and kicked off the team."

"My, my," Mac teased. "Aren't we cynical this morning?"

Dana's cheeks flushed and her dimples deepened in a guilty-as-charged grin. "Sorry. Way too many high-profile professional sports figures are ending up bad boys. They're being charged with everything from possession to rape. I don't have much respect for guys like that.

"Anyway," Dana went on, "Brad became estranged from his family for a couple of years after his arrest and was blackballed from the racing community. You'd have thought getting arrested would have straightened him up, but he went the opposite direction and hung out with what Vicki said were the wrong kind of friends. Friends who had a bad influence on him."

"Hmm." Mac sipped at his coffee. "Got to blame somebody, right? She accused Jessica of leading him down the wrong path."

"Yeah. Apparently these kids were high on parties and low on responsibilities. His parents had to make house payments for Brad on more than one occasion when he was between jobs."

Mac shook his head. "Lucky guy. I wouldn't mind having parents who paid my bills." That wasn't entirely true. Mac had a grandfather who was only too eager to share his wealth, but Mac wanted nothing to do with his grandfather or his money, which came from extortion and fraud and the spilling of a lot of blood. Mac had refused his grandfather's offer and made it through college on his own. He caught his drifting thoughts and reined them in.

"Well, you can't really blame the parents." Dana took a sip of her coffee. "There was a house at stake—they made the mortgage payments so Brad wouldn't lose the place. Vicki made a point of telling me that Brad had been getting back on track. He was skiing competitively and going to church again, at least until he disappeared. According to his mom, he'd been doing pretty well until he met Jessica."

"Have you talked to Jessica? It would be interesting to get her take on all of this away from Brad's family."

"She stayed home yesterday. Of course, that really impressed Brad's folks. The sister wasn't there either—Brad's mom said she's checking in with friends and places he likes to go."

"Maybe you should talk to Jessica—unofficially, of course." Mac lowered his leg, finished off his drink, and set the cup on the table. "You could write up all this stuff in case Brad turns up dead or is never found. That kind of information could come in handy."

"I'm way ahead of you there, Mac." Dana caught his gaze and

held it briefly; then she began to examine her cup. "I've been making notes."

Don't go there, Mac, Dana's demeanor told him. At the moment, he didn't want to listen. He remembered how much fun she was when they dated years ago. He wanted to ask her out again—maybe take her to a fancy restaurant. He wanted to unbraid her golden hair and watch it cascade around her shoulders. He leaned back in his chair again and studied her profile, thinking of all the reasons he couldn't.

She's dating a guy, Mac reminded himself. *And you are still engaged to Linda.* He needed to call Linda. He hadn't seen her since the counseling session. Avoiding the matter wasn't doing his stomach or his brain a bit of good.

"How's the sawmill murder case shaping up?" Dana shifted her gaze to the window, looking as though she wanted to leave.

"We have an ID. Escaped convict out of Nevada." Mac shook his head. "Whoever killed him was careful not to leave much in the way of evidence. There's really nothing we can use. We couldn't come up with a match on his prints. Kevin and I are talking to the guy who found the body today."

He glanced at his watch. It was eight-thirty. "I'm supposed to pick him up at nine."

"Then you'd better hustle. Traffic's a bear out there."

"Always is."

"You can follow me over the bridge if you want." Amusement lit Dana's eyes. "It's amazing how people slow down and get out of the way when they see me coming."

"A cop car tames traffic like nothing else," Mac chuckled. "Lead the way."

Mac and Kevin spent the day following up on leads and going over reports from various agencies regarding the murdered convict. Norton had apparently been hiding out at the abandoned mill since soon after his escape. So far no one had been able to come up with a link between him and someone from Oregon. Nevada authorities had only one known relative on file: Norton's mother, who was an inmate at the state mental hospital in Iowa. According to the staff there, his last visit had been ten years ago. "Not that it matters. Olivia doesn't even know she has a son," the woman from the institution had told Mac. "She has no other known living relatives."

By the end of the day, they were convinced the murder was a professional hit. Unless they got a break, the case would end up being shelved with the unsolved murders that plagued every department.

Mac wondered how many hits like this his grandfather had set up and executed without being caught. True, Norton was a loser, but so was his killer. Mac didn't want the murderer to get away even if, as Philly had said, "Good riddance. The guy got what he deserved. One scumbag snuffs out another scumbag. We ought to be happy—look at all the time and money the killer saved us."

Most of the guys agreed with Philly—even Kevin commented on shelving the case.

"Sounds like you want to give the killer a medal," Mac had shot back at Philly. He hadn't appreciated their comments and still didn't.

"That's not a bad idea," Philly said.

"All right, guys." Eric, Mac's redheaded Irish cousin, stepped into the foray. Tossing Mac a look of understanding, he said, "Maybe old Norton deserved the death penalty, but his killer deserves to be caught. Let's not forget that. Mac just wants to see justice done."

"Ah, the optimism of youth." Philly shook his head.

Later, Mac caught up with Eric and thanked him.

"No problem, Mac, but you might want to loosen up a little.

You're not going to be able to avenge them all." Eric sighed. "I get the feeling you're dealing with more than this Norton guy. Look, Mac, I know you have some skeletons in that closet of yours. You'd do well to practice a little thing called forgiveness and let God deal with the injustices."

Mac shook his head. "Forgive my father? Eric, the guy was dirty."

"I know, Mac, but you're not. You can't change what he did."

Mac hung his head. "Of course not, but . . ."

"But nothing." Eric slapped him on the shoulder. "Quit trying to make up for your father's shortcomings. It'll make you crazy."

His cousin was right—at least in theory. "Say, Eric, before you go . . . um . . . do you know what's going on with Kevin? I mean, he doesn't know about my dad and grandfather, does he? He's been acting strange lately."

"Mac." Eric paused in the doorway. "You're thinking I told him about Jamie or Antonio? I didn't. There's no need. You're a good cop and a decent guy. You're family, remember? Don't forget, your father was my uncle. We have some of the same skeletons in our closets. Besides, even if Kevin knew, it wouldn't make a difference. You should know that by now."

Mac shifted uncomfortably. "But have you noticed Kevin's behavior lately?"

"He's a little off. Maybe he's not feeling well. He took off yesterday afternoon to see his doctor. That's about all I know."

"Oh." *Doctor? That's more than I knew. Why didn't he tell me?* Mac kept the question to himself. "Okay then. I won't keep you."

"You and Nana coming over to the house for Thanksgiving dinner?"

"Really?" Mac raised his eyebrows. For the past few weeks he had taken his grandmother, Dottie, who they called Nana, to Eric's for Sunday dinner—with the exception of this past week, when he had to go to counseling with Linda. Mac enjoyed the visits with Eric's family, and so did Nana. He hadn't really thought about Thanksgiving. Linda hadn't mentioned it, so he wasn't locked into anything. "I'd like that."

"Great. You're in for a treat. I found a turkey deep fryer last month at a garage sale."

"Deep-fried turkey?"

"Yep. It's the latest craze."

"Craze as in crazy. Maybe there's a reason it was at the garage sale."

"What a skeptic." Eric laughed. "Just so you know, Philly and Russ will be there."

Mac frowned, picturing the unruly detective and his partner, Russ. "In that case, maybe I shouldn't bring Nana."

"Don't be silly. They'll behave."

Mac chuckled. "I wasn't worried about them offending Nana; I was worried about what Nana might do to them."

Eric howled. "Good one, Mac. And you're right. If anyone can keep those two in line, Nana can."

Nana wasn't Eric's grandmother, but his family called her Nana anyway, mostly because of her age and the fact that, other than her incarcerated husband, she had no family except for Mac. She loved that Eric's kids considered her their grandmother.

Mac grinned. "In that case, count me in. I'll have to check with Nana, but I'm sure she'll want to come."

Feeling somewhat relieved, Mac went back to his desk. Maybe he'd been paranoid about Kevin's actions of late. Could be his partner was nervous about having his physical. After all, he was talking about retiring. Mac hoped everything was okay. His partner was too important to the department to retire. Besides, Mac had learned so much from him and hoped to learn much more. It would take years to get to Kevin's level. Speaking of which, Mac intended to put the skills he'd learned thus far to crack this new case.

They weren't completely without evidence. They had that partial boot print and a couple of usable latents, along with one odd circumstance that appeared to link the convict to someone in the Portland area: Norton had been slaughtering wildlife. The blood and hides bore that out, along with carcasses buried in shallow graves around the property. He'd probably been poaching, but why? Why would a guy running from the law hunt down and slaughter more meat than he could use for himself?

9

THANKSGIVING AND CHRISTMAS came and went in a blur. The holidays, along with New Year's, had gone uncelebrated in the Gayneses' home, largely because they had nothing to celebrate. Brad was still missing.

Vicki peered out the kitchen window of her southwest Portland home as Todd eased out of the driveway, heading for work on the chilly winter morning. One of the area's infamous ice storms had blanketed the city with a shiny crust of beautiful, shimmering, treacherous ice. Todd was running late, as it had taken twenty minutes to defrost his older BMW. Vicki begged him to take the SUV with its four-wheel drive, but he'd declined, reminding her that she had errands and he wanted her to have the safer vehicle.

Vicki and Todd had lived in their modest home on the west side near Portland State University for the better part of ten years. It was the perfect place, except for those rare occasions when snow or ice turned their hills into slippery slopes.

"I can stay home. Nothing's going on out there anyway."

"Vicki, the weather is just one more excuse on top of the

hundreds you've already made. You need to get out. Holing up in here isn't going to bring Brad home any sooner."

She knew that. But since Brad had gone missing in early November, she hadn't felt like going out or doing anything. Today was no different, except that she'd promised Todd she'd at least go back to work. She'd all but abandoned her interior decorating business. Luckily, Rachael had stepped in to fill in the gaps. Maybe she should go on with her day as planned. Todd was right. Waiting around the house wasn't accomplishing anything. She needed at least to go to the fabric and craft outlet for supplies.

Still this wasn't a good day to start working—at least not outdoors. The City of Roses had been practically shut down the past two days while the winter storm passed through. And it wasn't as if she hadn't been working—she had. She'd spent endless hours trying to find her son. These past two months had produced nothing. After Brad's disappearance, the air search had ended after one day, but the ground search had gone on for the three full days. The searchers, explorer scouts, hounds, and law enforcement officers failed to come up with a single clue related to Brad's disappearance.

The search efforts had turned from search-and-rescue status to missing-person status. Family and friends had printed and handed out thousands of fliers to hikers and sightseers in the Columbia River Gorge area. The fliers, with a picture of Brad, offered a reward for any information leading to his whereabouts. With such inclement weather, they'd had to replace fliers routinely wherever they could along I-84 from Portland to the small town of Cascade Locks. Cascade Locks, about forty miles east of the metro area, was located near Bonneville Dam, the first of three dams on the massive Columbia River. Wah-kella Creek, fed by the falls, flowed into the Columbia a short distance above the dam.

Vicki dug into a cardboard box on her kitchen counter, where a dozen or so fliers remained. "Time to make new ones." She pulled out the handful of fliers and folded the empty box, smashing it into the recycling bin in the laundry room, next to a half-dozen other empty boxes.

Hopelessness threatened to end her efforts, but she fought it off. Picking up her hot tea and the fliers, she padded to the kitchen table, where she had set up a temporary workspace to track the reports and tips related to Brad's case.

Vicki set down her tea and powered up her laptop computer. She leaned back while it booted up, sipping her tea and making her list of things to do. *Go to copy place to make more fliers. Call Deputy Wyatt.*

Find Brad.

She crossed out the note to call the deputy. Vicki didn't want to hear his version of the story anymore, and he was getting tired of her almost daily calls.

"I'm officially listing Brad as a missing person," he'd said just two weeks after Brad disappeared. "Unofficially, I think we're dealing with a suicide." He hadn't changed his story.

Vicki hadn't wanted to hear that. She couldn't believe it. Brad had been raised to believe in the sanctity of life. His faith would prohibit him from killing himself. Even in Brad's darkest days, he'd call on occasion just to check in. Besides, there was no body. It wasn't unusual to lose a body on a river that strong and wide. The body could have floated downriver and gotten caught on something. She shuddered to think about that. The current was so strong and the river so vast. Vicki closed the door on those morbid thoughts. Brad was still alive. But if that was the case, where was he?

The theory that he left town and didn't want to be found was equally unlikely. Brad just wouldn't do that.

Vicki tossed the pen aside, got up, and walked down the hall into Brad's old room. She'd turned it into a sewing/guest room, but her son would always be welcome. It would always be his room. Sitting on his bed, she let her blurred gaze wander over the walls. Shelves on one side held Brad's trophies and mementos, photos of him winning race after race. Ribbons held medals of silver, bronze, and gold. She'd even hung the ribbons from his high-school sports competitions.

Rachael's medals were there too—the ones she'd won downhill skiing. She could have been an Olympian, but she chose a business degree and a husband and family over competition.

"Oh, Brad," Vicki said aloud, "you had so much promise. What happened? What went wrong? Did we push you too hard? Why the drugs and the drinking? Why did you feel you needed friends like that—why Jessica?" She brushed the back of her hand across her eyes and went in search of some tissues.

Jessica swore she had loved Brad. But where was she now? Less than a week after Brad went missing, Jessica packed her bags and moved back to California to live with an aunt and uncle in Crescent City on the coast. In fact, Jessica did a great deal more than just pack her bags. She also helped herself to some of Brad's sweaters and his watch, guitar, and collection of CDs and DVDs.

"Why would you do that, Jessica? Didn't you think he'd be coming back?" Vicki found some tissues in the bathroom and blew her nose; then she returned to the bedroom and went on lamenting Jessica's actions.

Of course, Jessica had taken all the money Brad might have had. She claimed she hadn't, but Todd figured Brad had a couple thousand in cash at the cabin. The money was gone, and Jessica claimed to know nothing about it. It was as if Jessica *knew* Brad wasn't going to be found. Why else would she leave so soon after his disappearance and take things Brad would want when he returned? Brad hadn't made November's house payment, so Todd covered it, saying they needed to protect Brad's investment. Vicki agreed, but she felt the reason was more personal—Todd wanted Brad to have a place to live when he came home. They'd made three payments now, and the cabin still sat empty.

Vicki dragged her thoughts away from the negative turn they'd taken. Every day—several times a day—she slipped into this ruminating mode, going over and over the circumstances surrounding Brad's disappearance. And every day, she prayed that things would be resolved and Brad would come home. She wanted it to be over, wanted to get on with life. She needed closure—some kind of closure. Any kind of closure.

Vicki pushed herself from the bed. With a heavy heart and legs of lead, she headed back to the kitchen table and sat at her temporary desk.

Work. You have to work. She picked up a white plastic binder and slipped on her reading glasses. Vicki thumbed through the pages, primarily at the bottom of the pile. She found the interview report for Jessica, written by Deputy Wyatt. The report indicated the deputy had interviewed Jessica the day following Brad's reported disappearance.

Vicki thumbed through the tattered pages of the search-and-rescue logs to get to the police reports, scanning the pages she had read a hundred times. In the report, Deputy Wyatt summarized his conversations with Jessica without going into much detail. There were no tape recordings, not even any challenges to Jessica's unusual reaction to Brad's disappearance. Vicki wondered why a detective wasn't called in to interview Jessica or at least to go over the reports of the officers involved with the search.

In the report, the deputy had written the same basic story Jessica had told her and Todd. There were a few additional details. Jessica reported that she and Brad went to the falls that day to talk about their relationship and that Brad had been drinking heavily. She also reported that Brad had smoked marijuana while they were talking in the parking lot. Vicki never read that part of the report without getting angry. She was so certain her son had gotten past the drinking and drug stage. Now Jessica had shifted the bulk of the blame to Brad.

Sweet, cute little Jessica apparently hadn't touched a drop. When Jessica told Brad to stop and that she'd have to drive home, he became angry. She told him basically to shape up or she was leaving.

Vicki rubbed her forehead. "What really happened out there, God? Will we ever know?"

Brad had assured them that he'd stopped smoking marijuana and had smashed a glass pipe in front of his father to confirm he was giving up the drug. Was all that for show?

What was it Brad had said? *"I'm trying to quit. I want to, but you don't know what it's like when your friends are addicted. And all Jessica wants to do is party."*

"You wouldn't lie to us, would you, Brad?" Vicki asked aloud. "And if you were telling the truth, then Jessica must be lying."

Going back to Deputy Wyatt's report, she read:

> *Jessica reported that during this conversation in Brad's car, she told Brad she was leaving him and was planning on moving out to stay with friends or return to live with her family. She said Brad had become physically abusive to her, and although she loved him, Jessica no longer wanted to be the object of his aggression. Brad became enraged when she told him their relationship was over. He reportedly grabbed her arm, and she told him to let go because he was hurting her. The alcohol and marijuana, mixed with the subject matter, caused Brad to grow increasingly irritable and threatening. Jessica claimed she was able to pull herself free from Brad's grip and get out of the passenger side door of the car. She began walking away when Brad again grabbed*

her arm. Jessica said she tried to push him away, but he was
too strong and too upset. Brad reportedly said, "If I can't
have you, then no one will."

Vicki shook her head. How melodramatic. Brad wouldn't act like
that. She'd told Deputy Wyatt what she thought of Jessica's so-
called statement, but there it was, still in the report along with the
strange story of an elusive truckdriver who deputies had never
found.

During the altercation Jessica said a trucker got out of his
tractor-trailer rig and walked over to them, carrying a
large flashlight. Because he didn't need it for light yet, he
appeared to be carrying it as a weapon.

The truckdriver, a man in his fifties, intervened, asking
Jessica if she needed any help. Brad told the man to back off
and mind his own business, then he shoved the driver back
with clinched fists. The truckdriver's straw cowboy hat fell
to the ground as the man struggled to regain his balance.
Brad and the would-be hero squared off, with the driver
flipping the large flashlight from hand to hand as though
he'd used it in a fight before. The trucker asked Brad repeat-
edly if he wanted a "piece." Brad stood in the parking lot in
a fighting stance, saying, "Come and get it, man."

Vicki rolled her eyes. Every time she read the account, it sounded
more unbelievable.

Jessica said she was hysterical at this point, telling the
truckdriver she was okay and begging the man to leave
Brad alone. The driver finally backed off and went to his
truck, yelling threats at Brad as he stormed off. Jessica said

the driver even cussed at her for causing such a fuss. Brad didn't want to let it go. He challenged the driver to come back. She said the trucker told Brad, "I'm not done with you, boy," and climbed back inside a red semi truck tractor with a silver trailer.

Brad went back to the car and grabbed another beer from the backseat, took several long drinks, then threw the can into the parking lot and slammed the door. Brad was crying at this point and yelled, "Why!" Then he started walking up the trail to the falls. When Brad disappeared into the thick brush along the trail, Jessica went back to the Subaru and ended up taking a nap out of exhaustion. When she woke a couple of hours later, Jessica reported being scared because it was getting dark and Brad was still gone. She said the truckdriver who came to her aid hours earlier was still sitting in his truck, watching her, which frightened her more.

Jessica drove back home to see if anyone had heard from Brad.

That was when Jessica had called the police, then Vicki and Todd.

What bothered Vicki most about the report was the very end, when the deputy had asked Jessica what she thought had happened. *"Maybe he jumped. People kill themselves at places like this all the time, don't they?"*

How dare she imply that Brad would end his life!

Vicki tossed the report on the pile. She knew that report by heart—she could recite it in her sleep. Still she read it every day, hoping it would trigger something, reveal a new clue.

"What a load of bunk." Vicki slammed the binder shut. The daily ritual of reading the report brought the usual anger and frustration—at the deputy, at Jessica, and even at Brad. And then there was the issue of his car keys. Jessica said he'd left them with her. But Brad always kept them in his pocket—he wouldn't have gone off without them.

Had he tossed her the keys before he went off in this alleged rage? "How did you get those keys, Jessica?" Vicki asked aloud. "Why did you move away so quickly? And why did you tell Deputy Wyatt about the marijuana and the mysterious truck-driver, but not us?"

Vicki folded her arms on the table and dropped her head to them, weariness overtaking her despite the caffeine. Jessica had avoided talking to them that first week. She hadn't even come out to the falls except for the first day. How could the authorities just let her walk? Couldn't they see she was lying?

"You are not getting away with this, Jessica. You know what happened to Brad, and I'm going to hound you until I have some answers."

Vicki grabbed a pen and a clean sheet of paper.

> *Dear Jess,*
>
> *I hope this letter finds you well. The weather is treacherous here, although beautiful with all the ice on the trees and power lines. The sun came out this morning, but it is still well below freezing.*
>
> *Jessica, please tell me what happened to Brad! I know you know more than what you told us and the police. I will forgive you if you only tell the truth. We treated you like family, Jess, because Brad loved you. Was there an accident? Did Brad fall or take some type of drug that harmed him?*
>
> *If you ever really loved Brad, call me and at least talk to me. I need to know what happened to my son. Not knowing is worse than death. Unless you are a parent, you could*

never understand the hurt inside a mother's heart when her child is missing, hurt, or even worse.

Jessica, I pray for you every day. I pray you will find it in your heart to tell me the truth, even if it is just me. Todd and I don't want you to get into any trouble, and we won't ask the police to get involved if you are afraid.

I fear the worst, Jess, and I know in my heart that you hold the key to Brad's disappearance, if only you would talk to me.

Why did you move away after Brad went missing? How come you didn't stick around and see what happened to him? And Jessica, why did you take Brad's clothes and guitar when you left? You knew he would want them when he returned.

Jessica, is Brad dead? He is my son, and I need to know. I need to know. Call me anytime. Call us collect, Jess, or write. Please.

May God guide your actions.

Victoria

Ignoring the tears streaming down her cheeks, Vicki folded the letter and enclosed some stamps and a blank envelope before stuffing the package into another envelope. She tapped the letter against her hand, wondering if sending it was the right thing to do. The deputies had told her to let them handle the investigation and to run any ideas she had through them. Vicki had lost patience with the deputies—with everyone, for that matter. Sending the letter wouldn't hurt. She doubted Jessica would respond, but she had to try.

Leaving the letter on the table, she walked over to the kitchen counter, picking up her now-cold tea. She took a sip and grimaced, then poured the tea down the sink. Maybe she would grab a chai tea on her way to mail the letter.

10

Mac squinted through the rain-soaked trees and tried to control his breathing. *In through the nose; out through the mouth.* He jogged up to a fifty-gallon barrel, lifted the muzzle of his Glock .40 over the top, and peered over the sights.

"You ready, Mac?" Kevin asked, keeping his voice low. He slid in next to Mac behind the hard cover.

"Ready as I'll ever be," Mac whispered back.

Kevin slumped behind Mac. Placing his left elbow on Mac's broad right shoulder, the senior detective lifted the muzzle of his handgun to eye level and advanced on the threat.

"Let's move in. I'll follow your lead." Mac rose slowly, still peering over the sights of his semiautomatic pistol.

"You step, then I'll step. We'll move as one unit."

"Wait." Mac peered at the figure to their left. "Is that guy holding a camera or a gun?"

"I can't tell. We need to move in and take a look." Kevin inched ahead. "Let's move in behind that second barrel." Mac shadowed Kevin, the detectives moving together.

"Police! Don't move!" Mac ordered. "Oregon State Police.

Drop the weapon or you may be shot!" He and Kevin jumped for cover behind a second metal barrel. Before Mac could give a third command, Kevin's weapon exploded. Mac discharged his weapon a heartbeat later.

"Drop the gun, drop the gun!" Kevin fired two rounds into the chest and one more to the head. Mac double-tapped two in, the first hitting the torso and the second hitting the shoulder.

"Get down on the ground! Let me see your hands!" Mac yelled. The suspect still hadn't flinched and still pointed a submachine gun at the two detectives.

"Cease fire, cease fire." The range master's monotone voice preceded a shrill whistle. The Oregon State Police training instructor looked at his stopwatch and headed toward Mac and Kevin on the gravel firing range. "Not bad for a couple detectives," he said. "Just shy of forty-five seconds, with five of six rounds in the kill zone."

"Five of six, what five of six?" Kevin asked.

Mac eyed the target. They'd fired six shots, and one of them had missed the target's center mass. Mac was certain the missed shot hadn't been his.

"Ask your partner." The senior trooper lifted his pen from his clipboard and pointed it at the "bad guy" silhouette at the end of the pistol range.

Kevin walked from the fifteen-yard line to examine the paper target. "Humph." He gave Mac a crooked grin. "One of us threw a round out into the shoulder. Looks like there are two in the head and three at center mass. If I had to guess, I'd say this shoulder shot was fired by the officer on the left side of the fire line."

"First rule of detectives, partner—never guess." Mac smirked and shoved a fresh magazine into his pistol. "I deal in facts, old buddy. I'd say an aging detective with bad eyes is more likely to put a round into a shoulder than a young officer with twenty/twenty vision."

"Possible, yes," Kevin replied. "Likely, no. See this?" He pointed to his gold-colored OSP baseball cap. The gold hat was rewarded to troopers in the agency who have shot a perfect score on the twenty-five-yard handgun qualification course. Mac had been close a few times, but never higher than the ninety-eighth percentile.

Phil Johnson, a.k.a. Philly, sidled up to Kevin and slapped him on the shoulder. "Yeah, but tell Mac when you won that hat, you old buzzard." Philly pulled out his earplugs and smashed them into his pocket. "I think we were, what, half a year out of recruit school?" Philly tried to knock the hat off Kevin's head. "That hat's older than you, Mac."

Kevin ducked and blocked Philly's hand before it connected. "I don't remember you ever having an expert cap, Philly." Kevin held onto his hat while he picked up his spent casings.

"I'm a lover, not a shooter," Philly joked, finally grabbing the hat with his thick fingers and tossing it over to his partner, Russ. "Look at that—still got my catlike reflexes." Philly struck his best Bruce Lee pose.

"Better ease up, Karate Kid, before you split your pants again." Russ handed the cap back to Kevin with a laugh. "You look like a constipated goose when you do that, Philly."

"Lucky for me I don't value your opinion." Philly tried his best to look offended.

Mac shook his head. Russ and Philly had been partners since Russ made detective two years ago.

"All right, all right," the range master interrupted the banter. "Can I get you ladies together for a few minutes so we can review? I have some real troops arriving at noon, and I'd like to get the range ready for them, if you don't mind."

"Get the range ready?" Philly looked around. "It's freezing out here. If you think I'm picking up my brass in this ice and snow, you got another think comin', troop. Who picked this range date, Frosty the Snowman? I'm freezing my tail off."

"That's senior trooper to you, Detective Johnson." The instructor slapped his clipboard. "And you know darn good and well the captain sets up training for the quarterly shoot, one per season. The last time I checked, winter is still a season." The instructor, an ex-Marine, glared back at Philly, almost daring him to complain again. "And yes, you will pick up your brass, Detective."

"My brass is frozen out here," Philly mumbled, no doubt needing to get in the last word.

The instructor glared at him again.

"What?" Philly feigned innocence.

"Okay, let's review," the firearms instructor continued, apparently deciding to ignore Philly's whining. "First, let's review our deadly physical force policy. Deadly physical force may only be used when you, or another, are in danger of serious physical injury or death. Any questions?" he asked before continuing. "Any of you guys want to give me the department force continuum?"

"Shoot first; ask questions later." Russ folded his arms, apparently bored with the review.

"No," the instructor growled. "Any other guesses?"

"Better to be tried by a jury of twelve than carried in your coffin by six?" Philly said, not wanting to be outdone.

"Good one, partner." Russ elbowed Philly, offering his approval of the one-liner.

"Come on, you guys," Mac interrupted. He'd had his fill of their goofing off like a couple of high-school dropouts. Wanting to bring the training session to an end and give the instructor a break, he recited, "Officer presence is first, verbal commands is second, and empty-hand custody technique is third."

"Thank you." The instructor looked relieved. "Go on, please, Detective McAllister."

"Chemical spray or cap stun is fourth, strikes and kicks is fifth . . ."

"Teacher's pet," Philly grumbled as he blew into his cold hands. "And baton blows is next, followed by deadly physical force at seven on the force scale. Blah, blah, blah, the same thing every time. And the precursor for use of force is means, opportunity, and intent."

"Sorry to bore you, Detective Johnson, but this is required material."

Philly pulled a piece of Nicorette gum from his pocket and shoved it in his mouth, providing company to the two pieces he was already chewing. The gum and a nicotine patch were his latest attempts to stop smoking.

"Any more words of wisdom before we shut this thing down?" Philly glanced at his watch.

The instructor removed his safety glasses. "If I could leave you with just one thought. Did you all hear the verbiage Detective McAllister used?' Something to the effect of, 'Don't make me shoot you; let me see your hands'? That was good material for possible witnesses. I'd rather be involved in a shooting and have the public hear that than the alternative statements I heard today." He tossed a warning glance at Russ and Philly.

"What? I got my point across, didn't I?" Philly squatted to pick up a piece of spent brass.

"I don't think the captain would want a potential witness hearing a trooper say, 'Eat lead, sucker,' or 'Say hello to my little friend.' Do you?"

"I don't know what you're talking about." Philly pouted as he began to walk away. "Come on, Russ, I can't stay here a second longer and face this abuse."

"What about your spent rounds and brass?" the instructor barked. "You need to help clean up."

Philly raised his arm and waved the comments off.

"I'll get his casings," Mac said, already picking them up. Philly had almost earned the right to be sarcastic, having been involved in two shootings in his career. The first had occurred when he was still a road troop, working 82nd Avenue outside Portland on the border of Clackamas and Multnomah Counties. This route was also State Highway 213, so the troopers worked the area often, giving it the nickname Felony Flats due to the high crime rate and the number of criminal interdictions in the area.

Philly had been on patrol in the area when he stopped a Plymouth Duster for not having a front license plate. Since this was the late 1970s, police technology and budgets did not yet allow for portable radios, or Philly would have known dispatch was calling him to let him know the car he'd stopped was stolen out of Umatilla in a strong armed robbery. Philly walked up to the driver, only to be met by the business end of a snub-nosed revolver.

Philly instinctively threw his ticket book at the driver. Shielding his face with his left hand, he drew his sidearm. The driver fired a round, blasting a hole through Philly's left hand and tearing away his earlobe. The driver fared much worse. The single .357 round from the police revolver did its job, sinking into the guy's temple. Philly lost some blood, but there was one less bad guy on the street.

The second officer-involved shooting happened about two years ago. Kevin, Philly, Russ, and Sergeant Frank Evans were hitting the front door of a suspected drug dealer's house in Molalla. While the sergeant and other detectives waited by the entrance, Kevin had made a cell phone call to the suspect, advising him that they had a search warrant. Kevin commanded him to come to the front door and give up. The suspect was believed to be handling large amounts of cocaine, in addition to having inappropriate relations with a twelve-year-old runaway who was staying at the house. The suspect came to the door all right, armed with an AK-47. The door splintered from the fire of the automatic rifle. Philly kicked in the door after the initial burst, just as the suspect was loading a fresh magazine. As the door exploded from its frame, Philly fired at point-blank range. Frank and Russ fired over Philly's shoulders. As the dust settled, the trio backed out and called for the OSP SWAT team.

Several calls were placed to the house, although there was no answer this time. The SWAT negotiators finally gave up, and the team decided on a dynamic entry on the house, firing flash bangs into the lower and upper stories of the home. The tactical team entered the home, only to find a dead suspect and a dead twelve-year-old girl. Ballistic tests showed the girl was killed by the suspect's weapon, and the detectives were exonerated from her death.

The medical examiner performed an autopsy on the suspect and concluded he was shot several times, although the fatal shot was a single round that severed the aorta. The suspect, who had a high level of cocaine on board, should have died immediately, but he lived long enough to continue firing through walls and kill the young girl in the next room. When the medical examiner asked the detectives if they wanted to know who fired the fatal round, they all agreed they didn't want to know.

Philly was front and center for the shooting and knew he connected on several rounds, but he would rather have the doubt than the assurance he was forced to take a second human life. Two lives were more than he signed on for when he joined this outfit. Mac hoped he'd never be placed in that situation.

"Philly pulls this stunt every time." Kevin helped Mac pick up the rest of the spent cartridges. "Sarge will probably get on his rear."

"If he ever gets out of his car." Mac glanced to the top of the gravel slope at Sergeant Evans, who was seated in his car gesturing wildly as he talked on his hands-free cell phone. "He's spent half the shoot sitting up there in his hammer wagon on the phone."

"Probably still working with Eric on that murder-for-hire case in Salem," Kevin said.

"The one where the woman tried to hire someone to kill her husband by calling that company down in California?" The training instructor pulled down the paper targets to place in the burn barrel.

"That's the one." Kevin stood up and rubbed his back. "This woman actually looks up a company called Hired Guns on the Internet and calls them at their Hollywood business, telling the manager she wants to hire someone to kill her husband. This company is a stuntman outfit that supplies guys to fall off roofs and jump out of cars for filmmakers. They think this gal is kidding, but she calls back several times and ends up sending pictures of her husband to the business and a couple of grand in front money."

"You gotta be kidding me," the instructor shook his head.

"Truth is stranger than fiction in this case," Kevin said. "Anyway, this company calls the local cops and they hook us up on the case. Eric and Frank write a warrant for a body wire and call this woman, telling her they are in town to kill her husband and want to meet to go over the details. She agreed, and they're planning to meet her at a motel in Oregon City to go over the plan to kill her hubby. Eric will be wearing a body wire so they can get the whole thing on tape."

The trooper shook his head. "That's the darndest thing I've ever heard of."

"Sure is," Kevin agreed. "Let's just hope their meeting with the wife goes as planned."

Mac and Kevin threw their spent shotgun hulls in the burn barrel with the paper targets, and they tossed their spent handgun brass into a large cardboard box for reloading.

"Where's Eric?" Mac asked. Ordinarily his cousin would have been in the training session with them.

"Probably returning the ex parte warrant for the body wire at the courthouse and running down Frank's last-minute orders." Kevin sniffed and rubbed his nose.

Mac stuck his numb fingers into his jacket pockets to warm them. Eric would have to make up the shoot later. "Looks to me like the boss is in overdrive up there—he's gesturing all over the place."

Kevin groaned. "Try not to make eye contact with him when you walk up to our car, or we'll be working on some goofy lead."

Mac and Kevin had earned a break, just ending a lengthy trial at Multnomah County Circuit Court on the Megan Tyson murder case. It had been Mac's first murder case as an OSP detective, and finding Megan's killer had given Mac a real sense of accomplishment.

"Throw your eyes and ears up there on the table," the instructor yelled after them. "I'll wipe them down for the next crew."

"Thanks," Mac replied. The two detectives removed their safety glasses and ear protection and set them on the large wooden table inside the range shack. The ten-by-ten cabin had two door-ways, without doors, separating the gravel range lanes and the parking lot area inside the large rock quarry. The state police troopers and detectives from the Portland-Metro area qualified four times a year with their firearms at the small range near Clatska-nine, a small mill town along the Columbia River between Portland and the Oregon coast.

Before going back to work, Mac emptied his Glock and his pockets of the range practice rounds. He didn't want any of the full-metal-jacket hardball rounds getting mixed up with his duty ammo. Mac and Kevin walked up to their unmarked Crown Victoria, and Kevin popped the trunk. Kevin loaded their shotgun with slugs and secured the weapon in the bracket that was mounted on the underside of the trunk lid. Mac slipped out of the waist-length raincoat he wore when he was a patrol officer and tossed it in, the raindrops still visible in tiny beads on the Gore-tex material. Kevin was wearing a long yellow slicker that came down to his knees, making him look like an oversized kid on his way to school.

"Did you actually wear that outfit when you were on patrol?" Mac grinned.

"What, the old banana coats? Didn't they issue these things to your academy class?"

Mac laughed. "Not ours. I don't think those things have been issued since the early eighties. I didn't think anyone actually wore those ugly things anymore. What good is a long slicker that doesn't let you get to your gear on your duty belt?"

Kevin slipped out of his coat. His damp dress shirt showed evidence that his twenty-year-old raincoat wasn't exactly the best for repelling water. "You have to remember that back in those days we didn't have mace, portable radios, and asp batons. All we needed was that little slit in the hips that our revolvers poked through on one side and our cuff case on the other."

"I don't think you'd catch any of the troops wearing them nowadays." Mac pulled his tie out of his dress shirt and adjusted the knot. "It'd be like working in a dress."

"Ah, to the untrained eye." Kevin smiled. "This coat's been a lifesaver on more than one occasion."

"How so?"

"When you were on patrol, were you ever on an accident or perimeter assignment and had to go to the bathroom, with nowhere to go in private?"

"Yeah, the center lane of a freeway doesn't afford much privacy. I don't see your point."

"That's the beauty of the long raincoat, my friend. It's built-in privacy when you have to go to the bathroom. Just look like you're busy and take care of business."

"I've heard far too much." Mac shook his head. "And get that nasty coat off mine." Mac grimaced, pushing Kevin's coat over to the side of the trunk with a lug wrench from the trunk.

"I'm kidding, I'm kidding." Kevin laughed. "I've never done it, but I know a few guys who have."

"No way. Who would . . ." Mac glanced over at Philly, who had unzipped his slacks out in the middle of the parking lot to tuck in his shirt. "Never mind. I think I know."

Philly reached in the backseat of his car and grabbed his pistol, racking the slide to charge the gun with a fresh hollow-point round. After securing the gun in his shoulder holster, he turned to Mac and Kevin. While adjusting one of the widest ties Mac had seen in years, Philly said, "You guys want to come with me and Russ to that Mexican joint down on Highway 30?"

"We all ate a huge breakfast on the way out here." Kevin loaded his magazines with duty rounds, as did Mac. "You can't be hungry again, Phil. How about something a little lighter?"

"My blood sugar's low, man. I've got to feed this high-mainte-nance machine." Philly patted his ample stomach.

"You hungry, Mac?" Kevin asked over the top of the car.

"I could eat something, but I don't know about Mexican," Mac replied. "How about that deli in Scappoose? They have pretty good sandwiches."

"Hey, Mac!" Sergeant Frank Evans yelled through the open window of his beat-up Chevrolet Caprice, which he affectionately referred to as the "hammer wagon." Come here."

"Uh-oh." Kevin adjusted the brim of his cap. "We should have run while we had the chance."

Mac ambled the few feet to Frank's car, placing his hands on the hood. Frank was still on the phone, and he gestured Mac to get in.

Mac went around to the passenger side and folded his lean frame inside.

"Look, I'll call you back." Frank frowned, his tone rough and louder than it needed to be. "I said, I'll call you right back. You just get that thing sealed or we'll have a media frenzy on our hands. I'll call you back in two minutes. Let me know what the judge says." Frank pressed a button on his cell phone, ending the conversation.

"CAN I HELP WITH ANYTHING?" Mac asked.

"No, just a glitch in the Salem case. This is my problem. You have another situation to take care of."

"What's that?" Mac turned slightly in his seat, catching his pants on the ripped upholstery.

"I got a page from dispatch. They got a call regarding a floater down at Kelly Point. I need you and Kevin to go out and take a look. Call dispatch and get some details, while I take care of this murder-for-hire case."

"You two coming or what?" Philly yelled from his car as he was pulling out of the parking area with Russ.

Mac rolled down the window. "Sarge just got a call on a floater down at Kelly Point. Kevin and I got the ticket."

"Let us know if you need any help," Philly hollered. "We'll probably swing out that way after lunch and check in."

Frank opened the car door and stepped halfway out. "You and Russ are going to finish those judicial backgrounds for the governor's chief of staff today, Philly. You aren't going to do a single thing until those are on my desk."

"Come on, Sarge. Judge backgrounds? What a lame assignment," Philly complained. "You can't waste my level of talent on doing some stupid background on a judge wannabe."

"Ha," Frank retorted. "You know good and well what level these backgrounds come from. Every detective in the back room got one, and you two are the last to get yours in. I'll expect them on my desk by the end of the day."

Frank slammed his door shut and picked up his cell to make another call. He gave Mac a thumbs-up as he began his conversation.

Mac headed back to the car, where Kevin was waiting in the passenger seat. "Sarge said dispatch sent him an alpha page on a body down at Kelly Point. Sounds like it may be a drowning victim or at least a body that's been in the water. He wants us to get the details then go out and take a look."

"Didn't I tell you not to make eye contact?" Kevin grumped.

"Yeah." Mac grinned at his partner. "Like that's going to stop him."

"Well, make the call and let's see what we've got."

Mac reached for his cell. "Hopefully this one's not too involved. I've got plans for tonight."

"Seeing your fiancée?" Kevin raised an eyebrow.

"Um . . . not exactly." Mac was hoping to connect with Dana for some mentoring, but he didn't want to elaborate. He'd been giving Dana pointers on making detective. Linda was another matter. He'd managed to sidestep any more premarital counseling sessions, but sooner or later he'd have to decide: stay with Linda or break up.

11

Mac scrolled his speed dial on his department phone until it read *RDC*, or Regional Dispatch Center, located in Oregon's Willamette Valley. The dispatcher answered, "State police. Is this an emergency?"

"No, this is . . ."

"Hold, please," the dispatcher interrupted. Moments later she came back on the line, asking Mac what the nature of his call was. The Oregon State Police handled everything from traffic accidents to homicides, so the call screener never knew what to expect.

"This is Detective McAllister from the Portland office, radio number eleven-fifty-four. Sergeant Evans said to call in about a twelve-forty-nine in Multnomah County."

"Oh, hi, Mac; this is Shirley. How's detectives?"

"Beats working the slab in the rain." The *slab* referred to Interstate 5, which ran from the Canadian border through Washington, Oregon, and California, and into Mexico. The freeway carried more than one hundred thousand cars through Portland every day. Truth was, Mac loved being a detective. He just didn't want to seem too enthusiastic. His eagerness usually earned him nothing but a hard time from the other detectives.

"I hear you. Let me get you over to the supervisor. Have a good one."

"Thanks." While Mac waited, Kevin reached over and turned the ignition key, starting the motor. Then he turned on the car's defroster full blast in an attempt to get rid of the growing condensation.

"Thanks for holding; this is Toni. How can I help you?" The civilian dispatch supervisor sounded clipped.

"Hey, Toni. Detective McAllister out of Portland. Detective Bledsoe and I have the ticket on that floater at Kelly Point. Sergeant said to call you for details."

"Yeah, sorry about having you on hold. We had a lengthy pursuit from Springfield to Florence. The troops finally got the guy spike-stripped before he got to Highway 101."

"Everybody okay?" Mac asked. He was still fresh enough off patrol to remember the adrenaline rush of a car chase.

"Yeah, they're all code four. Just a few flat tires. The sheriff's office had a canine on scene, so the guy didn't get far."

"That's good to hear." Mac glanced at Kevin, who gave him an impatient, get-on-with-it look.

"Let me pull up the info on the death investigation, Detective. Ah, here it is. We received a call at about 0900 hours. A floater in the Columbia, just upstream from Kelly Point. A fisherman called it in, and we dispatched a game trooper to check it out. They confirmed it was a floater and towed it into the bank on the Oregon side of the river. The only information I have is that it is a nude white male adult with no obvious sign of death."

"Nude?" Mac shuddered and glanced over at Kevin.

"Yeah, the game troop said he's in pretty bad shape. Looks like he's been in the water for a while. They're standing by with the body until you arrive. What's your ETA?"

"About thirty to forty-five minutes. I'm en route with Detective

Bledsoe from the Columbia County range. What channel are they running on?"

"Channel nine. I'll let them know you're on the way. Just for info, I talked to the game officer, Trooper Ferroli. He told me about a barge accident two weeks ago on the Columbia near Rooster Rock. The tug stalled going upriver and accidentally reversed into the barge. Two men fell overboard. The Coast Guard was never able to find them. That's all I have."

"Sounds good. Would you get the medical examiner on the way, please?"

"Notify M.E.," the dispatch supervisor repeated. Mac could hear her typing the directions into the computer-aided dispatch, or CAD, as the dispatchers called it. "Anything else?"

"That'll do it." Mac thanked her and ended the call. He turned his police radio to channel nine just as the dispatcher was calling the game troopers. Eleven-seventy-one responded.

"Who's eleven-seventy-one?" Kevin asked. "I can't put the voice together with a game officer." The eleven prefix meant the trooper was assigned to Portland, and the secondary number in the seventies designated him as a game officer, just like the fifties series were set aside for detectives. That way, every other station would know the station and work assignments of other troopers as they traveled around the state.

"Chris Ferroli. He runs that big jet sled on the Columbia and Willamette Rivers."

"Oh yeah, I know Chris. Sharp guy. Too bad he's a stump jumper. He'd make a great detective. Is he waiting with the body?"

"Yeah. Dispatch says it's a white male adult." Mac relayed his conversation to Kevin.

"I remember hearing about the tugboat accident." Kevin wiped down his glasses with a chamois cloth. "Or read about it, I can't remember. Something's always happening on those rivers. I can't count the number of times I've worked on accidental drownings or body dumps. The water is always cold, as I recall. The Columbia never warms up."

"Guess you wouldn't have fared very well with Lewis and Clark as they traveled and mapped the river by canoe." Mac eased over the chunky gravel lot onto the paved road that led to Highway 30. "If it had been the Lewis and Bledsoe expedition, St. Louis would have been mapped as the West Coast."

"Not if I would have had that yellow raincoat—nothing would have stood in my way." Kevin chuckled.

Frank was still on his cell phone as they left the parking lot. Mac shook his head. "Sarge is going to amp out one of these days."

"Frank is one of those guys who runs on stress. He was made for the job." Kevin glanced over his shoulder at Frank's shabby old Chevy Caprice. "You always know where you stand with Sarge. He's not interested in promotion or fanfare, just in getting the job done. I have a lot of respect for the man."

Mac nodded.

Kevin leaned back in his seat with his eyes closed.

"You taking a nap?" Mac asked.

"Just talking to the Lord before we get knee-deep in this thing. You want to join me, partner, or are you just going to let me do all the work?"

"All the work?" Mac shook his head. "Since when is praying work?"

"I'm praying for you too—figure it's about time for you to carry your own weight." Kevin opened one eye and peered at Mac.

"Tell you what, partner—you do the praying and I'll stick to the driving." Though Mac was getting used to Kevin's prayers, he wasn't ready to talk to God on his own. While he respected Kevin, the counseling session with Linda's pastor had left a bad taste in his mouth.

"I hope for our sake I pray better than you drive," Kevin teased. He turned down the fan on the defroster and added, "Better get going, driver."

Kevin prayed aloud for wisdom and justice as well as for the safety of all involved. He also prayed for the soul of the unknown victim and finished with a robust amen.

They drove east on Highway 30 through northwest Portland, taking Marine Drive to Kelly Point Park. Kelly Point marked the confluence of the northerly flowing Willamette River into the westerly flowing Columbia River. The back eddy at the merge of the two massive rivers often trapped river debris and dead animals, occasionally those of the human species.

"I think he's out at the end of Lombard." Mac scanned the riverbank of the Columbia for signs of the big silver jet sled that was operated by Trooper Ferroli. The jet sled was a popular fishing and enforcement boat in the Pacific Northwest, a steel-hull boat powered by a jet pump rather than the traditional prop-and-propeller mode. The jet pump allowed the boats to run over sandy river bars as low as four inches deep. The state troopers who worked the area had three at their disposal. The largest, a twenty-six-footer, ran on the tide-influenced Columbia River.

"There he is, Mac." Kevin pointed out the large silver boat with a blue canopy, identified by the words State Police written in black around a silver star on the hull. It was anchored less than fifteen feet from the sandy beach. The white-tipped waves licked at the sides, reminding Mac of how choppy and dangerous the river could be.

Mac parked above the beach to avoid getting stuck in the soft sand. "We better walk from here," he told Kevin. "I don't want to end up digging our car out of the sand."

"Good thinking." Kevin shoved open the door. "You grab the camera, and I'll get the crime-scene kit."

"You got it." Mac slammed the car's gear shift into park.

"Let's go ahead and get a crime-scene log started." Kevin checked his watch. "Call it 1200 hours for our time of arrival. Dr. Thorpe should be the only other person on the scene, but go ahead and get the paperwork started." Kevin glanced over at the state patrol unit pulling up beside them and grinned. "And Dana Bennett. Now, why am I not surprised?" Giving Mac a wink, he added, "I tell you, Mac, she's following you. Is there something you're not telling me?"

"She's following us—or to be more precise, the crime scenes. She wants to make detective." Mac felt his face flush and blamed it on the cold wind.

"So you've been telling me." Kevin nodded a greeting to Dana. "She's relentless; I'll give her that."

"So when's she going to make detective?" Mac hoped it would be soon. Dana had worked hard—above and beyond. She was logging in more overtime than he'd ever thought of doing. He wondered how her boyfriend handled that. She'd never said. Hopefully better than his own fiancée. Mac's time on the job was one of Linda's biggest complaints.

"You'll have to ask Frank about that," Kevin said.

"Hey, guys." Dana ducked into the backseat to grab her heavy OSP jacket then shrugged into it. The blue Gore-tex waistcoat fitted like a waiter's jacket to sit above her gun belt. It had a zip-in fleece liner with silver reflective letters spelling out State Trooper on the back. Her silver badge was pinned on her left chest exactly where it should be. Her grin widened as she approached them. "Anything I can do to help?"

Mac waved the clipboard. "Just in time, Dana. How about keeping the crime-scene log for us?"

"Sure."

Mac opened the back door and snapped open his briefcase,

securing blank log sheets, which he placed under the wide metal clip. "Here you go." His words came out in puffs of steam as his warm breath connected with the frosty air.

"Pop the trunk, would you?" Kevin stood at the rear of the Crown Victoria and rubbed his hands together. The wind was blowing the icy rain downriver.

Mac reached over and depressed the dash-mounted trunk release. Then he joined his partner at the trunk.

Kevin pulled out his long yellow rain slicker. "Want to make fun of my coat now?" Kevin slipped up the collar and fastened the snaps down to his knees.

"I stand corrected." Mac shrugged into his own rain jacket, pulling a knit cap and gloves out of the pockets. "Of course, my jacket does come with a matching pair of Gore-tex pants." Mac pulled the blue waterproof pants from his large black duffel bag and tugged them on over his dress slacks. He tied the drawstring around his waist and donned gloves.

"When did the department start issuing those pants?" Kevin reached for the plastic crime-scene box.

"About five years ago to the patrol division. They're pretty nice. They have short waists so they snug up right under your gun belt. Maybe you ought to start reading the memos." He chuckled. "I'll help you fill out the stockroom request form. I'm sure the back-order should arrive with your rain gear around mid-July."

"Watch it, smart-mouth. Remember who's the senior detective here. I could order you to hand them over." Kevin opened the box, which contained rubber gloves, evidence collection equipment, and markers. "In fact, that's not a bad idea."

"It's a terrible idea. They wouldn't fit. Face it, partner, you've got about twenty pounds on me." Mac waited until Kevin had snatched his cap, then he closed the trunk.

"Humph." Kevin pulled a black sock hat over his ears. Mac and

Kevin were close in height, but Mac was thinner. Kevin had a stocky build, trim and muscular, and had once been a boxer.

Serious now, the detectives left Dana with the clipboard and headed toward the police boat. The dark-haired Fish and Wildlife trooper, wearing green hip waders, was standing in a few inches of water near the bow of the boat. Wearing the department's all-blue water survival suit and baseball-style cap, he walked up the beach to meet the detectives.

"Hey, Chris. How's it going?" Mac pulled off his right glove to shake the trooper's hand.

"Pretty good, Mac. A little cold. The wind chill must be down around ten degrees on the river."

Mac nodded. The primary mission for wildlife troopers was to protect wildlife and natural resources. Bad weather brought salmon, so they would be on the big rivers eight or ten hours a day during fish runs. It was also hunting season, which meant troopers needed to be in the woods as well. All that, on top of arresting DUIIs or any other crime that crossed their path in the remote areas.

"You out on the river all by yourself today?" Kevin asked, shaking hands with the officer.

"Yeah. I thought it would be a quick trip before I got tied up in this thing. A commercial fishing gill net came loose from an outfit owned by some Native American fishing boats upriver, and I was hoping to corral it. I wanted to grab it before it ensnared any seals or sea lions."

"I'm sure the commercial fisherman wouldn't mind if it did," Mac said. Fishermen who netted for a living hated sea lions and seals that followed the fish runs because the sea mammals cut down on profit by eating the salmon or killing the fish for fun. Troopers often found dead seals and sea lions with bullet holes in their heads.

"Too true."

Wanting to cut their frigid investigation short, Mac bypassed the possibility of more shop talk by asking, "Where's the body?" He squinted at the waterline but couldn't see anything unusual.

"He's tied to the back of the boat." Chris pointed to the bobbing water craft. "A bank fisherman called it in, and a road troop took down his info. I found our floater about thirty minutes later in the eddy on the Oregon side of the river. He was bobbing facedown with a bunch of foam and river debris around him. I tried to heave him into the stern of the boat, but his skin is like tissue paper. It started to tear around his shoulder blade."

"Skin slippage." Kevin frowned. "The skin is waterlogged and will slide off like mush if we aren't careful. We can't remove the body until the M.E. gets here, even though this weather is miserable. I'll get on the horn and see how far out she is."

"I'll stay and get some info from Chris for the initial report," Mac said. "Let me know if it'll be long, and we'll wait with you back in the car."

"Sure thing." Kevin raised his shoulders as protection against the icy rain and hurried back toward the car.

"The boat's heated if you want to wait under the canopy," Chris offered.

"Nah. I'm doing okay right now." Mac turned his back to the biting wind, wishing he were wearing a survival suit. He'd had one when he'd done a stint with Fish and Wildlife. The Mustang suit was good to thirty below.

Mac turned his attention to the back of the boat and the gruesome cargo in tow. "Is the guy pretty bad off?"

"I've seen worse. I'll bet you a week's pay it's one of those guys who went overboard off the barge up near Rooster Rock."

"Dispatch gave me a little on that. Can you give me some details?"

Chris pointed upriver. "A tug out of Astoria was pulling an empty grain barge upriver. They were idling downriver from a hogline of fishermen, waiting for them to give the right of way when the tug stalled."

Mac nodded. *Hogline* referred to salmon fishermen who anchored alongside each other in their boats, sometimes reaching nearly all the way across the river. The big chinook salmon were called hogs, hence the term *hogline*.

"Anyway," Chris went on, "this tug is working to get started and is in a free-float heading downriver. The tug captain finally gets his rig started, but it looks like he may have had the tug in reverse. He ends up lurching toward the barge and knocks these two hands into the water."

Mac grimaced. "They lost both men?"

"Unfortunately neither of them was wearing life jackets or survival gear. They went under pretty fast. Weather didn't help. With the wind and choppy water, they didn't have a chance. The Coast Guard bird went up almost immediately, but they called off the search after about an hour—it was storming too bad."

"Do we have descriptions of the victims?"

"Yeah. One guy was Latino, short as I recall—around five-three. The other was a white male with blond hair. I'm pretty sure that's our guy."

Nodding toward the floating corpse, Chris said, "I tore a towel into a long strip and wrapped it around one armpit and his neck, then tied him off with some rope and towed him in. The body is nude and has a bunch of weird shapes on it, like someone drew on the skin."

"Like a tattoo or something?" Mac asked, trying to get the information down on his now-damp pad. It had finally stopped raining and looked like they might get a sun break.

"It's more of a depression. Like the lines you get on your face after waking up on top of a wrinkled blanket, but these have more of a design. I'll have to show you when the M.E. gets here; it's kind of hard to explain. The designs are on the guy's back and shoulder area. He's pretty ripe, Mac. It's going to be bad when we get him out of the water."

Mac nodded. "At least we don't have to do the autopsy. Don't know how the medical examiners do it."

Chris shrugged. "We do what we have to do. That's not a profession I'd choose, but then we get our share of bad stuff too."

"Yeah."

"Hey, Mac, you still seeing that nurse? Linda something or other?"

"Linda Morris. Yeah. We're engaged."

Chris raised an eyebrow. "You don't sound too excited about it."

"I've been thinking about breaking it off. She's having a hard time with my hours."

"I have a hard time with my hours too." Chris's face split into a grin. "Seriously though, if you don't think it'll work, it's better to bow out now."

Mac shrugged. "I told her I'd work on it." Mac had told Linda and Pastor Jim that he'd try to do better at keeping in touch. He'd tried, he honestly had—when he thought about it, which wasn't often enough. Chris was right. One of these days he'd have to face facts and come to a decision. It wasn't fair to Linda or to him to keep things in limbo.

Kevin emerged over the dune at the top of the sandy beach, unsnapping his raincoat as he came toward them. "Kristen is just pulling in." Looking at the sky, he said, "We may get lucky on the weather for a bit." As he joined Mac and Chris, he added, "Mac, you want to go up and give our good doctor a hand?"

"Sure." Mac trudged back through the loose sand, glad to be

busy, glad to have Kristen there. Glad for this new case. He'd completely dead-ended on the sawmill murder. As much as he hated to, he and Kevin had shelved it. It shouldn't have affected Mac quite so much, but it did. His first case as lead detective, and he'd failed. Of course, the case wasn't officially closed, but it might as well be. All they had was a latent print and no match.

12

Dr. KRISTEN THORPE swung her Dodge pickup behind the detectives' sedan and crunched on the emergency brake. She checked her reflection in the rearview mirror, though she wasn't sure why. Nothing had changed since she left the office thirty minutes before. Except that her heart was beating a tad faster. Detective McAllister was in on this one, and she liked the idea of seeing him again. He liked her—or at least found her interesting. So what if he was engaged? He wasn't married yet. She still had a chance.

Thorpe, you are out of your mind. The last thing you need is a relationship with a cop. She had a kid at home, for Pete's sake. She also had needs—needs that weren't fulfilled by the job. She liked her work, but she sometimes longed for the company of a man—someone nice, like Mac, who didn't find her work offensive. At least not too offensive. He respected her—that much she knew.

Kristen rolled her eyes and grabbed an ink pen from the sun visor, pulling off the cap with her teeth. She wrote down a few notes on a form attached to her metal clipboard and then pressed the cap back on the pen. Climbing out of the cab, she waved at the dimpled trooper. "Hey, Dana. I see you're still trying to make an impression on these guys. You must really want to make detective to stand out here in this frigid weather."

Dana nodded. "I do. But at the moment, I'm thinking I ought to have my head examined."

"Yeah, me too." Kristen liked Dana. Liked her attitude. She'd make a good detective, if and when she could get past the good old boys.

Mac jogged toward them. "Hey, Kristen, need a hand with your gear?" He stopped at the back of the truck. As usual, his gaze went to Kristen's spiked hair and triple earrings.

"Why thank you, Mac. Chivalry isn't dead after all." She sidled up to him, placing a hand on his sleeve. "You come here often?" she asked in a sultry voice, batting her long eyelashes at him. A femme fatale she was not, but she enjoyed teasing Mac. Enjoyed seeing his handsome face flush as she teased out his gorgeous smile. Her hand slid off his sleeve, and she wiped her wet palm on her jeans.

"Um, occasionally."

"Oh, Mac, relax. I'm really not as fearsome as I look." Kristen always managed to fluster him and wasn't sure if that was the right modus operandi. Maybe she should change her tactics. She grabbed the handle of the large plastic box, containing her camera, film, rubber gloves, and various other tools of the trade.

"Got a floater, huh?"

"Afraid so. It looks like he's been in the water for a while."

"Skin slippage?" Kristen squinted her eyes and plugged her nose.

"Yeah."

"That's just great. I hate floaters; I can never get the smell off me. My cat wouldn't even go near me after the last one I handled. No wonder I'm single." Kristen slipped on her rain jacket, momentarily exposing a pierced navel and a small tattoo on her hip as her shirt climbed up her midriff.

I don't think that's the only reason. Mac kept the remark to himself.

He liked Kristen, but she seemed a little too much on the wild side. Besides that, the woman was as intimidating as a Bengal tiger.

Kristen grabbed the handle on the large box that held her evidence equipment and then walked to the rear of the truck and opened the canopy. She pulled the steel cadaver gurney from the back of the truck with a grunt, extending the collapsible legs. She then locked the legs open and unfolded the black plastic body bag, then threw the box on the stretcher's surface.

"Like my new sticker, Mac?" Kristen pointed to the lid on her plastic box, which she'd covered with unusual bumper stickers.

He craned his neck to see the lid and spotted the sticker in question. The round yellow sticker had the familiar smiley face with black eyes and big grin. Only this smiley face had a red bullet hole in the center of its forehead.

Mac shook his head and rolled his eyes.

Kristen laughed. "A homicide detective with the Portland Police Bureau gave me that one. Isn't it just too tacky?"

"That's an understatement," Mac muttered.

Kristen's grin faded as she turned serious and looked over her gear. "Let's see—gloves, body bag, envelopes . . ." She went on to list the needed equipment. "You guys got the photos?"

"Yep, we'll handle that end. Kevin has the thirty-five, so why don't you let me shoot your digital?"

"Why, Mac." She grinned up at him and winked. "You can shoot my digital anytime."

Not waiting for his response, Kristen handed Mac her digital camera out of the toolbox. "Okay, lover boy, let's roll."

MAC AND KRISTEN carried the metal gurney to the shoreline, its heavy black wheels rendered useless in the sand. "Hey, Kev, how have you been?" Kristen asked, extending her hand.

"Can't complain."

"Do you know Chris?" Mac asked Kristen.

"I don't believe I've had the pleasure." Kristen shook the trooper's hand.

"Chris Ferroli, this is Dr. Kristen Thorpe. Kristen's the medical examiner." Mac gestured to the back of the boat. "She'll be taking your friend off your hands."

"What happened to 'finder's keepers'?" Kristen slipped on a pair of white cotton gloves and then topped them with purple latex gloves.

"What's with the double gloves?" Mac asked. "Do they make handling the victim easier?"

"It's a brand-new technique, Mac." She held up her hands and examined them. "It's called keeping your hands warm while you handle wet dead things."

"Check." Mac cleared his throat, feeling embarrassed.

"What about your feet? You're going to get soaked." Mac gestured toward her brown leather hiking boots.

"These feet aren't going in the water, that's how. One of you is going to bring the body to me." She gave Mac a sly smile.

"It's not going to be me," Kevin said.

Mac frowned. "These are my new boots."

"Looks like I'm elected." Chris said, slapping the rubber-coated legs of his water survival suit.

"What kind of shape is he in, Chris? Can you get him to shore by yourself?" Kristen asked.

"Yeah, I've got some cloth around his shoulder and armpit. He seems to float pretty well." Chris moved into the murky water, holding onto the rail of the heavy boat. The water was thigh-high when he reached the stern and reached over to untie the tether that held the victim. The trooper began pulling the bloated corpse to shore.

"Try to get some speed while he's still in the water so he slides up on the beach," Kristen told him.

"Right." Chris high-stepped out of the river, pulling the body up on the beach, about halfway out of the water. "He's bogging down. Want me to keep coming?"

"You're doing fine. Hoist that sucker all the way out if you can."

Chris turned and faced the body, walking backward onto the beach while tugging on the makeshift tow rope until the body was totally out of the water. The body undulated after reaching the shore, the water-saturated skin tearing in some places in its weakened state. The sight and smell proved too much for Chris. He made it less than three steps back into the river before succumbing to dry heaves.

"Such a pleasant job we have, don't you think, boys?" Kristen walked toward the body. "Help me roll him over, will you?"

Mac and Kevin both slipped on purple rubber gloves from Kristen's supply. Chris walked back toward the bank with watery eyes, carefully skirting the body. "Sorry about that. That's never happened to me before."

Kristen smiled, "Happens to the best of us. You okay?"

"Yeah. I guess the smell along with the sloughing skin got to me." Chris wiped his mouth on his shirt sleeve.

"There's some menthol cream in my box over there. Rub some under your nose, and you'll be fine." Kristen motioned with her head. "There are some mints in there too; you might want to grab some."

Chris made a beeline for the bag, and so did Mac. He didn't want to admit it, but Mac had almost lost his cookies as well. He rubbed some of the strong-smelling salve under his nose.

"I think I'll stick to fish and deer carcasses." Chris's eyes were still watering. "This is too much."

Mac joined Kristen and Kevin. Mac snapped a few photos with

Kristen's digital camera, while Kevin used the small 35 mm camera.

"I'd better take some backup shots. I don't trust these digital things." Kevin snapped several more shots before slipping the camera into his pocket.

Kristen stepped back from the body, scratching an itch on her chin with her upper arm—careful not to let her gloved hands get anywhere near her face. "I'll get some more at the autopsy," Kristen said. "This will do for now." Mac nodded and stowed the digital back in Kristen's field kit.

Kristen pulled a large thermometer from her toolbox and slid the sharp end of the instrument inside the skin on the upper right thigh of the bloated corpse. The purple skin tore as she slid the metal point in several inches. "Got to get it close to the bone for an accurate reading," she told them.

"What do you make of those lines on his stomach and shoulder?" Chris asked, still standing back away from the body.

"These striations?" Kristen pointed to the chest.

Chris nodded.

"These are all postmortem; it doesn't look like a man-made ligature shadow. My bet is some type of fishing net or even a sturdy piece of river grass wrapped around our victim. When the body begins to rot from the inside, it's like you start to ferment. The cavities expand and cause this bloating. Plant life or other things that restrict the body from bloating in certain areas cause indentations like this. Kind of like when you've had on a tight pair of socks and they leave temporary lines behind when you take them off."

"See any signs of blunt force trauma, Doc?" Mac asked, trying to get a better look at the bruised, swollen face.

"Nothing overt." Kristen moved the head from side to side. "My money is on that barge accident victim we've been waiting to float up. We'll know more when we get him back to my office for a post, but I don't see any obvious signs of trauma."

"When are you scheduling him in?" Kevin asked.

"This afternoon is fine with me, if you two can make it." She pulled the thermometer from the body's thigh and placed it back in the case. "He's enviro-temp, no surprises. I'll have to check my rigor charts with this water temp and get you an estimated time of death. With the greenies on the skin, I'm betting at least two weeks, though with this weather it could be more."

"That would be about right for our barge guys then," Chris said. "Only thing is, they were wearing clothes."

"I've seen these rivers and ocean currents strip the best of them, so I'm not too concerned with the nudity." Kristen rummaged through her case, pulling out a giant syringe and a small plastic cup. She removed the white plastic lid from the clear cup and set the cup in the sand. "I'm just thankful this one was lost below the dam. If he was upriver and went through the turbines, the body would be fish food by now."

"You have such a way with words." Kevin grimaced and shook his head.

"Flattery will get you everywhere." Kristen winked at Mac, then turned serious again as she plunged the syringe into the victim's abdomen.

Chris stepped back, turning a shade of green. "What are you doing now?"

"I need a little urine from the bladder to see if this dude was smoking any herb superb or taking any other drugs we can detect." She filled the giant syringe, emptied its contents into the plastic container, and sealed the lid.

"Can you check for the presence of alcohol in the urine too?" Chris asked.

"Not in this state. His blood and urine will be far too degraded.

Remember that fermenting I was talking about earlier?" Kristen asked.

"Fermenting." Chris bit into his lower lip.

"Well, I meant that in the literal sense. The body ferments just like grapes in wine, which will affect the blood-alcohol content readings. This guy is so degraded, I bet he comes back a three-point-five—four times the legal driving limit—without ever taking a sip of beer. That test is out of the question, but I can have the crime lab test for amphetamines, cocaine, and cannabis for THC content."

"Marijuana." Chris nodded.

"You got it. I prefer calling it the herb superb." Kristen chuckled. "It rolls off the tongue." She placed the container of urine in her case after sealing it with evidence tape and wrapping a small cardboard box around it.

"Okay, ready for the fun part?" Kristen clasped her hands together and raised up on her toes, rocking back and forth. "Let's get him bagged and tagged."

"How do you want to do this?" Mac grabbed the black body bag from the gurney.

"Let's unzip it and lay it out next to our friend here." Kristen snagged the other end of the bag and pulled it apart. She and Mac waved the bag until it was reasonably flat, laying it next to the corpse. "Unzip the top of the bag all the way, Mac." Kristen walked around to the torso of the body. "Okay, let's do this on the first try if we can. Mac, since you're the strongest, take the midsection."

Kevin rolled his eyes at this comment as Mac swaggered over to the body like an overdeveloped bodybuilder. "You have no idea what you just did to my ego," Kevin pouted.

"Sorry, Kevin. I was just trying to butter him up because of the handhold I'm making him take." Mac grimaced as he looked down at his section of the work. "Chris, you take the legs, and Kevin, take the shoulders. Roll him to me, and I'll make sure the bag stays open. Try to step on part of the body bag when we roll him or it'll just keep sliding up the beach."

"You want to roll him all the way over or just back on his face?" Mac asked.

"Just onto his face and stomach. We'll put him right side up when we get him back to the office. Everyone ready?" Kristen asked.

The three men nodded.

"Okay, on three. One, two, three."

The men pushed the body over into the bag with a grunt. Mac's hand sank into the victim's midsection. The move almost made his stomach give up its last meal.

"Good job." Kristen zipped the body bag around the victim, while Kevin pulled the steel gurney over to the body and collapsed the legs. They easily slid the bag and its cargo aboard the now-flattened stretcher. Kristen zipped a second, rubberized external bag around the body and clasped the belts around the feet, mid-section, and chest. They extended the legs again, and Kristen locked them into place.

"That's about it for here." Kristen pulled off her rubber gloves with a snap, then removed the cotton glove from her right hand and extended it to Chris. "Very nice to meet you, Chris. Thanks for the business."

Chris offered a wide grin, holding her hand a little longer than necessary. "I'll have to remember that double-glove trick. Your hands are pretty warm."

"Ah yes, the miracles of the medical field," she said with a laugh. "All right, cool. Let's get out of here."

Mac and Kevin carried the gurney with the body up to the parking area, then helped Kristen load the gurney in the back of her truck. The wildlife trooper started the jet sled, giving them a final wave as he eased the boat off the bank. Once clear, he started upriver to his truck and trailer.

"You guys want to head back to the office and wrap this up today?" Kristen asked. "If this guy's our deck hand, we should be able to get the body taken care of pretty quick, while we're already messy."

Kevin looked to Mac, who nodded and shrugged his shoulders. "I'm game." He made a mental note to call Linda to let her know he'd be late.

"Okay," Kevin said. "Let's put this one to bed today. We'll meet you there, Doc."

"It's a date." Kristen winked at Mac and put on a set of headphones, then started her truck and rolled along the river road, moving her head to the wild rhythm of the music.

"You up for an autopsy?" Mac asked Dana after thanking her and retrieving their crime scene log from her.

"Love to, but I have to get back on patrol. Catch you later."

After saying goodbye to Dana, Kevin and Mac settled back in their car. Kevin had his hand on the heater knob before Mac even got the car started. "Cold?" Mac grinned.

"The old blood doesn't flow like it used to." Kevin turned the heater fan to full blast. "I better call Sarge and let him know we may run into a little overtime with the post. You up for a voluntary adjust, Mac?"

"Okay by me. Maybe we can both get Friday off if we put in enough hours on this."

"Good thinking." Kevin punched in the numbers to Sergeant Evans's mobile phone. Seconds later, Kevin had him on the line.

"Sarge, this is Bledsoe. Yeah, I can hear you." Kevin cupped his hand over the mouthpiece and muttered to Mac, "I can hear him screaming without the phone. I hate that hands-free phone system he has in his car."

Kevin resumed the conversation with his boss. "Say, Sarge, any problem with Mac and me adjusting our itinerary and hitting the post on this floater today? We've got him loaded up with the M.E. and want to put an ID on the guy."

He hesitated then said, "Yeah, pretty sure that's our guy. Great, I'll send you a page when we're done. Should be off by six or seven." Kevin flipped his phone shut.

"Sarge said no problem. He wants us to ID the guy if we can and get to the next of kin for the death notification. I think these bargemen were out of Washington State, so we can get WSP to do the notification."

Mac nodded, though he'd overheard most of the conversation.

"Got time for a cup on the way?" Kevin asked as they reached the paved road again. "Doc Thorpe will take awhile getting prepped for the autopsy."

"Sure. I could use some coffee after dealing with that body."

"Don't I know it. I'd suggest we grab something to eat too, but maybe we'd better save that for later."

Mac groaned. "Much later. I don't know how you can even think about eating."

13

MAC EASED THE CROWN VICTORIA into a parking slot on the east side of the old brick building where the Oregon State Police medical examiners perform their somber work.

Kevin tossed his sport coat in the backseat, checking his 35 mm camera for film. "You mind grabbing . . ." Kevin stopped midsentence when he saw Mac was already holding the evidence-collection kit. The partners walked quickly in the drizzle to the north side of the building, where the front of Kristen's truck was peeking around the corner, backed into the loading dock.

Kevin and Mac walked in through the back door, propped open by one of the staff members. Kevin set his camera on the wood shelf that supported an ancient-looking sign-in book for the facility. He logged them into the building, noting the time on his watch before signing the form.

Mac peered into the autopsy room, seeing that the body they had just recovered at the river was still on the gurney next to one of the two steel tables. On the other, a male physician was just finishing up an autopsy on an infant. Mac turned the other way, averting his eyes. He hated it when they autopsied children.

Mac tried to put the scene from his mind—tried not to think about the children he'd seen during his child-abuse detail. He stopped in front of a giant poster of the circulatory system, trying to look interested until his peripheral vision caught a glimpse of the tiny package being wheeled to the cooler.

"Afternoon, Kevin." The doctor paused on his way out.

"Oh, hey, Drew. How have you been?"

"Same stuff, different day." He motioned toward the cooler. "Got a bad one." His Adam's apple shifted up and down.

"SIDS or stillborn?"

"Worse. Young mother never told her parents she was pregnant. Had the baby in the bathroom at her school and ended up leaving the infant in the toilet to die. The baby still had the umbilical cord attached when we found her."

Kevin closed his eyes. "Children having children. I'm sorry."

"Yeah. The worst thing is that the girl's parents are heartbroken. They would have taken the baby. Senseless."

Kevin gripped the younger man's shoulder. "How's the girl doing?"

"She's okay. Up at Emmanuel giving detectives an earful. D.A. is probably going for murder."

"That's an ugly one. Not your typical murderer, but there's no doubt she intended to let the child die." Kevin put the camera strap over his head. "You assisting with the post on our drowning victim?"

"No, I've done three today already. Kristen is going to do the honors." The doctor closed the cooler door after wheeling the infant inside to wait for a trip to the funeral home.

"What was her name?" Mac asked, his throat feeling thick.

"The mother?"

"No, the baby. Did she have a name? What are you going to put on the death certificate?"

"Jane Doe." The doctor paused. "But I named her Alice. Every child should have a name."

Mac swallowed hard, wishing he could shut down the compassion rising in his gut.

Kevin sighed. "At least the baby is safe and at home now."

"Home?" Mac frowned in momentary confusion. "Oh, you mean in heaven."

Kevin nodded.

"How do you know? That she's in heaven, I mean?"

"God is a father to the fatherless," Kevin said. The line sounded familiar—from Scripture, no doubt.

Having gone to parochial school, Mac had fair knowledge of the Bible. "What about the argument that we're all born in sin and we need to ask forgiveness and be born again to get into heaven?"

Kevin folded his arms. "Do you remember reading the story in the Bible where Jesus gathers the children around him and says, 'Let the little children come to me, and do not hinder them, for the kingdom of heaven belongs to such as these'?"

Mac nodded. He hadn't meant to turn the situation into a theological debate. Maybe he needed clarification himself.

"Grace, Mac." Kevin stepped into the autopsy room. "All of our questions can be summed up in one word: *grace*. God's grace is sufficient."

Mac hoped that was the case. Truth was, he didn't know God well enough to make that kind of judgment.

Kristen came out of her office and walked down the narrow hallway toward them, wearing her customary rubber apron with white lace sewn around the chest piece. "You guys ready?" Not waiting for an answer, she went into the autopsy room, where her assistant, Henry, had already prepared the large stainless-steel table.

"Hey, Henry. I didn't see you come in," Mac said.

"That's the way I like it." Henry's wide grin split his wrinkled coffee-colored skin. "That way Doc Thorpe can't pile more work on me."

"I can always find you, Henry. All I have to do is open a package of cookies from the vending machine, and you come running."

"My one vice and the woman's found it." He shook his head and rolled his eyes. Henry had worked at the medical examiner's office for years; he was probably the oldest and longest-tenured employee they had. He stepped back from the table, examining the tools he had set out. Henry had proven to be an invaluable assistant to the doctors. He always seemed to know what they wanted before they asked for it.

Kristen slipped on her gloves and pulled her foot-activated tape recorder to the center of the room. "I'm going to start dictating now, so no burping or anything. I don't want anyone to think it's me."

"I'll try not to, but no promises for Mac," Kevin joked.

Kristen looked at Mac. "Okay, let's get started." She stepped on the foot pedal. "This is Dr. Kristen Thorpe, Oregon State Medical Examiner, beginning an external examination on John Doe. Subject is approximately sixty-nine to seventy-four inches in height, with a postmortem weight of about two hundred and fifty pounds. Subject is a white male adult, nude upon examination." Kristen released the foot pedal and walked up to the head, lifting the eyelids. She then stepped on the pedal and continued, "Eyes are blue, hair blond with nothing remarkable. Head, neck, and chest evidence signs of ligature contact, although nothing that would indicate a cause or manner of death." Kristen touched and prodded the body as she gave her external exam. "Sternum, nothing remarkable. Abdomen, nothing remarkable. Hips, more ligature evidence from water exposure, nothing remarkable.

Genitalia, nothing remarkable." She smiled and looked up at her audience. "Isn't that every man's nightmare? To get the old 'nothing remarkable' label?"

Mac could feel his cheeks redden. He struggled to keep his mouth shut and his features nonexpressive.

"Don't answer her; that's her favorite joke," Henry said. "Don't give her the satisfaction of letting her see you squirm."

"Oh, pooh on you, Henry." Kristen stuck out her tongue and quickly resumed her exam. When she'd completed the legs and feet, she glanced over at Henry.

"You ready for x-ray?" Henry asked.

"You got it. I don't want to have to roll this dude over more than once, so let's get pictures before we get him off the gurney."

Henry grabbed hold of the steel gurney and wheeled it down the hall and into a room identical in size to the one holding the autopsy tables. The room was used to store the large x-ray machine, in addition to serving as an overflow room if more bodies arrived than they could handle at the office. The cooler was adjacent to the x-ray room, holding an assortment of unclaimed body parts and corpses that were awaiting transportation to a funeral home.

Henry moved the bloated body into place under the large x-ray machine, pulling the glide arm down over the torso. He pulled on a protective vest and stepped back several feet before activating the hand-held control, taking the x-ray. Henry quickly slid the glide arm down to the midsection and eventually to the legs as he completed the task.

"Should be just a few minutes," Henry told the detectives as he pushed the gurney back into the autopsy room. Once inside, he rolled the corpse onto the large steel table and rinsed sand and other foreign objects off the body. The runoff was trapped in the table's custom-made drain trap, in the event detectives wanted to review the contents.

Mac and Kevin slipped on rubber gloves, getting small envelopes and evidence tape ready to collect hair and skin samples, or whatever else Kristen found to be of interest. Kevin snapped a couple more pictures of the body, probably more out of restlessness than necessity. Mac let his gaze linger on his partner. He'd only known Kevin for a few months, but he had the feeling something had been bothering him lately. Several times he'd wanted to ask Kevin about his unusual behavior but hadn't felt like it was the right time or place. He figured whatever it was, Kevin would tell him eventually.

After several minutes, Kristen returned with the x-rays, affixed the three plaques on the lighted board, and snapped on the light.

"Houston, we have a problem," Kristen said while Mac was still trying to figure out what part of the body they were looking at.

"What?" Mac asked. "Where?"

Kristen pointed it out. "See this white mark under the scapula? That's a piece of metal." She grabbed a small ruler from the counter and held it up to the x-ray. "This is actual size, so we are looking at about half an inch. Let's get inside and see what it is."

Henry handed Kristen a long metal rod that looked like a two-foot-long knitting needle.

"You thinking what I'm thinking, Henry?"

"Yep." Henry nodded.

A bullet, Mac guessed. Not wanting to interrupt the team with his observation, he watched intently. Kristen turned back to the body then looked at the x-ray again. She lifted the victim's left arm and fingered around the armpit. "Bingo." Without explanation, Kristen placed the rounded point of the metal rod beneath her finger and gently slid the rod into the body. "Looks like you got about a ten-inch trajectory path, boys. My guess is it will go through both lungs and kiss the heart on the way."

Mac had been right. That pleased him. "So someone shot him.

Guess that rules out our bargeman theory." He looked at the x-ray again and then turned his attention back to Kristen.

Kristen nodded. "Hard to tell for sure until we open him up, but that would be my guess. Henry?"

With a scalpel, Henry made the large Y incision in the body. Then he cut a pathway though the ribs and sternum, allowing Kristen access. Henry removed the section of chest and set it at the foot of the metal table. Kristen dictated her findings into the audio recorder before going any further. Mac watched Kristen's animated features rather than her hands. Fascination accentuated her eyes, making them a brighter blue and giving her look of a kid with a new chemistry set.

"I need to remove the organs before I can get to the tip of the rod," she explained. "The trajectory extends from the left side of the torso to the right shoulder blade."

"We're not going anywhere," Kevin told her.

Kristen removed the heart and lungs, placing them in the scale that hung over the top of the John Doe's feet. After weighing the organs, she dissected them into quarter-inch slices. "Aha. I was right, boys. Our victim was double-lunged by the metal object, and it took out the tip of his aorta. Unless this was some weird postmortem wound, this will be my cause of death. Poor guy wouldn't have lived sixty seconds with a wound like this." She went on to examine the large and small intestines, finding nothing of evidentiary value.

Mac motioned to where the metal rod was still sticking out of the torso. "We checked over the body down at the beach. How could we have missed the entry wound?"

"With the bloating and skin slip, it was easy to miss." Kristen nodded toward the x-ray. "That, my friend, is why we do the films." She examined the x-ray again. "Hmm, the rib is broken inside the cavity, and the wound is right behind the external opening. It would take considerable force to shatter a rib like this."

"Like a bullet." Kevin came forward, and Mac thought he looked pale. His colorless face hadn't come from being around the autopsy—Mac knew that much. Kevin was a seasoned cop.

"Yep." Kristen raised an eyebrow, looking at Kevin as though she'd noted the pallor as well. "I'm still thinking gunshot wound. If he is one of our barge guys, there's more to the story than meets the eye."

Henry moved into position at the head of the table with the electric bone saw, preparing to remove the scalp so Kristen could examine the brain. He had previously made a circular incision around the head, level with the top of the eyebrows.

"Let's hold off on the head, Henry. I want to get that metallic object out of him before we get carried away."

Henry put down the saw and placed all the dissected organs into a clear plastic bag, eventually to be placed back inside the body for burial or cremation. With forceps, Kristen went searching for the metal object she found on the x-ray. "Here we go; I've got it." Kristen grunted as she twisted her arm around the body cavity of the victim. She pulled a small red glob of blood and metal from the body, held up to the light, then set it on the shiny table.

"Let me get a shot of that before you wash it down." Kevin inched forward and snapped a photo. He then set a small plastic evidence ruler on the table for perspective and took two more photos. "Okay, thanks."

"Here you go." Henry handed Kristen a pair of tweezers and a small plastic cup, half-filled with water.

"Thanks." Kristen picked up the piece of metal and tissue with the tweezers and placed it in the cup, swirling the water gently at first then more vigorously. She then poured the contents of the cup into her gloved left hand, holding it out for Mac and Kevin to examine. Mac eyed the mushroomed bullet. "Huh. Looks like a .38 or .357 to me."

Kristen placed the bullet on the table while Kevin took several more photos. Using the tweezers, she picked it up again and held it up to the light. "Looks like murder to me." Excitement of the find lit up her eyes as her gaze flitted from Mac to Kevin, then back to Mac. Mac caught a challenge in her eyes but wasn't sure what it meant.

Kevin dropped his camera, letting the leather strap catch it. "At best, a very suspicious death. We better get to work finding out who this character is. If it is a murder, we're way behind the eight-ball on catching the killer—by at least a couple of weeks."

14

Mac, go ahead and let Sarge know we are going to be a couple more hours, at the earliest. Tell him we're gonna try to get some fingerprints off this guy. See if he can grease the skids for us and get someone from the latent print unit to standby for us."

"You got it," Mac said, already halfway out the door.

"Grab the print kit, would you?" Kevin yelled after Mac.

"You bet." Glad to get out of the room for a few minutes, Mac jogged through the icy rain to their car, climbed in, then grabbed the cell phone off the dash and hit the speed dial to Frank. He summed up their findings to the sergeant and repeated Kevin's message. Frank agreed to make a call to the crime lab and let them know the detectives would be bringing in some inked prints and a bullet for examination. The ice was already building up on the windshield, so Mac started the car and put on the defrost. He'd have to leave the car running or they'd never be able to leave the parking lot.

Mac popped the trunk and reluctantly stepped outside. He pulled his jacket tighter around him and lifted his shoulders, hoping for a modicum of protection against the sleet. Rummaging through the damp clothing, he pulled out a small metal case from beside the spare tire. He locked the car and jogged back into the autopsy room, slipping on the icy step and almost taking a header. As he entered the autopsy room, he found Kevin and Kristen bent over and examining the victim's left hand.

"I've got the ink kit." Mac set it down and joined them. "And Sarge is going to make those calls to the lab so they'll wait for us downtown. Might take us awhile to get there, though. We got us a full-blown ice storm out there."

"Neither hail, nor rain, nor snow, nor ice will keep our OSP guys from their appointed rounds," Kristen said.

"That's the post office, not OSP." Mac brushed away the cold droplets on his forehead with the back of his hand.

"There's a clean towel on the counter over there, Mac. You might want to dry your hair," Kristen offered.

Mac took her advice, mopping up the ice that had accumulated on his head and shoulders. When he finished, Kevin was holding the victim's index finger. "Let's try to roll one, Mac."

"While you two are working on that," Kristen said, "I'll check the fax and see if those Coast Guard documents have arrived with the description of the two bargemen." Kristen dropped her rubber gloves on the empty exam table and walked out of the room. Henry left as well, his job finished there until they were ready for him to remove the body.

Mac opened the box and slid a white-and-pink fingerprint card from a manila envelope. "You want to try the ink pad, Kevin, or the real stuff?"

"Better try the ink pad first, before we make too big of a mess. This guy's got fairly long fingernails, so it should make for a good grip with the print spoon."

Mac pulled a metal fingerprint spoon from the kit and handed it to Kevin. The spoon looked like a shoehorn with a trigger guard on one end. He then grabbed the circular black ink pad from the box, taking off the lid and setting the pad on the edge of the table next to the victim's arm.

"I'll hold the fingers, and you try to roll the card." Kevin turned slightly for a better vantage point.

Printing a live person was difficult enough; printing a dead one was awkward at best. Kevin hooked the print spoon under the left index finger and pulled it over the back of the hand until it made a distended arch. "Give it a try, Mac."

Mac moved in next to Kevin, grabbing the ink pad off the table and rolling it over the pad of the finger. He then folded the print card around the box labeled for the left index finger and rolled the paper card on the top of the inked finger.

"How's it look?" Kevin asked, still holding the lifeless hand.

"Not great." Mac showed Kevin the card. "What do you think?"

"That's what I was afraid of. Poor quality." Kevin let the hand rest on the table and stepped back. "The prints don't have enough ridge detail. We've got to get the skin off his index finger and thumb, then dry them before they will roll."

Kristen came in, holding a stack of papers. "Looks like our guy may not be one of the drowning victims after all."

"Why am I not surprised?" Mac stepped over to the empty autopsy table where Kristen was laying out the faxes she'd gotten from the Coast Guard.

"Vic number one on the drowning was Latino, only about sixty-four inches, and had some false teeth. Our guy's got a perfect smile and may have gained some water weight, but he couldn't have grown over a half a foot."

Mac and Kevin both looked over the grainy fax pictures of the drowning victims. "What about the second guy?" Mac asked. "From what Chris said, he was about the right height and weight. Right hair color."

"He does, or did." Kristen slid a piece of paper to the front of the table where Mac was standing. "But take a look under the scars, marks, and tattoos section on the NCIC report."

"'Drowning victim number two had his appendix out and had a shamrock tattoo on his right shoulder,'" Mac read the report over her shoulder. Kristen turned for a moment, her face inches away from his. In that moment, Mac wanted nothing more than to pull her into his arms and kiss her. He stepped back and looked away, annoyed by his animal instincts and feeling like he'd gotten caught stealing.

Kristen didn't seem the least bit offended. In fact, she seemed to enjoy the moment. He expected a smart remark, but none came.

Kevin rounded the corner of the table and took a look at the victim's shoulder. "No tats on the shoulder or anywhere else I can see."

"And no appendix scar," Kristen added, not missing a beat. "This guy is a totally new unsub." Glancing at Mac, she added, "That's slang for unidentified subject."

Mac knew that but didn't trust himself to speak. He clamped his jaw and tried to focus on what Kevin was saying rather than on the testosterone-induced state he'd fallen into.

"We tried to roll a set of latents." Kevin showed Kristen the print card. "The skin's just too saturated."

"I'll get the blow dryer." Kristen tossed Mac a knowing smile. "Help yourself to one of my scalpels on the counter, boys."

Kevin selected a scalpel. "You ever done this before, Mac?"

"Done what?"

"Guess that answers my question." Kevin handed the scalpel to Mac.

Mac frowned. "Are we cutting his fingers off?" Mac remembered reading something about obtaining fingerprints by removing the dermis.

"No, *we* are not. You are going to do the cutting. I'll hold the print card and the ink. All you need to do is cut around the dermis on three or four of the fingers below the first knuckle and remove the skin."

"Oh." Mac's tone seemed a little too high and uncertain. He slipped on a fresh pair of gloves as Kristen returned to the room with a vintage blow dryer that had duct tape wrapped around the handle.

"You actually use that thing?" Mac nodded toward the dryer. "Doesn't look too safe."

"Me use a blower? Are you kidding?" Kristen touched the tips of her spiked burgundy hair. "This is the lab blow dryer. It came in with a woman three or four years ago, tucked inside the body bag. Bathtub incident—either it fell into the tub with her or someone threw it in. Of course, the other possibility is that she was using it as a bathtub toy. However you look at it, I don't think she ever missed it. It may not look so good, but it'll dry those prints out after you get the skin off."

"I guess my lucky number came up." Mac glanced down at the victim's hand and braced himself. "I get to take them off."

"This I've got to see." Kristen grinned in Mac's direction, not meeting his eyes.

Mac wondered at her sudden shyness, but only for a moment. Determined to keep his mind on the task, he held the tip of the middle finger, cutting around the base with the scalpel, and then tried to slip the skin off the bone. It wouldn't give.

"Twist it a little," Kristen said. "It'll break loose."

Mac set down the scalpel, held his breath, and twisted the skin on the finger, eventually sliding it off the end.

"Good." Kevin extended his gloved right hand, sticking his index finger toward the skin sample. "Go ahead and slip it on."

"This isn't a forefinger. Does it matter?"

"No," Kevin answered. "I'll just make sure I roll the print in the right box. It's easier for me to roll prints with my right index finger."

Feeling queasy, Mac slid the piece of finger skin from the victim over the top of Kevin's extended finger. This would not go down as his favorite part of being a detective.

Turning toward Kristen, Kevin said, "Doc, would you mind doing the honors?"

"Be happy to." Kristen turned the blow dryer on low speed, holding it about six inches from the skin sample and waving it back and forth. After about five minutes of drying, Kristen turned it off. "That should do it."

Kevin then rolled the ink pad over the finger and applied the print to a fresh card. Smiling at the results, he said, "That's more like it." On the card was a clean latent fingerprint that was quality enough to run through the AFIS computer at the crime lab and hopefully get a match.

"Let's get a few more, Mac."

Mac removed the skin from both thumbs and the index finger on the right hand, going through the same process to recover several more quality fingerprint samples.

"I'm impressed." After blowing dry the last one, Kristen wrapped up the cord around the dryer and set it aside. "Nice job, Mac."

Kevin slipped off his gloves after the skin samples had been set neatly on the edge of the autopsy table. "Mind hanging on to those for a while?" he asked Kristen. "At least until you release the body?"

"No problem. I'll have Henry wrap them up in the body cavity with the internal organs after he bags them. We still have to get a look inside his noggin, but I'd be surprised if anything comes of it. I'll get heart muscle samples and a dental mold before he goes into the freezer, in case we need DNA or a dentist to ID this guy later."

Kevin thanked her. "Mac and I are going to get these prints and the bullet to the lab, so page one of us if you turn up any more surprises."

"Sounds like a plan. I'll hold on to the corpse until I hear from you on the next of kin. There's plenty of room in the freezer if we need to hold him for a while. I'll also grab some head and pubic hair samples for you in case they come into play later."

"Great." Kevin nodded. He seemed stiff, his jaw set. Again Mac wondered what was going on with his partner. Since this wasn't the time to ask, he pushed it to the back of his mind, thinking he'd talk to him later.

Mac and Kevin walked out in the hall to collect their gear. "You okay to run with this one, partner?" Kevin asked.

"Sure, but two in a row?" Mac secured the latent prints inside a paper envelope, placing it back inside the print kit so not to smudge the acquired samples. He didn't want to have to repeat the process again.

"You need the experience." Kevin rolled the bullet inside a paper fold and placed it into a plastic evidence bag.

"Yeah, whatever." Mac rubbed his forehead, trying to assimilate all the mismatched details ricocheting in his head.

"You okay, partner?" Kevin frowned. "You look a little unsettled."

He looked unsettled? "Nah. I'm fine. Just not used to slicing up fingers." Mac shot a glance back inside the autopsy room as Kristen was weighing the brain from their victim. Henry had placed the internal organs inside a clear plastic bag and neatly tucked the little package inside the body cavity. He had just begun his closing handiwork on the body, stitching up the chest and sternum with nylon thread in preparation for transfer to a funeral home, once the body was released.

The men stopped on the steps.

"Looks treacherous out there." Kevin slipped a pair of wool

gloves out of his coat pocket and carefully made his way down the ice-coated stairs. The rough concrete gave them minimal traction.

Mac pulled on his own gloves and grabbed the metal railing for balance. "I left the motor running, so the car should be warm and the windows thawed."

"Good. Let's give it a shot. We've got good tires, so as long as there aren't any crazies besides us trying to drive in this stuff, we should be okay."

Mac clicked on the remote to unlock the Crown Victoria, then he half-walked, half-skated to the driver side door. Ice had formed around the doors and crackled as Mac and Kevin yanked them open.

Inside, Kevin snapped his seatbelt and warmed his hands on the heater. Mac shivered as droplets of ice melted and trickled down his neck.

"Hang on." Mac eased the car out of the parking space. "So far, so good." He tossed his partner a grin and turned south onto Grand Avenue in North Portland.

"Smart-mouth." After a few minutes, Kevin leaned back in the seat and closed his eyes.

"Praying again?" Mac asked.

"No. Thinking. It's none of my business, but are you and Kristen involved?"

"Me and the doc? You've got to be kidding." Mac was glad for the darkness. Even with the frigid weather he could feel his temperature rise. "She's just a big flirt—you know that. I was playing along, that's all."

"Yeah." He grunted and shifted slightly in his seat. "So, you're still seeing Linda?"

Mac hesitated. "Sort of."

"What kind of answer is that? Did you break off the engagement? What?"

"I don't know, Kev. She's still ragging on me to go to counseling with her, and I keep making excuses."

"Do you love her?"

"I don't know. Sometimes . . . I guess." Mac sighed. "I'm not sure what I want. Linda is a beautiful woman, and she's been more understanding about my work lately. I feel like I need to give her a chance."

"Ah, Mac, I'm glad I'm not in your shoes. I stopped having girl problems more than thirty years ago when I met Jean."

"You lucked out, Kevin. Jean is great."

"She is." He smiled. "Don't settle for second-best, Mac. If you're not sure, maybe you need to let things cool off. Date other women. I have a feeling Kristen wouldn't mind. Or Dana, for that matter."

Mac felt his cheeks flush. "What makes you think that?"

"Discernment, my boy. Both those women get all starry-eyed when you're around. Don't know what they see in you, but . . ."

"Dana is dating someone, and Kristen is . . . strange."

"You won't get an argument from me there, partner. All I'm saying is follow your heart."

My heart? Right. Mac had no idea which direction his heart was taking. One minute it leaned toward Linda, the next toward Dana, and today he'd even found himself tilting in Kristen's direction.

Mac tried to stop at a red light, but the wheels had other ideas. Fortunately, there were no cars at the intersection. He managed to regain control of the car and set off again, moving at a decent clip once he reached a heavily traveled road where the ice hadn't had a chance to settle in. Fifteen minutes later they were downtown, parking in a Police Only space in front of the Justice Center on SW 4th Avenue. The multistory building served as the county jail and a Portland Police Bureau precinct. The twelfth floor was home to the Oregon State Police forensic lab scientists for the entire metropolitan area. The crime lab, one of many maintained by OSP, satisfied several forensic needs of the criminal justice system, including DNA testing, ballistics, drug testing, and latent print comparison.

Kevin grabbed their evidence, and he and Mac entered the building through large glass doors at the street level. Once in the foyer, Kevin flipped open his wallet badge to show the security officer at the front desk. Mac pulled his sport coat aside to display the badge he had clipped to his belt. The officer buzzed them through the electronic lock and went back to his paperwork. They rode the elevator to the twelfth floor then hurried down the long, carpeted hallway, which displayed large photographs of crime-scene investigations dated fifty years or older. In the pictures, officers were shown using large cameras on tripods with flash powder.

"This one is my favorite." Kevin paused and pointed to a black-and-white photo of a dining room that had several overturned chairs. The room looked like a rustic cabin with hundreds of holes in the walls and furniture, connected by countless strands of string.

"Hmm." Mac rarely took time to look at the pictures. He promised himself he'd check out the history behind them someday. "I've always wondered what that was all about."

"That was in the 1940s in the central Oregon area. Some desperado killed a local lawman—I can't remember which one, but it wasn't a trooper—and was holed up inside this cabin. The local sheriff rounded up a posse, and they turned the house into Swiss cheese. They're using string to work out trajectory patterns."

"That's a lot of string," Mac said.

"Isn't that something? Here we are sixty years later, and string is still the best thing we have to work the same type of investigation," Kevin said.

"We have lasers."

"Those things are nice for measurements, but give me string any day if you want to see what went where and who shot who."

Mac and Kevin entered the forensic lab and stopped at the receptionist's desk. The receptionist was gone, so Mac reached over the counter and buzzed them in.

A lab tech saw them come in and stopped. "Can I help you?"

"I'm Detective Bledsoe and this is Detective McAllister from the Portland office."

The lab tech nodded. "We're closed for the day."

Kevin lifted his bag. "Detective Sergeant Evans phoned ahead to let you guys know we were bringing in some homicide evidence in for exam. Could you let the criminalist supervisor know we're here?"

"Sure. Hang on a sec." He disappeared around a corner and returned a minute or so later. "Criminalist Sprague will be right with you."

"Thanks." Mac dug in his pocket for a tissue to wipe his dripping nose.

"You're welcome, and I'm going home." He shrugged into a leather bomber jacket. "I heard the weather's pretty bad out there."

"Freeway's still open, but watch the side streets," Mac responded. "Come morning I have a feeling we'll be locked in."

Moments later, Allison Sprague, a forensics supervisor at the lab, emerged from around the corner in a white lab coat. "Hey, Mac and Kevin. How are you guys doing?"

"Been better. It looks like we jumped out of the frying pan and into the fire," Mac answered. "We fished a floater out of the river today, and it turns out he picked up a bullet somewhere."

"Sergeant Evans said you needed an AFIS run on some prints and a bullet frag entered into IBIS."

"Yeah." Mac placed the envelope containing the print card on the counter. "We thought our victim might be one of two men who fell off a barge in a tug accident, but the cursory identification didn't match up at the lab. So we lifted some prints."

"That shouldn't be a problem." Allison opened the envelope.

Kevin placed the plastic bag containing the bullet on the counter. "Doc Thorpe pulled this out of his chest during the autopsy. He's been dead for at least a couple of weeks, maybe longer."

"I can run these prints through AFIS tonight. Hopefully your guy has a criminal history or a military background. If so, he should pop right up. The bullet will have to wait until tomorrow, though. Both our ballistics guys are out of the office until morning." She glanced at the window. "At least I hope they'll be in tomorrow. Weatherman says we're probably going to wake up to about two more inches of this."

Mac groaned. "Tell me again why I live in the Northwest?"

"We'll worry about ballistics later," Kevin said. "Right now I'm more concerned with the prints. If we can get a starting point on the owner, it'll give us a lead on the investigation. Hopefully we won't have to pore over missing-person reports for the western United States—that could take weeks."

"If we get lucky, I could have them in about thirty minutes." Allison took the bag from Mac. "You guys are welcome to wait here or grab some dinner and come back."

"I'm sorry for the trouble, Allison," Kevin said. "Hope you didn't have plans."

"Don't worry about it. I was staying late anyway; I have some quality-control tests to perform on some instruments. It's easier after hours."

"You hungry, Mac?" Kevin asked.

"Starved."

Kevin nodded and turned to Allison. "I think we'll take your suggestion and grab a bite. Can we bring you back anything?"

"No thanks; I'm fine. My fifteen-year-old is always up for a late bite, so I'll eat with her in a couple of hours."

"Okay. We'll be back in about thirty."

15

THE SAME OFFICER they'd encountered on their earlier trip, with the same deadpan features, waved them inside the Justice Center. Upon reaching the twelfth floor, Kevin and Mac found the crime lab door locked. Kevin knocked, and Allison let them in.

"Sorry about that. One of the lab guys must have locked up on the way out."

"That's okay." Kevin stepped inside, looking to Allison to break the news.

Mac had the same anticipatory feeling—wanting to know, yet not wanting to know. Identifying the victim meant telling the family.

"I've got a match for you. Come on back." Allison motioned for the two detectives to walk around behind the front counter.

"After you." Mac held the half-door open, trying to subdue his eagerness. They followed Allison to a small office, containing only a desk with a computer and printer.

"Here you go." Allison held out a computerized printout. "AFIS hit on him right away—on the first thumb I sent through."

Mac grabbed the computer sheet and read the name aloud. "Bradley Gaynes." He handed the sheet to Kevin. "The missing hiker." Mac recognized the name immediately.

"You know him?"

"No, but I helped look for him. He went missing more than two months ago. Dana's been following the case pretty closely. Don't know why I didn't think about him right away."

"Our Dana?" Kevin raised an eyebrow at the implication and then turned his attention to the printout. "The kid was twenty-five. Looks like he was arrested for dope a few years back; he has a criminal history out of Deschutes County."

Mac remembered his conversation with Dana where she'd gotten that information from the mother.

"There's more." Allison handed a second page to Mac while Kevin studied the first. "Our guy is a listed missing person in LEDS. Looks like he's been AWOL out of Hood River County since November. His criminal history caught the prints through AFIS, but I had to run the name to check his status."

"So the sheriff's office has him entered as missing?" Kevin asked, moving in shoulder to shoulder with Mac to read the fax.

Mac's mind reeled with the news. His stomach twisted in knots as he tried to assimilate the information. He thought about the Gaynes family, feeling sick at the thought of having to tell them. He needed to call Dana—maybe since the two of them had helped with the search, they should be the ones to break the news. "Can I use a phone, Allison?" Mac took both printouts.

"Sure." Allison pointed to her office down the hall. "Use mine."

"Calling out to Hood River County?" Kevin asked.

The question jolted Mac. Luckily, his back was already turned to them. Of course he had to notify the sheriff's office first. Then he could call Dana. He glanced back over his shoulder. "You know it."

"I'll get the firearms guys on that bullet first thing in the morning, Kevin," Allison said.

"Appreciate it. Say, how's the better half?"

"Joe's doing great. I'll tell him you said hi. He's off on some fishing trip on the John Day River right now. Probably freezing his you-know-what off."

"Going after some winter steelhead, or are the chinook that far up yet?" Kevin envied the man—not that he was out in this weather, but that he took the time to do what he loved most. Kevin needed to do that. He needed to back off before it was too late. On the other hand, maybe it was already too late. Kevin shoved the morbid thought from his mind.

"Who knows," Allison laughed. "Joe doesn't catch much. With the money he has tied up in fishing gear and the price of gas nowadays, the fish he brings home run us about a hundred dollars a pound."

"I bet he has a blast, though."

"Yeah, he does; so I don't complain. Besides, Beth and I get a chance to do some heavy-duty bonding and shopping when he's gone."

Kevin nodded. "Thanks a million for staying late. I know you don't get overtime."

"No problem, Kevin. I'm glad to help a friend. Besides, I'll have an excuse to come in late tomorrow after staying up late tonight."

Mac caught the tail end of their conversation as he walked back into the room. "Looks like we're going to be up a little late too."

"Why, what's up?" Kevin asked.

"I talked to Deputy Sam Wyatt with the S.O. Since I was working on the sawmill case, I was only able to search that one day. Dana kept me up to speed for a few weeks. Wyatt says they did a full-blown search-and-rescue mission but didn't turn up a scrap of evidence. They speculated that there may have been an accident or maybe Gaynes committed suicide up at Wah-kella Falls."

"I remember that case now," Allison said. "Joe and I hike the

Eagle Creek trail system. He likes to hunt around there. Wah-kella is the first big falls when you go past Bonneville Dam."

Mac nodded. "The sheriff says the family is still searching for this guy, going back to the falls and posting fliers."

"So as of right now, the family thinks there may be hope for their son," Kevin said, as more of a reflective statement than a question.

"Afraid so. We have to make some notifications tonight. His parents live here in the Portland area."

"Looks like you two have work to do, so I'll get out of your hair." Allison gave Kevin a pat on the shoulder as she walked past.

"Thanks again, Allison. We'll be in touch on the bullet," Kevin said.

"You guys can lock up if you need to stay."

"We're heading out now," Kevin said. "You have the address, Mac?"

"Yep. It's over by Portland State. We're only about ten minutes out."

Mac and Kevin walked out to the elevator with Allison, but she continued past the doors. "You going down?" Mac asked.

She pointed to the stairway door. "I always take the stairs. It's the only exercise I get some days."

Mac smiled and waved good-bye as Kevin hit the first-floor button. Before the door shut, Kevin was formulating his game plan. "Did you tell the deputy what we found in the body?"

"You mean the bullet?"

Kevin nodded.

"Yes, I had to. When I first told him about Brad's body, he wanted to gear up his crew and start working this thing, still thinking it was an accident or a suicide. So I told him about the bullet and said we were working it as a probable murder. Wyatt is still under the impression the guy went over a waterfall after his girlfriend broke up with him, and his body floated downstream to the Columbia."

"That's doubtful," Kevin said. "I'd lay odds that this Gaynes fellow didn't go into the river above Bonneville Dam. The turbines would have turned him into mincemeat, unless he somehow navigated the fish ladder or sneaked through the locks. My guess is this guy took a bullet and was dumped in the lower river."

"Wyatt didn't have any information on a firearm from the family or girlfriend, although I didn't specifically ask. He wasn't too thrilled about us working the case—looks like he's been on it for some time."

"Did you tell him we were OSP?"

"Yep."

"We'll touch base with him again after making the death notification to Brad's mom and dad."

"He's working until four in the morning, so I told him we would give him a call. Apparently he hears from the mother a lot." Mac folded the papers and stared at the floor, remembering Brad Gaynes's distraught mother, father, sister, and girlfriend.

"Kevin, do you mind if I call Trooper Bennett in on this? She's been following through with the family on her off time. Besides that, she's been through the grief counseling training."

The elevator door opened when they reached the ground floor of the Justice Center. They stepped out, their wet soles squeaking against the marble floor.

"That's a good idea, Mac." Kevin hesitated a moment and then added, "In fact, why don't you and Dana go? I'll sit this one out."

Mac frowned. There it was again, that tired, strained look. "Sure, if you tell me what's going on with you. You've been acting strange for the past couple of weeks—more so today. Is everything okay?"

Kevin sighed and shook his head. "No, it isn't." He pinched the bridge of his nose. "I'm tired. I'm getting old. Been thinking about retiring—but you know that."

"Yeah. I just don't believe it."

Kevin clamped his hand over Mac's shoulder. "We'll talk. Soon. Just not right now."

They left the building and hurried to the car. The ice had turned to snow and was building up fast. Once they'd gotten into the car and buckled up, Kevin folded his arms around himself and leaned forward. "Just drop me off at my house, Mac. You can pick me up there in the morning."

"Why don't you want to drive your car?" It seemed an odd request, since Kevin lived across town and Mac's car was still parked at the OSP office. Usually they went back to the station, got into their separate cars, and went home.

"Like I said, I'm just tired. Now go." The words were clipped.

Are you angry with me? Did I do something wrong? What's going on? Mac wanted to ask those questions and more, but he didn't. Kevin didn't want to talk. He'd made that clear enough.

Mac grabbed his cell phone, not bothering to hide his annoyance. Partners were supposed to trust each other. They were supposed to confide in each other. He speed-dialed Dana's cell phone.

"Hey Mac, what's up?" Dana asked after his greeting.

"You know that floater we picked up this afternoon?" Mac said.

"It's Bradley Gaynes, isn't it?"

"How did you know?" Mac straightened and instinctively glanced in the rearview mirror.

"Intuition. I thought about him after you guys left. I hoped it would be one of the bargemen, but I had this feeling. Brad had blond hair and was about the same height." She hesitated a moment. "You're sure?"

"We have a fingerprint ID."

"Do you want me to notify the family?" Empathy swathed her voice, and he could almost feel the magic soothe his hurt feelings.

"That's why I called. I thought it would be good if we talked to them together." Mac glanced at Kevin's reclining form. He'd leaned back, lowered the seat, and had his eyes closed. "I'm dropping Kevin off at home and then heading over there. Do you have the address?"

"Yeah. I've been there a few times. We've got a guy out here on S.E. Powell who's had a little too much holiday cheer. I'll let Perkins take him in. I can get there in half an hour."

"Sounds good."

Mac closed the phone and slipped it into his jacket pocket. "Think I should call the Gayneses first?"

When Kevin didn't answer, Mac thought he might be asleep. After several long seconds, he said, "No. Just head up there, Mac. It's better to tell them in person—that way you're there to handle any problems."

There was no anger in his voice now, but Mac thought he saw a tear glisten on Kevin's cheek as they went under a streetlight.

"Why don't you give Sarge a call and bring him up to speed?" Kevin suggested.

Mac did, but when he couldn't reach Sergeant Evans, he left messages on his mobile and at home.

After driving his partner to his home in Milwaukee, Mac drove back to the city, through traffic on Broadway that was surprisingly heavy on such an icy night, past the various performing arts centers, and eventually passing the campus of Portland State University.

"I hate these," Mac muttered as he thought of the dozens of times he had to make death messages while working as a uniformed trooper. He disliked delivering messages to family members that their loved one had died in a car wreck or other unusual circumstances.

Mac thought about the last message he delivered, the very

evening he learned he had made detective and would shed his uniform patrol job. An older couple had been serving as foster parents to a child after the State had taken him from his violent parents. The father of the child had somehow learned where the child was staying. After murdering the foster mother in a bloody rampage, he kidnapped his son from the home.

Mac had drawn the short straw and had to tell the victim's husband that, while he was at work, his wife of thirty years had been killed by a madman. Mac met the man in his office and saw the look in his eyes right after they shook hands. The husband knew—somehow they always seem to know.

Mac found the address without any problem, probably because of the OSP vehicle parked on the street. He pulled alongside the curb behind Dana and glanced at the house. Judging by the cars in the driveway and the lights inside, the Gayneses were home. Mac took a deep breath and let it out again, willing his tension to dissipate.

The dome light on Dana's car came on as she opened the door. Her hair shone gold, creating a halolike aura. She stepped out of the car and grinned. Mac again felt drawn toward her. But then, he seemed drawn to a lot of women lately.

"Thanks for calling me, Mac." Dana opened her arms for a hug, holding him a bit tighter than usual. When she let go, he realized she'd been crying.

"Are you sure you're up for this?"

"No, but I need to be here. I know they'll appreciate hearing about Brad from us."

They made their way up the snow-covered walk, made more treacherous by the thick layer of ice.

Straightening his tie, Mac rang the doorbell and pulled out his badge wallet. Dana stood beside him, her badge fully visible on her jacket. The door swung open and Vicki Gaynes stood in the entryway, shifting her gaze from Mac to Dana. She was wearing a suit but had taken off her shoes. She'd probably just come home from work.

"Hello, Mrs. Gaynes," Mac said. "I'm Detective McAllister and this is . . ."

"I know who you are, Detective. You were on the mountain that first day, helping to look for my Brad. And you . . ." She pulled Dana into an embrace, her eyes filling with tears. "How are you, Dana?"

"Good."

"Mrs. Gaynes," Mac tried again. "May we come in and speak with you?"

"Of course." Vicki opened the door. "Let me get Todd. He's in the kitchen. Can I get you something? Eggnog, hot chocolate . . ."

Women so often did this. They knew why the officers had come, yet they wanted or needed to postpone the inevitable. Mac wanted to get it over with. He started to say so, but Dana interrupted.

"Hot chocolate sounds wonderful, Vicki." Dana tossed Mac a look that clearly indicated that he should follow suit.

"Sounds good to me too." He'd have preferred coffee, but apparently that wasn't an option. As Mac and Dana followed Vicki down the hall, he caught a glimpse of a family portrait and paused briefly to study the photo of the healthy-looking young man seated in front of Vicki. Why hadn't he thought about Brad sooner?

"Todd," Vicki said as she passed the kitchen, "we have company. You remember Dana, and this is Detective McAllister. He helped with the search that first day."

"Call me Mac," he offered.

Todd lowered the newspaper, folded it, and set it on the table. "It's about Brad, isn't it?" Todd stood and shook Mac's hand.

"Oh." The cry was sharp and tiny, like a puppy's yelp. Vicki's hand shot to her mouth as she sought to regain control. "P-please, sit down. I'll get the hot chocolate."

The kitchen was cozy and warm. Six chairs surrounded the rectangular table set in a bay window. "Mind if we all sit at the table?" Mac asked.

"Sure." Todd glanced at Vicki, who was pulling four large mugs from a glassed-in cupboard. "Vicki?"

"I'll just be a minute." She poured boiling water from a teapot into the cups and dumped spoonfuls of Swiss Miss into them. "Luckily the water's ready. I was boiling some for tea. It's so cold outside."

Vicki set the mugs on a tray and carried it to the table. "Sit down, honey." Todd held out a chair. When she was seated, Todd placed his hands on her shoulders. Vicki placed her hands on his.

Dana took a drink off the tray and handed it to Mac. Then she set one in front of Vicki and another at Todd's place. The big man sat down and wrapped his hands around the steaming mug.

They knew. Of course they did. Most people would ask what they wanted or why they were there before allowing them into their home. Todd wanted answers now. Vicki didn't want to hear the horrid news that she had outlived her son. But it was time. The only way to deal with this sort of thing was to be direct—no beating around the bush. "Mr. and Mrs. Gaynes," Mac began, "could you just verify for me that you are the biological parents of Bradley Gaynes, who is reported as a missing person by the Hood River County Sheriff's Department?"

"We are," Todd answered, his voice barely audible.

Mac swallowed back the emotions welling up in his chest. "Vicki, Todd . . . I am very sorry to have to say this, but your son is dead. His remains were recovered today in the Columbia River near Kelly Point."

Vicki hid her face in her hands and began to sob. Todd

squeezed his eyes shut, then rose and lifted his wife to her feet, wrapping his arms around her.

Feeling awkward, Mac stood. "We'll be in the living room. Take as much time as . . ." He stopped midsentence when he noticed the Gayneses weren't listening. Mac and Dana went into the next room to wait, allowing the parents to deal with the initial shock in private.

About fifteen minutes later, Mac set down the *National Geographic* magazine he'd been thumbing through. "Did you know flies taste with their feet?" he asked in a whisper.

"Is that what the magazine says?"

"No. I just heard that somewhere and was wondering if it was true," Mac said with a halfhearted attempt at a grin.

Dana rolled her eyes.

"They're taking it pretty hard," Mac whispered.

"Wouldn't you?" Dana shot him an annoyed look.

Mac splayed his hands. "What did I do?"

"I'm going back into the kitchen." She stood and turned back to him. "You coming?"

Mac reluctantly stood.

"On second thought," Dana said, "you stay here. I'll let you know when it's safe."

That hurt. He followed Dana as far as the kitchen door, where they found the couple sitting next to one another at the table, touching foreheads and holding hands. Todd was saying something Mac couldn't hear.

Vicki looked up and smiled. "I'm so sorry to neglect you two. Please come back in."

Mac was taken aback by the smile. He wasn't expecting that kind of reaction.

Dana sat down at the table with them. Mac leaned against the doorjamb, watching Dana work her magic. She'd help them through the whole shock, denial, and anger thing loved ones always went through. Mac had gone through the grief counseling training as well, but it had been awhile—and truth be told, he'd always felt that women did a better job. At any rate, it was better this way. He couldn't be a friend. He had to stay objective; emotions got in the way of analytical thinking. Mac went back into the living room and half-listened to their conversation while he thumbed through an *Architectural Digest* magazine. He wondered if Vicki Gaynes had decorated her own home. It looked sophisticated yet comfortable.

He hoped to be able to build or buy a home one day. It wouldn't be as elegant as this, but it would be homey. He wanted a fireplace and a Jacuzzi, a big kitchen, and a wife who liked to cook. He placed the magazine back on the table. Linda worked a lot of evenings. Well, so did he. Would they eat out most of the time?

Mac grimaced at the thought. He didn't want that kind of life. He'd never really thought that much about hearth and home, but he knew he wanted the kind of home his grandmother Kathryn had provided for him while he was growing up. A stay-at-home wife and mom. *Fat chance of getting a woman like that,* Mac thought bitterly. *All the women you know are career-driven.*

"Mac can answer those questions better than I."

Hearing his name, Mac tuned back into the conversation in the kitchen. He started to go back into the room but stopped when Dana came to him.

"Todd and Vicki are ready for you."

"Ready?" He frowned. "What are they expecting? We weren't planning to interview them now."

"I think it's the other way around, Mac," Dana said. "They want to know what happened to their son and what you're going to do next."

"Okay," Mac said. "That I can handle."

Mac started for the kitchen when Dana stopped him. "Hold on; you're crooked."

Mac raised an eyebrow. "What?"

"Here, let me," Dana's dimples went deep as she smiled up at him. She dropped her gaze to his tie, reaching up to adjust it. "There you go." She straightened his collar.

"Thanks." Mac rubbed the back of his head, hoping he didn't look as red as he felt.

"You're welcome."

Mac used the walk back to the kitchen to gather his thoughts and focus on the reason for their visit. He sat down at the table again and realized he hadn't touched the hot chocolate Vicki had made for him.

Dana walked around the table and slid into the chair next to Vicki.

"I understand you folks have some questions," Mac said. "Would you rather have me start from the beginning, or would you rather not hear the details? I know everyone's different—"

"I want to know what happened to Brad, Detective," Vicki interrupted. She clasped Dana's hand. "Can you tell us that much?"

16

MAC GLANCED AT DANA then returned to Vicki's expectant gaze. "We can't say for sure right now, Mrs. Gaynes. But I can tell you what we know so far."

"Please, call me Vicki." Her intense features eased to a furrowed brow. "I'm sorry. I don't mean to put you on the spot."

Mac nodded and smiled. "My partner, Detective Kevin Bledsoe, and I are playing catch-up at this point. We were involved in the recovery of Brad's remains today . . ." He paused when Vicki closed her eyes, obviously in grief. "Are you sure you folks are up to hearing about this right now?"

"Yes. We want to hear everything." Vicki squeezed Dana's hand. Todd also nodded, giving him the go-ahead.

Mac sighed. "About midday today, we received a call from a fisherman who found a man floating in the Columbia River in the Portland area. One of our wildlife troopers recovered the body near the confluence of the Willamette River. The state medical examiner, my partner, and I met the trooper at Kelly Point and examined the body. We found no obvious signs of foul play at the riverbank and thought it might be the body of a deckhand who drowned in a barge accident with a tug."

"I think I read about that in the paper." Todd leaned his arms on the table. "Are you sure it wasn't him?"

"We're sure it's not him. We transported the body back to the medical examiner's office for a comprehensive examination. That's when we learned some disturbing information." Mac paused again.

"It was our Brad." Vicki stared at some unknown spot across the room.

"Yes, ma'am. We eventually learned it was Brad's body after taking some fingerprint samples. But there's more. During the autopsy we discovered Brad had been shot with a large-caliber firearm. We recovered a bullet from his chest. The medical examiner says that the gunshot is likely the cause of his death."

"He—he was shot?" Vicki covered her face with her hands, sobbing again.

Dana rubbed the hand Vicki had been holding.

"I think maybe we should speak later," Todd said, choking back his own tears. "Do you have a card or something?" Mac pulled a business card out of his badge wallet and set it on the table. Then he picked up his briefcase.

"Would you like me to stay with you?" Dana asked.

Vicki nodded. "Please."

Dana walked Mac to the door. "I'll hang out here for a while."

"Do you want me to wait outside?"

"No. I'll give you a call later and let you know when they want to talk. I'm sure they'll have questions for you."

Mac nodded.

"Thank you." Vicki came into the entry and extended her hand. "Thank you for speaking to us in person. I know it must be difficult to deliver that kind of news."

"Yes, but it's harder to receive it." Mac left then, eager to get to the confines of his car.

"Boy, I could have done without that one," Mac muttered as he walked to his car. Once inside, he adjusted his rearview mirror and pulled into the deserted street. He blew out a long breath and loosened his tie. It was eight o'clock, and he wanted to go straight home. Instead, he picked up his cell phone and dialed Linda's number, arranging to stop by her apartment. On his way there he had dispatch put him through to Deputy Wyatt of the Hood River County Sheriff's Department. He told Wyatt that he'd made the notification. "We'll need to set up a time to meet. How about I give you a call after I talk to my partner? We'll need copies of the case jacket."

Mac then called Kevin to fill him in on the notification process, partly because he wanted to keep him informed and partly because he was miffed that Kevin hadn't been there to suffer through the notification with him.

"Appreciate the call, Mac," Kevin said, though Mac suspected he was just being polite. "Thanks for handling the notification. Why don't you call the deputy back and have him meet us in the morning, say around nine, at the falls? I'd like to head out to that waterfall area and get a look for myself."

"I'll do that." Mac entered the 405 Freeway, setting his sights for Vancouver.

"Maybe we can talk Philly into collecting reports tomorrow while we do a little background work. Let's start off with a cup of coffee and the trip to the gorge, then we'll check back with the crime lab and see if they have a match on that bullet for us."

"Sounds like a winner." Mac hung up, feeling a little better about Kevin. His partner had seemed more like himself, eager to move ahead with the investigation. Mac called the deputy and then made a call to Chris Ferroli. He left a message on Chris's voice mail to meet him and Kevin as well. Wouldn't hurt to have someone from OSP who knew the area well.

Linda greeted Mac with a smile, a kiss on the cheek, and a look of censure in her eyes. "You didn't call me all day."

Her tone was light, but Mac was in no mood for criticism. "I didn't have time."

Her lower lip went out in a pout. "But you promised."

"Don't start, Linda," Mac said gruffly. "I was thinking maybe we could talk, but . . ."

"We can, honey." She pulled him in and started to take his coat.

"No, we can't. Coming here was a mistake." Mac pulled his coat back on. "It's over. There's no use pretending we can make it work, because we can't. I can't."

Her mouth formed an O, but no sound came out. Seeming to recover, she said, "Mac, I don't understand."

"Yes, you do. For the past couple of months we've been playing games . . ."

"I'm not playing games. I've always been honest with you." She folded her arms, turned away from him, and walked into the living room.

"Well, I haven't been honest with you. I kept making excuses not to go back to see your pastor. Well, the truth is, I have no intention of going back." Mac licked his lips. "I don't want to get married, Linda. I'm not ready. I thought I was in love with you, but now . . . I . . . I don't know how I feel."

"You're seeing someone else, aren't you?" She turned an angry gaze on him.

"No . . ."

"It's Dana." Linda's eyes filled with tears. "I knew something was going on between you that time I went to your place and caught you together."

"And I explained that Dana came to me for advice. She wants to make detective, and I want to help. She's a friend." Mac realized that Linda had never really been a friend. Maybe that was the missing element—friendship.

"Don't give me that, Mac. I saw the way you looked at each

other. You're right. I haven't been honest—at least not with myself. I kept clinging to the hope that you loved me, and I refused to believe that you were cheating on me."

"I never cheated on you." *At least not in real time—not unless you count being attracted to other women.* Maybe he really was the sleazeball she seemed to think he was.

"Get out." Linda closed her eyes and turned away from him again. "Just get out."

Mac didn't want to leave like that. He hated confrontations with the women in his life. Part of him wanted to apologize to Linda, but he didn't. He'd told her how he felt and was glad he had.

"I never meant to hurt you." Mac said the words softly as he opened the door and stepped outside, but he wondered if she'd even heard.

17

MORNING, SUNSHINE." Philly greeted Mac as he walked into the detective office at a little after seven, carrying his tie and briefcase. "You sleep in your car last night?"

Russ laughed, retaining his position as Philly's biggest fan.

"I pulled a late one last night." Mac rubbed his eyes. Actually he'd gotten home reasonably early but had stayed up until two o'clock watching television. It had taken that long to get past the guilt over breaking up with Linda and determining he'd done the right thing. "You guys seen Kevin this morning?" Mac received an alpha page from Kevin earlier, letting him know he didn't need a ride to work after all.

"Yeah," Philly answered, but he apparently didn't feel led to expand on his answer.

Russ picked up the thread. "He's in a closed-door with the sergeant right now; he's been in there for over a half-hour."

"Oh yeah, what about?" Mac glanced at Frank's office door.

"I think he's asking for a new partner," Philly teased.

"Good one." Russ slapped Mac on the back as he walked past Philly to his cubicle.

"You're a ton of laughs, Philly, and I do mean a ton," Mac

muttered as he entered his cubicle and set his briefcase on the desk.

"Was that a jab at my weight?" Philly followed Mac and stood beside the partition, rubbing his ample belly. "Better come up with some fresh material, newbie. I'm shedding the pounds on that all-protein diet."

Mac looped his tie around his neck and tucked it under his collar. Philly did look like he had lost weight. "How much have you lost, Phil? You do look like you're slimming down."

Before Philly had a chance to answer, Russ piped up, "Five more pounds, and he won't have to stop at those truck scales on the highways."

"You take a look in the mirror lately, SWAT boy?" Philly turned his sights on Russ. "Looks like that belt of yours is loosened a few notches."

Russ, no longer amused, hooked his thumbs on his belt. "That's because I'm wearing a belt holster today."

"And your hairline's receding too." Philly tried to look concerned as he examined his partner's hair.

"I just got a haircut," Russ snapped, apparently able to dish it out better than he could take it.

"Don't be so sure. Someday you're not gonna be so young anymore, partner." Philly laughed, seizing his victory in the contest of insults that he coveted so highly.

With Philly's focus on Russ, Mac took the opportunity to duck into the break room for a cup of coffee. He was more concerned with waking up than bantering with Philly. Not that he'd ever come out on top—especially not in the morning.

Taking his cup of java back to his desk, Mac turned on his computer, listened to his voice messages, and began checking e-mail.

"Get some rest last night?" Kevin entered Mac's cubicle.

"Not really." Mac took a sip of the hot brew.

"You work late on this case?" Kevin sat on the corner of the desk.

"No. I went over to Linda's after I talked to you."

Kevin smiled. "I wish I had your energy."

"What energy? I'm drained. We ended up having a fight and broke up."

"Hmm. How are you feeling about it?"

"Okay, I guess. I'm not jumping for joy, but I'm not crying over it either."

"Well, I can't say I'm surprised. I'm just wondering what took you so long."

Mac pinched his lips together. "I kept thinking I needed to hang in there. Part of me wanted it to work."

"And now?"

Mac shrugged. "I did the right thing."

"I think you did, Mac." Kevin stood up. "So, you still up for a cup and a trip to Wah-kella Falls?"

"You know it. Ready when you are." Mac grabbed his black leather police notebook from his desk.

"Why are you still carrying that thing?"

"Old habit from patrol. I tried the day planner thing for a while, but it never really took with me." Mac rubbed the smooth leather cover with his initials stamped on the cover. "Me and this old note-book have spent a lot of years together. I guess it just suits me."

"Huh," Kevin nodded. "I can understand that. My wife says the same thing about me."

Mac chuckled. "Hey, why were you meeting with Sergeant Evans? You in the blue room?" *Blue room* was slang for a disciplinary meeting with a supervisor.

"No, nothing like that. I'll tell you on the way." Kevin rubbed the back of his neck. "Say, how'd the call to the deputy go last night? Are we going to get our hands on that case jacket today?"

"Yeah. He's adjusting his shift and will meet us out at the falls. I told him we'd be there around nine unless he heard otherwise."

"That's a pretty tough turnaround from his late swing shift. I got to thinking after we talked that we could have made it later."

"Wyatt said it wasn't a problem. He has grand jury anyway, so he said he would be up. Seems like a pretty good guy." Mac straightened his tie and tossed his notebook in the briefcase. "I also left a message for Chris to meet us up at the falls."

"Chris?" Kevin frowned.

"Yeah, Chris Ferroli, the game troop who towed the body in for us. I thought he would be handy with his maps and knowledge of the Columbia River and the creeks that flow into it."

"Oh. Good idea, Mac."

Mac and Kevin started for the Columbia River Gorge after a quick stop at the Starbucks at SE 122nd and Division. Following the routine they'd established, Mac drove. He rather liked the arrangement, as he'd become accustomed to driving while working as a patrol officer.

"Whew, that's still too hot," Kevin said, taking a sip of his coffee of the day—an Irish Cream blend.

Mac couldn't help but smile. When he and Kevin had first met, Kevin was a no-nonsense coffee drinker—black and straight up. Mac had been that way as well, but living in an area with a specialty coffee shop on every corner had broadened his horizons and sense of taste. Mac still liked plain old coffee, but he'd grown accustomed to his raspberry latte, as well. Philly teased him to no end about that.

"So, what's the deal with you and Sarge?" Mac skillfully maneuvered a curve with one hand, holding his coffee steady in the cupholder in the other, glad the snow plows had been out and the roads graveled.

"Right. I almost forgot." Kevin glanced over at Mac then to the road. "We talked about you, mostly."

"Me?" Mac kept his gaze on the road and the view of the Columbia River opening up ahead of them, trying not to let on that his heart had picked up speed or that his palms had started sweating.

Kevin laughed. "Relax, Mac. It's a good thing. Has to do with making you lead detective on this case. I told Sarge I thought you were ready and had already asked you."

"And?" Mac sat up straight in his chair, not knowing what to say.

"He agreed. We both have a lot of confidence in you."

"I appreciate that, but I'm pretty new out of the chute."

"I'll be with you every step of the way, but I think it's important you get the call on this one. Philly and I have been around for a while, and we aren't going to be here forever. It's guys like you and Russ who will carry this office over the next ten years."

"Does Philly know about this?" Mac asked.

Kevin nodded. "I ran it by him before talking to the sergeant."

"And?" Mac asked, taking a sip of coffee.

"He agreed, Mac. Philly thinks you're top-notch. The work you did on the Tyson case really impressed him—impressed a lot of people."

"Humph. I didn't do much impressing on the sawmill investigation."

"True, but we can't win them all. We aren't the first detectives to come up short. Have you taken a look at the list of unsolved murders lately?"

"I know. We're not supposed to beat ourselves up over it, but it still bugs the heck out of me. We've got fingerprints and a partial boot print."

"Yes, we do, and who knows, maybe we'll end up with a match someday."

"Maybe we will." Mac took a long drink of his latte. "I appreciate the vote of confidence."

"Well, I just hope you stay detective and don't get the heat from the brass to promote."

"Not me, pal. I'm going to stay a working troop till the day I hang it up." Mac felt a wide grin spread across his face.

"We'll see." Kevin lifted his coffee cup in a toast. "Right now, we need to focus our efforts on this case. The admin reports and court work will all reflect you as the lead investigator."

"Thanks, partner. I don't know what to say."

"Don't say anything. Just buy me coffee for the next couple of weeks, and we'll call it even."

"We'll never be even. I owe you a lot."

"Yeah, yeah. Don't go getting all maudlin over it, or I'll have to change my mind."

Kevin winked and went back to his coffee, his gaze settling on the view.

Mac adjusted the visor, blocking out the blinding sun. It had been cloudy when they left the office, and the forecaster had predicted freezing rain again. Heading east, they'd escaped the clouds and driven straight into blue skies. The locals had a saying about Portland weather: "If you don't like the weather, just wait ten minutes and it will change."

As Mac drove east on Interstate 84, they passed numerous waterfalls on the scenic cliffs on the south side of the freeway. The north side of the freeway was bordered for hundreds of miles by the massive Columbia River, which separated Oregon from Washington State.

"You ever been to the fish hatchery at Bonneville?" Kevin asked as they approached the giant concrete dam on the river, near the Multnomah and Hood River County line.

"Fish hatchery, no." Mac glanced over at the dam. "I've been in the dam area, down at the fish viewing area, but never to the hatchery. That fish ladder window sure is something to see, though."

"Yep. Especially when the chinook and the chad are running. Thousands of fish, all trying to get over the dam. You should visit the hatchery sometime; it's downriver from the dam at Tanner Creek. You take the same exit, just make a left at the fork instead of a right. There are these big ponds of hatchery fish in various stages, but the real attraction is the giant white sturgeon. Some of those guys live to be over a hundred years old. They have a couple of sturgeon in there that are over twelve feet long and forty years old."

"I read in the dam tour area that the divers who poured the footings for the dam reported sturgeon estimated to be some twenty feet."

Kevin whistled. "I bet they look a lot bigger when you are nose to nose with one. But twenty feet? Humph." Kevin set his cup in the holder and stretched. "I've heard there are men buried in the concrete of the dam."

"No way. I don't remember reading about that on the tour." Mac raised an eyebrow. "You're kidding, right?"

"Well, it might be a rumor. But it's possible. Not all that unusual for workers to lose their footing. Since there was no way to save them when they fell into the concrete, the workers just kept building the dam on top of them."

"Sounds pretty far-fetched to me." Mac took the Wah-kella Falls exit. "Here we are."

MAC PULLED THE CAR into the large lot and parked close to the base of the falls. As Mac and Kevin exited the vehicle, a Hood River County sheriff's vehicle pulled in next to them.

"That's Deputy Wyatt," Mac said.

The deputy stepped out, pulling on a brown ball cap that matched his dark brown uniform. "Hey, Mac." Sam extended a hand. "Good to see you again."

"You too. Sam, this is my partner, Kevin Bledsoe."

The men shook hands and exchanged pleasantries, finally getting down to business. "So you guys got our boy, huh?" Sam asked.

"Afraid so." Mac said. "Too bad it wasn't just a cut-and-dry floater. That bullet really threw us a curve."

"Us too. I've got the files in the car." Sam ducked into the back-seat to retrieve the paperwork. "I gotta tell you, the sheriff isn't too happy giving up the investigation. We could handle it, you know."

Politics wasn't Mac's strong point, and he looked to Kevin for guidance. When Kevin wasn't forthcoming, Mac went ahead. "We realize that, Sam, but the fact is, we don't know when or where our victim was killed. We know he lived in Clackamas County, was last seen in your county, and was found in Multnomah County in a river that divides two states. It only makes sense that OSP works the case. Believe me, if I had half a chance, I'd dump this murder investigation. You know how time-consuming they can be—the pressure from the family and the hundreds of hours of reports and court time involved if we make an arrest."

Sam paused for a moment. "To be honest, Mac, I haven't actually run with a homicide investigation before, and I have no problem with OSP taking it on. The sheriff is dragging his feet. You know how elected officials like to keep their names in the papers."

"I'm glad you agree."

"Most of our contacts live on the west side anyway." Sam handed Mac a two-inch stack of files. "These are all the reports to date. We didn't have much to go on without a body."

"Was this the area you based the search on the first day?" Kevin asked.

Since he'd only been up there the one day, Mac let Sam answer. "Yep. Most of those reports are search-and-rescue logs for our department and the search efforts of private citizens and outside agencies. We had a couple birds up, hounds, searchers on foot and horseback, the works. We didn't turn up anything on this guy."

"Did you interview many people outside of the family?" For not being the lead, Kevin sure had a lot of questions. Mac was content to listen and learn.

"Yeah, it's all in the reports. Besides Brad's mom, dad, and sister, we only talked to a couple friends, and of course, to his girl-friend, Jessica. She was the last one to see him alive that we know of." Sam clicked his tongue. "Bet you got an earful from Brad's mother; there's no love lost there."

"Actually no, we just delivered the bad news last night. Didn't figure they were up for an interview." But Mac did remember Jessica and the antagonistic attitude the family had toward her.

"Jessica was Brad's live-in girlfriend," Sam went on. "She and Brad had come up here to talk. Jessica says she broke up with him. He took off in a huff and headed up the trail. That's the last she saw of him—or so she says. Her take is that he fell or jumped off the cliff."

"Or was pushed," Mac added.

"Well, we gave that a lot of thought. Thing is, suicide isn't that far off. We get jumpers from the valley here all the time. The place is actually included on some Web site that lists ways to commit suicide."

"No kidding?" Mac shook his head.

"You can find just about anything on the Web these days. The Web address is in the reports. I checked it out one or two jumpers back."

Kevin looked up at the waterfall and then down at the pool at its base.

"Anyhow, Jessica reports her boyfriend missing after driving all the way home to the Mount Hood area. That and the fact that Jessica didn't help with the search got Mrs. Gaynes into a tizzy. To make a long story longer, Jessica ended up leaving town less than two weeks into the search."

Kevin frowned. "Where did she go?"

"California. Crescent City. She has family there. Brad's parents said that Jessica cleaned out the house on her way out of town. Took everything of value, including clothing and possessions that belonged to Brad. They took it as a sign she knew Brad wouldn't be coming back."

"What kind of read did you get from her?" Mac asked. He remembered his encounter with Jessica. She'd been cool and apathetic.

"Hard to say," Sam said. "She was pretty standoffish. Good-looking gal. She was the kind of kid you wanted to believe. I'll tell you this much: she stuck to her guns, no real discrepancies in her story. One thing she did say, though, was that Brad got into an altercation with a truckdriver."

That piqued Mac's interest. "How so?"

"Jessica said Brad was getting verbal, and the truckdriver thought he would rescue a damsel in distress. Brad told him to butt out. They argued, and the driver finally went back to his rig after threatening to get even."

"You followed up on it?" Kevin asked.

"We tried. We were never able to track this guy down, so he's still a loose end."

"Has anyone interviewed Jessica since she moved?" Mac tucked the reports under his arms and blew on his hands, wishing he'd put on long johns and gloves. The frigid air whipped right through his wool slacks.

"Nobody had any reason to, until now. Brad's been missing for a while, and we ran out of leads. You'll see in the reports this guy was a little rough around the edges, so the possibilities were endless."

"Yeah, we identified him from his criminal-history prints," Mac said. "Did some dope a few years ago. Anything else you can tell us?"

"He ran with a snowboarding crowd up on Mount Hood. Struck me as a bunch of wannabe or has-been skiers who didn't want to grow up and get real jobs. Brad seemed to have real talent, though. He had a bunch of downhill-skiing medals from all over the country."

Mac thumbed through the stack of reports. Other than the info on the trucker, Sam hadn't given him much more than what he'd learned from Dana. "We'll start by reviewing your reports and go from there. Will you be available to work this with us if the investigation points back to your territory?"

Sam's eyes lit up. "You bet. Just tell me when and where, and I'll be there. The sheriff would like to be kept abreast."

"We'll be in touch after we look through the case file." Mac thanked him for coming, then he and Kevin shook hands with him.

"Oh, one more thing," Sam said. "I don't know if there's a connection, but the second day of the search, our guys came across some hunters. We interviewed them, checked their licenses—all legit. None of them had seen our missing hiker, so we just asked them to keep an eye out. Reason I mentioned it was that our guy might have taken a stray bullet. Lots of hunters that time of year. It's all in the report."

"Hunters, huh? That's a real possibility." Mac tucked his hands into his pocket. "Thanks for the heads-up. We'll check it out."

18

PRETTY SMOOTH, Mac; good to include him," Kevin said as Deputy Wyatt pulled out.

"I know what it's like to lose a case you've put a lot of work into. I hated it when I was in patrol and would start a good drug case or an involved investigation from a traffic stop then have to turn it over to detectives."

"He seems pretty squared away, so it's good to have him on our side if we end up spending much time up here," Kevin said.

Kevin looked up at the trail. "Hey, I know you're familiar with this area, but I'd like to get a feel for the place. You can either walk it with me or sit in the car."

Mac opted to walk with him, but only after getting his gloves out of the trunk and putting on his heavy jacket. Kevin did the same. Though Mac had hiked a good portion of the trail during the search, he wasn't all that familiar with the lay of the land. His trip up with Dana had been a first. One of the problems with living in the Northwest was that there were just too many great places to visit and not enough time to see them all.

The parking area nearest the trail to the falls was striped with spaces made for passenger cars, the other half of the lot for big rigs. That was where Jessica's trucker would have been parked—assuming there was a trucker.

The top of the waterfall seemed to hold its own clouds amid the relatively clear winter sky. Mac and Kevin studied the falls and the pool from the parking lot, then they walked along the creek fingering out from the pool.

Trooper Chris Ferroli pulled into the parking lot in his white Ford F-150 pickup. Mac easily recognized the truck as a State Police Fish and Wildlife vehicle by the three antennas on the roof and the two spare tires mounted upright in the bed of the pickup behind a large white toolbox.

"There's Chris," Mac said.

Kevin turned momentarily to look, then he continued out of the parking lot to examine the creek more closely. "Go ahead. I'll join you in a minute."

"Hey, Mac." Chris jumped down from his elevated pickup. He was dressed in the department field uniform: wash-and-wear navy blue pants and shirt that didn't require dry cleaning. Due to their rustic assignments enforcing poaching laws and back-country investigations, game troopers were the only uniformed division of the OSP allowed to deviate from the spit-polished leather requirement. Mac missed the more casual dress but would never consider going back. He'd found his niche in detectives; and if what Kevin had said was true, he wasn't the only one who thought so.

"Thanks for coming out, Chris." Mac reached for the trooper's hand as he approached the truck. "I really appreciate this. I didn't know if you'd get my voice mail in time."

"No problem. Glad to help. I still can't believe what you guys found at autopsy."

"Yeah, pretty wild." Mac glanced back to Kevin, who seemed fixated by the thick wall of cascading water. "I hope you didn't put anything on hold to come out here; I really didn't know what to expect. Neither of us knows the area very well. I've hiked the trail above the falls, but that's about it."

"Actually, I had some follow-up to do near Bonneville. I've been sitting on a report of a dumped black bear carcass. Sounds like it may be gall poached. The ice storm kept me out of the gorge for a while."

"Gall poached?" Kevin asked, as he joined the two men.

"Howdy," Chris greeted. "Detective Bledsoe, right?"

"Right. Morning, Chris." Kevin shook his proffered hand. "What was that about bear gallbladders?"

"Yeah, there's a ring working right now on black bears. They kill the bear for the gallbladder and paws, then they leave the rest to rot."

"Seems like an odd thing to do." Kevin grimaced.

"The gallbladder is prized in some cultures as having high medicinal value," Mac told him. He'd learned about the prized bladders during his stint with Fish and Wildlife. "Once those things are dried and ground, they can go for hundreds of dollars an ounce."

Chris nodded. "Between the novelty value of the paws and the gallbladder, a poacher could make over a thousand dollars a bear."

"First I've heard of it." Kevin shook his head. "What some people will do for money."

"You got that right."

"Say, Chris, do you know much about this area—the falls and the water flow in particular?"

"A little." The men walked to the trailhead. "What do you want to know?"

"What can you tell us about Wah-kella Falls?" Kevin again studied the waterfall.

"Probably not much more than you already know."

"You'd be surprised." Mac chuckled. "About all I can tell you right now is that the land drops off up there and the water falls by gravitational force."

Kevin rolled his eyes. "My partner, the genius."

Mac ignored the jibe. "And we know we're just inside Hood River County."

"Well, I'll see if I can enlighten you." Chris nodded toward the end of the parking lot. "Take this trail to the east and you'll find yourself on the Eagle Creek trail system. The west trail winds up around to the south and eventually takes you up a steep grade to the top of the falls. Quite the hike, but the view from the top is worth the work. You guys know about the history of the falls and the jumpers?"

"We met a deputy here earlier who brought us up to speed," Kevin said. "Sounds pretty grim."

"A Hood River County deputy?"

"Yeah. Sam Wyatt," Mac said. "You know him?"

"Sure do. Sam's good people."

Kevin agreed. "Does this creek flow all way to the Columbia River?"

"All the way and at about the same depth and width as you see here." Chris stepped to the side of the creek, pointing north along its banks.

Mac estimated the creek to be about two feet deep in the middle and only about twelve feet wide. There were a few small waterfalls and some white water as it cascaded over rocks hiding just beneath the surface.

"The creek is pretty much the same year-round," Chris went on. "We get a nice steady coho salmon run in here in the fall. I have to keep pretty close watch on it when the run's in. Snaggers come out at night and drag 'em out left and right."

"What's the weight on our victim, Mac?" Kevin was focused on the falls again.

Mac jogged to the car, pulled out the report, and thumbed through the preliminary pages. "About one-hundred-and-eighty pounds." He put the report back and hurried to where the two men waited. "He was listed as being muscular and in good shape."

"You think this creek would carry a man that size to the Columbia, Chris?"

"Hard to say." Chris squinted at the flowing water. "My guess is no, unless there were some heavy rains."

"It was raining pretty heavily during the search," Mac said.

Chris wagged his head from side to side. "Yeah, but it would take a lot for this thing to rise much. I spent a few nights here in November when the coho were in, and I don't remember much of a difference. We can check with ODFW and get the info on the water flow from the stream checkers if we need."

Mac nodded. The Oregon Department of Fish and Wildlife was the biology arm of wildlife management while OSP was the enforcement arm.

"Would you get that?" Kevin asked. "For all the days in November?"

"No problem. I'll stop in at Bonneville Hatchery today."

Mac followed Kevin's gaze. "You're thinking our victim didn't go over the falls?"

"I'm having a hard time picturing it. We need to prove or disprove that someone the size of our victim could go over the falls and make his way to the river by way of this creek."

"You volunteering to go over?" Mac grinned at Kevin. "You're about his same weight, aren't you?"

"Very funny."

Chris lifted a hand. "Don't look at me."

On a more serious note, Mac asked, "Want me to scare up a piece of wood?"

"I'm afraid we'll need something a little more lifelike," Kevin told them. "I've done this before with ballistic testing, but never with a waterfall. We need to round up a one-hundred-eighty-pound sheep, shave it down, and launch it over the falls to see what happens. My guess is it will end up with a few broken bones. Our guy didn't have any fractures—at least none that turned up on x-ray. And I'll bet there isn't enough current to float it out of the waterfall pool. We may want to try putting it into the creek first to see if it will float to the river."

"Where are we going to get a sheep?" Mac asked.

"I think I can help you out," Chris offered. "I do game meat inspections for a butcher up in Corbett. I'll bet he could hook us up."

"Perfect." Kevin rubbed his chin. "We need one that's close to the same weight; and it has to be sheared, so it doesn't get hung up on tree snags or rocks."

"Does it have to be alive?" Chris asked. "I really don't think we want the animal rights folks breathing down our necks. We have a hard enough time with them as it is."

"It should be humanely dispatched prior to our little test." Kevin started back to the parking lot. "I know this is a lot of work, but we have to put this possibility to rest before we look much further. We want to rule out suicide or an accidental fall."

"Understood. When do you want it?" Chris asked.

As if remembering he'd given the lead to Mac, Kevin nodded in Mac's direction. "Ask Mac."

"Why don't you check those water records at the hatchery and give us a call?" Mac asked. "If the water is close to what it was then, we can set a time for the test."

"Good enough. I'll head down there right now." Chris opened the door to his truck and climbed in. "Anything else you want me to check on?"

Mac glanced at Kevin, who shook his head. He elbowed Kevin and turned back to Chris. "There is one thing. Could you verify the size of those sturgeon Kevin claims are up at the hatchery? His story sounds pretty fishy to me."

"Oh, you mean the sturgeon general?" Chris chuckled. "I can vouch for him; they're still up there. One is eleven feet long; and the big one—the one they call Uncle Wally—is just shy of thirteen feet."

"I can't believe you ever doubted me." Kevin feigned despair.

"You fishermen always exaggerate the size of fish. I needed an objective account of these monsters from the deep."

"Hey, speaking of sturgeon, did you know that white sturgeon are a source of caviar? When the fish is mature . . ." Chris stopped. "More than you want to know, huh?"

Mac and Kevin both nodded.

"Okay, I can take a hint. I'll head down to the hatchery and get that information and page you."

"Thanks." Mac waved at him. "Kevin and I are heading down to the crime lab to get a workup on that bullet. Catch you later."

Chris cranked the key and notified dispatch he was back in service before pulling his door closed.

"You ready to head back to the lab?" Mac asked his partner.

Kevin nodded. "I'm ready—for my second cup of coffee too."

"Get in, then. Guess I'm buying, what with being lead detective and all." Mac glanced at Kevin. "Though with all the questions you were asking, I got to wondering if you really meant it."

"Sorry, partner. Some habits die hard."

"Don't worry about it. I'm glad you were there. I don't think I'd ever have thought of dropping a sheep over the falls."

Kevin's seatbelt clicked. "My pleasure. Now you'll owe me a month's worth of coffee."

Mac put the car in reverse. "I don't know if I can afford this lead detective thing."

19

IT WAS JUST AFTER TEN when Kevin and Mac made their way to the twelfth floor of the Justice Center. Mac asked to see the OSP crime lab supervisor, Allison Sprague.

Sarah buzzed them in.

Mac and Kevin had just entered the hallway as Allison rounded the corner. Her white lab coat flapped open to reveal an expensive-looking gray pinstriped pantsuit. "All dressed up today, Allison?" Kevin gave her an appreciative smile.

"Just hoping I can stay clean. I have court this afternoon on some DNA testimony." She greeted them in turn. "Come on back. I assume you're here for your bullet."

"Yep." Mac nodded. "Did you find a firearms scientist to run it for us stat?"

"No, but he made time. I've got Criminalist Wain Carver on the assignment; he just got started on it a few minutes ago. Why don't you two go on back and introduce yourselves?"

"I know Wain," Kevin said. "Thanks, Allison."

"You're welcome. I'm going to excuse myself, gents, so I can get ready for court."

"Not many of these scientists hold the criminalist rank," Kevin said as they meandered through the lab office.

"Why's that?" Mac gave a quick nod to Pete in prints.

"Has something to do with recruitment. When the brass decided the scientists should go through the academy with the rest of us, a lot of them quit. There aren't many applicants with a master's degree in molecular biology who want to march around in cadence for four months in the basic academy. So anyone with the criminalist rank—the ones who pack guns, anyway—have at least twelve years in the department. Far as I know, the new-hire scientists don't have police authority. They just run analytical tests."

"Can't say I blame them. I bet these guys don't want to go out to the range and qualify with their guns every three months either."

"Most of them." Kevin pointed through an office window to a stocky man with gray hair and a mustache who was firing a rifle into a metal tank filled with water. "But not him. That's Wain. A gun nut if there ever was one."

The scientist held up a hand, signaling Mac and Kevin to wait. Then he put on his ear protection and safety glasses before firing into the tank. After he took off his hearing protection, he waved the detectives into the room.

"Did you get a good bullet, Wain?" Kevin shook hands with the scientist.

"Hard to say. These .223 rounds are hard to get a good bullet from. Even in the water tank, these bullets are so fast they often break up."

"Wain, this is my partner, Detective McAllister. He goes by Mac."

"Nice meeting you, Mac." Wain set the weapon aside. "Did you wear out your old partner, Kevin? Where's Eric?"

"He's working on that bizarre murder-for-hire case."

"Where the woman hired the Hollywood stuntmen?" Wain drained the water tank to look for his bullet.

"That's the one. Things were going sour, so he and Sarge are trying to get all their ducks in order." Kevin peered into the water tank.

"Is that an M-16?" Mac asked, trying to get a look at the selector switch on the trigger guard, to see if the full auto option was available.

Wain let out a string of cuss words. "Another bad bullet." The scientist looked up at Mac and Kevin. "Sorry, this is my fifth try. And to answer your question, Mac, that's an AR-15. It's the civilian version of the military M-16; it's not fully automatic."

Mac was well aware of the difference in the firearms but opted not to comment.

"But some have been known to convert these Colt ARs to full auto." Wain wiped his hands on a towel.

"You don't know anyone who would do that kind of thing, do you, Wain?" Kevin raised an eyebrow.

"Why, Detective, that would be illegal." Wain grinned and then muscled his way past Kevin. "Bet you two would like to know a little about your bullet."

"We would." Kevin backed up so Wain could get to his worktable.

The criminalist pulled a chair in front of a microscope, then he turned on a large computer monitor on the shelf above the microscope. He picked up the bullet fragment collected by Mac and Kevin the previous day and slipped it under the lens. The enlarged image popped up on the computer monitor. Wain moved the bullet around with his ballpoint pen and then zoomed in on the side of the projectile.

"First of all, this little beauty is a hollow core .357 round. The bullet is over ninety percent complete, telling us it primarily had contact only with soft tissue on the victim. In other words, it didn't hit anything hard enough to peel any weight off of her. Do you guys have a barrel for me to compare this to?"

"I'm afraid we don't at this point," Kevin replied. "If we find one, do you have much to compare it to?"

"Oh yeah, this little dandy has several good forensic details. See these here?" Wain pointed at the striations below the bullet mushroom that looked like the curved ridges on a piece of licorice.

Mac nodded, studying the monitor.

"These are called lands and grooves. The soft lead bullet received the print from the rifling on the barrel of the firearm. Each land and groove is unique to the firearm that projected the bullet, as detailed as a human fingerprint under the microscope. We are looking for a .357, probably a revolver, with a counterclockwise twist inside the rifled barrel. You bring me the gun or another bullet shot from the suspect's gun, and I'll be able to match them up for you."

"That's great," Kevin said. "Hopefully we'll be bringing you some business."

"I ran the bullet schematic through the IBIS computer database, but nothing came back, which means it was never tested or logged into our computers. And that, gentlemen, means your shooter probably still has it."

Kevin and Mac left the bullet fragment in the custody of the ballistics expert and headed back through the maze of offices toward the lobby.

"I need to answer some pages," Mac said, examining the numbers. "One is Dana's cell phone; the other is a 541 area code, probably Chris."

"Why don't you make the calls while I make a pit stop?"

Mac ducked into the first empty office while Kevin aimed for the nearest restroom. Five minutes later, the two met in the lobby and started down the elevator.

Mac pressed the button for the first floor. "That 541 was Chris calling from Bonneville. He said the creek is running about the same today as it was two months ago, a little harder due to the ice melt. He checked with the butcher in Corbett. The guy is willing to sell us a sheep, but the biggest he has is around 150 pounds."

"Hmm. I wish it were more, but I guess it will have to do. If it makes its way all the way to the Columbia by way of the creek, we'll probably have to float a heavier animal. Will the butcher bill us?"

"I didn't ask. I can put it on my credit card if he won't," Mac volunteered. "Then I can put it on my expense account. I wonder what a sheep costs?"

"I guess we'll find out. You want to call him back and give him the go-ahead?"

"I told him I'd call him over the radio. He was leaving the hatchery when we got off the phone."

"Sounds good, Mac."

The two detectives left the building and got into the Crown Victoria.

"What about Dana's call? I presume she called about the victim's family." Kevin drew up his seat belt. "On the other hand, maybe she called to ask you out. Now that you're a free man . . ."

Mac rolled his eyes. "She called to tell me that Vicki Gaynes would like to speak to us this afternoon. I thought we could be there around four. She'll tell Mrs. Gaynes and page me if there's a problem."

Mac started the car and headed east toward the Columbia River Gorge and Wah-kella Falls. He picked up the radio mic and called for Trooper Ferolli. "Eleven-seventy-one from eleven-fifty-four."

Chris answered immediately. "Eleven-seventy-one, west at Rooster Rock."

"Go ahead with the purchase, Chris. We'll twelve-six you at the falls. Just leaving city center now. Page me if there's a problem on the payment of the package."

"Eleven-seventy-one, copy. The butcher has the sheep ready

for carving, sheared and hanging, so we're in business. ETA about one hour." Chris signed out.

Mac and Kevin stopped for lunch then drove back out to Wah-kella. Chris arrived shortly after with the sheep carcass in the back of his truck. "Sorry I'm late, guys. I stopped off at the hatchery and borrowed a handcart. I figured you didn't want to haul a bloody sheep carcass up to the top of the falls on your backs."

"You assumed correctly. Thanks." Kevin removed his coat and tie in trade for his long yellow raincoat.

Mac eyed the yellow slicker and grinned.

"You're not going to make a big deal again, are you?" Kevin frowned.

"Of course not. I don't know what you're talking about . . . Old Yeller."

Kevin shook his head. "Just wait, kid. Your time is coming."

"You wanted to try the creek first, right?" Chris took out his hip waders.

"Right." Mac pulled on his rain gear as well.

Chris pulled on the waders and secured them with suspenders. Then he and Mac dragged the sheep carcass out of the truck and pushed it over to the trailhead on the handcart.

Chris pushed and Mac guided the cart to the edge of the creek. "This should be a good place to put him in." Chris then dragged the dead animal into the center where the water reached his knees. The carcass drifted a few inches then stopped. Chris stepped over to it, dragged it downstream a bit, and gave it a shove. Again it shifted in the current, but the water just moved around it.

"That's what I expected," Kevin said. "Now for the fun part. We need to take it upstairs."

"Why not stop now?" Mac asked. "We know Brad's body couldn't have made it to the river."

"True, but let's make doubly sure."

"You got it. First I'll need to change back into my boots." Chris pulled the sheep carcass to the bank, where Mac helped him load it back on the cart. He quickly shed the waders and pulled on his heavy-duty work boots. "Which one of you is going to help me wrestle that thing up the hill?"

"How about I go with you?" Mac offered. "I could use a little exercise. Besides, Kevin might trip over the flaps of his fancy coat."

Kevin shrugged. "I was going to volunteer before you made the coat crack."

"Let's do it." Chris pulled the laces tight and double-tied the knot. Then he started up the trail with Mac, the cart between them.

In the meantime, Kevin secured the base of the falls to keep any hapless hikers from coming into contact with a falling sheep. It took Mac and Chris the better part of forty-five minutes to lug the carcass to the top of the falls. Chris radioed Kevin on his portable radio, and Kevin gave him the all-clear.

Moments later, the test launch cascaded over the falls and splashed into the pool, sending a huge spray of water in Kevin's direction.

"Where'd he go?" Mac shouted. After securing his arm around a tree, he leaned closer to the edge but couldn't see beyond the heavy cascade of water from the top of the falls.

"I don't see him," Kevin yelled back. Going to the pool's edge, he thought he saw the carcass floating in the pool behind the falls. The back current of the waterfall held the carcass in check.

Kevin wondered how well the search-and-rescue team had searched the back of the waterfall. Mac and Chris made their way down in half the time, meeting Kevin at the base of the falls. The carcass was still floating at the back of the pool with one leg sticking up, just above the surface. Chris changed back into his hip waders then returned to the pool's edge.

"Go ahead and yank it out, Chris," Kevin said.

Chris waded into the water, making his way along the edge to the back of the falls, where he waded into thigh-deep water. He grabbed the sheep by its protruding leg and dragged it around to the front of the falls and onto a flat rock.

Mac gave him a hand with the animal. Spray from the falls saturated his hair and dripped down his collar. Even without an x-ray, Mac could see compound fractures of the ribs and legs.

"I think this proves beyond a reasonable doubt that our guy never went over the falls, dead or alive. Whoever shot Brad Gaynes probably dumped him straight into the river, most likely below the dam." Kevin brushed the mist from his hair.

"I'd have to agree." Chris pressed a hand to his back. "There's no clean way to go through the dam unless he happened to pass through a lock when a ship or a barge was going through. It's possible, but not likely because the main current goes straight at the center of the dam and the turbines."

"Can you dispose of our test project, Chris?" Mac leaned over and shook the excess water from his head.

"No problem. I have a place where the coyotes come to dine. They'll enjoy the change from rotten game evidence." They loaded the carcass back into the Ford pickup, and the detectives again thanked Chris for his help.

"Let's get cleaned up, Mac." Kevin glanced at his watch. "We'll need to hustle if we're going to make our four o'clock with Mrs. Gaynes."

"This will be tough." Mac pressed his foot to the pedal, moving the speedometer up to seventy-five.

"Tough? In what way?"

Mac sighed. "The family has been through so much. Now that we know their son has been shot, we're going to have to interview them from the angle of a murder investigation. We need to find out if anyone they know owns or has access to a .357 handgun."

20

DANA ANSWERED THE DOOR at the Gayneses' home when Mac and Kevin arrived. She was wearing a faded pair of jeans and a sweatshirt with the department logo on the front. Her hair, usually tucked neatly in her campaign hat, hung loose around her shoulders. Mac caught himself staring, which would have been okay if Kevin hadn't noticed. His partner gave him a knowing smile.

"I hope you don't mind my being here, guys." Dana ushered them inside and closed the door. "The family asked me to stay."

"The family?" Kevin asked. "More than the parents?"

"Yes. Brad's sister, Rachael Skinner, is here, along with her husband, Kip. Vicki asked them both to come so you could talk to all of them at once."

"The sister and her husband know Brad's dead, don't they?" Mac asked. "And that we recovered the body?"

"Yes, but they don't know the details about the bullet or the condition of the body." Dana looked from Kevin to Mac. "Do you have any suspects yet?"

"Several possibilities. Nothing firm. We haven't eliminated

anyone." In fact, they'd barely gotten started. Kevin had scanned the reports during their drive back into Portland, highlighting incidents for Mac, most of which he'd already heard.

"Come on back. They're waiting in the kitchen." Dana led the way through the entryway into the kitchen and introduced the detectives.

Brad's parents were seated at the table with the younger couple. A plate of cookies sat next to a floral centerpiece. Placemats held napkins and cups.

"Welcome, detectives. Please sit down," Vicki said.

Dana plucked her jacket off the back of one of the chairs.

Rachael, who was holding a baby, offered Mac a wan smile. She wore no makeup, and the blotches around her eyes left no doubt that she'd been crying. "You helped with the search."

"Only the first day, I'm afraid."

"What's the little one's name?" Kevin asked, looking as though he wanted to pick up the kid and cuddle him.

"Michael."

"Hey there, Michael." Kevin bent down and gave the kid an animated smile. "How old is he?"

"A year last week," Rachael answered. "I need to put him down for a nap. I'll just be a minute." She let Michael wave good-bye to his audience before leaving the room.

"Can I get you something to drink?" Todd asked. "We have a fresh pot of coffee and some cold drinks."

"I won't turn down a cup of coffee." Kevin pulled out one of the six chairs.

"Sure, I'll take a cup. Black, please." Mac took the empty chair between Kevin and Todd.

"Would you like anything more, Dana?"

"No thanks; I'm good." She lifted what looked like a glass of cola from the table and took a sip. With no available chairs, Dana claimed a stool at the island that separated the kitchen from the eating area. A gas fire made the adjoining family room look warm and cozy. The television set was tuned into a sports channel, but the sound had been turned off. Mac noticed that Kip had the remote at his elbow. He tried to remember if the Blazers were playing. He hadn't been keeping up lately.

From the looks of the son-in-law, Kip had done some playing in his high school and college years. He was stocky and about six-two. He confirmed Mac's suspicions when the talk turned to football and Kip confessed his affiliation with the Oregon Ducks.

By the time Rachael returned, they all had their coffee. Rachael settled into the chair next to Vicki and held her mother's hand.

Vicki sighed. "I guess we should get started. I asked Rachael and Kip to come so we could all get an update and share some of our suspicions with you."

"Sounds fair enough." Mac placed his briefcase on the table and opened it. "As you know, Brad's disappearance last November has been a mystery to the Oregon law enforcement community for some time. My partner and I have secured the reports from the sheriff's office in Hood River County and are familiar with the extensive search conducted at the location where he was reportedly last seen by his girlfriend." Mac said.

"Jessica," Rachael said with venom in her voice. "Her name is Jessica Turner."

"Right."

"Detective." Vicki placed a hand on her daughter's arm. "We're painfully aware of the reports. I've read them so often I can recite them by heart."

Mac glanced over at Dana. Her understanding brown eyes put him at ease. "Yes, well . . . Regretfully, Brad was still missing up until yesterday and was presumed to be deceased by way of accidental death or a possible suicide. Yesterday the state police recovered Brad's body in the Columbia River in North Portland. We identified him through his fingerprints and have come to the conclusion he died as a result of criminal homicide."

"Criminal homicide?" Rachael stared at him. "What does that mean?"

Kip got up and stood behind Rachael, hands on her shoulders. He said, "It means someone killed him, honey."

"Any unnatural death is considered a homicide by definition," Kevin told them. "In this case, we believe Brad's death was caused by criminal means. We think someone murdered Brad by shooting him with a large-caliber handgun. Of course, there is the possibility of an accident or unusual circumstance. Hunting season was in full swing when Brad disappeared."

"You're saying a hunter may have accidentally shot him?" Todd ran a thumb up and down the side of his cup.

"It's possible, though there is no evidentiary basis for anything other than murder right now."

"I knew Brad would never take his own life, Mom. We all knew." Rachael reached up and grabbed hold of Kip's hand.

"Without going into too many details, there's no evidence Brad committed suicide or ever went over Wah-kella Falls. There was no trace evidence on the body to support a self-inflicted gunshot wound, though we have no evidence to conclusively rule it out either. However, we feel that's unlikely."

"Where was he shot?" Todd asked.

"We'd rather not release that information right now, Mr. Gaynes," Mac answered. "We like to keep details like that inside the department."

"Understood." Todd said the word but didn't look like he understood at all.

"Detective." Vicki leaned forward, arms on the table. "How do you know he didn't go over the falls?"

Before he could answer, Rachael asked, "And how did Brad get into the Columbia River?"

"The wounds on his body are not consistent with a fall from that height," Mac explained. "We've determined that in all likelihood, the creek could not have transported a man of his size down to the river. Also, the falls and creek are above Bonneville Dam on the river. There would be little chance that Brad's body would be found intact if he were to have gone through the dam. In fact, if he had gone through the turbines, we'd probably still be looking for him."

The horror reflected on their faces made Mac wish he could take the last comment back. These people didn't need to know that. "I'm sorry." He sighed. "This is some pretty raw information and may not be something you want to hear right now."

"Don't be sorry, Mac," Todd assured him. "We want as many details as you can give us."

"Please, go on. Tell us everything, Detective," Vicki answered. "This is why I wanted us all together."

"Outside of knowing your son was killed, all we really have are theories at this point." Kevin's comment reminded Mac that Brad may have been killed by a family member.

"Can you explain why it took so long to find him?" Kip asked. "Um . . . assuming he was killed the day or week he was reported missing?"

"The Columbia River is vast. There are countless possibilities, but the one thing science can tell us for sure is that Brad's body was consistent with someone who had been in the water for some time."

"I heard he was nude." Rachael held her mug with both hands and stared at the contents. "Why? Where were his clothes?"

"Where did you hear that?" Mac cut a quick look at Dana, who shook her head to verify it wasn't from her.

"I told her," Vicki said. "The medical examiner's office called me today and asked about making arrangements for Brad's funeral. They said he had no personal effects and had arrived at the morgue without any clothing."

Kevin nodded, obviously a little perturbed that they had released pertinent information. "We don't want that kind of information to get out, in the event there is some clothing evidence out there. We especially don't want the media to know and then have the evidence disappear. We don't plan on doing a press release on this yet. We want the killer to continue to think the body is at the bottom of the river." He paused and took a sip of his coffee. "On the matter of the clothing, though, it is entirely possible the bloating of the body or the river current tore the clothing from his body. Water victims often are recovered nude, even ones who have tight clothing like jeans or neckties."

"I think we've heard enough." Rachael pinched her lips together. "What I want to know now is where you're planning to go from here. I mean, it's been two months. Isn't the trail going to be cold?"

Mac got a nod from Kevin to go ahead. "You're right to a certain extent. We are at least two months behind. We don't know much about Brad, so we have to learn everything we can about him rather quickly. We already have a great deal of background from the county reports. We know he was an accomplished skier and was living up in the Mount Hood area with Jessica. On the forensics side, we know the caliber of weapon that inflicted the wound; in fact, we possess the bullet and will be able to compare it if we obtain a suspect weapon."

"Assuming there is something to compare it to." Todd leaned back in his chair.

"That is a concern, Mr. Gaynes. Hopefully it's not twenty feet underwater or sawed up and dumped."

Kevin cleared his throat as a signal to Mac to back off. They needed to be careful not to give the family members any ideas. They couldn't eliminate anyone at the table or within Brad's circle of friends without a thorough investigation. The truth was always stranger than fiction. Kevin had experienced meetings with grieving family members before, only to end up arresting one of them down the road. "The topic of the firearm leads me to ask a rather uncomfortable question," Kevin said. "Do any of you own a handgun?"

Rachael and Kip looked immediately at Todd.

"Yes." Todd folded his arms, his jaw set. "I have two deer rifles and keep a handgun in my bedside table. If you're suggesting I killed my son, you're crazy."

Vicki smoothed her slacks over her thighs with both hands. "Why don't you go and get them, Todd? They're only doing their job."

"Would you mind showing us?" Kevin asked. "It will only take a few minutes."

"Sure, come on upstairs." Todd pushed back his chair and seemed none too happy. Kevin followed him.

"Anyone else?" Mac directed the question toward Kip and Rachael.

"We don't own a gun," Rachael said.

"How about Brad?"

"I don't think so," Vicki answered. "Um . . . do you know about his arrest record?"

"Yes, the arrest for drug possession?"

"That's a long story," Vicki replied. "But yes, he was arrested for drug possession. Because of the felony conviction, he couldn't possess any firearms. To my knowledge, he and Jessica didn't have any guns in the house."

"Brad didn't like guns," Rachael said. "And I won't allow one in our house. Kip would have to find a new place to live if he wanted one, especially with the baby."

Kip's jaw moved in annoyance. Mac suspected that even though Kip didn't own or want to own a gun, he didn't like his wife telling another man what she would or wouldn't allow him to do.

Kevin and Todd returned. From Kevin's demeanor, Mac suspected that Todd's firearms were in the clear.

"Folks," Kevin said, "you asked where we're going from here, and I'll be blunt. Speaking from a purely statistical viewpoint, most people who are murdered in our country are killed by someone they know. With that in mind, we would be negligent if we did not conduct a thorough interview with each one of you to document your stories and account for your time."

"You're not suggesting that one of us . . ."

"We are not suggesting anything, Mrs. Gaynes. We work for Brad at this point, and we intend to do our duty. I'm sure you can see the logic in our reasoning. Mac and I need to start with Brad's family and friends before we move on to strangers."

"I understand." Vicki dropped her gaze to the table.

"It isn't fair." Rachael scowled at Kevin. "We've been through so much, and then to have you question us like this . . ."

"Rachael," her father said, "they have to get the whole story." He returned to his seat at the table. "We were all at home when the call came from Jessica. Vicki and I met Jessica and the authorities at the falls area. I called Rachael and Kip. They wanted to come, but I told them not to. I promised I'd keep in touch, and Rachael came out the next day to help with the search. Kip stayed home with the baby."

"It isn't that we suspect you; it's just that you may hold the key or have information that is crucial to the case without knowing it," Kevin added, seating himself in the chair next to Mac.

Rachael nodded and looked into her cup, swirling the drink with her hands.

"Can you account for the hours prior to Jessica's call?" Kevin's tone had softened some. "He was last seen at four-thirty. Jessica didn't call until nine."

Kip cleared his throat, anger evidenced in the color of his cheeks and the set of his jaw. "Incredible. You're thinking that we had plenty of time to find Brad and Jessica—somehow watch for Brad to leave, kill him, dump the body, and get home?" He shook his head. "I'm going up to check on Michael."

Rachael watched him go then got up. "I'll be right back."

Mac made a note to find out how Brad and his brother-in-law got along.

21

SORRY ABOUT THAT," Vicki offered. "Kip gets a little hot-headed at times. I know how he feels. It's a stretch by any means to think any of us had anything to do with Brad's death. We loved him. You should be looking at Jessica."

"We will, ma'am." Kevin took a sip of his coffee. "As I said, we'll be ruling out the family and spreading out from there."

"Sounds like you have some pretty strong feelings about Jessica," Mac said.

"I never have liked her; she was such a drain on my Brad. Every step forward he would take, she would drag him two steps back. I suppose you know she went back to California."

"We're aware of that, yes. Has anyone talked with her since she moved south?" Mac asked.

"Never." Vicki spat the word out. "I've tried calling a few times, but she's never there. At least that's what her aunt tells me."

"Would you folks mind giving us formal statements?" Kevin asked. "It would be helpful if each of you gave your account of Brad's disappearance individually."

"Of course," Vicki said. "You can use the front room."

At that point, Dana decided to leave. "I have an early shift tomorrow."

Mac gave her an I'll-see-you-later look.

Vicki hugged her. "Thanks so much for being here for us."

"Happy to do it. You have my card, so give me a call anytime."

Kevin and Mac split up then, interviewing Brad's relatives one by one. Kip had gotten over his anger and apologized for the scene. Mac questioned him about his relationship with Brad.

"You want the truth; I'll give it to you straight. Brad was a spoiled brat. He refused to get a decent job—I even offered to bring him into my computer business as a partner as a favor to Rachael. Don't tell any of the others I said so, but Brad's been going down the wrong road for a long time. He was irresponsible. He drank too much and I don't know for sure, but he might have still been doing drugs too."

"His family seems to blame Jessica for his problems."

"Humph." He looked around before answering. "When I first met Jessica, I thought she'd be just what Brad needed. If you ask me, it was him corrupting her."

"Really?" Mac noted the comment on his pad. "So despite what the family says, you liked Jessica."

"Just don't let my wife know. Todd and I have kept a low profile about her, seeing how Rachael and her mom feel. We both figured Jess was okay. Bottom line? I don't think Jessica killed Brad."

"Do you have any ideas who might have?"

He slapped his palms on his thighs. "Not a clue. Maybe that trucker Jessica told the sheriff about. Maybe Brad did get hit with a stray bullet. Stranger things have happened."

"That's true." Mac nodded. "Thanks, Kip. I appreciate your being up-front with me about Jessica."

"Look." He stood. "I'm sorry I blew up earlier. I don't have a lot of patience with things like that."

Mac got to his feet and shook Kip's hand. "If you think of

anything that might help us with the investigation, give my partner or me a call."

"I'll do that."

Mac and Kevin completed their interviews in less than an hour then obtained a signed consent-to-search form for Brad's home in the Hoodland community of Brightwood.

"No one has been there since just after Jessica left." Todd opened a kitchen drawer and withdrew a key ring. "There's one for the front and back doors. His car keys are on there too. We left the place as is and locked it up. Brad's Subaru is parked in the garage."

Vicki leaned against her husband. "We kept making payments, in case Brad came back."

Todd wrapped an arm around her shoulders. "Guess now we'll have to put it on the market."

"We'll have our crime lab go out to the house tomorrow to assist us with a search," Kevin said. "We want to make certain that there is no evidence of a crime at that location."

Since Jessica had been the only person, thus far, who placed Brad at the waterfall, they would need to do a thorough investigation of the house and car.

"Do you need us at the house tomorrow?" Todd asked.

"You are welcome to come along." Mac hesitated in the doorway. "It will take us about four hours to go through it."

"Victoria and I may stop by, but again, make yourselves at home."

Mac nodded. "You folks have my number. Call me if you think of anything else."

"Thanks, Detective." Vicki wrapped her arms around herself. "Just please, find whoever did this to our son. Please."

"We'll do our best." Mac ducked outside and headed for the car. He just hoped their best was enough.

"You ready to call it a night?" Kevin asked as Mac climbed into the car.

"You know it, partner. Tomorrow is going to come early." Mac stretched. "My muscles are feeling the strain from yanking that old sheep around."

"You're getting old, Mac."

"Ha. And what does that make you?"

"Beyond old, I'm afraid." Kevin winced as he got into the car. He had that odd look about him again.

Before Mac had a chance to comment, Kevin asked, "Did you give Mr. and Mrs. Gaynes our numbers?"

"I gave them my card yesterday, and it has my cell and pager numbers on it. Why?"

"Just checking. I gave Vicki and Todd Gaynes one of my cards when I interviewed them." After snapping down his seat belt, he went on. "We need to make sure we cover all the bases."

"Well, sure. What are you getting at? Did I do something wrong?"

"No, no. Nothing like that. Even though we have a signature, the consent-to-search form could be revoked at any time. That means any evidence we find in the cabin could be suppressed."

"I'm not sure I get your meaning."

"Consent is only valid if the person providing the consent has the continual option of revoking the consent. A guy can't say you can search his house and then you lock him up in jail where he can't call you and take it back. The family needs our numbers so they can revoke consent at any time, in case we find condemning evidence for one of them."

"That doesn't seem right."

"You're telling me. Ask Philly. He was jammed up on a search of a car during a suppression hearing because the guy who gave consent was hauled off to jail. His defense attorney planted the notion in his brain after the fact. Philly nearly lost the case because of the suppressed evidence, which, by the way, was a bloody towel the stabbing suspect used to clean his hands. It's a good thing he had other evidence."

"Hmm. I don't see the Gayneses pulling the plug on us. They seem like decent people. And they really want the killer caught."

"What did you think of the son-in-law?" Kevin asked.

"Actually, I meant to talk to you about him. Apparently, he doesn't share Vicki and Rachael's feelings about Jessica?"

"How so?"

Mac detailed the conversation. "Did Todd say anything to you?"

"No, but then he didn't say anything negative about Jessica either. Vicki pretty much took care of that part."

"Same with Rachael. I wonder why there's such a discrepancy there. If Jessica's as bad as Vicki and Rachael make her out to be, why didn't the guys notice anything?"

"I'm not surprised, Mac. Guys aren't always as perceptive as women. Maybe Kip had a thing for Jessica."

Mac shrugged. "Maybe. He seemed pretty up-front about her, though. Maybe the dislike on the women's part is due to jealousy."

"Could be." Kevin held his hands in front of the heater, which was now blasting out almost too much hot air.

"What do you think we ought to do about Jessica?" Mac asked. "We'll need to interview her."

"That's a tough call. Do we go to California to interview her or have a detective from down south hit her up?"

"I'm for going to California." Mac turned the heater down. "We could use a break in this weather."

Kevin smiled. "Ain't that the truth."

Mac headed downtown to the OSP office, where he would drop Kevin off at his car then head home. Bed sounded good about now. Especially after the sleepless night he'd had.

Mac wondered how Linda was doing and whether he should call her. Better not to, he decided. Break-ups should be clean and quick.

"Does this case sound familiar to you, Mac?"

"Hmm?" Mac glanced at his partner.

"Remember a case our Astoria detectives had a few years back? The one where the woman was convicted of pushing her boyfriend off the cliff at Ecola State Park?"

"Yeah, I do. In fact, that first day of the search I thought about it. Probably because we had such a similar scenario. Boy leaves girl in the park and doesn't come back. Family can't stand the girlfriend and blames her for the guy's troubles."

"You don't suppose Brad's mother is making comparisons, do you? That could explain some of the animosity." Kevin rubbed the back of his neck.

"She might be." Mac said. "That Ecola State Park case got a lot of press time. I'd be surprised if she didn't know about it."

"Two of our guys were assigned the case after the boyfriend floated up on the Washington coast several months later. That guy's girlfriend moved back to the Midwest somewhere, right after the boyfriend went missing at the beach. Our guys put together a great plan that had the victim's parents invite the girlfriend back to Oregon to attend the funeral under the guise that they were paying her way. In reality, we paid for the plane ticket and got a chance to interview her."

"Right." Mac nodded. "Good play. She confessed, didn't she?"

"Yep. Told the detectives she pushed her boyfriend over the cliff during an argument."

"You're right; this is very similar." Mac turned toward Kevin. "You think we ought to try the same thing with Jessica? Pretend the Gayneses are flying her home for the funeral, then interview her?"

Kevin shook his head. "I'm not a big fan of that approach. For one thing, our guys caught a lot of flak during the trial. People don't like the police being dishonest during investigations, no matter how legal it is."

"How are we going to do any undercover work then?" Mac said sarcastically. "Do they think we should send our narcotics guys into a sting wearing uniforms?"

"Humph. Very funny. I'm just stating a fact. Juries don't like police lying to suspects. I think we'll make a call tomorrow morning and get a detective to Jessica's home in Crescent City. Hopefully the address Vicki has is still good. We need to let her know Brad is dead, no matter what the family thinks. If she won't consent to an interview with us, we'll fall back on the locals. If we're lucky, she'll come back to Oregon on her own accord and we can do a face to face. That's the way I'd rather conduct business, but then again, you are the lead on this. Your call, Mac."

Darn. I was looking forward to a trip to a slightly warmer climate. But Kevin was right. It would be more efficient to have a local cop talk to her. Besides, Mac didn't feel secure enough to take a different approach. "Sounds like a plan, Kev. Let's hit the house tomorrow, and I'll get the California cops to inform Jessica."

"Good. Sounds like a plan." Kevin parroted one of his youthful partner's favorite lines.

"Smart-mouth."

22

YOU GUYS MAKING ANY HEADWAY on that Salem caper, Sarge?" Mac asked as he walked past Sergeant Evans's office. His question was partly curiosity about the murder-for-hire case and partly wanting to make sure his boss noticed he was at work at 6:30 A.M.

Frank looked up from a stack of police reports and peered over the top of his reading glasses. "Oh, hey, Mac. This thing grew wings, but I think we have the old gal nailed. Eric got the request for the hit on a body wire tape."

I bet a jury won't have a problem with that bit of "dishonest" undercover work, Mac thought. "So Eric was able to pull it off? You guys make an arrest yet?"

"Yep. We got the husband in the loop. Had him holed up in a Motel 8 down in Marion County. The wife fronted us ten grand for the hit, with ten more when she got the proof."

"Proof?" Mac asked. "How did you pull that one off?"

"By consulting with the master," Philly said, as he maneuvered his large frame into the cramped office.

"Something like that." Frank rolled his eyes. "Now get lost. I gotta get these reports proofed and signed off. I'm sure Philly will share the details, Mac."

"Sure. Let's get some coffee first." Mac followed Philly out of the office and into the break room, where they filled up their coffee mugs and Philly hooked a couple of donuts.

"What happened to your low-carb diet?" Mac asked, raising his eyebrows at Philly's donuts.

"Too restrictive," Philly mumbled around the powdered donut he'd stuffed in his mouth as they entered his office.

"Okay." Mac settled into a chair. "Tell me what went down."

Philly dumped creamer into his cup. The air swooshed out of his oversized executive chair as he sank into it. "Russ and I dolled up the husband like a dead guy—the dude actually let us put makeup on him and everything. A little dirt on the face and some ketchup in his hair, and there you go." Philly opened a file and showed Mac a few photographs.

"These are good. He really looks dead." Mac grimaced. "Did she fall for it?"

"Hook, line, and sinker. Eric showed her the pics, and she handed over the money. End of story."

"I'm impressed."

"As well you should be." Philly bit into another powdered donut, spraying sugar all over his suit and dark tie.

"How's your case coming along, Mac?" Frank stood in the doorway, holding a cup of coffee.

"So far, so good." Mac got to his feet. "We have an ID on the victim and are starting interviews with the family. The main person of interest right now is the victim's girlfriend. She's already moved out of state."

"You know the governor's restriction on out-of-state travel, so don't even ask," Frank warned. "Our budget's in pretty bad shape. No out-of-state travel unless it's an emergency."

"Not to worry, Sarge, I called the S.O. down south last night and asked them to make contact with her. I asked if they would send an experienced investigator to note her reaction to the death notification and interview her if she permits. I also asked him to have her call me, but I don't know if that will happen or not."

"Good. You and Kevin getting all the help you need?"

"Right now, yes. We have Chris Ferroli, a game officer, helping on some of the follow-up, but we are just getting started on the interviews."

Philly scowled. "What help can a stump jumper be to a murder investigation?"

Mac took exception. "For your information, wise guy, Trooper Ferroli has been a great help. He recovered the body and has given us some invaluable information on the falls area, where the victim was last reported missing."

"He knows, Mac." Frank laughed. "Philly just likes making derogatory remarks."

"You know me too well, Boss Hog." Philly sighed. "I'll let you and Gramps bumble around for a day or two, Mac, and then give you some tips to wrap up this gig, just as soon as Russ and I are done with this murder-for-hire case."

"Thanks a bunch." Mac picked up his lukewarm coffee. "I need a refill."

"Don't mention it," Philly called after him.

"Yeah, thanks a lot." Kevin appeared in the doorway, blocking Mac's exit. Mac jumped at the sound of his voice, sloshing coffee on his jacket.

"And what's this Gramps stuff? I'm only a few years older than you."

"You just look a lot older," Philly laughed. "And quit sneaking up on me."

"If you'd ever stop bragging about yourself, you might actually hear the door to the office open."

Kevin grinned at Mac. "Hey, partner, you ready? We need to be in Brightwood in about an hour."

Mac finished dabbing the coffee off his jacket, staining his white hanky. "You bet. Just let me grab my briefcase and get rid of this." He tossed the stained hanky in a side drawer and left his half-empty cup on his desk. Briefcase in hand, he joined Kevin at the main door.

The detectives started east on SE Powell Boulevard, which was US Highway 26 in Portland city limits. After stopping for real coffee, they drove through Gresham and Sandy on their way to the small community located twenty miles from Mount Hood.

"Everything go okay with the sheriff's office in California?" Kevin asked.

"They were glad to help. I expect to hear back in the next couple of hours."

"Good." Kevin sighed, taking a sip of coffee. "Morning came early today."

"Hey, I meant to ask, what type of guns did Todd Gaynes have?"

"Just a couple of rifles, like he said, and a .22 pistol in his nightstand. His rifles were a 7 mm magnum and a 300 Winchester, nothing close to what we're looking for."

"I ran a check through the firearms verification unit in Salem last night. None of the other family members have firearms registered to them. Jessica doesn't either."

Kevin raised his brows. "That would be helpful if it were accurate. That database is only about seven years old and only captures guns purchased by law-abiding citizens. You're not going to find most of the guns bought at gun shows or on the street or in garage sales." He shook his head. "It's just too easy for crooks to get guns."

"Yeah, I was just hoping for a lucky strike." Mac felt a bit defensive. Maybe the two of them were spending a little too much time together. Maybe Kevin was having second thoughts about giving him the lead.

The detectives didn't talk much during the drive east on

Highway 26. Mac exited on Brightwood Loop Road, near the Oregon Department of Transportation truck weigh station. Using the directions Brad's parents had given them, they easily found the small house Jessica and Brad had lived in. The one-story chalet was nestled amongst ferns and moss-covered fir and cedar trees. Because it was located so close to Mount Hood, the community along the Hoodland corridor was popular with skiers and others who enjoyed alpine living. On a clear day you could see the snow-covered twelve-thousand-foot peak.

"This must be the place." Mac eased into the gravel driveway. "Looks like Allison's already here." Mac pulled alongside the crime lab Ford F-250 pickup and parked.

"Morning, guys." Allison stepped down from the passenger seat of the truck. A male crime lab technician climbed out of the driver's seat. After greeting each other, Kevin opened the front door with the key Vicki had provided. "We'll run video on the outside if you can get started on the inside," Mac told Allison.

"Sounds good. We'll go over the inside with the lights, both white and blue. I don't see much need to spray chemicals unless we find something suspicious."

"Agreed." Mac popped the trunk.

Allison and her assistant disappeared inside the small house while Mac and Kevin examined the outside grounds.

"Not much of a housekeeper." Mac scanned the hundreds of beer bottles and cans that littered the back of the house, next to a fifty-gallon burn barrel.

"You said it. I wonder why they didn't return these for the deposit?" Kevin peered inside the barrel. After rummaging around in the barrel with a stick, he tipped it over to take a look at its contents. Then he pulled a pair of latex gloves from his jacket pocket and slipped them on, preparing to look through the debris.

Mac continued to walk around the cabin, taking videos and

photographs and looking for anything out of the ordinary.

"No outbuildings; nothing much to look at," Mac said as he returned to the small garbage dump Kevin was kneeling over.

"Good. Help me dig through this burn barrel stuff. There's a lot of paperwork here that someone tried to burn, but you can make out some of it." Mac slipped on gloves and began to search through the papers, mainly bills and late notices from collectors.

"Hello. Take a look at this." Kevin held up a singed piece of white paper and handed it to Mac. "I wonder who Jeremy is?"

Mac read the handwritten note.

Dear Jess,

I know our situation is a little weird right now, but I wanted you to know I'm thinking about you. I'm here for you if you need me. I'm willing to be your friend for now, but you know I would like to be more. You deserve so much better.

Love always,
Jeremy

"Romeo's got my interest," Mac said. "I hope someone knows who this guy is so we can find out what this letter is all about. I'm wondering what that 'situation' is."

"And the 'you deserve so much better' comment." Kevin grimaced as he straightened. "I'll get an evidence bag. I don't see much else of interest, except for those phone bills." He pointed to some singed documents. "Let's seize those. The phone numbers might be important."

"See anything else you want me to bag, Mac?" Kevin asked.

"This is tough for you, isn't it?" Mac chuckled.

"What do you mean?"

"Come on, Kev. You're having a hard time remembering to let me take the lead."

"Maybe a little, but I'm trying. Just remind me if I start step-ping on your toes, okay? I want you to feel comfortable with this. Now answer my question—do you want me to bag anything else?"

Mac suppressed a grin. "I think that's it for the outside. Nothing else of evidentiary value that I can see."

"Whatever you say, boss." Kevin slipped the paperwork into clear plastic evidence bags, sealed the envelope, and then placed the items in the trunk of the Crown Victoria.

"You think we ought to have the lab run some ninhydrin testing on the note? Maybe this Jeremy has some prints on file." Ninhydrin was a chemical mist to lift latent fingerprints.

"Either that or iodine fuming," Kevin said. "We'll have to see what Allison thinks." Kevin dumped his gloves in the waste receptacle.

"Iodine fuming?" Mac chuckled. "Do they still perform that test? I thought that went out with Dick Tracy."

"Newer isn't always better, Mac. Sometimes the old mousetrap can't be improved upon." Kevin pursed his mouth. "Fuming doesn't ruin the document like ninhydrin; the only color change is the actual fingerprint when it meets the fumes from the iodine crystals, reacting to the oil on the print. Ninhydrin works pretty well on most documents, but it's messier. You can always run ninhydrin after fuming, but not the other way around."

"Once again, partner, I'm impressed by your never-ending storehouse of knowledge." Mac peeled off his gloves and tossed them in the waste bin on top of Kevin's.

"Yes, I can tell you are very sincere." Kevin threw the evidence tape at Mac. "Besides, I've been using iodine fuming for twenty-plus years and I don't quite know how that ninhydrin junk works."

"Aha!" Mac threw the tape back at Kevin, who caught the bulky roll and set it in the trunk then closed the lid. They were still laughing as they made their way up the walk and into the house.

"All clear to come inside?" Kevin yelled from the front deck.

"Yeah, come on in," a male voice came from a back room. As the detectives entered the small home, Mac said, "When the Gayneses said Jessica cleaned it out, I wasn't expecting this. Looks like she even took the furniture."

"It's pretty sparse all right."

The residence had a small kitchen and a dining area, located next to a family room. There were a few scattered dishes on top of a card table in the dining area and a futon in the family room area. The carpet indentation indicated that other items of furniture had once been in the family room—probably another chair, a coffee table, and a television, by the look of the prints.

"Nothing remarkable yet, fellas." Allison stood in the entrance to the bedroom, holding a bright white light and examining the wall. "As you can see, there's not much to look through. My partner is in the bedroom taking a look around with the lights, though I didn't see anything unusual on our cursory search."

Mac peeked in the bedroom, noting only two mattresses on the floor and a makeshift bedside table. The CSI tech was going over the walls and carpet with a blue light, looking for blood spatter evidence. "You guys can start the physical search of the kitchen area. It's the only room ready right now," Allison said.

Mac and Kevin searched the kitchen, eventually moving into the front room and the single bedroom and bathroom. Their search proved fruitless, though the techs did pick up some trace items from the carpet and paint in the event they needed some samples for future comparison. Allison finished packing up, then she collected the evidence Mac and Kevin had stored in the trunk. "See if you can get prints off the letter from Jeremy," Kevin said.

"Right. I'll make copies and fume it before spraying the destructive chemicals on it."

Kevin sent Mac a wink as the lab people left. "Was I right or wasn't I?" Kevin looked entirely too smug, but Mac's comments were cut off when a familiar car turned into the driveway.

"Look who's here." Kevin nodded toward the Ford SUV.

Todd and Vicki stepped out of their car, and Mac walked out front to greet them. "Anything new to report, detectives?" Vicki asked.

"I'm afraid we didn't find much to aid us in the home," Mac answered. "It looks pretty well cleaned out."

"I know. Jessica and her friends did a number on the place." Vicki looked past Mac to Kevin, who'd gone back to lock the front door. Kevin greeted the parents and handed the keys back to Todd.

"Mrs. Gaynes was just telling me about Jessica and her friends cleaning out the house," Mac said.

"Friends? What friends? You told us about the items Jessica removed from the residence—Brad's guitar, clothes, and ski equipment. I don't remember you saying anything about furniture items or that she had friends helping her."

"We don't really know any names, just that Jessica had people over at the house after Brad went missing." Vicki ran a hand through her hair. "They may have been mutual friends, but they were all very disrespectful, if you ask me."

"How so?" Mac asked.

"Well, take a look around. They must have partied hard and trashed the place. You can see the stains all over the carpet and the beer bottles and cans out back. None of that was here when Brad lived in the house. He kept the place fairly clean."

"Yeah, we saw the trash." Kevin placed his hands on his hips. "Can you give us any names?"

"Sorry, I don't know." Vicki deferred to her husband.

"Me neither." Todd shrugged. "When he wasn't working at Timberline Lodge, he was skiing. I know Brad had friends, but he never brought them around us. I guess he knew we probably wouldn't approve of them."

"Does the name Jeremy ring a bell?" Kevin asked.

Interested in their response, Mac's gaze shifted from one to the other. There was no look of recognition.

"Sorry, it doesn't," Vicki said. "Should it?"

"Maybe. It's just a name that came up in some paperwork we found in the residence," Mac offered. "Probably nothing."

"The crime lab went through the home also," Kevin said. "We didn't find any obvious signs of a struggle or crime evidence. Since Brad lived here, there is no real value to taking prints or initiating additional testing at the house unless we have specific information that would require it."

"So what's next?" Todd asked.

Mac looked over at Kevin then back to Todd. "Our next step is to talk to coworkers up at Timberline."

"What about Jessica?" Vicki asked.

"In the works."

"I hope you talk to her soon, detectives."

"Why's that?"

"Because as soon as she hears that Brad's body was found, she's going to run. I'm afraid if you don't act fast, that young woman is going to get away with murder."

23

STATION TWENTY from eleven-fifty-one," Kevin called in over the car radio as Mac drove east on Highway 26 toward Mount Hood.

"Eleven-fifty-one," the dispatcher answered.

"Fifty-one, please advise if nineteen-eleven is on," Kevin said, trying to reach the Government Camp patrol sergeant. The village of Government Camp was located at the base of Mount Hood at over four thousand feet. The accident-plagued snowy pass was patrolled by a rugged group of state troopers, led by the outpost sergeant. Before the dispatcher could answer, the sergeant came on the radio.

"Nineteen-eleven, Warm Springs." The sergeant gave his location as being farther east, on the Warm Springs Indian Reservation.

Kevin gave the sergeant his cell phone number and asked him to call.

"Copy, eleven-fifty-one. It'll be a few minutes."

"These mountain pass troopers have a rough job," Kevin said while he waited for the call. "There's snow on Mount Hood year-round, and they never get a break from the traffic crashes."

"Which is why they call this section of Highway 26 Blood Alley." Mac slowed down at a curve. "Beautiful and treacherous."

"These troops handle more death investigations than we do."

"I hope the sergeant has a contact for us up at Timberline Lodge so we can get some work history on our guy. And maybe he knows this Jeremy guy."

"Ask him about Timberline road too, Kev. We may have to chain up east of Rhododendron." Mac eyed the snow-covered peak in the distance.

Kevin's cell phone rang moments later. The sergeant provided them with the name and location of the lodge personnel manager. He also warned of a snow-packed road but said the mountain ODOT crews had dumped a fresh load of gravel on the highway. "We should make the lodge okay if we stay on the highway, but the parking lot may be a little rough."

"Thanks, Sarge." Kevin snapped his phone shut. "Our contact at the lodge is Drake Kessler."

Mac maneuvered the Crown Victoria over the winding, snow-packed road to Government Camp. Luckily, the line of cars moved along at a good forty miles an hour. A half-hour later, they turned onto Highway 173, better known as Timberline Road. The steep grade through a winter wonderland led up to the base of Mount Hood and to the historic Timberline Lodge.

The landmark building was heaped with snow, the roof seeming to touch the ground at some points with its pristine white covering. Mac drove along the lines of cars and SUVs, finally finding a place to park. The parking lot was crowded with sightseers, skiers, sledders, mountain climbers, and snowmobilers. Mac and Kevin wound their way through the throng of people.

"I wish I would have worn boots," Mac said, high-stepping through the knee-deep snow. He also wished he could be up here skiing and promised to make it happen soon. He thought again about Linda. She didn't like winter sports. Did Dana? Mac squelched the idea. He didn't need to bring a date.

Kevin and Mac entered the giant stone-faced building, going from the dark tunnel to a great room with one of the biggest fireplaces he'd ever seen. Mac made his way through the crowd to the information counter.

"May I help you?" the friendly attendant asked.

"Sure. We'd like to speak with Drake Kessler," Mac answered. "We don't have an appointment."

"Let me check." The teenager gave Mac a wide smile. "Can I tell him who you are?"

"Oregon State Police." Mac displayed his badge.

"Oh." Her smile disappeared. She hit a speed-dial on the phone. While waiting for someone to pick up, she asked, "Are you guys here about the stolen ski equipment?"

"Not exactly," Kevin answered, "but we might be able to take care of that too. Is Mr. Kessler in? It's rather important."

After a brief phone conversation, she pointed up a set of stairs at the end of the rustic entry. "Right up to the top, third door on the right."

"Thanks."

The men climbed the wide wooden stairs and were greeted at the top by a man wearing casual yet expensive-looking clothes. He eyed the detectives suspiciously. "You're with the Oregon State Police?"

"That's right," Mac answered. "Detectives McAllister and Bledsoe." They both displayed their badges and photo identification.

"You're not here about the ski equipment, are you?" Kessler shook hands with each of them.

"No. Actually we're working on a murder investigation."

"Really. By all means, come on in." Kessler lead them into his tidy office. "Please sit down. Can I get you some coffee—a soda?"

They both declined the drinks and settled into the comfortable chairs at a large round table that sat in the corner of the office, just to the right of a mahogany desk. "We talked with Sergeant Jon Walker a short time ago and he gave us your name. Said you might be able to help us."

Kessler smiled. "Right. Jon and his family come up to the lodge often." He sat in the third chair at the table.

Mac and Kevin spent the next few minutes telling Drake about Brad Gaynes's death and their subsequent investigation.

Drake shook his head. "I read about his death in the paper. A number of us went out to help with the search when we could take the time off. I remember at the time thinking he'd probably be found dead somewhere."

"Why's that?"

Drake shrugged. "You come to expect it. We live in some pretty rugged country. So when a guy goes missing, especially someone like Brad, who had wilderness survival training . . . Well, he wasn't the type to just up and leave."

"That's pretty much what the family thought," Mac said. "Turns out they were right."

"Brad had a lot of friends here, and he was a good worker. He worked hard, and I imagine, like a lot of these guys, he partied hard."

"Tell us something about his work habits."

Drake pursed his lips. "Like I said, he was a good worker. Always came in when he was scheduled. Never missed a lesson. That's saying something. His students liked him—we never had any complaints."

Mac made a few notes on his pad. "Can you supply us with a roster of employees who knew Brad?"

"Sure. How about I get the info together and fax it to you tomorrow?"

"That would be great. Are any of his friends working today?"

"I couldn't say right off, but I can check for you." Drake checked his watch. "Why don't you guys go on down to the restaurant? Lunch is on us. By the time you're finished, I should have some answers for you."

"Sounds good." Mac nodded. "I'm afraid we can't accept gratuities, but we'd be happy to pay for our own meal."

Drake shrugged his shoulders and smiled.

Mac cleared his throat. "Um, before we go, could you tell us anything about Jessica Turner, Brad's girlfriend?"

Drake's face lit up in a smile. "Jessica worked in the bar. They made a real nice couple. She and Brad hit it off right away. I wasn't surprised—Jessica was a special gal."

"Really." Mac didn't tell him that not everyone thought so.

"Upbeat, good personality. Good worker, someone you could count on. In fact, she came to me just before Brad went missing and asked if she could get a job in the administrative offices. Said she and Brad were getting married, and she wanted a full-time job. She had good timing, since my assistant was moving. And I was pleased to get her. Jessica was thrilled." He frowned. "After Brad disappeared, Jessica changed—got pretty depressed. She quit her job and moved back to California with her family."

Mac glanced over at Kevin, who was busy writing. "Did you notice any problems between Jessica and Brad before he disappeared?"

"Not that I recall. I don't see my employees every day, though. Some of the others might be able to tell you something."

Mac tapped his pen against his hand. "Do you know anyone named Jeremy?"

He rubbed his chin. "Jeremy . . . I know several. Popular name. You mean someone who works here?"

"Right."

He smiled. "Jon Walker's son and a Jeremy. Um, Larson, I think. His name should be on that roster."

"Okay." Mac turned to Kevin. "You have anything?"

"Not right now." Kevin pressed his palms against the arms of the chair and pushed to his feet. "Mr. Kessler, I think we'll take that lunch break now."

"All right." He went to his desk, took out a pad, and scribbled something on it. Handing it to Kevin, he said, "Just give this to the waiter. At least allow me to seat you at my personal table. It has the best view of the slopes."

"We really appreciate your cooperation, Mr. Kessler."

"Hey, anything I can do to help. I'll get that information for you and bring it down to the restaurant." He walked them to the door. "I'll arrange to have any of my people who knew Brad come in and talk to you if you want."

"That would be great, thanks."

AFTER LUNCH and three unproductive interviews, Mac and Kevin plodded back out to the parking lot. It had snowed heavily while they'd been inside, and the going was even tougher than before. "I think we're going to need sled dogs to get back to our car." Mac made a wry face.

The car was barely visible in the snow, with at least six inches of fresh powder on the ground. Mac opened the driver side door carefully. A huge chunk of snow thumped onto his seat.

"Oh, great. Just what I need." Mac brushed out the snow, his hands freezing in the process.

Kevin chuckled. "You may want to dust the snow off the car before you open the door, Daniel Boone." He caught the edge of his coat sleeve in his hand and brushed the snow from the top of the passenger side door and the windshield. "You do have tire chains, don't you?"

"Chains? Didn't you put them in the trunk?" Mac cast Kevin a concerned look as he finished clearing his seat. "If you didn't, we may have to spend the night."

"Are you serious? You came up here without chains?"

It was Mac's turn to laugh. He clipped his pager to the visor so it wouldn't fall and get lost in the deep snow before brushing the white stuff off his side of the windshield. "Of course I have chains. I'm just not sure I know how to put them on."

"Marvelous." Kevin popped the trunk with the dash button then went back to retrieve them.

Mac pulled the box of tire chains from the trunk and dropped it on the ground. Kevin pulled his yellow slicker from the trunk, snapping it on over his clothes. "Never put on chains, huh? You didn't grow up in the country, did you?"

Mac shivered and slipped on his rain gear, wondering when Kevin would realize he'd been joking about putting on the chains too. During his stint as a trooper he'd helped dozens of stranded motorists chain up.

"Still want to make fun of my coat?" Kevin pulled a chain from the box and wrapped it around the right rear tire. Less than fifteen minutes and numerous grunts later, Mac and Kevin had chained the rear wheels.

"Thought you didn't know how to chain up," Kevin huffed when they were finally back in the car.

Mac grinned. "I didn't say I couldn't. I said I wasn't sure I knew how."

"Okay, wise guy. Next time you get to do both wheels."

They plowed through the snow and out of the parking lot. Mac took his pager off the visor and checked it before clipping it onto his belt. "Darn. Missed a page."

"Who called?" Kevin asked, rubbing his hands over the heater.

Mac frowned as he tried to place the number. "I think it's Jessica."

24

J ESSICA? Are you sure?" Kevin asked, apparently as surprised as Mac was.

"I think so." Mac examined his pager again. "The area code is right. I'm pretty sure it's the same number Mrs. Gaynes gave me. I gave it to the detective in California. Where do you think we should call from? I don't want to make the call on a cell phone; we may want to tape it. And I'm not sure if we even have cell coverage up here."

Kevin agreed. "Let's head back down to Highway 26 and use our outpost office in the ODOT shop. The Portland office key should still fit the Government Camp office." Mac traveled slowly down the icy Timberline Road to the highway shop. Even with chains and using extreme caution, his tires spun in the fresh powder when he tried to catch traction and cross Highway 26 to the shop entrance.

The Oregon Department of Transportation kept sand and gravel, used by the highway workers to maintain the icy road, piled in small mountains under covered ports. The parking lot to the highway shop led into a narrow alley between huge garage bays where snowplows and sand trucks were housed much of the year. In the winter, however, the vehicles were in service 24-7. At the end of the alley stood a familiar blue highway sign indicating an OSP office was nearby.

The small office wasn't much more than a couple hundred square feet, just big enough to hold a coffeepot and a report writing desk when the winter flares and boot chains were stacked inside. The A-frame design was popular in the Hoodland community, where heavy snowfalls were the norm. This year was no exception, and the area around the OSP office was piled high in snow. Mac and Kevin parked and took out their briefcases before stepping again through knee-deep snow to the door. Once inside, they stomped off the snow and headed for the desk.

Mac pulled a pad out of his briefcase and began to set up for the important call. "Looks like these phones aren't set up with recorders."

Kevin pulled a small ear recorder and wire from his briefcase. "You can use my mobile device."

"I've never seen one of these before. Where did you get one that small?"

Kevin shrugged. "ATF insisted I keep it after I worked an armed career criminal assignment with them. The feds get all the neat stuff; this recorder is almost ten years old."

"They insisted, huh?" Mac raised an eyebrow.

"Well, maybe more like they forgot I had it. I've put it to good use over the years. Just put this little speaker in your ear and plug the male end into your mini cassette recorder. This little beauty picks up your voice and the one on the other end. It's pretty slick."

"I don't know if California has laws that prevent recorded phone calls. Is that going to be a problem?" Mac slipped the tiny padded microphone into his ear.

"Nope. Testing—one, two, three," Kevin said into Mac's ear

then played the recording back. "Oregon doesn't require us to notify the person that you are recording over the phone, so that's all we need to worry about. Just as long as one end of the conversation is in Oregon, we're good to go."

"Humph. Are you sure about that? I'm probably violating some federal law," Mac mumbled.

"Sure I'm sure." Kevin slapped Mac on the back. "But if you end up going to prison, I'll deny ever having this conversation with you."

Mac rolled his eyes. "Maybe you better call."

Kevin chuckled. "I'm kidding. Of course I'm sure."

"Great." Mac took a deep breath and let it out in a swoosh. Then he punched in the number, saying the date and time into the microphone. The phone rang once.

"Hello." The female voice sounded out of breath.

"Uh, hello." Mac glanced at Kevin. "That was quick. This is Detective Mac McAllister with the Oregon State Police. I received a page to call this number."

"Yes, I paged you. This is Jessica Turner. Um, Mac? You helped search for Brad that first day, right?"

"Right. I'm surprised you remembered."

"Oh, well, you and Dana were nice to me and . . ." She sighed. "Anyway, I'm here with Officer Rodriguez from the sheriff's office. He said I could get hold of you at this number. He said you found Brad?"

"Yes, I'm afraid so, Jessica," Mac said. "I'm very sorry for your loss."

"Um, thank you. How are Brad's parents handling the news?"

"They're understandably upset."

"Still blaming me, no doubt."

Mac ignored the last comment, hoping to establish a rapport with Jessica before getting into the meat of the questions.

"Okay, thanks," she said. "I can reach you at this number, right?"

"Excuse me?" Mac asked, surprised by the statement.

"Oh, sorry," Jessica said. "I was talking to the officer here at the house. He just handed me his business card and said he was leaving."

"I'd like to speak with him before he goes." Mac leaned back in the chair.

"Sure," said Jessica. "Hang on."

A few seconds later, Mac heard, "Rodriguez here."

Mac introduced himself. This wasn't the same person he'd talked to earlier. "Can you tell me about the conversation you just had with Ms. Turner?"

"Yeah. I just came out here to tell her this Brad Gaynes fellow had been found dead. I gave her your pager number in case she wanted to talk to you about it. The detective you talked to originally was sidelined by another homicide and assigned the death notification to me."

Mac held back a few choice words. *If you want something done right, do it yourself.* The pager number hadn't been for Jessica's use, but for the detective's. Still, Mac was glad she called.

"How did Ms. Turner react when she received the news?"

"Yeah, things are a little cold down here. Not what I would expect this time of year."

"So she was indifferent to the news?"

"You could say that."

"All right. Thanks for your help. I'll give you a call at your office." Mac wrote down the officer's phone number. "Go ahead and put her back on."

Jessica told Rodriguez good-bye again then came back on the line. "So now what?" Jessica asked. "I guess I'm suspect number one, huh?"

"I wouldn't say that. I do have several questions for you, but they can wait. The purpose of this call is to answer any questions you may have about Brad's death."

"Deputy Rodriguez didn't have many details. He just told me that Brad had been shot and was found in the river."

"The officer told you Brad was shot?" Mac glanced up at Kevin and rubbed his forehead.

Kevin tipped his head back and threw out his arms, obviously upset that key evidence had been released.

"That's what he said. Is that true? Was Brad shot?"

"Yes. Brad was found in the Columbia River. The medical examiner is ruling Brad's death a homicide. We—um, Detective Bledsoe and I are playing a little catch-up now. The best information out there is that you are still the last person to see Brad alive."

"So . . . what? Do you want to arrest me or something? I'll take a lie detector test or whatever; I didn't kill Brad."

Mac couldn't help but smile at her naiveté. "We're not going to arrest you." *At least not yet.* She sounded young and sweet, not like a cold-blooded killer. "We would like an interview. We could really use your help in catching the person who did this." Kevin gave Mac a thumbs-up.

"Okay. I was planning on coming to Oregon soon; I have some things in pawn and wanted to pick them up. I'll tell you right now, some of the stuff is Brad's. I needed cash to get to California, so I hocked a few things. My boyfriend has loaned me some money so I can get the things out and, you know, give Brad's stuff back to his family."

"Boyfriend?" Mac asked, again for Kevin's benefit.

Kevin raised his eyebrows and whispered, "Don't ask about Jeremy; let her talk."

"Yeah, I met someone here in California. He's a really nice guy. Um . . . I don't know if you know this, but Brad was abusive." She huffed. "I bet Vicki never told you about that."

"He hurt you?"

"Mm. He was mean—especially when he drank and did drugs."

"I see." Mac decided not to press it. Plenty of time to talk with her when they were face to face. "When did you say you were coming to Oregon?"

"I didn't. I haven't made any real plans yet. If you need me to be there right away, I could catch a bus in the next day or two. Will that work? I can't drive that far right now, and I can't afford a plane ticket."

"That would be great. I hope you aren't feeling like you're getting the third degree. Unfortunately, Brad's killer has a real head start on us, and like I said, we can really use your help."

"It's okay. I don't mind."

"Listen, Jessica, would you mind telling me what happened the night Brad disappeared?"

"Can't you get my statement from the reports? Nothing's changed."

"I know, but sometimes if you tell a story again, new memories come back to you. Besides, the officers early on didn't know where Brad was and they may not have documented something that is important now."

Kevin nodded, obviously impressed that Mac was going to lock her into a statement on tape. A provable lie was just as valuable as hard evidence.

Jessica sighed. "All right. Whatever you need. I want to help as much as I can."

"Good. Rather than play twenty questions, why don't you take it from the top?"

"Okay. Brad and I met at Timberline Lodge. You know where that is?"

Mac looked out the window at the towering mountain and smiled. "Yes, go on."

"I fell pretty hard at first. Brad had the looks and the reputation, the total package. We had a lot of fun. One thing led to another, and we ended up moving in together—actually, I moved in with him at his cabin in Brightwood. We had some great times at that place. Our friends were really into the party scene."

"Would the parties sometime include drugs, Jessica?"

She didn't answer.

"Jessica, let me make one thing clear. I'm not a narcotics officer. I work homicide. I don't care if you and Brad slept in a mattress stuffed with weed. That's not what I'm after."

"Um . . . yeah, there was some drug use. Brad and I both smoked a few bowls now and again."

"Bowls of marijuana or crank?"

"Just marijuana, nothing serious," Jessica answered, sounding a little offended. That always amused Mac, when drug users would minimize their vice and have an example of some type of drug or conduct that was more serious. Kevin had taught him to utilize this human trait in interviews, minimizing their crime and giving an example of something more serious to keep the perp talking.

"A little marijuana doesn't concern me."

Kevin smiled and shook his head at Mac's comment. Mac held his finger up to his lip and waved Kevin away.

"I don't do drugs anymore. I never did a lot. It was mostly Brad. I don't drink either. Brad liked to drink and have a good time, you know, get high. I wanted him to quit. We argued about that a lot, and at the falls that day I broke up with him. He didn't take it well."

Jessica went on to tell Mac about her argument with Brad and the trucker who had intervened. Her story was the same as what Mac remembered reading. No discrepancies, no changes.

"Tell me more about this truckdriver," Mac said.

"Well, Brad was really mad. I got out of the car, and so did he. He grabbed my arms when I tried to walk away—told me I wasn't going anywhere. This truckdriver decided he was going to play hero, I guess, and came to my rescue. He asked me if there was a problem, and Brad said, 'There will be if you don't mind your own business.'"

"How did the truckdriver react?" Mac asked.

"He just sort of stared at me, like he was still waiting for me to answer."

"Can you remember what he looked like?"

"About fifty, kinda like Todd, but shorter and with a potbelly. He was wearing a cowboy hat. I didn't answer quick enough, I guess, and the guy asked me if I was okay. Brad freaked out. Shoved the guy backward, and his hat fell off. Brad asked the guy if he was deaf and if he wanted a piece of him. I couldn't believe he actually said that. It sounded so corny I started laughing. It reminded me of some cheap movie or one of those fake wrestling shows."

"I bet that went over well."

Kevin caught Mac's attention, holding up his pager and indicating with his other hand he was going out to the car to make a call. Mac nodded.

"Not at all. I had both of them mad at me." Jessica paused a moment before going on. "The truckdriver had to bend over and pick up his hat. Wait a minute. The guy's hair was all matted, black with gray streaks in it."

"Good observation, Jessica."

"You're right." Her voice brightened. "I forgot about that part when I told the story to the deputies at the falls. Anyway, the truckdriver had this disgusted look on his face. His face was bright red when he stood up, and he didn't say a word. He just smashed his hat back on and went back to his rig."

"Was this guy holding a weapon or anything that you could see on him?"

"No, nothing I could see, other than a flashlight he was holding. I didn't really think of that as a weapon. Do you think this guy had something to do with Brad's death?" Jessica sounded close to hysteria. "Oh my gosh, what if we made him so mad he . . ."

"If he was responsible for Brad's death, it wouldn't have been your fault, Jessica. At this point we haven't eliminated anyone. We still have a lot of questions. On that note, could you tell me if you or Brad owned any firearms?"

"I didn't, but Brad did. He had a pistol; I don't know what kind. It was black and had one of those clip things that you put in."

"Do you know what happened to his gun?"

"Yeah, I pawned it. That was one of those things I was telling you about that I wanted to get back."

"Can you remember which pawnshop you left the gun with?"

"I pawned everything in Portland, in one of those shops down on Division. It's the one by David Douglas High School. I can't think of the name, but I have a card somewhere."

"I think I know the one. So tell me how you came to possess the gun."

"Well, like I said, when Brad went missing I was left to deal with his neurotic parents and sister. After a week, I figured Brad had skipped out or had an accident or something. I wanted to come back home, so I took a few of his things to hock. I took his guitar and some skiing and snowboard equipment, along with the gun. I only ended up with about eight hundred dollars for the stuff, but it got me home. I planned on paying him back once he showed up, but he never did."

"Did you use your name on the pawn slips?" Mac wanted to secure Brad's possessions himself.

"Not exactly. I used a fake ID. I didn't want to get busted for stealing the stuff. Sorry, I wasn't thinking."

"So what name did you use? And why do you have a fake ID?"

"I've had this fake card for years so I could get into bars before I was twenty-one. It has the name Cynthia Richardson on it.

That's the name on the pawn slip. Sorry, I know it looks bad, but I wasn't thinking very clearly then."

"I understand. Like I told you earlier, I just want to find out who did this to Brad. Anything else you can give me to work on before we meet in person?"

"I can't think of anything. Would the day after tomorrow be okay? I'm pretty sure I can catch the bus to Portland."

"That would be fine. Tell you what, you tell me the bus number and time you arrive, and I'll pick you up myself. I'll take you to wherever you want to go."

"I have your office number and your pager. I'll give you a call when I get the time firmed up, if that's okay."

"Perfect. We'll see you in a day or two."

"Thanks, Mac. I'm glad you're on the case."

Mac hung up the phone, then he pulled the earpiece from his ear and gave the time into the microphone to indicate the conversation was over.

"How'd it go?" Kevin asked, startling Mac.

"Okay. I didn't hear you walk in."

"What's the scoop?" Kevin sat down.

"Brad owned a gun after all. I guess he wasn't as concerned about being a felon in possession of a firearm as his parents seemed to think. She described a semiautomatic though, so probably not a .357. She pawned the gun along with a bunch of other things Brad owned. I'll call and get a uniform down to the pawnbroker before we leave here. She used a fake name to pawn the goods. Said she was scared she would get pinched for the stolen stuff."

"What's this new boyfriend business?"

"I didn't make issue with it, but she says she met him in California. He gave or loaned her money to get Brad's stuff out of hock. I'm meeting her the day after tomorrow at the bus station in north Portland."

"She actually agreed to come back for an interview?" Kevin looked surprised.

"Not agreed, she offered. Maybe a little too cooperative?"

"Maybe, we'll see." Kevin stood up. "Anything else raise any hairs?"

Mac looked over his notes then shook his head. "Nothing really. You can listen to the tape on the way down the mountain. Her story was still pretty consistent after all this time. We still have her and this truckdriver to clear out of the person-of-interest column. Not much to go on with the trucker, I'm afraid, but she was able to remember a couple of details about him." Mac pulled the mini cassette from the tape recorder, punching out the plastic tabs on the cassette with a pocketknife so the tape couldn't be recorded over. "And we still don't know who this Jeremy character is," he added as he stuffed the tape and knife back in his pocket.

"We do now." Kevin waved a piece of paper with a name and address on it and slid it over to Mac.

"What's this?"

"That's our next stop, Mac. We're heading to Estacada to contact Jeremy Matthew Zimmerman. He goes by J. Z., according to his CCH anyway. That page was from Allison at the lab. She hit that love letter from Romeo with the fume gun and lifted a print right away. She said AFIS churned out old Jeremy Zimmerman in less than forty-five minutes. He's got a minor rap sheet, mostly misdemeanors for theft. Here's the interesting part. Get this: our pal J. Z. has a handgun registered to him, a little purchase he made at the Expo Center."

"Expo huh? A gun show?"

"That's my bet. Looks like he purchased the gun from one of the few dealers who register their sales like they are supposed to. And you'll never guess what old J. Z. bought just ten weeks ago."

"Let me guess, a .357."

"Bingo, a .357 Smith and Wesson Chief Special, one of those little five-shot jobs with no hammer spur. Great little gun for concealing in your pocket, no hammer to hang up on your clothes when you pull it out. I wouldn't mind owning one myself."

"You think he still has it? What do you want to bet it's conveniently lost or stolen?"

"Only one way to find out."

25

As MAC ROARED WEST on Highway 26 to the Highway 211 junction in Sandy then turned south toward Estacada, he phoned the office and spoke to a patrol sergeant, asking for an officer to hit the pawnshop Jessica had described. He wanted to see if Brad's handgun was still in hock. If so, the gun would go to the ballistic tank at the crime lab, where Wain would run tests to see if the bullet was a match.

At the same time, Kevin was on his mobile phone, lining up a polygraph examiner in the event they needed one. Cutbacks had forced the Portland poly detective back into patrol work, so the closest examiners were now stationed in Bend and Salem. Mac, thankfully, had escaped the cuts. Kevin claimed Mac's luck was due solely to his prayers.

"Patrol sergeant has a car on the way," Mac said as they entered Sandy. "He'll call when the troop gets some info. Do we have a polygraph available?"

"Sarge thinks so; he's working on it. Looks like they wrapped up that murder-for-hire caper, so Philly and Russ are back in the loop. The detectives down in the valley can clean their own fish now."

"Clean their own fish?" Mac asked. "I haven't heard that one before."

"Do their own follow-up." Kevin grinned. "We're going to have a remedial class for you so you can catch up on all the lingo."

"That could take a while. You guys make up most of it as you go along." Mac slowed as the highway wove through town. "Where in Estacada does our friend Jeremy live?"

"DMV and the handgun unit both have him living out by Faraday Lake, up on Moss Hill Road. You know that area by now, don't you? It's less than two miles from the abandoned sawmill."

"Yeah, I know the place." Mac let out a long breath. He knew the area all too well, the sawmill murder only adding to his grim list of memory markers. "I responded to a fatal automobile accident on the highway by the lake a few years ago. A boozer was driving back from Ripplebrook after an evening of drinking and popping pills. He dozed off at the wheel and swerved off the highway, killing two boys who were riding their bikes."

"I'm sorry, Mac. That was a tough one. I remember reading about it."

"Yeah." He didn't tell Kevin about the highway worker crying or about his own tears at seeing the mangled bicycles on the white fog line. Mac also remembered being disappointed that the driver had only sustained some injuries. "The driver should have been the one to die, but the drunks always seem to live while the innocent pay the price."

Mac glanced over at Kevin, hoping his disparaging remarks wouldn't open the door to one of Kevin's sermons. It didn't. Kevin nodded in agreement. "Moss Hill intersection is right up here on the left."

Mac's gaze took in the stark wooden crosses on the highway shoulder. One of the fathers of the victims still maintained the makeshift memorial after all this time.

Mac eased the car off the highway, reading the scattered addresses on the mailboxes. This rural part of Clackamas County was a gateway to the Mount Hood National Forest and offered a place for people who liked a little space. Some of the residents liked their privacy for more reasons than one.

"There's the place."

Mac glanced at the homemade wooden sign attached to a tree trunk at the top of the drive. He turned in. Both officers unbuckled their seat belts as they started down the gravel drive—a habit from their patrol days. If something went down, you didn't want to be strapped in your seat belt when it happened.

"You want a crack at J. Z., Kevin?" Mac asked.

"I know that sly grin. You just want me to have to write the report."

"Guilty as charged." Mac climbed out of the car, and the two of them walked to the front of the two-story farmhouse. "It's only fair." Truth be known, Mac figured the younger man might have more respect for an older detective than one close to his own age.

"Sure, I'll take a crack at lover boy. I want to get hold of that handgun and see if he has any other guns in the house. Folks out here like their pistols." Kevin knocked on the front door, while he and Mac positioned themselves on either side of the doorway. The door swung open immediately, startling them both.

"What can I do for ya?" a forty-something woman with about a hundred pounds of extra padding asked, apparently out of breath. A stepladder stood just behind her.

"Hello. I'm Detective Bledsoe and this is Detective McAllister with the Oregon State Police. We were hoping to talk with Jeremy Zimmerman. Is he at home?" Kevin showed the woman his identification.

"Wonderful." The woman pushed the ladder back and put her hand on her chest. "What's J. Z. done now?"

"Are you his mother?"

"Stepmother."

"We don't believe he's done anything. We were hoping he might have some information on a case we are working on. Can I get your name?" Kevin asked.

"Sure. Sorry, I forgot my manners. I'm Donna Zimmerman. Come on in. J. Z. is home; I'll get him. I was just dusting the light fixture in the entryway. Sorry about the ladder and the mess."

"No problem, Mrs. Zimmerman," Kevin said as he and Mac stepped into the entryway. "Does J. Z. live here with you then, or . . ."

"Yeah." She didn't sound happy about it. "He still lives with us. Almost twenty-five and still no plans to do anything except play video games and snowboard. My husband, J. Z.'s father, is a long-haul truckdriver. He's in the Midwest right now on a route." Donna walked to a railing at the top of some stairs and yelled for Jeremy to come up.

Moments later, a tall, thin young man with a navy blue stocking cap sauntered up the stairs. "What do you want?" J. Z. was unshaven and unkempt, with jeans sagging below his hips, baggy bell bottoms that rested on his unlaced tennis shoes.

"J. Z., these men are police officers, and they want to talk to you." Donna motioned toward Mac and Kevin.

"Jeremy is it, or do you prefer J. Z.?" Mac shook his hand and Kevin followed suit. He'd noticed a flicker of fear in the guy's eyes, but that gave way to a disinterested yawn and a stretch.

"Either is fine. What's this about?" In an awkward gesture, he yanked off his hat, allowing his thick black curls to fall around his face.

"Jeremy," Mac said, "we want to assure you that you're not in any trouble or anything. We'd like to talk with you about a case we're working on."

"Sure, grab a seat," Jeremy flopped onto a sofa in a slouch, crossing his arms and yawning again.

"Did we wake you?" Kevin asked.

"Nah, just zoning—watching the tube."

"Hmm." Kevin sat at Jeremy's right and Mac took a seat on his left. "Like my partner said, you are not under arrest or anything like that. If you don't want to talk to us at any time, just say so and we'll get out of your hair. Okay?"

"Okay. So what's this about?"

"We're looking into your relationship with Jessica Turner right now. She's helping us with an investigation, and we thought you might have some information for us."

Mac caught Kevin's eye. *Smooth move.*

"Jess?" Jeremy came out of his slouch. "Is she in town?"

"Like I said, she's been very cooperative, and we're hoping you will be as well. We're looking into a situation involving Bradley Gaynes. Do you know him?"

"Yeah, I know Brad. We go back a ways." Jeremy folded his arms. "I'll tell you right up front, there's no love lost between Brad and me. I helped look for him when he went missing—more as a favor to Jessica. The guy just, you know, disappeared. Weird scene all the way around. I only know what Jessica told me."

"And what was that?" Kevin pressed.

Mac leaned back, suspecting Jeremy would be a weak interview—easy to manipulate and easy to catch in a lie.

"Just that Brad got rough with her and she broke it off with him. Guess he went for a walk and never came back. That's it, man; that's all I know."

"And when did she tell you this? Have you talked to her lately?"

"Sheesh, I wish. Jess went stone cold when she moved out. Went to live with some family members in California or something. I haven't talked to her since she left. Did you say she was in town?"

"No, I didn't say." Kevin made a note on his pad. "I heard mention of some letters you wrote to Jessica. Some letters that indicated you would like to be more than friends?"

"Did she show you those?"

Neither Kevin nor Mac answered.

After a moment, Jeremy said, "Yeah, I wrote a few letters. See, I used to ski with her and Brad. We would party at their place, have some drinks. Some of the guys smoked a little bud now and again." He shrugged. "A few went with crack."

"But you didn't?"

"Nah. I drink sometimes but never got into the drug scene. That stuff messes up your brain, you know what I mean?"

Mac nodded. Jeremy's answer surprised him.

"Jess didn't do drugs either," Jeremy went on. "She was okay with Brad doing dope for a while, but then she started getting on him. She wanted Brad to quit everything—the smoking, the drinking, the drugs. He didn't like her telling him what to do. Jess was really unhappy, and sometimes when everybody else was bombed, she'd tell me stuff."

"What kind of stuff?" Kevin settled back in the chair, obviously giving Jeremy some room.

"Personal stuff." Jeremy frowned. "Man, what do you need that for? I told you I don't know anything about Brad going missing."

Kevin sat forward. "Brad isn't missing anymore, Jeremy. He's lying in a freezer in the morgue. We pulled him out of the river two days ago."

"No way." Jeremy turned a pale shade of gray. "Is that why you guys are here? You think I had something to do with it? I swear I didn't. You gotta believe me."

"We don't 'gotta' do anything, Jeremy," Kevin said. "But I would love to eliminate you as a person who would have the means, opportunity, or intent to pull this off. Are you going to help me do that?"

"I'll do anything; just let me know what."

"Have you ever taken a polygraph test?"

Jeremy sighed. "Once, when I was accused of stealing money from work."

"How did that turn out?" Mac asked.

Jeremy shifted in his seat. "Well, I never actually finished the test. Before they were through with their questions, I admitted to taking out a loan."

Kevin glanced over at Mac, trying not to smile. "So, are you willing to take one again?"

"Sure, I'll take it right now. Hook me up."

"We'll have to make arrangements for that," Kevin said, "but we appreciate your cooperation. Tell me more about the letters to Jessica and your romantic interest in her. You were talking about sharing. She shared what, thoughts, emotions, body fluids? You tell me."

"I wish. We just talked. Jessica had a lot on her mind. For a while, after Brad disappeared, I tried to convince her to go out with me. She said she couldn't be with me because it would look bad. She said she was going to take some time in California and then come back, or I could go south if she found a good job. But like I said, she took off and I never heard from her again—no call, no letter." Jeremy dipped his head and examined a spot on his jeans.

"I see." Kevin looked at his notes, more for dramatic effect than anything else. "So tell me, Jeremy—just so I can understand correctly. You don't know anything about Brad's death, is that correct?"

"I swear on a stack of—"

"Don't say that, please. I don't want you regretting those words. A simple yes or no works fine with me."

"Okay, then—no."

"Good. Then it's safe to say you have nothing to hide."

"Right." He spread his hands. "Nothing."

"Good, very good. Tell me about that five-shot revolver you bought at the Expo."

He looked from one detective to the other, surprise registering on his features. "How'd you know about that?"

"Those forms you fill out and the electronic fingerprint imaging scan you used when you bought the gun."

Jeremy grinned. "Oh, yeah."

"Those records are maintained by our department, so I know what you bought and how much you paid."

"It's legal, right? I don't have any felonies on my record, so I can have a gun."

"Yeah, you're okay. I just don't want you going sideways on us. Tell us about the gun, Jeremy. Why did you buy it, and where is it now?"

"There's not much to tell. I bought it when I was with my dad at a gun show. He loaned me a little cash, and I'm paying him back. The gun is downstairs in my nightstand. You want me to get it?"

"Not right now. We'll get to that in a minute." Kevin looked Jeremy in the eye. "So why did you buy the gun—a .357 Smith, right?"

"Yeah, that's right. I've been working a little security up at the mountain at night, you know, watching over some of the ski-run grooming machines. Some guys were messing with their snow cats and other equipment, so they hired me to watch the yard at night. I make a few bucks, mainly get vouchers on some food and lift tickets. It gets a little spooky out there at night, so I decided to start carrying the gun with me."

"Do you have a concealed weapons permit?" Kevin asked.

"Um . . ." Jeremy winced. "No, but I should have, right? Are you going to take my gun?"

"We'd like to take your gun and run a couple of tests on it," Kevin said. "With your consent, of course. And I would be willing to forget about that permit thing if you're willing to help us out."

"Sure, but what kind of tests? Will it wreck the gun?"

"No, not at all. I just want to have one of our gun experts examine the gun. You'll have it back by week's end if it checks out okay. Then I suggest you get that permit."

"Sure, okay then. Do you want it now?"

"Mac will go with you to get it." Kevin motioned toward Mac.

Mac accompanied Jeremy downstairs to his living quarters and asked him to point out where the gun was stored. "Thanks, Jeremy. Now I'm going to ask you to stay right here while I get it, okay?"

"Whatever you say."

Mac retrieved the handgun from a bedside table and secured it before following Jeremy back upstairs. Once he was in better light, Mac opened the cylinder and extracted five hollow-point cartridges into his hand, rolling them around momentarily for his partner to see. When Kevin saw the hollow-point bullets atop the shiny aluminum casings, he raised an eyebrow. They were the same type of bullet found in their victim. The same caliber firearm.

"Any more guns in the house?" Mac asked.

"Lots. My dad has a gun safe in his bedroom." Jeremy glanced toward a closed door. "He's a big-time hunter."

"Could we take a look at those guns too?" Kevin asked.

"Sorry, I guess Dad isn't the trusting type. I don't have the combo."

"Any more .357s or .38s in the safe to your knowledge, Jeremy?"

"Dad carries a .357 Chief Special, just like mine. That's why I bought that one. I think he has some more handguns, and he has about five rifles for different game, but I'm not sure what caliber. He won't be back for a couple weeks, sorry."

"Will he be calling in while he's gone?"

"Probably. You'll have to ask Donna."

"We'll do that," Mac said.

"Will you be at this residence for a while, and can we contact you here?" Kevin asked.

"No immediate plans, and yeah, you can call me here."

Kevin jotted down the phone number, telling him they would be in touch about the gun and a polygraph examination. Mac gave Jeremy a business card. After talking briefly to Donna, the detectives left the residence. Donna promised to have her husband call them if and when he contacted her.

They then headed for the crime lab to meet with Wain Carver and his ballistics water tank.

26

"I THOUGHT YOU WERE DOWN SOUTH," Mac said to Philly as they entered the twelfth-floor crime lab entrance at the Justice Center.

"I heard you were trying to cut me out of the loop and thought I better get over here and make sure you and Gramps weren't messing things up." Philly gave them a look of almost genuine concern.

"Where's Russ?" Kevin ignored Philly's comments.

"Down on the first floor, sniffing around some latent-print tech he's been dating. He'll meet me down at the car when he's done slobbering all over the hall. I brought in some handwriting evidence for comparison from our caper in the valley and heard a uniform get the dispatch to hook a gun at the pawnbroker, told him I'd bring it down to the lab if he found it."

It took Mac a moment to realize the gun in question was the one Jessica had hawked. "Did he get the gun?" Mac asked.

"I'm here, aren't I?" Philly opened his briefcase and produced a stainless semiautomatic. The slide was locked back and a metal tag ran from the magazine well to the ejection port, a required safety mechanism if you wanted the lab to accept the evidence for testing.

"Looks like a 9 mm." Kevin eyed the weapon.

"Right on the money. One stainless steel finish, 9 mm Beretta. The gun had no magazine when the troop recovered it, so there are no cartridges to compare." Philly slid the gun on the evidence bar over to Mac. "No way that peashooter's going to throw enough lead to be confused with that magnum round, but you better run the test anyway. You never get lucky on the first gun. It'll take at least . . ."

Philly stopped midsentence when Kevin pulled out J. Z.'s revolver, dangling the prize in front of him. This gun had the same metal evidence tag through the open cylinder of the five-shot revolver.

"You would get lucky, Bledsoe. Where'd you skin that hog's leg?"

"Off a punk who was making time with our vic's girlfriend," Mac answered.

Kevin gave Mac a glance of disapproval. *It's okay to talk with Philly without talking like Philly.*

"You're kidding me," Philly said. "I bet that's your weapon right there. Means and motive, huh?"

"We shall soon see." Kevin scanned the floor for the firearms expert. "Is Wain available?"

"Yeah, he's around. I already asked for him. The receptionist said he'd be right up."

"You guys all wrapped up on that murder-for-hire business?" Mac asked.

"All the brainwork's done, so Sarge cut me loose; the valley boys can clean up the rest. Man, that was one slick piece of work on our part. You guys should have seen this broad when Eric showed her the picture of her 'dead' husband." Philly made the quote marks with his fingers. "She laughed and said she hoped he suffered big-time. Then she cut Eric a check for another ten grand. The husband was sitting in the next hotel room with Russ, listening in the wire. I thought he was going to stroke out right there he was so angry. Eric gave the arrest signal over the mic, right? Then we walked in with the husband and pinched her for conspiracy to commit murder. Her jaw almost hit the ground when she saw her husband." Philly laughed. "She started yellin' she wanted Eric arrested for fraud. I almost split a gut watching the whole thing. This gal was a real beaut."

"Is she in custody now?" Mac asked.

"At Clackamas County jail as we speak. Sarge has been on the phone with the district attorney, trying to go over the evidence for the grand jury. The woman tried to hire a high-powered attorney, but her husband pulled the plug on the funds. This is going to be one for the books when she's convicted. Sarge thinks she'll pull an insanity plea."

"What was her motive, insurance money?" Mac leaned against the counter.

"That may have been part of it, but I think her friend, the pool boy, also had something to do with it. According to the guys on surveillance, she had the cleanest pool on the block, if you know what I mean. That pool guy was showing up at the door the minute the husband took off for work. I guess she was looking to trade in her old man for a newer model."

"Did the pool guy have anything to do with the wife's plan?" Kevin asked.

"Nope—the guy had other clients to service, I guess. He never missed a beat."

Kevin looked over the evidence submittal counter as the clerk sat back down and pulled her chair up to her desk. "Wain's on his way up now," she said without looking at the detectives, as she answered the phone.

"What about this handwriting exemplar?" Philly asked.

"What about it?" The clerk sighed. "I'll log it in when I'm ready, Phil. Just keep your shorts on."

The ballistics expert walked around the corner, the tails of his white lab coat whipping as he motioned for Mac and Kevin to come back. Philly snorted a complaint as the two men shuffled past, obviously upset Kevin and Mac were receiving service before him. "It will be today, won't it, Wanda, when you get around to logging in this evidence? Logging in this single sheet of paper?"

"I just thought of something else I need to do first." The clerk winked at Mac as she stood up and walked away from the desk. Philly tapped his fingers on the counter. "I'll get you for this."

"Come on in, guys—the door's open." Wain went right to his microscope. Kevin and Mac entered the cluttered but organized room. Mac placed the revolver and pistol on a clean spot on the table.

"Sorry I'm late. I needed to run a quick check on a gun barrel for Medford Police Department. That should do it." Wain placed the four-inch barrel from a semiautomatic in a plastic evidence bag and spun around on his stool. "What have you brought me?"

Mac motioned to the handguns on the examination table.

"These are on the bullet that killed Brad Gaynes?" Wain asked.

"Right."

"Are we worried about prints on these guys?" Wain slipped on a pair of rubber gloves.

"No, just bullet and barrel comparison. We already know who owns them; they have legit reasons for latents already."

"Good." He picked up the 9 mm gun first. "This one's no good, no way, not large enough caliber. I'll shoot the barrel so we get a bullet into IBIS, but this isn't the gun that put the bullet into your victim. But that's not to say the gun didn't put a bullet into someone else, so we'll get a sample. Any ammunition for either weapon?"

"Not on the nine," Mac answered, "but the Smith had these with the gun. The kid had the rounds in the revolver, stored in his nightstand drawer." Mac handed the examiner five cartridges.

"Humph. These look like cheap factory rounds."

That fit with Jeremy's persona. Mac didn't peg him as a gun collector. Most gun nuts preferred hand loads instead of cartridges purchased over the counter. That didn't mean Jeremy hadn't done any hand loading. Especially since his father seemed to be into guns big-time.

"These aren't the same bullet, but we'll see if the gun is a match." Wain removed the metal evidence clip from the cylinder, then he removed the cylinder from the gun. He placed a small fiberoptics camera at the end of the barrel, projecting the view on his big-screen monitor that amplified the view hundreds of times. "She's a real Smith and Wesson barrel, got the right twist direction for our suspect bullet. Let's take a spin through the water tank; this guy is looking good so far."

Mac looked over at Kevin, trying to conceal his excitement. Kevin had been disappointed far too many times to share Mac's enthusiasm.

"You guys mind waiting around the corner?" Wain nodded toward the opening. "I'm going to put a couple rounds into the water." Mac and Kevin walked out of the exam room to a small hallway that led to a storage closet. Through the Plexiglas wall, they watched Wain assemble the cylinder into the frame and dry fire the gun several times into a Kevlar box. Satisfied the gun was operating properly, he loaded a single cartridge into the cylinder and secured the gun into a contraption that looked like a cement mixer with a rifle rack mounted at the opening. After securing the gun, Wain put on a pair of safety glasses and ear muffs, then he closed the door to the soundproof room and slipped a ballistic vest onto his torso.

"He doesn't take any chances, does he?" Mac tipped his head toward Kevin.

"You can't afford to in this business," Kevin said. "Wain has probably investigated every type of weird shooting accident known to man."

Wain signaled for the detectives to stick their fingers in their ears, which they both did on cue. With a thumbs-up from Wain and a nod from Mac and Kevin, the examiner pulled the trigger.

The revolver erupted, firing a single round into the water tank. He removed his ear protection and immediately opened the cylinder of the gun to allow the hot gasses a chance to escape without going down the barrel and potentially altering the pattern on the subsequent test fire. Wain fished the bullet from the tank. After slipping on his ear protection, he repeated the process a second time.

Mac and Kevin returned to the room while Wain dried both bullets and placed them on his microscope bench. "We'll give them a second to totally dry under the light then take a look at them and see how they match up."

"Any guesses with the naked eye?" Mac asked.

"Sorry, no guesswork in here. Too many variables."

"Hmm. I hope you don't mind asking, but why fire two rounds for testing?"

Wain smiled up at him. "Don't mind at all, Mac. If we make a match, the defense will ask for a test sample to use at a private lab. With two samples, we can't lose our only test piece. We can supply them their own for some hack to destroy in his lab."

Mac suppressed a grin at Wain's obvious disdain.

Wain tapped on his computer keyboard, bringing up a split-screen image on the large monitor. On the right was a large-scale view of the bullet pulled from the victim, looking as big as a loaf of bread on the magnified screen. "See these striations in-between the lands and grooves?" Wain pointed to the screen. "These little beauties will make or break the case for us. Let's take a look at the first test fire." Wain slipped the first bullet under the scope, displaying the familiar licorice twist shape on the big screen. He manipulated the bullet on the test tray with a large pair of tweezers until the grooves lined up on the split screen. Wain rotated the bullet for several moments before setting down the tweezers and crossing his arms.

Mac felt his earlier excitement drain away.

"Sorry, guys. That's not our gun." Wain confirmed what Mac already observed. "Our suspect bullet has deeper grooves and sharper land ridges. None of the scarring is the same either. You guys are going to have to keep on searching. I'll run the bullets through IBIS with the 9 mm, but I won't need the guns after today."

"I should have known it wouldn't be this easy." Kevin sighed. "Looks like Jeremy's off the hook—at least where this weapon is concerned."

"Yeah." Mac examined the bullets on the screen. "But we've still got his dad's stash. Maybe Jeremy wasn't being honest with us when he said he couldn't get to his dad's guns."

"Could be."

"Say, didn't Donna say Jeremy's dad was a truckdriver?"

"You thinking maybe there's a link?"

"Well, Jessica did report seeing a trucker. It's a reach, but . . ."

Kevin chuckled. "Stranger things have happened. We may have to obtain a search warrant to get those guns ASAP."

"Ha, what'd I tell you?" The loud voice startled Mac, and he turned to find Philly poking his head in the door.

"You said we probably had the gun."

Philly slapped Mac on the back. "No, I didn't. I said, you never get the gun on the first try. Guess it's back to the drawing board, ladies."

27

TWO DAYS LATER, Mac attacked his pile of paperwork with the same vengeance the squirrel outside his office window was attacking the feeder on the large oak.

"I wish the patrol troops would quit feeding those things," he muttered to himself. "They're getting aggressive." The squirrel ran back down the tree with his prize, two filberts stuffed in his inflated cheeks.

The past two days had been exhausting. Mac and Kevin had interviewed almost all of Brad's friends and coworkers. They'd gained nothing more than speculation, and Vicki and Todd Gaynes were getting impatient for results. Mac was backed up on reports and needed a little time to himself. He was down eleven interview reports. Bad, but it could be worse. Fortunately for him, Philly, Russ, and Kevin had done some of the interviews. Even Dana had helped out on several contacts. Of course, she had somehow managed to get all her reports in the next day.

She's got to be doing these things at home on her own time, Mac thought as he peered at the neat stack of paperwork Dana had left for him to review. Her home phone number was at the end of her note, asking for advice on her work. Maybe she should be mentoring him—at least when it came to writing reports.

"Detective McAllister, line 101," the receptionist's voice came across the office intercom.

Mac forced his gaze away from the window and picked up the phone. "This is McAllister."

"Um, Detective, this is Jessica. Jessica Turner from California."

"Yes, Jessica." Mac fumbled for his tape recorder and plugged it into his special phone adapter. *Shoot, no fresh tape.* "How are you doing?" He stood to rifle through his drawers, looking for a new mini cassette tape. *There are dozens of these things lying around until you need one.*

"I've been better, I guess. Anyway, I'm at the Amtrak station. I lost your number and had to call information."

"You're at the station now? Right now in Portland?" Mac paused, his hand still in the top drawer. He could hardly believe it.

"In the flesh. You still want to talk to me?"

"You bet." Mac worked at getting his tone in the normal range. He didn't want to give her the impression that he was anything but calm and efficient. "Where exactly are you? I'll come pick you up, if that's still okay."

"Sure. That's cool. To be honest, I just want to get this whole thing over with. I'm wearing a black Adidas sweat suit. I'll meet you in the big lobby area by the big indoor tree."

"I know the spot. I'll be there in about twenty minutes." Jessica ended the call without a good-bye.

Mac grabbed his jacket off his chair and jogged down the hall, looking for Kevin. After checking the patrol and wildlife offices, he asked one of the reception staff to page Kevin over the intercom. Moments later, a narcotics detective popped his head out in the hall and told Mac he recently saw Kevin going for coffee with the region captain.

Region captain? I'll have to page him on the way. Mac double-timed it out to his car and sped out of the parking lot, asking dispatch to send Kevin an alpha page to meet him at the office in thirty minutes. He took Burnside Street east across the Willamette River into Portland's Old Town, heading north to Union Station. Mac parked in the loading zone, draping his raid jacket over the steering wheel in case the Portland Police Bureau officers were in the neighborhood and thought about towing his car. He adjusted his tie and walked briskly into the depot. Mac saw Jessica almost immediately in her black Adidas knit pants and hooded jacket. She waved and stood up.

His jaw dropped and his eyes widened in disbelief. He was glad she'd told him what she was wearing because he'd never have recognized her. He gathered his wits and tried to greet the woman with some kind of normalcy. When he'd seen her at the waterfall she'd looked like a waif—no makeup, blotchy cheeks, swollen eyes. Her hair had been damp and stringy.

Now her face glowed, and her hair was clean and shiny, swept up in a ponytail. But it wasn't Jessica's attractiveness that caught Mac's attention.

She laughed at his discomfort. "What's the matter, Mac? You've never seen a pregnant woman?"

He grinned, relaxing a little. "I just didn't expect . . ."

She nodded. "Bradley Junior is part of the reason I decided to come up here."

"So this is Brad's baby?"

"Of course. I think Brad's family needs to know the whole story. I probably should have been more up-front with them in the beginning, but they were treating me so awful."

Mac rubbed his chin. He didn't want to get too much information without Kevin there or without his tape recorder. "Can't say I blame you. They were a bit cool."

"Well, I've had a lot of time to think, and Aaron—my boyfriend—thought I should come up and clear the air. He's such a neat guy. He wants little Brad to know his real grandma and grandpa."

"I'm anxious to hear all about it, but we need to get going. My partner and I want to get a statement from you, and it's better if we do that at the office."

"Are you arresting me?"

"No." Mac smiled. "We just want to talk with you."

"And record my statement, right?" She swung a bag over her shoulder and started to pick up a larger duffle bag. "You don't have to worry, Mac. I said I'd cooperate, and I will."

"I'll get that for you." Mac scooped up the bag. "Anything else?"

"I travel light. I probably won't be in town long. I understand Brad's funeral is tomorrow?"

"As far as I know. The body has already been cremated and the ashes scattered. I think they are calling it a life celebration—something like that." Mac wasn't into that sort of thing, and apparently neither was Jessica.

"Sounds weird." She bit the corner of her lip.

Mac shrugged. "People deal with loss in their own way."

"I guess."

"All set?" Mac asked.

"Yeah. I already called the people I'm staying with. Will we be done by two or so? I told them that was my best guess."

"Oh, I'm sure we will." *Unless you are under arrest.* "We can head on over to my office and meet up with my partner. Like I said, we need to take a formal statement from you for the official record, so we can put that requirement to rest."

"Am I a suspect, Mac? Do I need to contact a lawyer?" Jessica asked as they headed for the car. "The friend I'm staying with told me not to talk to you without a lawyer."

"Is that friend by any chance Jeremy Zimmerman?" Mac went on the offensive to defer the question.

"Jeremy? How do you know about him?"

"We've questioned most of the people you and Brad hung out with."

She nodded. "So do I need a lawyer? I'm sure Vicki and Todd have filled your case file with their speculations and suspicions about my actions."

"Actually Jessica, the Gayneses have been very cooperative during this difficult time. They just have a great deal of love for their son and a lot of unanswered questions that must be driving them insane. The last time they spoke to me, they welcomed the idea of your coming to the funeral. They know how much you apparently meant to Brad and wanted to respect what he would have wanted."

"Really?" Her face brightened.

"Yes."

"I'm sorry if I sounded rude. I'm feeling pretty stressed out about seeing them again. Especially since Brad was killed and . . ." Jessica glanced down at her rounded abdomen.

Mac tossed Jessica's bag in the trunk and opened the passenger side door for her.

She slid in and waited for Mac to close the door before putting on her seat belt.

Interesting turn of events. Mac removed his jacket from the steering wheel and folded himself in.

"Back to your question, Jessica. I don't know if you need a lawyer; only you know that. We just need to ask you some questions. As far as we know, you were the last person to see Brad alive. To be honest with you, our interview may take more than two hours. I was hoping you would accompany us back to the falls and show us exactly where Brad walked and where you had the run-in with the truckdriver. You are not under arrest, and I have no intention of arresting you with what I know right now. You are free to leave, or I'll take you anywhere you want to go. All my cards are on the table—no secrets, no surprises. So what's it going to be?"

Jessica looked out the window; it had begun to rain. The chemicals the office fleet manager put on the officers' car windows made the water streak down the glass with amazing speed, to allow for a clean windshield while on patrol in the rain.

"Like water off a duck's back, huh?"

"What?" Mac frowned at her odd comment.

Jessica smiled. "What makes the water on the windshield shoot down like that?"

"Some spray our car guy puts on them. I don't even have to use my windshield wipers in the rain. At freeway speeds you wouldn't even know it was raining."

She chuckled. "Okay, let's do this. Anyone nerdy enough to put rain chemicals on his car windows seems harmless enough."

"Ouch. Nerd, huh?" Mac smiled back as he looked over his left shoulder to back out into the parking lot. Although he'd turned away from Jessica, he could sense her studying him. As discreetly as possible, he touched his gun with his right elbow, bracing himself should the need arise. She looked and acted harmless enough, but you just couldn't tell.

Mac took the freeway back to the office. Portland, the City of Roses, has also been called the City of Bridges. Scores of bridges cross the Willamette River that divides the city, running from the south to northern confluence with the Columbia River. Mac occasionally still got the names of the bridges mixed up, even though he had crossed them countless times.

He and Jessica arrived at the Portland patrol office in less than fifteen minutes. Kevin's car was in the back lot. Kevin, a perpetual passenger, didn't care much for driving—probably due to the years on uniform patrol, where it was not uncommon to drive two or three hundred miles in a shift. Mac thought about the poor guy who would inherit Kevin's car when he retired. The car would be fifteen years old before it had enough miles to turn in to the fleet manager for a new one. Only Sergeant Evans's Caprice was older and uglier. Seeing his partner's car reminded him of Kevin's odd behavior of late. *Why was Kevin hanging out with the brass? Was he discussing retirement?*

"Here we go," Mac said to Jessica. "Let's go inside, and I'll introduce you to my partner." She held her bag close to her chest.

"Anything in the bag I need to be concerned about?" Mac asked. "You seem awfully attached to it."

"No, just my things." She loosened her grip. "I guess I'm kind of nervous."

"Before we go inside, do you mind if I take a look? You know, just to put my mind at ease to make sure there's nothing in there that will hurt me."

"Do I have to? I mean, there's no gun or anything."

Mac noticed Dana's patrol car in the parking lot, recognizing the stuffed teddy bear she kept on top of her dash-mounted radar. "Would it be okay if a female trooper looked in the bag, just as a precaution?"

"Sure." She glanced down at the asphalt. "I guess that would be okay."

Mac opened the back door to the office after punching in the keypad code, leading Jessica into the patrol briefing room. Fortunately, Dana was nearby. "Dana, this is Jessica—you remember, Brad Gaynes's girlfriend."

Dana smiled and reached out her hand. "Hi, Jessica. Of course I remember you."

"Jessica is here for an interview," Mac said, "and I wonder if you'd look through her things before we go in."

"Sure." Turning to Jessica, Dana said, "Come with me. And don't look so worried. It's standard procedure."

Moments later, Dana came out of the briefing room with Jessica and directed her to the women's restroom.

"Anything in the bag?"

"Nothing dangerous, Mac. I think she's just frightened, but I'm doing a personal search just to make sure."

"Thanks. Would you bring her down to the back room when you're done?"

"You got it. Need some help with the investigation?" Dana looked hopeful.

"Not right now, but thanks." Mac hesitated. "By the way, you did a great job on those reports; they're first-rate."

"Thanks." Dana grinned, then followed Jessica into the bathroom.

Mac took the stairs down to his office and met with Kevin. They agreed to ask Jessica to accompany them to Wah-kella Falls right off the bat, getting her version of events while en route. Mac had already established a rapport, so he would ride in the back of the car with Jessica while Kevin drove. This would probably be their only shot at a complete interview with her. Even if she wasn't the one who pulled the trigger, she might know who did.

Mac thought about the case Philly told him about where the wife paid to have her husband killed. Somehow he couldn't visualize Jessica killing anyone, but he'd learned the hard way that you couldn't always trust your impressions.

"Here we are," Dana said as she and Jessica entered the detectives' office. "All clear."

Dana lingered for just a moment. "If you guys don't need me for anything else, I'm off to hit the road and patrol."

"Thanks." Mac turned his attention to Jessica as Dana left the room.

"I told you there wasn't anything in my bag." Jessica looked from Mac to Kevin.

"I'm sorry about that. We have to be careful."

"So." She sank into a nearby chair and looked at Kevin. "Are you Mac's partner?"

Kevin nodded and shook her hand. "Detective Bledsoe. You can call me Kevin."

The older detective gave Mac a stern look. "Mac, can I see you for a minute?" Then turning to Jessica, he said, "We'll be right back."

Once they were out of earshot, Kevin stopped Mac. "Why didn't you tell me she was pregnant?"

"I didn't have a chance. It took me by surprise too."

Kevin ran a hand through his graying hair. "She looks to be about five, six months along, which means the baby is probably Brad's."

"Yeah. That's what she said."

Kevin drew in a deep breath and let it out. "Okay, here's the deal. I think we should try to set up a poly and get her statement first, then depending on the results, take her out to Wah-kella and see if she has anything to add. I don't want her hiking up the trail. It won't serve any purpose that I can see, and we don't want any complications down the road."

Mac agreed. "I guess I was looking at that case up at Ecola State Park. The detectives took their suspect up the trail and actually got a confession."

"I'm not saying it isn't a good idea, but let's take first things first."

"Right."

The men walked back into Mac's office. Jessica was gone.

28

Mac had a moment's panic until he found Jessica in the break room with Philly, who was handing her a cup of hot water. Jessica looked up at Mac and smiled. "Philly asked me if I wanted something to drink. Tea sounded good."

"Great." Mac didn't know whether to hug the big detective or hit him.

"Always willing to help a lady in distress." Philly left the room armed with a large mug of coffee for himself.

Mac shook his head and grabbed a cup of coffee for himself. "Help yourself to a donut, Jessica."

"No thanks. I have to eat a nutritious diet for my baby."

"Good. That's good." Mac ushered her back to his cubicle. He had to side with Todd and Kip on their impression of Jessica. She seemed like an okay gal. Maybe she was a victim in all this as well.

"Where's your partner?" she asked as she took the chair she'd been sitting in moments before.

"Kevin went to see about scheduling a polygraph test while you're here. It will save you a trip. He should be back in a minute and we can get started."

Kevin came in before Mac finished the sentence. "Sarge is arranging for an exam at the Portland office this afternoon."

While they waited, Mac and Kevin sealed Jessica's interview by getting it on tape. There were no real changes other than the addition of her wanting Brad to make some changes. "I told him I was pregnant. He got upset and said he wasn't ready to be a father. I told him I was keeping the baby no matter what he decided to do. All I wanted was for him to stop drinking and doing drugs. He wasn't willing to do that for me or for the baby. I couldn't marry him under those conditions, and I told him so." Jessica sighed. "I know it looks strange. I mean—I guess I was the last one to see him."

"Jessica," Mac began, "I have to ask, why were you so standoffish when everyone was out looking for Brad? You didn't help with the search, and you didn't seem interested."

"I was mad at him. I thought maybe he'd walked out on me. And I had morning sickness really bad. I had to stay close to the bathroom."

"Why didn't you tell anyone—primarily Brad's parents—about your pregnancy?" Mac asked for the tape.

"Like I told you earlier, I was angry. They were treating me like I'd done something to him. Vicki and Rachael treated me as if I were a lowlife. They never took the time to get to know me."

"That must have been hard on you. Did you ever want to get back at them?"

"No. I just wanted to get away. That's why I left for California so soon after Brad disappeared. I'd had it with the calls and the dirty looks. Besides, I figured if Brad had left me, there was no point in my hanging around."

"Did you ever wonder if he'd been hurt?"

"Yes. I worried that the trucker had gone after him."

"You mentioned to Deputy Wyatt that you thought he might have killed himself or fallen."

"I didn't know what to say. I had no idea what had happened to him. Brad liked the legend of the falls, so I said that. Later on I

260 Patricia H. Rushford and Harrison James

wondered about a hunting accident, but then no body was found, and I really did think he'd run off somewhere." She frowned. "I never heard a gunshot. But then I had fallen asleep for a while . . ."

Mac nodded. "Thinking back on it now, Jessica, would you tell us what you think happened?"

She shook her head, tears gathering in her eyes. "I have no idea. All I know is that my baby's father didn't want him." She looked out the window at the squirrels.

"Do you know anyone who might have wanted Brad dead?"

"No. I can't think of a soul. People loved Brad. They didn't know him like I did. I loved him too—even when he drank and . . ."

Kevin handed her a tissue.

"Thank you."

"Jeremy told us that Brad hit you." Mac watched her face.

"A few times." She turned to look at him. "I know this probably sounds terrible, but I'm glad I'm not with Brad anymore." She caught Mac's raised eyebrows. "I'm not glad he's dead," she quickly amended. "But I'm happy now. I have a boyfriend who loves me and who's clean. I met him at church and . . ."

"Church?" Mac leaned back. "Vicki told us that you refused to attend church with Brad."

"I wasn't into it then. See, Brad was a hypocrite in a lot of ways. He pretended to be this nice Christian guy around his parents and his sister, but he didn't practice what he preached." She shrugged. "Aaron does. I wish you could meet him."

At noon they ordered deli sandwiches and drinks for themselves and Jessica. By one o'clock, they had her in with the polygraph detective from Salem. After back-to-back exams, Detective Matt Manza showed Mac and Kevin his findings.

"I think she's telling the truth, guys. She has no knowledge of Brad's murder."

"Nothing at all?" Mac asked. He didn't really want the pregnant woman to be guilty of murder, but he wanted the investigation to be over. And Jessica was their best source for finding the killer.

"There was a hang-up on one question," Detective Manza said, looking through the one-way glass in the interview office at Jessica, who brushed her hair behind her ears. "When I asked, 'Are you in any way responsible for Brad's death?' Jessica provided an affirmative response, which deemed to be truthful."

Mac frowned. "But . . .?"

"She explained later that she felt their argument and failed relationship contributed in some way to his disappearance and eventual death. She's feeling guilty, which under the circumstances is entirely normal."

"Okay." Mac took the preliminary results from Detective Manza and shook his hand.

"I'll get the formal results to you in a day or two," Manza said.

Mac nodded. "Right. Thanks for coming on such short notice."

"Not a problem. You guys take care."

Mac quickly looked over the results, then he and Kevin wrapped up their interview with Jessica, deciding not to take her to the falls at this point. They did, however, have her fingerprinted and mugged for comparison standards, as she had no criminal record. This was a precaution in case she became less than cooperative down the road.

"Where can we drop you off, Jessica?" Mac asked when they got to the car. "Jeremy's place?" Kevin took the driver's seat as he and Mac had agreed, while Mac joined Jessica in the backseat.

"Jeremy's?" She frowned. "Why would you think I'd be staying there?" She dug into her purse and fished out a piece of paper with an address on it. "I'm staying with Aaron's sister and her family."

"I'm sorry for the assumption. Jeremy indicated the two of you were friends."

She laughed. "'Friends' is the operative word, Detective. I know he would have liked us to be together, but he isn't my type. Besides, I really don't have much contact with the old gang."

"It's just as well." Mac told her about the firearm they'd recovered from Jeremy's house. Jessica didn't seem surprised. "And just so you know," Mac continued, "the property you had in the pawnshop has been seized."

"So I don't have to pay to get it out?"

"Not at this point."

"What will happen to it?"

"Since we signed for the gun," Mac explained, "we'll have to make sure the pawnbroker is reimbursed what he paid you for the gun. You or Vicki and Todd can pay the store or allow us to return the gun; the broker just won't make any money off the exchange."

"I'll pay for it." She sighed. "Why did you take the stuff—because of the gun?"

"Primarily yes. But it's all being processed for trace evidence by our lab."

"Huh—like they do on that CSI show?"

"Yeah." Mac smiled. "Like that."

"I'm glad I took the lie-detector test." Jessica watched the street signs. "I did okay, huh?"

"You did." Jessica seemed more relaxed now, and Mac could see more of her personality. Warm and kind, with a nice sense of humor. Opposite of the time he'd first met her.

Aaron's sister, April, met them in the driveway and enveloped Jessica in a welcoming hug. Apparently the two hadn't met face to face. April asked Mac and Kevin to come in, but they declined.

"That was interesting," Mac said once he and Kevin were on the road again.

"Jessica seems like a sweet girl."

"Yeah. Different than when I first met her."

"Maybe not so different," Kevin said. "Maybe different circumstances. The kid's been through a lot, and you have to admire how she's gotten her life together."

"You mean the church thing?"

Kevin chuckled. "That's part of it."

Mac laughed. "I'll remember that. All I have to do to get on the good side of you is tell you I'm going to church."

"Would you be telling the truth?" Kevin asked in a hopeful tone.

"Nope. I tried going to those counseling sessions with Linda and . . ." He frowned. "Well, you know about that. It didn't work out so well." Mac had told him awhile back how the pastor and Linda had basically ganged up on him.

"I'm sorry about that, Mac, but don't base your decisions on the actions of a few. Not all pastors are equipped to counsel people. Seems to me he should have been neutral and not taken sides."

"Yeah, well, that episode of my life is over."

"You sound bitter."

"Maybe I am—a little. I really tried to make it work." But had he? Linda wanted phone calls. He could have given her more of those. He didn't much like the idea of quitting.

"It wouldn't have worked, Mac. Not very many women can deal with the life we lead, the work we do. They might say they understand, but they don't—not really."

"So what do you think about Jessica?" Mac asked, wanting to change the subject. "Was it wise for me to turn her loose?"

"I would have. I know it's tough to give up your best lead, but something will shake loose if we keep dogging it. Don't lose faith, partner."

"I just hope I made the right call." Mac yawned.

"You made the decision—a very hard decision, which I happen to support. We had nothing to hold her on, and you followed your gut instincts. Without that, you wouldn't be worth a plug nickel as a major case detective. You have to follow your heart, Mac. And rest assured, I would have said something if I had any problem with the call. This thing is going as well as can be expected, and the family will have to understand that. There isn't a detective in the back room who doesn't support Sarge's decision to give you the lead rope."

Mac swallowed hard and managed to say, "Thanks, Kev. I appreciate that."

"You been getting much rest?" Kevin glanced over at Mac, pushing at his shoulder.

"Some, why?"

"Not that I'm concerned; I'm just tired of driving," Kevin teased, effectively changing the mood. He pressed his back against the seat, stretching his legs.

"I'll bet. It's been what, almost half a day now?" Mac chuckled. "Seriously, I'm doing okay."

"I think it's time you worked a short day, Mac. You've been burning the candle at both ends for months now."

"A short day sounds good. A day off sounds even better." Mac folded his arms and focused on the car in front of them. "But I can't. I'm up to my eyeballs in reports. Sarge is going to have me in the blue room like Philly if I don't have them on his desk soon. The late reports were in my last evaluation, remember?"

"Tell you what. Why don't we both knock off early? I'll give you a hand in the morning and we'll get them wrapped up by noon. What do you say?"

"Sounds like a plan, partner," Mac yawned his response. "Say, what was the deal with the captain today?"

"What, coffee with John?"

"Yeah. Are you bucking for promotion or something?"

"Please, I want to work for a living. John and I came on

together; we're both eligible this spring and were comparing retirement plans. We may joke about the brass, but I would have certainly gone for that promotion if I'd thought about retirement twenty years ago. John will pull about a thousand more a month in retirement than me."

Mac whistled. "Yeah, but with his job, you'd have to work sixty-hour weeks and live by the pager all day every day."

"And that's different than our job?" Kevin eased the car around the corner. "You better get ready, the pressure is going to come for you to promote someday. The captain already asked if I thought you might be interested. They test next summer, you know."

"Sergeant McAllister." Mac grinned. "Has a nice ring to it. But, I don't know—we'll see when the time comes. This place won't be the same without you around. Depends what kind of partner I get strapped with."

"What if it's Dana? I'll bet you'd stick around for that."

"I might." Mac laughed out loud. "She'll be good, Kev. In fact, much as I'd hate to admit it, she'd probably already have this investigation wrapped up."

"Don't sell yourself short." Kevin pulled into the back lot of the patrol office and pulled up behind Mac's car. He sighed. "I'm not even going into the office."

Mac sat there a moment. "Kevin, can I ask you something?"

"Sure. What's troubling you?"

"You," Mac ventured. "I know something is going on, and I don't have a good feeling about it."

"You're right, Mac. Something is going on."

"But you're not going to tell me?"

"I was going to wait until morning. Planned to tell all of you together."

"All of us." Mac frowned. "As in Russ and Philly and Eric and . . ."

"And you. My friends, Mac."

"So you are retiring?"

"No, Mac. Not unless I'm forced to." Kevin paused. "There's no easy way to say it. I have cancer."

29

MAC SAT IN STUNNED DISBELIEF, his head reverberating with Kevin's announcement. "That can't be." Mac finally found his voice.

"That was my reaction at first. I've suspected it for a while. My wife finally made me go in a couple of weeks ago, and the doc ran a bunch of tests. I have prostate cancer."

"Why didn't you tell us sooner?"

"Guess I didn't want to say it out loud. Talking about it made it too real." Kevin ran a hand through his hair and rubbed the back of his neck. "I'll be starting chemo next week, so I thought I'd better let you all know so you and Philly wouldn't start teasing me about losing my hair." He offered a tense smile.

SOMEHOW Mac managed to say good-bye to Kevin and get into his car. Robotlike, he turned the key, belted himself in, and headed out, following his partner as they drove toward the freeway. Mac honked and waved as he went north on I-205 and Kevin took the opposite ramp to the south.

Cancer.

Mac would never have come up with that scenario. Not in a million years. Even having heard it from Kevin's own mouth, he still couldn't believe he'd heard right. Shock followed him all the way home and came inside with him. Mac took off his shoes and turned on his gas fireplace, then settled into his chair. Lucy, Mac's golden retriever, seemed to sense something was wrong and curled up at Mac's feet, occasionally putting her head on Mac's lap.

"What's a matter, old girl—you worried about me?" Lucy's big brown eyes stared lovingly back at him. Mac rubbed the dog's ears and scratched her head. Lucy placed her right paw on Mac's left forearm to make sure the cuddling didn't end anytime soon. Mac rested his hand on the dog's head, stroking her silky fur.

"Why Kevin, God?" he murmured, his gaze fixed on the fake log. "It isn't fair. Kevin is one of the good guys. He even believes in you and in those prayers he says. How could you let this happen to him?"

Mac remembered what Kevin had told him about the rain falling on the just and the unjust. How the world was in a mess and bad things happened. *The important question isn't why, but how,* Mac remembered Kevin saying. *"How can I be a better person because of what has happened?"*

God will turn your mourning into joy. Mac wasn't certain where that thought had come from, but he recognized it as a Bible verse he'd memorized as a child. He tipped his head back, wishing he were still at work. Maybe he'd go back over to the office and work through the night.

He closed his eyes and within seconds felt himself drift off.

MAC AWOKE AT SEVEN P.M., feeling hungry and at odds. He didn't want to go out to eat but hadn't bought any groceries either. He thought about calling Dana, but he didn't think he could hang out with her for very long before she figured out something was wrong. Dana tended to be very perceptive. He didn't want to talk about Kevin. Instead, he decided to drive to the retirement inn to visit his grandmother.

As usual, Nana welcomed him with open arms and listened intently as he brought her up to date on everything that had happened in his personal life during the last two weeks.

"You look so sad, Antonio. Because of Linda?"

"A little, mostly about my partner." He told Nana about Kevin's diagnosis and got about fifteen minutes' worth of people he should talk to. "Half the people here have had cancer. There are so many options. You tell Kevin to come see me. I'll introduce him to some survivors." She smiled and patted his arm. "I know it's a hard word to hear, but your friend will come out of this. You'll see."

"I wish I had your faith."

"You do, Antonio. It's all inside you. All you have to do is admit it."

Mac hung around until eight-thirty, when Nana's eyes began to droop. "I should go."

"Don't wait so long next time." She kissed his cheek and gave him the usual hug.

"I won't."

"And bring Kevin."

"I'll try."

Driving home, Mac had to smile at the irony. He visited Nana to cheer her up, but nearly every time he went, it was he who ended up feeling better.

"YOU GOTTA BE KIDDING ME." Mac glanced at the nightstand alarm clock. Two o' clock in the morning. The audible tone on his pager went silent after three choruses. Mac leaned over and pressed the readout button on the digital pager, squinting to read the alpha message.

The page from dispatch read, TROOPER DOWNEY REQUESTS 12-4 AT TROUTDALE P.D. ASAP.

"Now what?" he grumbled. "Probably a car full of stolen property, and they want me to write the warrant again."

Mac reached for the phone, calling dispatch to have them patch him through to Troutdale. No sense in spending his dime on the call; it was long distance from his place.

"State police dispatch. Is this an emergency?" the dispatcher answered.

"This is Detective McAllister out of Portland. The supervisor sent me a page to call a troop at Troutdale. Would you patch me through, please?"

"I think the desk supervisor wanted to talk to you when you called in. Hold on a sec, and I'll transfer you."

"Who's the . . ." Mac stopped, realizing she'd already put him on hold.

"Is this Mac?" a woman asked.

"Yeah. I was paged to call TPD."

"Hi, Mac; this is Sue. Trooper Downey called a few minutes ago and said he needs you to respond to TPD instead of calling. He said it is important, related to the twelve-forty-nine Adam you are working."

"The murder case? Really? Did he say how it was related?" Mac was suddenly wide awake.

"Nope. He arrested a DUII out on Highway 30 just after 1:00 A.M. and went to the PD for a breath test when he called in. He said he wanted a call from you, then he said he couldn't talk and wanted you to respond ASAP."

"Okay, I'm en route. My ETA is about thirty. Would you alpha page eleven-fifty? Tell Sergeant Evans I'm out and about. I'll have my cell on if he has questions, though you know what I know at this point."

"Will do, Mac. Take care." The dispatch supervisor ended the call.

I wonder what this is all about. Mac slipped into his jeans and running shoes, grabbing his Glock and cuffs off the top of the fridge on the way out. He made good time as he crossed over the Glen Jackson into Oregon and headed east on I-84 to Troutdale. The small town, located at the confluence of the interstate, the Columbia River, and the Sandy River, had really expanded in the past few years. The towns of Gresham and Troutdale had grown together, providing a gateway to the Columbia Gorge. Mac parked next to the trooper's marked Crown Vic and rushed inside. He was buzzed through and met with Trooper Downey inside the DUII processing room.

"Hey, Tom. I came as soon as I could." Mac noted the time on his watch out of habit. "What's up?"

The trooper pulled a finger to his lips, indicating he wanted Mac to keep his voice down, and pointed to the next room. "Thanks for coming, Mac," the trooper spoke in a low but deliberate tone. "I have a guy in the Intoxilyzer room. Arrested him for DUII out on Highway 30 about ninety minutes ago. Nothing remarkable at first. I stopped him for driving with his high-beam lights on when he passed by me without dimming. When I walked up I knew I had a keeper—slurred speech and blurry eyes. I arrested him after field sobriety tests and took him back to the PD for the Intox. The guy's name is Troy Wilson. He gave a breath sample then started bawling like a baby. Still nothing too far out of the ordinary, right? He's a two-time loser on probation, and I figure he's just upset because he may go to jail for thirty days for the probation violation. He had a no-alcohol package as part of his probation. His probation officer wanted him revoked and lodged."

"How's this connected to my case?" Mac kept his voice down, but it wasn't easy. "You're killing me here."

"I was getting to that." Tom gestured toward the room where Troy Wilson was being detained. "Wilson starts telling me about how he's going to lose custody of his daughter because of the arrest. I guess he has some custody hearing this next week and will lose by default because he's in jail and his ex-wife will get their girl for good this time. Out of the blue he starts telling me he has information about some body recovery that's been in the paper. He hasn't said much else, except that it's the one where the guy turned up in the river, and he called it a murder. Your case, I think, but I didn't think the media knew it was a murder investigation."

Mac struggled to maintain his composure. Could they finally be getting a break?

"He clammed up after that. Says he'll only talk to a guy that has the authority to deal with him. I thought you would want to know right away, so I had dispatch call you. I was recording him and decided to have dispatch have you come out. I knew you would want to talk to him."

"Thanks, Tom. You bet I do. Does this guy sound credible?"

"He sounds pretty straight up to me," Tom said.

"What did he blow?"

"A .10 blood alcohol content, but he's not drunk out of his mind."

"Could you introduce me?" Mac thought about calling Kevin but figured it would take him almost an hour to come from south Clackamas County after a wake-up call. No sense in getting him up at this hour—especially with what he was going through. Mac could handle the interview with Wilson for now.

"Sure. Come on in." The trooper opened the door to the Intoxilyzer room, introducing Troy Wilson to Mac. Wilson was still cuffed behind his back, slumped down in the chair next to the Intoxilyzer machine. "Mr. Wilson, this is Detective McAllister with the Oregon State Police. He was the one you wanted to speak with."

"You got the authority to deal?" The demand came via slightly slurred speech and eyes as red as a fire engine.

"Thanks, Tom. I'll take it from here."

"I'll be right next-door when you're ready to transport." Tom walked out of the room, shutting the door behind him.

Mac turned to Wilson, his gaze drifting to arms that had been secured behind his back. "Why don't you stand up, and let me switch those to the front?"

Wilson shot him a look of surprise. "Yeah, that would be great. Thanks."

"You can call me Mac. Do you mind if I call you Troy?"

"Sure, that's fine."

Mac removed the handcuffs and motioned for Troy to sit down.

"Thanks." Troy rubbed his wrist. "You never answered my question—do you have the authority to deal or not?"

Mac pulled up a chair next to him. "Let's just say I am the conduit for the person who does, but he's not going to talk deal before I know what you have to offer. Only the district attorney can cut deals, but if I call him up right now he's just going to want to know what you have to say and go back to bed. So I'm the guy you want to talk to first. Got that?"

"Yeah, I got it. I spill my guts and you get the chance to stiff me if you want." Troy frowned, adjusting his grimy baseball hat.

"I'm afraid that's the way it works." Mac almost felt sorry for the guy. "How old is your daughter?"

"She's six." His features softened. "Her name is Julie. I've got to get her back, man. I've got to. That little girl is my life." Troy met Mac's gaze. "My ex has hooked up with a real loser, Detective. I've got to get my baby girl back."

"Maybe you should have thought about her before you picked up the bottle."

"I know. I got a problem, but I'm trying to quit."

"I'd like to see you get a fair shake at that hearing, Troy, but I need to know what you have to offer. That's the way the system works. Are you willing to give me a shot? I can tell you this. If you have good information for me, I'll go to bat for you."

Troy fixed his gaze on the ceiling.

"I give you my word on that," Mac added.

"Okay."

"First of all, this murder you claim to have information about. Are we talking about Bradley Gaynes, the man who was recently pulled from the Columbia River?"

Troy nodded, his eyes filling with tears. "He's the one, but you gotta know, I'm as good as dead if I tell you about it."

"How's that?" Mac asked.

"This guy will kill me. He even suspects I crossed him, and he'll . . . he knows where my little girl lives. The guy is ruthless."

"Sounds like your best bet is to put this guy in prison. Are you willing to help me help you?"

"I've got no choice."

"And you're sure the victim you're talking about is Bradley Gaynes?"

"I'm sure. I didn't know the name until it hit the paper, but I recognized his picture."

"Good." Mac took a long, deep breath and started the tape recorder. "For starters, I need to explain something to you. Because you are in police custody, I need to advise you of your rights. That's the rule."

Troy winced. "Twice in one night, great."

"You have the right to remain silent. Anything you say can and will be used against you in a court of law. You have the right to talk to a lawyer and have him or her present with you before any questioning. Do you understand these rights as I have explained them to you?"

Troy nodded.

"I need a yes or no for the audiotape," Mac said.

"Yes, I understand." Troy licked his lips.

"Having these rights in mind, do you still wish to speak to me?"

"Yes, I do. For my daughter's sake."

Mac began the interview with small talk, getting Troy's biographical information and discussing his daughter. When he thought Troy felt more comfortable, he asked for the information on the murder.

"Where do I start?" Troy asked.

"At the beginning. Let's just work through this together."

"Well, it all started about six months ago. I met this guy through a friend of a friend. Goes by the name Jayce. It's his nickname. I don't know his real name. That's the way he likes to keep it. I don't even know what it means or where it comes from; I don't ask and he don't tell. I needed some quick cash and my friend recommended me to this guy."

"To do what?"

"Act as a guide. I used to guide for black bear before I moved to Oregon. Jayce was looking for some help with his guided bear and cougar hunts, so we hooked up. It was pretty easy money, and all I had to do was keep my mouth shut."

Mac frowned. "Why the secretiveness? There must be hundreds of guides in the state for big game."

"Jayce doesn't go on those kind of hunts; they aren't as profitable. We poach animals, not hunt them. Mainly black bears for their galls and paws, but we take any trophy animal to sell on the black market. We use dogs for bear and cougar, but we wouldn't pass on a trophy elk or deer if we got the chance. People pay top dollar for big antler racks."

"How much were you pulling down?" Mac immediately thought about Chris Ferroli's comments about poaching.

"Depends. Fifteen to twenty grand a week. Jayce would cut me in at twenty percent. I'm good with a gun and fast with a skinning knife, but he had the contacts. Most of them were out of Portland area with overseas buyers. I know that was the case with the bear galls; I'm pretty sure they went to Asian countries."

"How does this involve Brad Gaynes? Was he a client?"

"Hardly. About two months ago we were hunting near Cascade Locks, running hounds for black bear. You can run for miles and not see another soul. I knocked down this big sow and her cub. She didn't die right away. She took off and ran a few miles west before the dogs finally caught and killed her. It was a shame; they messed her hide up pretty bad. Jayce and I were harvesting the galls when we saw this kid staring at us from about twenty feet away. The dogs alerted us or we might not have seen him."

"And this kid was Brad Gaynes?"

"Yeah. Like I said earlier, I didn't know his name until his picture was in the paper last week. I didn't even know he was dead until then." He squirmed in the hard wooden chair. "I had my suspicions, though."

"Why's that?" It looked as though Brad might have caught a hunter's bullet after all, but in this case it was no accident.

"Jayce walked over to the kid all friendly-like. Told him we were with Fish and Wildlife doing some tests on the bears in the area. Jayce told me to leash the hounds, then he told the kid to step back so he won't get bitten. Jayce put his arm around the kid's shoulders and led him away. It was dark by then, so I couldn't see beyond the lantern. After a while I heard a gunshot."

"So this Jayce was carrying a gun?"

"He always carries a gun. That night he was carrying a scoped revolver—some custom job with hand loads that he uses for shooting cats and bears from the trees."

"What happened after you heard the gunshot?"

"Jayce came back and said the kid tried to jump him, so he fired a warning shot and the kid ran off. Jayce told me to leave the sow and get the dogs back to the trucks. Once we got back to the rigs he told me to call it a night and paid me two grand in cash—twice the normal pay. We hadn't even harvested the goods from any of the animals that night. Jayce just said to take off and he would go back and get the gall bladder from the bear. He looked kind of nervous. When I asked him about it, he just said the shot might have drawn attention. That's when I knew he'd taken out the kid. I mean, we fired our guns all the time with no worries in that country; it's too rugged for the game wardens. And besides, there are legal hunters that time of year."

"Could you take me back out to the place where you saw Brad?" Mac wondered if the bear carcass was the same one Chris had told them about.

"I don't think I could find it. It was dark, and we took so many turns tracking the wounded bear."

"Have you seen this Jayce guy since that night?"

"Yeah. We've been out a few times since, even taken some customers on hunts."

"Tell me more about these customers." Mac leaned forward, elbows on his knees.

"People pay top dollar to shoot a trophy bear or cougar. Since hunting with hounds is illegal in this state, folks pay big-time to kill a trophy with us then claim they shot it during daylight hours. That way they get their names in the record books. I bet sixty percent of the top animals in every category are taken illegally."

"How much do these hunts go for?"

"Up to five grand a night, even if you don't shoot. We have several repeat customers."

"How does a person learn about this type of thing? I'm sure Jayce doesn't have a web site or newspaper ads."

"Humph." He smiled at the comment. "Word of mouth mostly.

If he doesn't trust you, no way. You have to know somebody to get in."

"Troy, is there any way you can get me this guy's real name, maybe a recorded phone call or a license plate?"

"No way. I'm telling you, Jayce is real careful. He only meets his customers in person. He never talks business over the phone. He even pulls off his plates when we hunt so no one can get a read if they call in the shooting."

"Has he said anything about the shooting incident with Brad since it happened?"

Troy rubbed his eyes. "No. But he knows I know. Sometimes he asks about my daughter and ex, ask if they still live at the same address. Jayce made it clear that I needed to keep my mouth shut. He's that way. In the beginning, he told me if I talked about the poaching gigs he would kill me, grind up my body, and feed me to his dogs."

Mac leaned toward the desk and picked up the phone.

"Who are you calling?"

"The Multnomah County D.A. I'll talk about a deal on your drunk-driving charge and parole violation in exchange for your testimony. Unfortunately, due to your criminal history, no judge in his right mind would sign a warrant using your testimony as probable cause. It would have helped if you had given us this information before you were jammed up. Now it will sound like you're making up stuff to save your skin."

"I'm not, I swear."

"I'm going to need hard evidence, Troy."

"What are you going to do?"

"I think you're telling the truth, and I'm going to try to convince the D.A. While I'm doing that, I want you to think about how you're going to get me on one of those hunts with Jayce."

30

"TELL ME AGAIN why you think this Troy Wilson guy is so believable?" Sergeant Frank Evans paced back and forth in his office. "Our informant has arrests for manufacturing dope, bribery, theft, not to mention the DUIIs. There's no way a judge in his right mind will sign a search warrant based on this character's testimony. We can't establish anything close to the reliable informant standard a judge would demand."

Mac listened impatiently, waiting for a chance to talk. "I understand that, Sarge, but I have a plan."

Kevin leaned against the doorway to Frank's office, sipping his morning coffee and grinning like a Cheshire cat. He had been in Mac's hot seat many times before and was enjoying watching his partner squirm. Kevin had postponed his announcement so Mac could share his pertinent information with Sarge.

"Oh, you have a plan." Frank cast a derisive look at Kevin, who raised his cup in a salute. "That makes me feel so much better. Does it you?" He shot Mac the same look. "You actually want me to cough up five grand in confidential informant funds?"

Mac nodded. "That's what it'll take."

Frank shook his head. "This had better be the plan of the

century. There is no way I'm going to the lieutenant without justification up the wazoo. Your guy didn't say squat until he was
hauled into jail, and now he wants to be your saving grace. How do
you know Wilson was even in the area at the time our victim went
missing? How do we know this Jayce character even exists? And
how do you know Wilson isn't the trigger man?" Frank stopped
and bent over Mac, his lined face inches away. "So tell me this plan
of yours, Detective."

When Sergeant Evans backed off, Mac cleared his throat and
sat up straight. He glanced at Kevin, hoping his partner would at
least give him some moral support. He had a hunch that Kevin,
standing there wearing that dopey grin of his, was praying for him.

I could use a prayer this morning. Mac cleared his throat again. "I
was getting to that, Sarge. I talked to the D.A. and convinced him
to give Wilson a shot. There will be no deal on the DUII charge
and the probation violation. The troop cited him for the charge
and his P.O. agreed to hold off on the custody situation while we're
working on the case."

"So how does this involve five thousand in confidential
informant funds?" Frank lowered himself into his chair.

"I want Wilson to book me a hunt with this Jayce, or whatever
his name is, so I can check him out and get a look at the gun he
packs—maybe pick up some prints. According to Wilson, Jayce
always carries a revolver with a scope; he uses it to knock animals out
of the trees when the dogs corner them. We're not going to get any
kind of a search warrant at this point. Heck, we have no idea who
this guy is. I want to get a look at him. We need an identity. Sounds
like this guy is pretty secretive, taking off his license plates and never
discussing business over the phone. Wilson is going to set me up on
a hunt, and I'll hopefully get a shot at a bear or a cougar."

"And you expect the citizens of Oregon to fund your safari so
you can get a look at the gun Jayce carries?"

"More than that, Sarge. I talked with Trooper Ferroli in our wildlife office about how they work poaching stings with unlawful guides. He tells me he can loan me one of their .308 rifles they use on undercover missions, one that already has the firing pin strike entered into IBIS for identification. Trooper Ferroli will give me some hand-load rounds with just enough powder to move a special copper bullet down the barrel, but not enough to kill an animal the size of a bear or cougar. The bullet is a hollow jacket that will frag once it leaves the barrel. Like I said, it won't kill or severely injure a big-game animal. With any luck we'll tree a big animal, and I'll take a shot with the altered rifle that will only wound it. I'll pretend to have a malfunction. Hopefully Jayce will make the kill shot with the suspect gun, and we'll get a bullet for comparison, and get some prints. At the least I'll get my own probable cause for a search warrant for the gun, instead of relying on the informant's information."

"You lost me." Frank sounded a little calmer this time. "How does that give you probable cause for a search warrant on a murder case?"

"It doesn't for a murder charge, but it does for a 'hunting game mammal prohibited method' charge."

"A hunting what?"

"Hunting game mammal prohibited method is a crime, and we can establish probable cause to search a residence or a vehicle. Hunting big game in Oregon with dogs or hunting them after dark is a misdemeanor. On top of that, bears and cougars are not even in season. We book our trip with the five thousand in flash money, and I go on the hunt. Even if we don't kill anything, I'll write a search warrant on the guiding and poaching charges for a solid search warrant foundation. In the affidavit we go looking for our marked buy money, the weapons, and records of other illegal guiding."

Frank sat back in his chair, hands folded and resting on his desk. At least he wasn't yelling or telling Mac it was impossible.

"It's risk-free on the money, Sarge," Mac assured him. "We'll recover it the next day. The only thing we're risking is my hide."

Frank picked up his phone, punched in some numbers, and leaned back in his chair. "Hey, Lieu; this is Evans. I need to talk to you about some buy money. Hang on a second, will ya?" Frank cupped the phone with his hand. "You two get out of here. I want to see your tactical plan on my desk in an hour. Let me know when this Wilson guy checks in. I'll convince the lieutenant we need the funds; you guys get me the details on paper. I want a plane up and at least four troops on the ground while you're playing big-game hunter, Mac. We don't have enough for an ex parte order on a body wire, but I want you wearing a GPS locator at all times."

"Those things are too bulky, Sarge," Mac grumbled. The Global Positioning System was as big as a pack of cigarettes. "It's a real pain."

"No buts, Mac—you wear it or you don't go. I don't care if you hide it where the sun don't shine, I'm not losing track of you in those woods."

"Yes, sir. Thanks for your support." Mac grinned as he turned to leave the office.

"Close the door on your way out." Frank flicked his hand and went back to the conversation.

"Yes, sir." Mac eased the door shut.

"Good job, partner." Kevin patted him on the back. "For your sake, I hope this works out."

"Me too." He had a lot riding on this one.

MAC SPENT THE REST OF THE AFTERNOON working with Chris Ferroli on the tactical plan. A fixed-wing plane equipped with the GPS monitor to keep track of Mac was placed on standby for the operation. Chris briefed Mac on poaching operations and some of the language he should use when hunting the animals.

Mac welcomed the refresher on the tactics used by the big-game poacher. It had been years since he'd worked a wildlife assignment, and even then his experience had been limited to fisheries enforcement.

"Avoid cop slang, Mac. And don't ask too many questions. We don't want to make Jayce suspicious." Chris went on to give Mac a brief anatomy lesson on big-game animals. "If you get a shot at a bear, aim for the shoulder. Even with a regular rifle load it would be hard to knock a bear down with those aim points—their skull and shoulder muscles are so thick."

"What about a cougar?"

"Hope for a bear. A big cat will spook and run, even with dogs. If you don't kill it, you'll have a chase on your hands. If you do get a cat, pretend to miss it so you don't send a wounded cat out on the public."

"Can't I just pretend to miss and have Jayce fire?"

"You could risk it, but I'd stick to plan A. This guy will get suspicious if you don't fire a round, even more suspicious if you miss a four-hundred-pound bear at ten yards. If the suspect sees that you're getting a shot at a trophy bear, then don't shoot at the head; go for the front shoulder. Aim forward to avoid any vitals. The heart and lungs are right behind the shoulder, so be careful in case the bullet does penetrate."

"Why not the head?"

"We measure trophy bears by the size of their skull, so you don't want to shoot there or he'll think something is up. It would be like shooting the antlers on a trophy elk."

"Got it. Anything else?"

"Let's take a look at the rifle." Chris produced a wood stock .308 Savage from the gun locker. "We'll be able to trace any bullets fired from this gun, so don't worry about that. The lab already has it in the database. This is the last round I want you to load into the magazine well. It has a thin red line on the casing. See?" Chris handed the cartridge to Mac to examine.

"Why the last?"

"These other rounds are factory and will shoot like any other cartridge, so keep them separate." Chris handed him a box of shiny cartridges. "This little beauty has a slightly enlarged casing. Make sure you really slap the bolt home when you close the action on it. Load it last so it comes out of the magazine first; the gun holds five, so it should be your fifth round. When the bullet is discharged from the rifle, the already tight-fitting casing will expand from the powder burn and will render the extractor useless in pulling it out to make it look like a stove-pipe malfunction. That should convince even the hard-core poachers you aren't scamming them. We've used this technique before."

Mac examined the rifle, going over the procedure a couple of times with Chris. They were about finished when Mac received a 911 page from a cell number he recognized immediately as his own. Wilson didn't have a cell phone, so Mac had loaned him his department phone to page him when the hunt was set up. "This is our guy." Mac stepped past Chris to use the phone in the wildlife office.

"Yeah," Wilson answered.

"This is McAllister; you paged?"

"You wanted me to let you know when I spoke with Jayce. Well, I left him a message on his cell phone and he got back to me. The hunt's on, man. Like I told you before, he won't discuss business over the phone, so I met him down at Sheri's Restaurant in Troutdale over a cup of coffee and set up the hunt."

"Good." Mac gave Chris a thumbs-up. "How did it go?"

Troy's breathing sounded a little ragged. He was probably nervous. If this Jayce was as bad as Troy indicated, Mac could see why. He just hoped Troy wouldn't let his nerves get the best of him. A slip-up could cost Mac and Troy their lives.

"He was a little concerned," Troy said, "but it went pretty smooth. I've brought in customers before, so it wasn't anything new. I told him you were a friend of Charlie Bonner. I'd set Charlie up a few times, so the connection is a natural one."

"Unless Jayce talks to Charlie." Mac frowned.

"That might be a little tough. Charlie's dead."

"What happened to him?" Mac had visions of Jayce shooting his client in the back.

"Old Charlie was a rancher out by Hermiston. He was killed in a skidder accident while he and his son were thinning logs last month. A widow maker from a previous logger fell on him when he was moving his skidding to another log."

"Widow maker?"

"You know, when a logger fells a tree and it only leans into the next live tree and doesn't come all the way down, they call it a widow maker. Anyway, old Charlie isn't going to spill the beans."

"How old was Charlie? Tell me about him so I don't trip up."

"He was in his sixties, lived with his wife on a fourteen-hundred-acre spread near Hermiston. His place was mainly a hay farm, but he had some timbered acres. He and Helen have three grown daughters and a son, all living in the valley now. Since it sounds like you don't know anything about trees or farming, I'd stick to something else. Maybe, say you were an investor or something and were taking care of Charlie's businesses."

"That would work. How many times had Charlie been out?" Mac asked.

"Three times, got two nice bruins and one dandy male cat. All three are hanging in his place in Hermiston. None are record breakers, but they got nice coats, no rubs on the bear hides."

"When is the hunt, Troy? Where do we meet?"

"Tonight, we have to go tonight. Jayce has a bait barrel . . ."

"Bait barrel?"

"Yeah. Bears are mainly scavengers. He puts out a barrel filled with dead things to attract them. He's got one on top of the bluff. We were going to go out this week by ourselves looking for bear galls, so Jayce decided to take you along. The hunt is still five grand, and we keep the gall bladder if you shoot a bear. I'll meet you in Corbett, in front of the Grange Hall, and take you to our meeting place. That's how we work things. Plan on being there at seven o'clock sharp. Don't be late."

"I'll be there. Just make sure you tell me if anything changes."

"We still good with the D.A.?"

"As long as you're square with me, we're good to go. If I get any indication you're lying, the deal's off."

"I'll do just what you said, I swear. I want my little girl."

"All right. I'll see you tonight then, and bring my phone with you."

"S-sure." He hesitated. "I made a few calls to my daughter; I hope you don't mind."

Mac sighed. *That will go over big with Sarge.* "Just bring it tonight."

Mac briefed Chris, who agreed to be one of the ground troops for the mission. He then called Sergeant Evans to make sure he'd been able to secure the confidential funds.

"You're all set, Mac," Frank said. "Just be careful."

Mac would wear the GPS so air support could monitor his location while ground units would standby in the gorge. He checked out a half-ton Chevrolet pickup with dead plates for the mission and loaded up his rifle and gear for the meet. After briefing all the involved detectives and troopers, Mac left for Vancouver. He had to go home and get into character for his acting role this evening.

Driving over the bridge, Mac did a little praying himself. He wondered if this is what a soldier felt like before going into battle.

He'd done a little undercover work, but nothing like this. Everything depended on his ability to make Jayce believe he was nothing more than an illegal hunter.

The butterflies he'd had in his stomach all day turned into combat planes.

31

MAC DROVE EAST on I-84 to the Corbett exit, glad they'd be taking Troy Wilson's vehicle from this point on. The old undercover truck he'd signed out was in dire need of brakes and a front-end alignment. The twenty-year-old truck had been seized from a dope peddler years ago. Mac pulled up in front of the Corbett Grange and found Wilson already parked there in an older-model red Toyota pickup.

Mac parked behind the building and grabbed his rifle, then walked around the other side of his pickup to make sure the small GPS unit was still functioning. He pulled out the front of his wool pants to check the glowing green light. He'd attached the GPS to the inside of his shorts. Not the most comfortable place, but probably the safest.

Mac saw no reason to give Troy details of the OSP plans. Truth be told, he didn't trust Troy Wilson any more than he could throw him.

Troy pushed open the passenger door of the truck from the driver's seat. Under the dome light, he had the look of a man heading for the gas chambers. Mac shared Troy's anxiety.

"You ready for this?" Mac climbed into the pickup, wishing

they were doing this hunt in daylight rather than the dead of night.

"No." He sighed heavily. "I just hope we can pull it off, or we're both dead. You got the money?"

Mac patted his right front pocket on his camouflage jacket. "Right here."

"Let's see it." Troy pulled a cigarette out of his front shirt pocket.

"I'm not your customer. I'm your ticket out of here, remember? Don't forget who's running this trip. You'll see the money when I pay Jayce."

"He'll kill me if he finds out. He'll kill both of us." Troy lit the cigarette with trembling hands.

Mac hated cigarette smoke. Another remnant from his father's bad habits. He didn't say anything, figuring Troy was barely hanging on as it was. The nicotine would calm the guy—at least for a while. "So you said. I guess you'll have to trust me, Wilson. Now let's get going. And if you have to smoke, at least crack open your window."

Mac felt for the small .380 semiautomatic backup gun he'd stowed in his hip pocket. It was there all right, but he doubted he'd get to it in time with all the clothes in the way.

Troy pushed the manual transmission into gear and started back down Corbett Hill to I-84, eventually turning east on the freeway toward Cascade Locks. They didn't talk much on the way except for the brief instructions Mac gave Troy on how he wanted the bear handled if they killed an animal: unskinned and whole. "I want Jayce's bullet in the animal."

They passed Bonneville Dam, entering Hood River County in less than twenty minutes. After taking the exit for Cascade Locks, Troy zigzagged up so many forest service roads that Mac lost his sense of direction. It didn't help that he couldn't see past the headlights. After more than forty minutes of back-country driving, Troy stopped in front of a rustic cabin. Mac could see a large four-wheel drive pickup parked in back, but he couldn't make out the model or color in the low light.

The lights were on inside the small hunting cabin, giving it a warm, homey look. Mac's heart pounded so hard, he could feel it pulse through his neck. He took several deep calming breaths as he followed Troy up the gravel path to the front door.

Troy knocked. "Hey, Jayce. It's me."

"Come on in, it's open," a gruff voiced boomed from inside.

Troy and Mac walked in the front door. Mac wasn't sure what he'd expected, but it wasn't this. The cabin was tidy and clean. A warm fire crackled in the fireplace. On the wall above it was a fine collection of mounts—a black bear made into a rug, a large bull elk with an enormous rack, a handsome mule deer buck, and a trophy antelope with long black horns.

"Hey, Troy, and you must be Steve." A large man in his fifties with the look of a grizzly sat at a large wooden table in the kitchen area. Mac hoped he wouldn't have to tangle with the guy.

Mac smiled, hoping it looked genuine. Steve was the name Mac agreed to use for the undercover operation. On Trooper Ferroli's advice, he carried no identification on him.

The big man was pumping a lantern full of fuel. Wiping his hand on his suspender-supported jeans, he stood and came forward to shake Mac's hand.

"I am, and you must be Jayce." Mac noticed how the hand was nearly double the size of his own.

"That's Jay-cee," he corrected. Then with a surprisingly kind expression on his face, he added, "It only sounds like that when Troy here says my name with that southern accent of his. Pleased to meet you. Troy tells me you're a friend of Charlie's."

"That's right. Too bad about his untimely death." Mac rubbed his chin and glanced toward the wood floor.

"You two were pretty tight, huh?" Jaycee went back to his lantern. "I didn't catch your last name."

"I'd prefer not to use last names," Mac replied. The best defense in these situations was a good offense. "You stand to make a lot of money in our business relationship, and I'd rather keep us on a first-name basis."

"Good, good, that's the way it should be." Jaycee chuckled. "I'm glad to hear you feel that way."

Mac glanced at Troy, whose upper lip and forehead were beaded with sweat. Mac could feel the heat too, even though the cabin temperature was probably around sixty. "Charlie and I were only business partners, and let's just say we made some profitable investments. It is a shame about his death, though. He owed me a substantial amount of money, but I couldn't collect because we were dealing under the table—if you know what I mean."

Jaycee nodded. "Too bad. So how did you meet old Charlie?"

"On a guided hunt. He told me I might be able to get some trophies. I'm hoping to acquire all the native cat species for my taxidermy collection. I already own most of the African cats. I need a cougar for my collection, preferably a big male. I also want a black bear. I have others, but I am looking for a full body mount."

"All right!" Jaycee grinned. "You bring the money?"

"Yep. I brought five thousand, not a penny more, and I'm prepared to book subsequent hunts if this evening goes well."

"I'm sure we will be able to do business. How about you show me the five thousand, and we'll go hunting."

Mac produced the five thousand dollars in hundred-dollar bills. The serial numbers on each bill had been inventoried earlier. "It's all there; you can count it."

"I will. Why don't you and Troy take a listen while I'm counting? The dogs are already on a scent." Jaycee eyeballed the bills as he spread them in his thick fingers. Mac listened intently, hearing the baying of Jaycee's hounds in the distance. "They caught a scent on the way to the cabin and I let them out. Sounds like they've treed something already."

"How far away?" Mac asked, his pulse quickening.

Jaycee stuffed the cash in his pocket then reached for a canvas pack from behind the table. He removed a black piece of electronic equipment with a large antenna. "About twelve hundred meters, maybe a little more." Mac recognized it as a Global Positioning System unit and felt a moment's panic. He let out a long slow breath, realizing that Jaycee could only track his own GPS boxes, not the one on him.

"Let's start hiking." Jaycee headed for the door. "You got your rifle?"

"Sure do!" Mac tried to sound enthusiastic. "It's in the truck." He zipped up his coat and removed a sock hat from the pocket before removing his rifle from the front of Troy's truck.

"You have your .30-.30, Troy?"

"I didn't bring it, boss." Troy stuffed his hands in his jacket pockets. "Didn't think we would be going out so soon. It's at the gunsmith's for a new front sight." Mac was glad he told Troy not to bring any guns with them on the hunt. He didn't want the hired help blazing away on the animals, and he for sure didn't want to get shot in the back. Watching one suspect in the dark would be enough of a challenge. Of course, that didn't mean Troy didn't have a concealed weapon. Mac hadn't thought to frisk him when they'd met up, and he certainly couldn't do it now.

"I'll shoot backup then," Jaycee said, opening a case on the wooden table. He pulled a heavy-barreled revolver from the case with a scope mounted on the frame. After quickly running a rag over the gun, Jaycee slipped it into a shoulder-holster rig. "Let's go hunting, boys."

Mac inspected his .308, taking careful notice of the rounds he pushed into the magazine well before slamming the bolt shut on the marked cartridge. Jaycee and Troy headed into the darkness with flashlights, and Mac followed close behind. Mac had never killed a large animal; his family wasn't into hunting—not animals, at any rate. At times, he couldn't tell if he was excited about the hunt or anxious about the case. He had done enough hiking and rescue work to handle the rough terrain. And it was rough maneuvering over and around the windswept deadfalls—fallen trees that produced a false ground when the ferns covered their rotting hulls.

"Should be just up ahead. We can just follow the dogs from this range." Jaycee handed the electronic equipment to Troy.

"Telemetry equipment on the dog's collars," Troy whispered to Mac before putting the equipment in his backpack.

Mac nodded. He'd figured as much.

"If we get separated, don't head north," Troy said. "You'll launch yourself off one of the cliffs before you know what hit you."

Great. Which way is north? Mac didn't get a chance to ask.

They followed the sound of the baying dogs for another thirty minutes. For Mac, the sounds seemed to be coming from all directions. The two experienced hunters walked a razor-straight line to the dogs. For now, Mac focused more on the dangers of the hike than the potential murder suspects in his midst. He had long since removed his sock hat and gloves, even unzipping his coat. It had to be close to freezing up here, but he was overheated and soaked with sweat.

"Right up ahead, boys. There they are." Jaycee shined his flashlight on a medium-sized Douglas fir that was surrounded by seven hounds, barking like maniacs and clawing at the tree. "Let's move in a little closer," Jaycee hollered. "See what they've cornered."

The three men walked to within twenty feet of the dogs when Jaycee announced their findings. "Hey, we're in luck. A nice fat bruin for you, Steve." Jaycee sounded as excited as Mac felt. "He'll be a keeper."

Mac followed the end of the flashlight beam, his gaze settling on the terrified bear that sat perched only about a dozen feet up the tree. His eyes reflected the light as he pawed the air. His shiny hide glowed in the light.

I can't do this. The plan had looked perfect on paper. How could he fire at this magnificent animal? He hated using the animal to further his case. *The man's a murderer,* Mac reminded himself. *You need this evidence.*

"It won't make the record books." Mac barely heard Jaycee above the pounding of his heart. "But it will make a fine mount. Take your time on the shot; he won't go anywhere with the dogs there. Once he falls, just stay back and let the dogs smell him. That's their little reward for the hunt; they won't harm the hide."

Mac brought the sling off his shoulder, taking a last look at the bear's black nose and glowing eyes before shouldering the rifle. *Sorry, old boy.* He found the bear's thick front shoulder in his 3 x 9 scope and took careful aim at the beefy target. Mac fired. The bear screamed in pain but didn't fall from the tree.

"He's hit; put another one in him!" Jaycee yelled.

"I can't!" Mac yelled back. "My gun's jammed!"

Jaycee swore, pulled his revolver from his holster, and took a quick aim before firing. The bear groaned and fell, lying dead before the crazed hounds. Jaycee holstered and looked at Mac. "He's down now. Let me take a look at that thing." Mac handed him the rifle, hoping Chris's plan had worked. He held his breath as Jaycee pulled back hard on the bolt, but the extractor wouldn't budge the casing.

"She's jammed all right. It'll come loose when she cools down."

"I must have loaded that one a little too hot." Mac breathed a little easier. "You made a great shot, though. Thanks. Where'd you hit him?"

"Right in the bread basket, should be a double-lung shot," Jaycee said proudly, approaching the bear.

Troy leashed the dogs. "Nice shot, boss."

The bear had been shot behind the front left leg. "Not bad, huh?" Jaycee slapped Mac on the left shoulder. "Will this do it for you?"

"Perfect." Mac forced a smile. "He'll make a fine mount."

"No pictures." Jaycee cautioned. "I'm sure you understand."

"Didn't even bring a camera. Thanks for the hunt." Mac shook Jaycee's hand, trying to look as thrilled with the shot as Jaycee did.

"I'll start to field dress it, Troy. Why don't you go get your truck? There's a skid road not far from here. We won't have much of a drag to the truck."

"You got it, boss." Troy began his hike back to the cabin with the dogs.

So far, so good. Mac breathed a little easier now.

"You're okay with a my taking out the gall, right?" Jaycee pulled a large-bladed knife with a gut hook on the end from his pack.

"Sure, just be surgical about it. Don't poke around any more than you have to, or I'll hear about it from my taxidermist."

"No problem." Jaycee chuckled. "I've had a lot of experience."

I'll bet.

Jaycee field dressed the bear, laying his prized inky-black gallbladder in a plastic container before placing it in his canvas bag. Troy arrived soon after Jaycee finished dressing the bear.

Mac watched as the two men used a ratcheted come-along winch and some cable to drag the bear to the pickup. He watched for any potential evidence from the carcass, not wanting a bullet falling out from the bear.

It took all three of them to lift the bear into the back of Troy's truck, even with the help of a winch.

Out of breath, Jacyee leaned against the tailgate. "Okay, Steve. Troy will get you to where you need to go. It's best if you don't get any blood in the back of your own rig. For an extra hundred, Troy can skin the bear and flesh out the skull if you want it scored. There's no one quicker with a skinning blade."

"Thanks, Jaycee." Mac shook his hand. "This was awesome. I can see us doing business for years to come."

"Good to meet you, Steve. You can go through Troy for future hunts or contact me directly. Troy can give you the number. Just tell me you want to go hunting and I'll meet you in person. I don't set up details over the phone—I'm sure you understand."

"Completely."

Jaycee went back to his hounds, disappearing into the thick woods, his flashlight flickering between the shrubs and tree trunks.

"He's walking back?" Mac asked.

"Yep." Troy jumped onto the bed and covered the bear with a blue tarp, securing it with brown twine. "He's the original mountain man." After taking a drink of water from an old milk jug, Troy got into the driver's side and started the truck.

Mac unloaded his rifle and placed it in the back of the seat, relief washing over him. His knees started to buckle as he climbed into the truck.

Troy drove back to the cabin in just a few minutes. It had taken them over an hour to walk through the woods.

"You get what you came for?" Troy asked.

"I don't know yet. Give me my phone."

Troy pointed to the glove box. Mac retrieved the phone and called Kevin, who was waiting at the base of the Bridge of the Gods in Cascade Locks.

"It's about time you made contact. I've been worried sick," Kevin said.

"You have?" Mac chuckled. "I didn't know you cared."

"Smart-mouth." Kevin then asked, "How was the hunt?"

"Great. We have a bear, hopefully with Jaycee's bullet inside. Hey, Kev. Meet me back in Corbett at the Grange. Bring me some coffee and a bottle of water. And bring Chris. We need a game officer to go through the carcass."

Troy and Mac pulled into the Grange parking lot to find Kevin and Chris already there, leaning against the undercover truck. Two patrol troopers were also waiting in the lot—Mac's cover if things had gone sour. Sergeant Frank Evans pulled in moments later, covered in mud. His car reeked of hot brakes.

"You okay?" Frank asked Mac.

"Fine, Sarge. Hungry for bear?" Mac pulled back the tarp.

"Nice one." Chris hopped into the back of the truck. "Did things go as planned?"

"By the numbers, Chris, thanks. Our guy put a round in with his revolver, and he's back in his cabin by now. I couldn't tell you how to get there, but Mr. Wilson can."

"Our plane has a pretty good lock on the position of the cabin, thanks to the GPS you were carrying. They made note of any positions when you weren't mobile," Kevin said.

"I can give you directions," Troy added. "Or draw a map."

"Thanks, Troy," Mac said. "That would be a big help."

They really didn't need the map, but Mac appreciated the man's efforts. He retrieved a blank sheet of paper from his briefcase in the clunker truck he'd driven out. "Directions and a map would be great."

Troy seemed relieved to have something to do.

Mac turned his attention back to the bear. Chris waved a metal detector over the carcass. "There's something in the right shoulder. That's the only read I get. Is that where you shot, Mac?"

"It was." Mac frowned.

"Let's take a look, I'll tell you if it was one of my bullets right here." Chris pulled a folding knife from his duty belt and began skinning the bear's shoulder hide. "Here's our entrance behind the left front." Chris pointed. "Hopefully it's not a through and through, and the detector was just getting a bullet jacket or a fragment." Chris skinned the bear's other shoulder after the others helped him roll the animal over in the truck. "Shoot. There's an exit wound in the other shoulder."

"Oh, no." Mac rubbed a hand over his head. *All that work for nothing?*

"Hand me that metal detector back," Chris said to Kevin. He waved the handheld device over the bear one more time, this time with no tone. "That's odd."

"Wave it over the hide that would have been by the exit wound," Troy suggested as he handed the directions to Mac.

Chris placed the round head of the machine over the bear hide that was lying flat on the truck bed. "Bingo!" Chris yelled as the detector chimed. "Give me some light right here."

A patrol trooper shined his light on the spot Chris was pointing to while he examined the thick black hide. "There's a bullet lodged in the hide; grab an evidence bag!"

Kevin produced a paper evidence bag from his pocket. Mac grinned at his optimism. Chris pulled a large-caliber bullet from the hide, bloodied by its course. "That's not one of mine, so it must be from the other shooter."

Mac released the breath he'd been holding as Chris placed the bullet in the evidence bag and handed it back to Kevin.

"Mac and I will be waiting on the front steps of the crime lab when it opens in, what . . ." Kevin looked at his watch. "Seven hours."

"I'll accompany the bear to our wildlife-evidence freezer at Bonneville," Chris said, "just in case we need to look it over again.

I'm not getting any other hits and don't see any more wounds. Looks like your round bounced off as planned, Mac."

"He probably missed," Frank grumbled.

"Thanks for the confidence, Sarge." Mac laughed, more from relief than from anything humorous.

"Don't mention it."

"It gets better. The suspect actually grabbed my rifle after it jammed and wrapped his meat hooks over the top of the barrel and the action. I made sure I didn't touch that part of the gun on the way back, so hopefully latents can lift some prints off it."

"Good. Now get your rears home and get some sleep. You guys have soaked me for enough overtime already." Frank slapped Mac on the back as they walked to their vehicles. "You better get working with the D.A. on the phone records for Jaycee's cell phone, Mac. Let them subpoena the cell company so we can find out who this character is."

Kevin gave Mac a thumbs-up. "See you in the morning, partner."

On the way home Mac reviewed everything that had transpired, from his first interview with Troy to Chris discovering the bullet. He felt certain Jaycee had killed Brad, but something else niggled at his mind. He thought about the unsolved murder case out at the sawmill and the animal carcasses they'd found buried out there. They figured the ex-con had been poaching. Had he been working for Jaycee? The idea wasn't that farfetched. One thing for certain, he planned to check the fingerprint they'd found on the tape at that scene against Jaycee's.

Maybe he was being too optimistic that the two cases might be related. The chances were slim, but if they were, it meant two successful cases with him as lead detective. He shook his head as he pulled into his driveway. Stranger things had happened. Mac opted not to mention his harebrained scheme to anyone just now. He'd bide his time and let the evidence speak for itself.

32

KEVIN WAS WAITING in their car in the front of the Justice Center in downtown Portland with the manila evidence bag containing the bullet. Mac had walked across the street for coffee and scones. He returned to the car holding two cups of coffee in his hands and the bag of scones in his teeth.

Kevin rolled the passenger side window down a few inches, making Mac wait in the rain. "You got a pumpkin scone in there?"

"Uh-huh," Mac mumbled around the paper bag.

"You may enter then." Kevin smiled and rolled the window all the way down, taking the cups and bag from his partner.

Mac was in too good of a mood to complain.

"Might as well make yourself comfy." Kevin set the bag on his lap. "The lab doesn't open for a few minutes yet. The crew is probably inside, but the doors don't open up until eight sharp."

Mac took a sip of hot coffee, staring out the window at the parking lot full of Portland Police Bureau cars. The sub floor of the Justice Center served as the Multnomah County jail, while the first floor was the Bureau's Central Precinct office for their agency.

"Did you get hold of anyone on that cell phone number Troy Wilson gave us for Jaycee?"

"Yep, taken care of." Mac had dealt with the phone as soon as he'd come into his office at seven that morning. "We'll see what name is on the contract for the phone number he gave. Hopefully it isn't stolen and we can get an idea who this guy is. It was a 541 area code, so I got one of the detectives at Hood River County on one of their contacts, to save us time on getting a grand jury subpoena or writing a warrant."

"Good work, Mac. I appreciate your being a jump ahead of me."

Mac wasn't sure what to say. He checked his watch. "We could go in now. It'll be about eight by the time we get to the twelfth floor."

"Yeah, you're right, but I haven't eaten my scone yet." Kevin opened the sack and sniffed appreciatively. "Ah. Something to be savored. Not eaten in a rush."

"So, you want to talk or something?" Mac asked, hoping that wasn't the case. He wanted to get the bullet into ballistics. Now.

"Yeah, that might be good. I kind of dumped a load on you the other night—telling you about the cancer thing."

Mac shrugged. He really didn't want to deal with that issue. He had efficiently shoved it into a corner of his mind. "Did you have a chance to tell the others?"

"No. With this case breaking loose, I haven't brought it up. Which was why I wanted to talk to you. I'd rather you didn't mention it to anyone. I'd like to tell them myself."

"Right. My lips are sealed." Mac grabbed the envelope containing the bullet from the dashboard. "You can go ahead and savor your scone, Kev. I gotta know if this is the winning bullet. I'll meet you up there." He opened the door, tossing Kevin an expectant grin.

"Oh, all right then." Kevin sighed. Taking the sack and his coffee, he joined Mac on the sidewalk.

Security passed them through, and they took the elevator to the crime lab on the twelfth floor. Mac had left a message so that

Wain would be expecting them. The receptionist was just coming in to work.

"Hi, Kevin, Mac. Wain said to go right back."

"Thanks." Mac hurried to the criminalist's office, with Kevin trailing behind.

"Morning, Wain," Mac said as he entered. He held up the envelope. "I've got a present for you."

"So I heard." Wain was standing in front of his microscope, booting up his computer and monitor. "Do you have the gun also so I can compare barrels?"

"Sorry, not yet." Mac frowned. "You don't need it to compare bullets, do you?"

"I don't need it. Helps if I have a bullet from a gun taken in a clinical environment. How'd you get this one?"

"Pulled it out of a bear." He chuckled at Wain's expression.

"Comparing bullets from bears and humans. Interesting." Wain took the bullet from Mac and, after removing it from the evidence envelope, placed it under his microscope. He examined the bullet for several seconds before photographing it with a camera attached to the microscope. He then removed it and set it in a solution. After cleaning the blood and bone from the bullet, he placed it back on the microscope and peered into the eyepiece. "It has the right twist to the barrel imprinted on the sample and appears to be made of the same material. Let me bring up the image of the bullet taken out of Mr. Gaynes on the split screen." Mac held his breath as both bullets sat side by side in the enlarged-image screen. They appeared to match, but Mac waited for Wain's expert opinion.

Wain peered through the microscope for what seemed like an eternity. "Gents, my professional opinion, based on the lateral striations I see here . . ." Wain paused for several more seconds and raised his eyes to look at the screen.

"Your professional opinion is . . .?" Mac repeated.

"These bullets were fired through the same gun. That's prima facie evidence. If the barrel is from the same gun, you have your murder suspect."

"Thank you!" Mac clinched his fists, trying to tone down his excitement but finding the task impossible. "So that's it!" Kevin and Wain probably thought he was nuts. "We've got him."

"Not so fast, Mac." Kevin shared his enthusiasm in part. "This test alone would have been good enough for a conviction five years ago, but IBIS will put the last nail in the coffin with a computer analysis."

"He's right," Wain said. "But for now, I can tell you without hesitation that these bullets are fired from the same barrel and you have probable cause for arrest—if you know the owner of the gun."

"We do." Kevin grinned. "We'll call back later on that IBIS info, Wain. Thanks for the quick work."

Mac and Kevin all but ran out of the crime lab to the elevator. Mac pressed the lobby button over and over until the door closed and the car began its downward journey.

"Pretty cool, don't you think?" Mac asked.

Kevin shook his head. "Do you always get this revved up?"

Mac's pager vibrated. "It's dispatch. We have an alpha page to call Hood River County. I bet it's that cell phone info."

"We can give them a call from the car," Kevin said.

Mac jogged ahead, taking back his place as the driver. Kevin called the sheriff's office as Mac drove. "I was speaking with a Detective Marty Keels; it was probably her."

"Yeah, this is Bledsoe with OSP. Dispatch said to call your office. Probably from Detective Keels."

Mac took some deep calming breaths as he raced back to the patrol office. They were close, thanks to his brilliant plan. *Yeah, but it would never have happened if that trooper hadn't pulled Troy Wilson over and brought him in.* The thought sobered Mac. They'd gotten a lucky break. Except Kevin wouldn't have called it luck—he'd have called it an answer to prayer.

Kevin covered the mouthpiece. "Deputy Sam Wyatt's the one who paged you."

"The original deputy to respond." Mac nodded.

"Yes, this is Bledsoe." Kevin listened intently to the information Sam gave him. "You're kidding. You don't say. Tell you what, why don't you and your crew put out a BOLO (be on the lookout) on this guy and try to hook him up." Kevin jotted something on his pad. "We'll be putting a team together and heading your way. If you find him at his house and want to hot-pop him for aggravated murder, we have probable cause for the arrest. Okay, thanks. I'll use this number. You can go through dispatch or we'll go to your radio net when we get close. Thanks, Sam. Be careful." Kevin slapped the phone shut.

"What was that all about?" Mac gripped the steering wheel.

"Found out who Jaycee is. Jaycee is not his name. It's J. C., his initials. Stands for Jack Clovis. He's a volunteer for the search-and-rescue crew Deputy Wyatt heads up. Lives over in Cascade Locks, east of Bonneville Dam."

"No kidding. He was out looking for Brad that first day. I saw his rig, but I never saw him. Good thing, or I'd have been dead meat last night." Mac frowned, remembering the truck he'd seen out at the cabin. It had been too dark to see it clearly. "He ran hounds on the search looking for Brad when he disappeared. I can't believe this. The fox was in the henhouse the whole time."

"Wyatt's crew is going to the suspect's home in Cascade Locks."

"So, do you want to head over there? This is our pinch."

"They'll be there in a few minutes; they know to hold him for us. If he's talking, they'll take notes but won't press him. Besides, you are out of the interview loop with your undercover stunt. He'll be too mad to trust you. I'll have to partner with the sergeant or give this over to Russ and Philly to tag team."

"Shoot," Mac muttered. "You're right. I want to be there when they bust this guy."

"Tell you what. Let's head east to Cascade Locks where Clovis lives and get some troops en route for support." He read off Clovis's address and the directions from his pad. "I'll have dispatch get Chris Ferroli going and our gorge patrols, maybe even some from The Dalles if they have any patrols out this way."

Kevin phoned dispatch, asking to have cover started out to the gorge. The radio ripped with activity as different troopers responded. Dana, who had gorge patrol, called in as she took the Cascade Locks exit. She'd get there ahead of them. Mac's chest tightened at the thought of Dana being involved. That annoyed him. She was a trooper just like they were. He shouldn't be that uptight.

Chris was also en route, along with a patrol from The Dalles. They'd all be going to assist the deputies at Clovis's home. Sergeant Evans had responded as well and would be steaming east in the hammer wagon. *The gang's all here,* Mac thought. Except for Russ and Philly, who were in Salem conducting interviews.

Just prior to Bonneville Dam, Kevin's cell phone rang. It was Deputy Wyatt. "Clovis isn't at his residence. They're rerouting to the cabin."

"Do they know how to get there? We have the directions." Mac had put Troy's map in the console.

"Says he does. Guess they've used it as a base camp in the past on SAR missions."

"Helpful son of a gun, isn't he?" Mac handed the directions to Kevin. "This will help." Troy had created a concise map and had even put in the numbers of the Forest Service roads in the Eagle Creek system.

"I'll let Sarge know. You have the uniforms meet us at the freeway exit. We'll get our vests on there. Then they can follow us to the cabin. Wyatt is heading this way with a couple of deputies, and he has a few more checking some other residences and businesses."

Mac and Kevin stopped at the eastbound exit to the freeway, briefing Dana and Chris, who arrived about the same time.

Kevin opened the trunk and slipped his heavy raid vest over his shirt and tie. Mac and the others followed suit. The vest was bulky and uncomfortable, but it afforded Mac some degree of assurance. Though if Clovis wanted to take him out, he'd have no trouble—he could put a bullet into Mac's head with the first shot.

Kevin gave some general directions, and the small caravan started for the cabin. Frank caught up with the group as they left the freeway exit and pulled in behind them as they hit the gravel road.

Mac drove as fast as the gravel road permitted. On the way he noticed dozens of small cabins dotting the hillside on the leased federal forestland. Last night it had been too dark to see much of anything. At the base of Road 16, Mac recognized a large boulder with white paint on the side. "Was Road 16 on the directions?" he asked.

"Yep. It should take us right to the front door." Kevin released a heavy sigh. Both men slipped out of their seat belts. Mac took the road at a slower pace.

"There it is." Mac recognized the mossy roof of the cabin as it came into view. Not wanting to alert anyone if they were inside the cabin, Mac pulled up a little farther and off the road, parking just short of the main driveway. The bevy of cars efficiently blocked the driveway.

They gathered behind the vehicles and out of sight. "Kevin and I will take the front," Mac said. "We've got the heavy vests." The vest worn under the uniform on patrol was lighter and more pliable, thus not as effective. His and Kevin's were heavy raid vests, similar to the military model soldiers wore. "I need one uniform to go with us and the other to hit the back. Is that okay, Sarge?" Mac sensed he was stealing the sergeant's thunder.

"We could use some more troops," Frank grumbled, "but we'll make do. A forced assault is authorized only on my say-so. I've got SWAT on standby if this turns into a standoff. Let's see if anyone is home right now." Sergeant Evans pulled his shotgun from his car and racked a round.

"I'll go to the front with you and Kevin," Dana volunteered, pulling her Glock .40 from her duty belt.

Mac wanted to object—to tell her to stay back—but he couldn't, wouldn't do that to her. She was a trained trooper and better than most. Mac trusted her. "Okay." Their gazes connected for a moment. Had she read his reluctance? He quickly refocused. "Chris, you take the back with the sergeant. Everybody ready?"

They all nodded, and the five officers started toward the tiny cabin. At first, it looked like no one was there.

"I've got a vehicle in back," Chris said over the radio.

"What kind of . . ." Mac stopped midsentence when the front door flew open. Troy Wilson staggered out, holding his hands over his ears. Blood covered his head.

Terror ripped through Mac as time stopped.

A shot exploded from inside the cabin. The bullet hit Troy square in the back, stopping him in his tracks.

Mac ran forward and caught Troy as he fell face-forward. Dana and Kevin fired through the open doorway. The shooter fired again, hitting Dana in the chest. She staggered and landed on her back, her head hitting the gravel.

Kevin emptied his magazine into the front of the cabin. Mac instinctively crouched down to lessen his exposure, while still cradling Troy with his left arm. He tried to level his handgun sights on the shooter and managed to get off several rounds. Tunnel vision had set in and he felt as though someone had flipped a switch, transporting them into a surreal, slow-motion world. He needed to get to Dana. He gently lowered Troy's lifeless body to the ground.

Kevin dumped his empty mag and ran to Dana, dropping down next to her.

More shots erupted from the back of the building.

"Twelve-ninety-nine, twelve-ninety-nine, officer down," Kevin yelled into Dana's spike mic.

Mac ducked as a big Dodge truck careened around the corner with Jack Clovis behind the wheel, firing from his window. A round hit the ground less than a foot from Dana's boots. Sergeant Evans and Chris sprinted around the corner.

"Is she bad off?" Frank yelled.

"Don't know. You guys okay?" Kevin yelled back.

"We aren't hit; the guy came out too fast. We got off a few rounds into the truck, but I don't think we hit him."

Oh God, make her be all right. Please. Mac raced to Dana's side.

"Talk to me, Dana." He dropped down next to Frank.

Dana opened her mouth, but nothing came out. Tears filled her eyes. "Hurts."

Kevin ripped her uniform shirt and vest off.

"There's no blood."

"I think the vest stopped the round." Kevin said. "She may have some broken ribs, though. Probably had the wind knocked out of her."

"I'm okay," Dana whispered. "Where is he?"

Mac looked at Kevin and got to his feet. "He won't get far." He motioned to Chris and Frank. "You guys stay with her."

"You ready, Mac?" Kevin scrambled to his feet, and the detectives reached their car in record time.

"Let's go." Mac crushed the gas pedal as he tore after Clovis, who left a handy trail in the wet dirt to indicate his direction. Their cars hadn't been a deterrent to the all-terrain vehicle Clovis drove.

Kevin prayed out loud as Mac pushed the Crown Vic for all it was worth. "Lord, give us the strength to finish this task and the courage. Please be at our sides, guide our actions, and help us do the right thing."

Mac's chin was set, and his hands were tight on the wheel. He didn't just want Clovis arrested; he wanted to kill him.

Mac came around a corner, nearly crashing into the back of the suspect's truck. Clovis had apparently gone out of control on the curve and hit a tree. The open door indicated their suspect had fled the scene.

"There he is!" Kevin caught a glimpse of Clovis running north.

"He's heading toward the cliffs." Mac pulled his shotgun from the roof-mounted rack of the car and ran after Clovis, yelling for him to give up. Kevin, gun at the ready, ran with him.

"How do you know there are cliffs?"

"Troy told me."

"That could be good or bad. Clovis knows the terrain better than we do. He probably knows a way out."

"We'll have to outrun him."

Or I will, Mac thought. Kevin was already breathing heavily.

"Or at least keep him in sight." Kevin closed in on Mac, pacing him step for step.

"His revolver has a scope, and he knows how to use it, so be careful." Mac sprinted ahead, pausing just fifty yards from their suspect. Clovis was trying to negotiate his way over the deadfalls along the cliffside. Mac hit the dirt, putting Clovis in his sights.

He was legally justified in shooting the fleeing murderer. But Mac didn't feel the moral justification. "Jack Clovis," he yelled again. "State police; stop where you are! Don't make me shoot you!" Kevin caught up to Mac again, diving to his side and leveling his Glock on Clovis.

Clovis got off another shot.

Kevin looked at his Glock. "This thing is just about worthless at this distance, Mac. You have a good sight picture?"

"I've got him." Mac leveled the post on the ghost-ring sight on the middle of Clovis's back. "Stop, or I'll shoot you where you stand!" Mac yelled again. Clovis stepped awkwardly over a large deadfall. They were at the edge of a cliff. Beyond Clovis, there was nothing but air. A strong east wind howled through the trees. The bear of a man stepped up on a log, his back to them. He held his revolver out to one side as if he were going to give up.

"Drop the gun!" Mac yelled. "Don't make me shoot you!"

In a fluid motion, Clovis spun around and aimed the barrel dead on them.

Mac fired in a heartbeat. Time once again stood still. Mac swore he could see the slug leave his shotgun muzzle, penetrating the smoke cloud on its way into Clovis's left shoulder. The massive shotgun slug tore into the soft target and spun Clovis around. The gun fell. To Mac's surprise, Clovis then picked up the gun and dropped out of sight.

33

HE'S GONE OVER THE CLIFF!" Mac tore out after him, not knowing if the man had fallen or had taken a trail down the treacherous slope.

"Don't hesitate to put another round into him." Kevin followed at a distance.

Mac reached the cliffside. No way could Clovis have walked down. Holding onto a tree limb, Mac leaned forward, expecting to see Clovis at the bottom. Instead he lay on a rocky ledge a few feet down, panting like a wounded animal. His jacket sleeve and shoulder were saturated with blood. The gun lay several feet away, but Clovis made no move to recover it.

Mac removed the sling from the shotgun and dropped to his stomach. "Clovis, grab the sling. I'll pull you up."

Kevin came up behind him. "Careful, Mac. Does he still have his gun?"

"It's on the ledge, but he's not going for it. Grab the sling, Clovis. Come on!" Mac yelled again.

Clovis spit a mouthful of blood on the rock next to his battered face. The wound from the slug was bad. Mac wondered if his bullet had shattered the bone. "No thanks. I'll take my chances here. Besides, isn't this where you ask me why I did it?" Clovis winced in pain.

"Just grab the strap," Kevin urged. "We'll talk when you're safe."

"You ever try to make a living as a logger in this country? Hard work. Hard work," Clovis gasped. "How's a man supposed to make a living with all these tree-hugging wackos crying over their spotted owls? You can't. I couldn't. I had to find some way—that's why I turned to the bear galls and hunts. It was the only way I could keep my place."

"I understand, Jack," Mac hollered into the howling wind. "Just grab the strap, and we'll work this out."

"No." He groaned. "I need to tell you this now. I didn't mean to kill the boy. He walked in on me and Troy on a bear kill. I was gonna try to bribe him—just talk to him—when he ran. I panicked and shot him. I didn't want to, but I couldn't have him telling anyone. I'm a respected man in the community. I have ties, even to the cops. Just ask Sam. I shot the kid on impulse."

"How'd Brad end up in the river?" Mac asked.

"I went back to pick him up later that night. Dumped his body in the Columbia below the dam. I burnt his clothes. I knew I was done for when I heard Sam Wyatt was at my place looking for me with a half-dozen other deputies. I figured right that Troy had talked. I picked him up and took him out to the cabin—told him I needed him for another hunt. I was crazy mad by then. Sorry about shooting at you guys; I was hoping you'd kill me first. Lost my nerve, I guess." Clovis wiped at the blood streaming from his nose.

"Troy said you threatened to kill him and feed him to your dogs if he talked," Mac said. "If you're such a nice guy, why would he say something like that?"

"Probably because of what I did to that ex-con. Norton threatened to turn me in if I didn't cut him a bigger share."

"Ex-con." Mac glanced over at Kevin. "The guy at the sawmill?"

"Unbelievable." Kevin shook his head. *Not so unbelievable,* Mac thought. He wouldn't tell Kevin he'd considered the possibility—at least not yet. Right now they had more important matters to attend to.

Mac had wanted to kill Clovis for shooting Dana and Troy. He'd even aimed for his chest when they'd exchanged fire. Now he wanted the guy alive—wanted him to pay for the lives he'd taken.

"Okay." Mac leaned forward, dropping the sling lower. "You got that off your chest; now let's get you off this cliff. You need a doctor."

Clovis stood up, weaving like a wounded bear. With what must have been his last bit of strength, he launched himself off the cliff.

"No!" Mac wasn't certain which of them yelled. Maybe they both did. They watched Jack Clovis tumble into the deep ravine. Then silence. There were no screams, no groans—nothing but the wind rustling through the trees.

Mac couldn't move. He was still hunkered down on one knee, holding the rifle sling over the cliff's edge. Kevin stood behind him. The wind tore through their hair and their clothes. Several long minutes later, Kevin grabbed Mac's hand, pulling him to his feet.

The landscape blurred. Mac couldn't have said why he felt the way he did—as though he'd lost a friend. Jack Clovis was a murderer. The man didn't deserve a second thought. He finally placed the blame on the aftereffects of nearly losing Dana and of losing his informant.

Kevin settled an arm around Mac's shoulders and hugged him.

Mac felt a little better seeing that his partner had been moved to tears as well.

Without a word, they headed back to the car. They still had work to do.

Mac and Kevin were more than happy to hand the crime scene over to a detective unit from the Oregon State Police office from The Dalles. They were witnesses in this one, all of them active shooters in the attempt to take Clovis into custody. Mac learned the only good part about being involved in an officer-involved shooting was he didn't have to type a report; that was left to the other investigators. All Mac had to do was come to grips with his actions and make sure Dana was all right.

34

S EVERAL DAYS LATER, Mac met Dana at their usual coffee shop. They were both off work for a while—Dana with broken ribs and a scheduled psych evaluation after having been shot, and Mac on administrative leave. Though Mac had accompanied Dana to the hospital right after the shooting, they hadn't gotten together for social time, or what Dana preferred to call mentoring sessions, until now.

"Hey, Mac." Dana settled into the chair next to Mac and closest to the big fireplace. "How's it going?" She was wearing a soft pink sweater that matched the flush in her cheeks.

Mac grinned. "Good. But I should be asking you that."

"I'll be fine, Mac." She settled a hand on his. "We need to talk."

He groaned inwardly. Her tone was reminiscent of the one Linda had used on him. What was it with women and their need to *talk?*

She laughed and pulled her hand back. "Relax, Mac. It's not what you think."

"How do you know what I'm thinking?"

"I just do." She gave him a knowing smile. "I didn't get a chance before to tell you how much I appreciated your treating me like one of the guys out there."

"What do you mean?"

"Don't play innocent with me. I know what was going through your head. You wanted me safe and out of the way."

Mac looked down at his coffee. "I'd want that for any of the people I work with."

"I saw that look in your eyes, Mac." Dana took a sip of her drink. "You were afraid for me."

Mac shrugged. "Okay. And when you went down I about went crazy. I care about you. So sue me."

"Oh, Mac." Dana's gaze turned watery. "We need to talk about that too." She licked her lips. "Just not right now. I need you to bring me up to date. I heard you had to take some admin leave."

"Right, just until the powers that be rule the shooting as justi-fied." No doubt he'd made a complete fool of himself. Dana had a boyfriend.

"Good. So you get a vacation."

"Of sorts. I'm using the time to catch up on paperwork and wrap up loose ends. The latent guys at the lab matched the prints on the duct tape and boot print from the sawmill to Clovis, so looks like his story checked out on the first victim. No wonder Troy was so scared of him, if that's what Clovis did to other asso-ciates in the poaching business. The prints Clovis left on my rifle, in addition to the confession he gave me before going over the cliff, tied the case up nice and tidy."

"Can I help? I'm sort of at odds too."

"Hmm." Mac considered her request. He'd already written a letter to Troy Wilson's daughter via his ex-wife, telling her how her father helped in the investigation and helped police catch a killer.

"I need to talk with Brad's family and answer any questions they have."

"Would you mind if I tagged along?"

"I'd like that." He'd been putting off the task, thinking it would be too emotional. "I was planning on heading up there this morning."

She nodded. "I have some good news." Dana's dimples deepened as she flashed him a wide smile.

He leaned forward, elbows on his knees. "You're getting married?" Mac wasn't sure why he'd said that. Maybe because she looked like a woman in love.

"Married?" Her smile faded. "No." She laughed then. "I made detective. Mac. When I'm ready to go back, I'll be working in your office."

Mac grinned and leaned back. "That's great." He wanted to be happy for her, and he was. But the position opening in detectives was probably Kevin's.

"Why in the world would you think I was getting married?"

He shrugged. "You looked so happy."

Dana rolled her eyes. "Mac, I'm not even dating anyone."

"You're not?" Mac studied her for a moment. "Did your boyfriend have a hard time with you being a cop?"

She sighed. "No. I broke it off. I decided Jason wasn't my type."

"Am I your type?" Mac asked hopefully. Her silence made him wish he could take the words back.

She smiled again. "It won't work, Mac."

"Why?" He set his cup on the table. "We had a lot of fun together once. We could again, if you'd give it a chance."

"We're too much alike. And now that I'll be working with you, it's just not a good idea."

"Professional ethics." Mac knew she was right. Still, he didn't have to like it.

"Something like that."

Mac finished his coffee. Lifting his jacket off the back of the chair, he said, "Well, Detective Bennett. Are you ready to make a visit to the Gayneses?"

MAC AND DANA CALLED AHEAD, and Todd and Vicki were eager for them to come. They arrived at the house at ten.

"Jessica?" Mac stared open-mouthed at the attractive young woman who opened the door. She was wearing a maternity top and had her hair hanging loose around her shoulders.

She smiled and reached out to shake hands with Mac and Dana. "Surprised to see me here?"

"Yes," the two detectives said together.

She leaned forward and, in a conspiratorial tone, said, "Me too."

Vicki came around a corner. "Mac, Dana. It's so good to see you. Thanks for coming."

She took their coats. "Come on in and sit down. Todd's in the family room."

Jessica led the way and asked if they wanted anything to drink.

Neither did. They greeted Todd and took the proffered chairs.

Vicki came in and settled an arm around Jessica's shoulders. "You don't need to wait on us, Jess."

"I want to."

Vicki gave her a warm smile. Her animosity was completely gone.

Jessica had apparently been vindicated, but Vicki seemed to have made a complete turnaround.

Vicki's gaze drifted to Mac. "Todd and I wanted to thank you for everything. Finding Brad's killer—well, it answers so many questions."

Mac nodded.

"And Dana." Vicki sat down next to her husband. "When I read that you'd been injured . . . Are you all right?"

Dana raised her eyebrows. "I'm sore, but thanks to my bullet-proof vest, I'm alive to tell about it."

Mac cleared his throat. "Did you have any questions or anything we can clear up for you?"

Todd shook his head. "We read the report you sent. The only bad thing is not being able to confront this Clovis guy. He should be in jail for what he did."

"I agree," Mac said. "It doesn't seem fair in a lot of ways. But if it's any consolation, Jack Clovis said he didn't mean for Brad to get hurt."

Mac still felt responsible for Clovis's death in a way. He'd been the one to pull the trigger. Maybe if he'd tried to lower himself to the ledge, he might have stopped the man from jumping. He'd never know. Clovis had jumped to his death. They'd airlifted the body out; he'd been pronounced DOA at the hospital. Mac had replayed the incident a hundred times over, trying to convince himself that, under the circumstances, he'd done the best he could.

"I met him," Vicki said. "That first day of the search. He seemed like such a kind, decent man." Tears filled her eyes. "He knew where Brad was the whole time. I don't think I'll ever be able to forgive him for deceiving us like that."

"Not to change the subject," Dana said, "but I have to know. What happened between you guys and Jessica?" Dana slid her gaze from one to the other.

Vicki took hold of Jessica's hand. "I made a terrible mistake. I was judgmental and cruel. Jessica's heart was breaking and . . . I can hardly imagine what she must have been going through."

"It was my fault, really," Jessica insisted. "I should have told you I was pregnant."

"No. You tried to tell us that it was Brad, not you, who was doing drugs. But I was so sure my son would never . . ." Vicki shook her head. "Anyway, I was wrong. Jessica was the best thing that could have happened to Brad. I'd like to think that had he lived, he'd have done the right thing. I think Brad would have given up drugs and alcohol. I think he would have chosen to marry Jessica and be the kind of father that his father is."

Todd watched his wife, admiration in his eyes. "Brad isn't here to look after Jessica and the baby, but we are." He smiled at Jessica. "She and the baby are welcome here anytime, and so is Aaron."

Vicki sniffed. "Aaron is coming in today. We just want to make up for all the grief we've caused Jessica and be the best grandparents a kid could have."

"I'm so glad it's worked out for you," Dana said.

Mac and Dana stayed for another hour. Then they headed back to Vancouver, where they both lived. "Want to have dinner with me tonight?" Mac asked. "Not a date. I just thought we might talk about your new job and all. We could go to that great Asian restaurant that serves sushi."

"I'd like that," Dana agreed. "Two old friends talking shop. Yeah, I can handle that."

"Good. I'll pick you up at six."

She frowned. "I'll meet you there. We wouldn't want anyone to get the wrong idea."

Mac suppressed a grin. "No, we wouldn't want that."

All in all, things had turned out pretty well, Mac thought as he headed for home. They'd caught their bad guy and ended up solving two cases. And he had a date with his favorite trooper—make that detective. If Dana wanted to believe they were just friends, that was fine with him. But Mac knew better. Being with her felt right—and best of all, Dana knew exactly what it was like to date a detective.

* * *

Open up the first of
The McAllister Files

With his newly minted detective badge firmly in place, "Mac" McAllister reports for his first assignment with the Oregon State Police Department: a particularly gruesome homicide. It's a headline case, as the victim—Megan Tyson—was brutally murdered mere weeks before her wedding.

The investigation and autopsy turn up far too many suspects, and too little hard evidence. Why would the beautiful Megan, engaged to a wealthy businessman, be involved with the seedy lineup of characters who seem connected to her? With more questions than answers, Mac and his partner try to uncover the secrets Megan took to her grave and sort through the lies and alibis before Megan's murderer strikes again.

Not sure that he can trust his instincts, Mac depends heavily on the advice of his partner—a seasoned detective with a strong faith in God. A faith Mac has no use for until he must come to terms with his own past and the secrets that haunt him.

Fiction that reflects the grittiness of real life . . . and the reality of faith.